PRAISE for…

Her Mother's Daughter
Crewe's talent lies in rendering characters that readers can actually care about. They have been hurt and they have hurt others, but their essential goodness shines through.—Atlantic Books Today

Hit & Mrs.
If you're in the mood for a cute chick-lit mystery with some nice gals in Montreal, Hit & Mrs. is just the ticket.—Globe and Mail

Crewe's writing has the breathless tenor of a kitchen-table yarn…a cinematic pace and crackling dialogue keep readers hooked.—Quill & Quire

Ava Comes Home
She expertly manages a page-turning blend of down-home comedy and heart-breaking romance.—Cape Breton Post

Shoot Me
Possesses an intelligence and emotional depth that reverberates long after you've stopped laughing.—Halifax Chronicle Herald

Relative Happiness
Her graceful prose…and her ability to turn a familiar story into something with such raw dramatic power, are skills that many veteran novelists have yet to develop.—Halifax Chronicle Herald

LESLEY CREWE

Kin

Vagrant PRESS

Copyright © Lesley Crewe, 2012

All rights reserved. No part of this book may be reproduced, stored in a retrieval system or transmitted in any form or by any means without the prior written permission from the publisher, or, in the case of photocopying or other reprographic copying, permission from Access Copyright, 1 Yonge Street, Suite 1900, Toronto, Ontario M5E 1E5.

Vagrant Press is an imprint of
Nimbus Publishing Limited
PO Box 9166
Halifax, NS   B3K 5M8
(902) 455-4286
nimbus.ca

Printed and bound in Canada

Cover art: Deanne Fitzpatrick (www.hookingrugs.com),
     courtesy of Donna Hutchinson
Cover design: Heather Bryan
Author photo: Sarah Crewe

This novel is a work of fiction. Names, characters, places, and incidents are either the product of the author's imagination or are used fictitiously.

Library and Archives Canada Cataloguing in Publication

   Crewe, Lesley, 1955-
   Kin / Lesley Crewe.
   Issued also in an electronic format.
   ISBN 978-1-55109-922-4

I. Title.

PS8605.R48K56 2012   C813'.6   C2012-903647-1

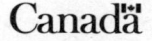

Nimbus Publishing acknowledges the financial support for its publishing activities from the Government of Canada through the Canada Book Fund (CBF) and the Canada Council for the Arts, and from the Province of Nova Scotia through the Department of Communities, Culture and Heritage.

For Paul Alexander, my kindred spirit.

And my grandparents, Kenzie and Abbie Macdonald

✼ ✼ ✼

CHAPTER ONE

1935

ANNIE'S BREATH WAS HOT AGAINST her hands as she covered her face and kept her eyes tightly shut. She leaned against the rough wood of the shed at the back of the house while counting to one hundred. It wasn't easy. A housefly kept on buzzing around her head and the back of her checkered dress was sticky with sweat, she'd been standing so long in the noonday sun.

"Ready or not, here I come!"

It took a moment for her eyes to adjust to the light, and then she was off like a rabbit, bounding around the neatly stacked woodpile to the middle of the dirt driveway. There she stopped and studied the situation. She knew her brother David was clever, so he'd be the hardest to find, but his two friends were dumb. They were probably somewhere obvious, like under the back porch or crouched down behind the old cart next to their neighbour's vegetable garden.

The screen door creaked open and her mother, a petite woman with sharp features and soft brown hair hidden by a kerchief, stood there with a basket of wet clothes. "Put these out on the line, please, and don't hang everything up with one peg."

"Can't! Gotta find Davy."

Annie tore off into the field towards the rock pile so her mother wouldn't be able to catch her.

"Leave your brother alone, Annie!"

Her mother's voice faded with each swish of the tall grass flying past her stick legs. She loved plowing through the field, but more often than not she got distracted by small wildflowers and stopped to pick them. Once she was so intent on her bouquet gathering that she didn't see the bush of nettles near the small creek that ran through the field. The new sweater her grandmother had knitted for her was instantly covered in small burrs. David found her rubbing her eyes so she wouldn't cry. He picked them off for her, but the sweater was never the same, and her mother wasn't pleased.

Annie ran up to the rock pile and sat on the highest flat stone, which served as the lookout for her pretend fort. As she peered around, watching for any small movement, she smacked her dry lips and fidgeted to keep the heat of the rock from pressing through her play dress.

Annie's world in Glace Bay was a good one, bounded by home; the neighbourhood triangle of South, Blackett, and Water Streets; Central School; and the Baptist church. She didn't know it was the dirty thirties and a lot of men were out of work. Her father was a mechanic in the machine shop of the roundhouse. They even had a maid, a girl from Newfoundland looking to make some money to pay for her way to the Boston States. There was always good food on the table, a clean house, and a peaceful atmosphere. No one drank and a good time was when family came over to play cribbage or a game of cards. The Macdonalds were good-living people.

She watched her mother hang out the last shirt. Soon she would be inside and Annie would be able to continue the game, but at that moment Mrs. Butts appeared from around the corner of the house and made a beeline for her mom. Even at the age of seven, Annie knew that Mrs. Butts talked a lot. Once she cornered them at Milne's Meat Market and by the time she walked away, Annie knew her mother was annoyed. Not that she said anything. Her mother always said that if you didn't have anything nice to say, you shouldn't say anything at all.

That was difficult when David's stupid friends were around.

While Annie waited, she lay on her stomach and peered into the rock crevices beneath her. Maybe a snake would appear. She loved snakes, especially when their tongues flicked. The two little girls up the road always screamed whenever Annie tried to show how nice snakes were, so she decided it was much better to play with boys.

When a snake didn't appear, she looked up and saw David and his two friends carrying fishing poles, headed for the shore.

"Hey! Hey! Wait up!"

Annie scrambled down from the rocks and ran like the wind, catching them four houses down.

"What are you doing?" she panted.

"Get lost," said the bigger of David's friends as they kept walking.

"But you said..."

"No one wants you around," said the other one.

Annie stopped and they kept going. She held her breath until David turned around and ran back to her. "We'll play after supper. Just you and me."

Then he shouted loud enough for his friends to hear. "Now scram!"

Annie grinned and skipped home. Her dad and maternal grandfather had built the house themselves; a four-square white home near the corner of Blackett and South Streets. Mom's brother, sister, and two cousins owned four houses a little further along the road and her paternal grandparents once lived on Water Street, just across the big field. That was the house where Annie was born one morning in the summer of 1928, just as the seven o'clock whistle blew for the men to go to work in the mines. The midwife told Mom not to push until the doctor got there, but Annie never did listen to a thing anyone said.

Back then Annie's parents lived on Water Street with her paternal grandfather, because he needed looking after. The house was large, or so Annie thought, with a long lane leading from the main street, high trees on either side. Her father built a swing for her, and there was a picket fence around the garden in the front and a big vegetable garden at the side.

Annie knew her mother hadn't been fond of her grandfather. She said he'd call her a snippet because she didn't scurry around like his daughters did when he slammed the table with his fist. Annie wasn't sure what a snippet was, but it didn't sound very nice, so she was glad she couldn't remember him.

Hunger told Annie it was lunchtime, and since it was a Saturday, her maternal grandma would be making a huge pot of soup. All the grandchildren would be sent over with pots to take back to their own households. Annie didn't mind going, as long as her cousin Blair didn't try and trip her going down the back stairs of her grandma's house.

The only time Annie did mind going over was when she had to dust for her grandmother—a thankless and boring job that always seemed to take forever, with all her knick-knacks and china.

The minute she stepped into the kitchen, her mother handed her a covered pot and pointed out the door. "Your father will want his lunch. Make sure you don't spill it all."

Back out she went, running the entire way. She spied her younger cousin Dorothy rushing towards the house too, so she made sure she was first up the steps. "Beat you!"

"Did not!"

Annie walked into the very warm kitchen first. Her grandmother turned from the bubbling pot on the coal stove. "How are my girls today? Do you have time to stop and have a cookie?"

"No, but thank you," Annie said.

Her grandma reached for a still-warm molasses cookie and placed it in Annie's pocket before ladling several scoops of thick vegetable-beef soup into the offered pot.

"I can have cookies," Dorothy piped up.

Annie managed to carry the pot of soup home without spilling a drop. By the time she got there, her dad was already at the table buttering his roll in anticipation. Annie loved it when her father was home for lunch. The kitchen felt cozier when he was there. The smell of baking coming from the coal stove and the pans of bread rising in the warming oven made it even better.

They ate in the kitchen every day and in the dining room on Sundays or special occasions, but even in the kitchen her mother set a good table, complete with napkin rings.

"Wash your hands before lunch, please."

Annie bolted to the sink and lathered up the hard piece of soap there. Then she slipped back to her chair as her mother handed her a bowl of soup.

Her father, Kenzie, was a tall man with big hands who wore round, wire-rimmed glasses and had a large, bald head, full lips, and a very quiet manner. He only talked when he had something to say. Her mother said he was very bright and read everything he could get his hands on. She said David was like that, too. Annie never had time to read, so she guessed she wasn't bright at all.

Her mother, Abigail, took off her apron before she sat down.

"Why doesn't Davy have to come in for lunch?"

"I wrapped up a couple of sandwiches for him."

"Would you say grace, Annie?" her father asked.

Annie bowed her head and clasped her hands in front of her. "God is great. God is good. Let us thank him for our food. Amen."

Her mother sipped a few spoonfuls of soup before she spoke. "Bertha Butts told me today that they're having a little girl come to live with them."

"How old is she?"

"Your age, I believe."

Her father shook his head. "Mrs. Butts doesn't strike me as the maternal sort."

"It can't be helped, apparently. The child is a distant relative whose father ran off long ago and whose mother just died of TB. It's a tragic story."

Annie's eyes got big. "Her mother died? Can mothers do that?"

"Sometimes, but don't you worry. I'm as healthy as a horse."

Annie dropped her spoon. "Mr. Tutty's horse died last week!"

"Your mother is fine."

This was something Annie had never considered. How did you survive without your mother? Then she started to think of the brother she'd never met, the one who died before she was born.

"Were you sad when Coll died?" she asked.

Her parents looked up and exchanged glances. "We were very sad," Mom said.

"I bet he'd be as nice as Davy."

"Speaking of David," Mom said, "I want you to stop pestering him when he has friends over. He's allowed to do things without you. He's ten now."

Annie frowned and fiddled with the butter knife. "Is it true that Grampy's hair turned white the day after Coll died?"

Her father cleared his throat. "Eat your lunch, please."

"And is it true you lost your hair in the war?"

"I'm not going to ask you again."

Annie finished her soup and the thick piece of bread with molasses on her side plate, and drank all her milk. Then she reached in and pulled out the remains of the crumbled cookie in her pocket and put it on her plate. "I forgot."

"I have some ginger snaps and sugar cookies in the pantry."

"No, thank you. May I be excused?"

Her parents nodded and Annie took off upstairs, but instead of going to her small room at the back of the house, she slipped into her parents' room. For some reason she was always a little nervous to go in there. It felt funny to know that her father slept in pyjamas. Not that she ever saw him wear them. He was up long before she was in the morning and she went to bed at 7:30 every night. When she was five she asked her mother why parents never slept. It became a family joke.

She sidled over to her mother's side of the bed and reached for the picture of her brother Coll on the bedside table. He was a year old, sitting on a little white bench, holding onto a toy dog and wearing a white jumper with a Peter Pan collar, knee socks, and black patent-leather shoes. His hair was neatly brushed into place and he had big, dark eyes, a button nose, and cupid's-bow lips. He was the prettiest baby Annie had ever seen.

She kissed his picture. "You can play with me when Davy isn't around, but I can't say Collie because that's a dog's name."

Annie put down the picture and picked up her mother's hand mirror to look at herself. She tried to see if she looked like her brothers. She had brown eyes like Coll, whereas Davy's eyes were blue. Her hair was darker than Davy's and her page-boy haircut always looked like it was ready to spring into action. The damp was her enemy, so living near the ocean meant that Annie was perpetually at war with her hair. Davy had only a slight wave in his hair, which she always thought wasn't fair.

The day Lila came to live next door was a Sunday. Sundays weren't Annie's favourite day, despite the fact that she got to eat leftover yellow-eyed beans and steamed brown bread for breakfast. The whole day was taken up with church, and Annie never could sit still for very long. In the morning Mom would take them for the eleven o'clock service at the local Baptist church, and then Annie and her brother trooped back to church at three o'clock for Sunday school, both of them still in their good clothes. Sometimes they accompanied their mother to the seven o'clock service as well, after a tasty roast beef dinner with Yorkshire pudding, but David was good at convincing their mother that they'd listen to the church radio broadcast instead. Their father usually didn't go to the evening service and sometimes even got out of attending the morning one as well. He was lucky.

On Sundays Annie and David weren't allowed to play cards, swim or skate, play ball or hockey, ride a tricycle or bicycle, or use a cart. Annie complained every chance she got, but her parents never changed their minds. David told her to stop asking because she was annoying. Annie wanted to know what annoying meant.

School was going to start that Monday, so this was the last day of freedom for Annie after a long and glorious summer. She tried not to get sick at the thought of being cooped up all day in a classroom. It seemed no matter how hard she tried, she always got into trouble with the teacher.

Now *that* was annoying.

Annie raced outside to wait for her mother and David. She headed for the new swing her father had made for her in the backyard, but out of the corner of her eye she spied a young girl sitting on Mrs. Butts's porch. This was something she should investigate, so she turned around and walked up to her.

"Hey."

"Hi."

"What's your name?"

"Lila."

"That's pretty. I'm Annie. How old are you?"

"Seven."

"Me too!"

Lila smiled the nicest smile Annie had ever seen. She was a real-live china doll, despite her old and mended clothes and scruffy shoes. She had reddish-gold hair that fell in waves down to her waist. She didn't look like a stick either, which is what everyone called Annie. And she had dimples. Annie had always wanted dimples.

"Are you the girl whose mother died?"

Lila's smile disappeared and she lowered her head and looked at the ground. Mom and Davy arrived on the scene just as Mrs. Butts came out of her back door.

"Good morning, Bertha," Abigail said.

"Morning. Lila, say hello to Mrs. Macdonald, please."

Lila kept her head down. "Good morning."

Mrs. Butts frowned. "Stand up and say hello properly."

"That's all right," Abigail smiled. "I'm sure it's very confusing to meet everyone at once. It looks like you've met Annie. This is her brother David."

David looked uncomfortable in his ironed shirt and tie. His hair was wet and combed to the side. He nodded but didn't say anything. Lila glanced at him and then looked away.

Mrs. Butts reached for Lila. "We're off to church. We'll make a good Catholic out of her yet."

"No!" Lila refused to take her hand.

Mrs. Butts looked mortified. "What on earth is the matter?"

"I don't want you to get a hold of me."

"Make sense, girl."

Lila burst into tears. "I'm not Catholic. I'm Protestant. Mama's with God and I have to pray in a Protestant church."

Annie went over and put her arm around Lila's shoulder. "That's okay, Lila. You can come with us. We're Baptists, right, Mom?"

Her mother hesitated. "It's certainly fine with me if Lila would like to come to church with the children. We'll keep an eye on her."

"This is nonsense. If she's going to live with me, she's going to a Catholic church and that's that." Mrs. Butts grabbed Lila by the arm and marched her down the driveway.

Annie felt sick.

"Bertha!" Mom walked over to Mrs. Butts and talked to her quietly. At first it didn't look like her mom was winning, but after a few more minutes, Mrs. Butts took her hand off Lila's arm and bent down to look at her in the face.

"I want you to behave yourself. And if you ever embarrass me again like that, you'll see what happens to you."

Mrs. Butts walked down the street grumbling.

Mom cupped Lila's chin with her gloved hand. "It's all right now." She looked back at her children. "We'd best go. We don't want to be late."

Mom held Lila's hand all the way to church. Annie ran circles around them the entire time, telling Lila everything she'd need to know about the neighbourhood. About how you had to be careful and not pick apples off Mr. Ferguson's tree because he'd set the dog on you and how you could get three honeymoons for one cent instead of two if you said thank you to the store owner. Then there was the rule that if you wanted to jump the brook, you had to take five running steps. Not four or six. Finally David told her to hush.

Annie was enthralled by Lila, who sat on the pew beside her and didn't move a muscle. She kept her head down and prayed the entire time the minister spoke from the pulpit. She was so still that Annie poked her, but Lila would not look or speak to her.

To be so devout was impressive. Annie tried to close her eyes and think about God without moving, but it didn't go well. She had to open her eyes and look at the sunlight streaming through the stained-glass windows. Then she had to count how many people coughed and how many times the minister licked his fingers as he turned the pages of his Bible.

To her great relief the number of the hymn "Onward Christian Soldiers" was announced. Annie jumped up and sang with great gusto. Normally David didn't open his mouth, but he liked this one because it was about soldiers. He and Annie would try and out-sing each other.

When Lila didn't move, Annie bent down and whispered in her ear. "You have to stand up and sing."

"I can't sing ever again. My mother is dead."

Annie sat down beside her. "Then I'm not singing either." She reached for Lila's hand and held it in her own.

At that moment the church organist sprang from her bench and ran down the church aisle in a panic. Five minutes later she ran back in. "Sorry, everyone, I left a pie in the oven." She went back to the organ and continued.

After Sunday school, Annie and David showed Lila the rock pile in the middle of the field.

"No one is sure why it's here," David informed Lila. "Dad said something about the property being owned by a farmer once, but that's as much as he knows. The thing is, if you stand on the top of it, you can see the ocean to the right, the baseball field to the left, and the tops of the buildings on Commercial Street in front of you. You can also see your friends' houses at the back and if you whistle, they can hear you."

"And this is where you come if you need to be alone," Annie said. "If you hide behind it, no one can see you from the kitchen window."

"I like it," Lila said. "It's a secret spot. Don't you just love secret spots?"

"I never thought about it," Annie admitted.

David was tapping the rocks with a stick when he quickly bent down and held up a toad. "Bet you don't like this."

"I love toads." Lila reached out and stroked its bumpy head. "He's beautiful."

"He's going to pee on you," Annie cried.

"I don't care," Davy said.

"I think he's frightened," Lila said. "You should let him go. He needs to go home."

David put down the toad. It was gone in a flash.

"Who are they?" Lila pointed to the two tall, thin women in flowered hats being greeted at the door by their mother.

"Those are the MacKenzie sisters, Minnie and Sadie. They're related to Dad. They always come for tea on Sunday." Annie reached into a paper bag and took out three oranges and passed them around. The trio was quiet as they peeled them open. Annie ate the white of the peel first.

"You shouldn't do that," David said.

"Why?"

"You'll get worms."

"You're lying."

"Don't believe me, then."

Annie spit out her mouthful. "You're annoying. Do you have an annoying brother?"

Lila shook her head.

"Do you have any kin?" David asked.

Lila looked away. "No."

"That's okay, Lila," Annie said. "We'll be your kin."

CHAPTER TWO

ANNIE LAY SNUGGLED IN HER wrought-iron bed. Although the frame creaked when she turned over, it was still comfortable, with its stuffed mattress, handmade quilts, and flannel sheets. It was beside the window, and sometimes if the window was open, she'd get a fine misting of rain on her feather pillow. She could get on her knees in bed and look through the blinds and spy on the people next door, but they didn't do anything exciting, so she usually flopped back in bed and listened to the wonderful sounds of her hometown.

Her favourite was the song of the spring peepers around Copper's Brook, but in the summer it was waking up to the *putt, putt, putt* of the single cylinder engines as the fishing fleet left the harbour at dawn. Her dad told her that in the summer, Glace Bay Harbour was so blocked with fishing boats that you could cross it by leaping from deck to deck.

The whistles of the busy S&L Railway announcing their approaches to crossings, the ringing of crossing bells, and even the distant sounds of trains shunting boxcars in the yard made up the background noise of Annie's day. That and the noon Caledonia Colliery whistle that signalled it was time to go home for lunch.

The loneliest sound was the mournful double-toned *BEE-OOH* of the foghorn in the distance, and the nicest was the music from the circus grounds in the summer or the skating music in the winter from the open-air rink on South Street.

Hands behind her head, she dreamed of what she was going to do that day. The possibilities were endless. She'd take her new friend Lila to feed her uncle's pony. Or they could jump rope or climb a few trees.

Her mother's voice drifted up the stairs. "David! Annie! It's time to get up for school."

Annie groaned and covered her head. She'd forgotten about school. She had to wear a new dress and new shoes today, which meant her feet would be sore and her neck itchy. But then she remembered Lila would be walking to Central School with her today, so she bounced out of bed and slipped into the bathroom ahead of David.

On the coal stove every morning was a big pot of thick, creamy porridge that had simmered in a double boiler all night. Annie always put lots of brown sugar and cream over it. Her mother would serve ham and eggs, toast with butter and homemade jam, along with milk and hot tea. Annie and David were always stuffed to the gills going out the door every morning.

When they came home for lunch, it was just as wonderful, with thick lobster, chicken, or egg salad sandwiches on homemade bread, a large piece of pie or gingerbread, an apple, and more milk.

No, David and Annie didn't know what it was to be hungry.

David came downstairs in his new duds—breeches with leather patches on the knees, a flannel shirt, knee-length stockings, and boots. His mother turned from the stove and saw him standing in the doorway.

"David! You look very grown up. You'll soon be as tall as your father."

David seemed pleased with the compliment. He sat at the table and grinned when his mom put a big plate of food in front of him. "Dad says I have a hollow leg."

"I wish *I* was going into grade five," Annie said with her mouth full. "That way I could miss grades two, three, and four."

Her mother sat the table. "Annie, you can't start off the school year with that attitude. Think of the fun you'll have with your friends and all the things you'll learn about the world."

"The only fun I have is at lunchtime and the only thing I learn is the boring alphabet and sums."

"It comes in handy if you want to read and count your money," Mom laughed.

"Davy can do it for me. He's smarter than me."

David nodded. "You're right."

"You are just as smart as your brother. You can do anything you put your mind to."

"My mind is out to lunch."

"I'll say one thing for you," her mother sighed. "You've got a smart mouth."

Lila was already outside when they left for school. She didn't have on new clothes and she didn't have a school bag.

"Hi, Lila."

"Hi, Annie."

"You better go get your things," David said.

"I don't have anything to bring."

"Why not?" Annie asked.

"Never you mind," David said. "I can lend you a pencil and notebook when we get to school."

Lila gave them a small smile, but she was obviously nervous as she and Annie walked behind David. "I don't know anyone here."

"You know me. That's all you need. And you've got Davy. If anyone says anything, he'll stick up for you."

"You think someone will say something to me?"

David turned his head. "Stop worrying her. No one is going to say anything."

Walking to school with a new friend was rather exciting. Annie couldn't wait for her classmates to meet Lila; Annie liked being the centre of attention, and a new kid in school was always a curiosity.

The day was a blustery one, with wispy clouds racing across the blue sky. Although it was early September, there was a touch of fall in the air and Annie wondered if Lila was cold in her thin sweater. She didn't want to worry Lila by bringing up the subject, so she resolved to carry an extra sweater with her at all times in case Lila needed it.

Lila did stand out from the circle of girls that swarmed around them in the schoolyard. Most of them had their hair bobbed like Annie. Lila's reddish-gold waves looked old-fashioned. A few girls tittered behind their hands, but stopped when Annie gave them a dirty look.

The boys looked at Lila too, but none of them approached her. It was as if they sensed that she was vulnerable, but it was more likely that they knew Annie would fly into them.

The first day of school was always an eternity for Annie. The outdoors beckoned through the windows and when they were cracked open she heard the birds singing in the trees, and smelled that intoxicating whiff of leaves and sunshine. How she longed to be a bird. Instead she was brought back to reality with a sharp word from the teacher to stop daydreaming.

The grade two teacher that year was Miss Coombs. She was dumpy and her ankles always looked like stuffed sausages coming out of her shoes. The students called her Miss Doom behind her back. She never smiled. It was going to be a long year.

Miss Coombs called Lila up to the front of the room. Lila got up reluctantly from her desk and did what she was told.

"Students, we have a new student this year, Lila Phillips, coming to us from Ross's Ferry, is that right?"

Lila nodded.

"Speak up, girl."

"Yes."

"Are you a good student?"

Lila looked terrified. She nodded again.

"In this class, Miss Phillips, we speak when we are spoken to."

"Yes," Lila whispered.

"I can't hear you."

Lila trembled and bit her lip before bowing her head in disgrace.

"Don't stand there whimpering...."

"She said yes!"

Miss Coombs turned to face the class. "Who said that? Stand up this minute."

Annie rose from her desk.

"Did I ask for your opinion, Miss Macdonald?"

"No."

"Then do not speak unless you are spoken to."

"But you just said to speak when you are spoken to."

"Enough! You will stay after class today and write a hundred times, *I am a rude little girl*. I'm sure your parents will be proud to know you have detention on the very first day of school."

Annie's heart sank.

But David and Lila were waiting for her on the steps when she emerged from the school doors thirty minutes after school ended. Lila's eyes brimmed with tears. "I'm sorry I got you in trouble."

"That's okay. It wasn't your fault. I used two pencils at the same time so it would go faster."

"I'm going to make you a gift," Lila said. "It's a surprise, so don't ask me what it is."

The three of them walked back home. Annie knew her parents would be disappointed that she was in hot water already.

The truth came out at the kitchen table over platefuls of salt cod, pork scraps, white sauce with sautéed onion, and boiled potatoes. Annie's dad asked them how the first day of school went. He looked confused when neither of them answered. Then he put down his utensils, clasped his big hands in front of him, and looked at Annie. "What happened?"

David spoke first. "She didn't do anything wrong. Lila told me Annie was sticking up for her."

"I'm asking Annie."

"Miss Coombs was frightening Lila so I spoke up. I had to stay in detention and write *I am a rude little girl* one hundred times. I'm really not, Dad. I didn't understand what the teacher meant about speaking when spoken to and I did speak when she spoke but then she changed her mind and said I shouldn't speak. It was very confusing."

Her parents looked at each other from across the table. Mom held up her napkin to hide her mouth. Dad nodded his head as if thinking deeply about the situation.

"Well, it's true that in school you only speak when the teacher asks you a question, so I can see why she thought you overstepped the boundaries of classroom etiquette. On the other hand, if you were sticking up for an injustice being done to a friend, I'm proud of you. But you must also realize that it is rude to talk back to an adult, however misguided they may be. Your best course of action is to keep quiet and then come and tell us if you think a friend is being abused."

Her dad always talked like this. It made Annie feel important. And she couldn't believe that she didn't get into trouble.

"I think you should stay in after supper and go to bed early. It sounds like you've had a tiring day. What do you think, Abbie?

"I think so too. Now, who would like some lemon meringue pie?"

That night after supper Lila knocked on their back door.

"Here Annie, I made this for you. And I made something for David too so he wouldn't be left out."

She handed over two small pieces of paper. Annie's was a picture of herself standing in the classroom in defiance of the teacher.

"You drew this? It's so good! It looks just like me."

David opened his picture of the toad he'd held in his hand. "That's amazing. It looks real."

Annie hugged her. "I'll keep it forever."

In just a few short weeks, Annie couldn't remember a time when Lila hadn't been in her life. Her new friend was still shy around others, but was very chatty when the two of them were alone. Lila didn't mind David either, but he wasn't around much; he was too busy playing baseball with his friends or building forts. Sometimes Annie got upset when the boys shooed them away, but soon the two girls made their own fun and forgot all about the boys.

Neither of them liked dolls, but Annie noticed that Lila always seemed happiest when there was an animal around. She loved every creature, be it worm, frog, snake, mouse, or rabbit. Cats and dogs followed her in droves, and the pony, Ginger, loved Lila to pat its soft nose.

Then one day Lila came screaming to their back door. Annie and her mother ran to see what was wrong. There was Lila, covered in ashes, holding two limp kittens in her arms.

"Someone threw them on their ash pile! No one wanted them. Are they dead?"

Mom took over and reached for the kittens while Annie tried to console Lila. "Mrs. Butts told me to throw them away! I can't do that. They didn't do anything wrong!"

Abigail reached for a dishtowel and wrapped up the kittens. Then she took a cloth and dipped it in warm water. The girls watched as she rubbed their tattered little bodies in the hope of some response.

Gradually, the warmth of her touch worked its magic and the kittens started to mew. Annie and Lila jumped up and down and hugged each other.

"May I keep the kittens here? Then I could play with them. I'm not allowed to have a pet. Mrs. Butts said so."

"Did she, now?" Mom's face softened when she looked at Lila. "Of course you can keep your kittens here."

Lila's dirty face was so happy. "I'll give one to Annie and then we can both have one. Which one do you want?"

"You choose. You're the mother," Annie said.

Lila reached for the marmalade kitten with white feet. "I saw her first, so I'll take this one." She held the tiny kitten up to her chin. "You'll be all right, Boots."

Annie took the orange and white one. "This is Squeak, because she's squeaking!"

"They'll be all right, won't they?" Lila asked. "They're so small."

"I'll tell you a little story," Mom said. "When I was born, in 1898, I weighed only two pounds."

"Two pounds?" Annie said. "I weighed seven pounds when I was born."

"I was so small that my arm fit inside my father's wedding ring, and he could hold me in the palm of his hand."

Annie's and Lila's eyes got huge.

"My mother wrapped me in cotton batting and put me in the warming oven."

Annie swivelled to look at the warming oven over the coal stove. "In there?!"

"It was warm and quiet and dark. I must have thought I was still in my mother's womb. So remember, it's not how big you are that makes you strong. Your heart is a mighty thing." Mom rose from her chair. "Your babies are going to need feeding. I'll warm some milk and you two get a box and make a comfy bed for them. There are old towels in the porch you can use."

After that, Lila was over all the time, but it was hard to say goodbye to her at night. Annie knew she didn't want to go home to Mrs. Butts and leave Boots behind.

And then Annie noticed that whenever Lila thought she wasn't looking, she'd sneak a cookie or a muffin from the racks of goodies cooling in the pantry. Her mother brought it up one day as she peeled apples at the kitchen sink. Annie was behind her at the table, struggling to do her homework and hating every minute of it.

"Annie, have you noticed Lila losing weight?"

"No."

"I think she's looking a little peaked."

"What does that mean?"

"Like maybe she's not feeling well."

"She's good."

Mom put down the peeler and sat across from Annie. "I noticed some of my baking disappearing and I thought it was David but when I asked him, he didn't know what I was talking about."

Annie didn't want to be a tattletale, but the worry on her mother's face alarmed her.

"Sometimes Lila and I take a few cookies."

"Are you sure it's not just Lila?"

Annie nodded, but she could tell her mother didn't believe her.

"I think Lila's hungry." Mom chewed on her thumbnail, deep in thought. "I have a secret mission for you. Do you think you can handle it?"

When Annie asked Lila if she could come over to her house for supper, Lila looked unsure and said she'd have to ask Mrs. Butts. Annie had only ever been in Mrs. Butts's porch. She never invited children in like some of the other women on the street.

The two of them walked into Bertha's kitchen. Annie looked around, stunned. There was a mess everywhere, on the counters and the floor and the table. Even the cupboard doors were open, revealing chaos inside. Annie's stomach felt funny.

"Where is she?" Annie whispered.

"She'll be in the parlour on the couch," Lila said.

The girls crept down the hallway. There were books and newspapers in piles everywhere. Annie thought she was in a dream and her mouth went dry. When they entered the parlour she grabbed Lila's hand. "Is she dead?"

Mrs. Butts was sprawled on the sofa, with her mouth open and spittle running down the side of her mouth.

"No. She likes to sleep."

Lila approached her guardian. "Mrs. Butts? Mrs. Butts? Can Annie stay for supper?" When she didn't respond, Lila reached out and touched her on the shoulder.

Mrs. Butts woke with a start and struggled to sit up. "Who's there? What time is it?"

"It's me. Can Annie stay for supper?"

"No."

"But…"

"I said no…oh, Annie, you're here." She gave a nervous laugh and tried to straighten herself up, while reaching for the nearly empty glass on the side table. "I didn't see you. Well, I suppose it's all right if Annie stays. You're over at their house all the time." Mrs. Butts drained the glass. "Play upstairs until supper is ready."

Annie was more than glad to escape that room. She followed Lila upstairs.

"There are three bedrooms up here, but I'm only allowed in my room."

They crept down the hall. One of the bedroom doors was open, and when Annie glanced inside, she saw Mr. Butts fast asleep across the bed with his work clothes on.

This was all wrong. Annie shivered and kept close to Lila. They reached her room and Lila closed the door behind them. The bedroom was gloomy and not very nice. There were no toys and her bed had a grey wool blanket on it. There was a bureau and a chair, but the rest of the space was taken up with boxes and unwanted items that were piled in the back corner. They crawled up on the bed together.

"This is my room."

"You don't have a lot of things."

"No. I had to leave most of it behind."

Annie couldn't imagine leaving any of her possessions behind.

"I do have this." She moved her pillow aside. There was a small brown bear and a nursery rhyme book. "My mom used to read me this book." She opened the pages and a photo fell out. Lila passed it to Annie. "That's my mother and me."

Annie looked at the small picture of a pretty young woman holding a baby. She was looking at the baby and smiling. The baby had her hand on her mother's cheek.

"Your mom is very pretty."

When Annie passed it back, Lila looked at the picture.

"Where's your dad?"

"I don't remember him. Your dad is nice."

"Is Mr. Butts nice?"

Lila shrugged. "I don't know, he doesn't talk to me, but he's not mean or anything."

"Is Mrs. Butts mean to you?"

Lila put her mother's picture back in the book before she answered. "She doesn't hit me, but she likes to yell. And sleep."

"So what do you do in the evening?"

"This."

Lila reaches down under her bed and takes out a pile of paper, labels, envelopes, and old school notebooks. "These are my friends."

On every scrap of empty space were pictures of animals, people, and landscapes. "These are places I want to go and these are the things I love."

"That's me!" Annie laughs at the picture of herself hollering out her bedroom window. "And there's Davy by the woodpile! I wish I could draw like you."

"And I wish I could talk like you."

The girls were eventually called down for supper. It was the biggest shock of all. There was no tablecloth or place settings at the kitchen table. It looked like Mrs. Butts had swept aside some of the clutter to provide them with a small space to eat.

"Aren't you going to eat, Mrs. Butts?" Annie asked.

"I eat later."

She served them bread with butter and brown sugar. Lila quickly ate hers up, but Annie couldn't choke hers down and offered it to Lila.

When it was time to say goodbye, Lila waved from the doorway. "I'll see you tomorrow."

Annie ran up her back stairs and threw open the door. The smell of roast chicken hit her in the face. The racks of cooling bread rolls only made it worse.

Her mother turned from the stove. "Annie! What's wrong?"

Annie ran and put her arms around her mother's apron. She hid her face in the warm and fragrant scent of her mother, that familiar and reassuring constant in her life.

Her mom touched her forehead. "You're burning up." Annie began shivering so hard her teeth rattled and she saw coloured spots in front of her eyes.

After that she remembered things out of sequence; her father came into her room and pressed a cool cloth on her brow, her mother wiped her down just like she did with the kittens. She cried out for Squeak, and David put the cat on the bed. Annie didn't know if it was day or night. Her mother lifted her head and spooned beef broth into her mouth. She made her drink, even when she didn't want to.

And then she fell into a deep sleep.

When Annie awoke her mom was sitting beside her on the bed, rubbing her hair.

"Hello, sleepyhead. Do you feel better?"

Annie nodded, but she didn't feel like getting up. It was as if her limbs were made of rubber.

"You had a bad fever, but it's broken now, and you should feel better in a couple of days."

Annie nodded again.

"I have something for you." Mom reached over and took a handmade card from the top of the bureau. "Lila made it for you."

The card was covered with drawings of flowers. It made Annie happy, and then she remembered.

"Mom?"

"Yes?"

"Can Lila live with us? Please? Please?"

Though Annie's parents didn't say yes to her request, it was obvious they were putting their heads together to sort something out. Every time Annie walked into the room, they stopped talking. And Lila was invited for supper every night. Mr. and Mrs. Butts didn't seem to notice. Mom even asked Lila to come home with Annie for lunch on school days. She also made Lila take a colourful quilt to put on her bed and an old jewellery box to put treasures in.

David kept an eye out for her, too. One weekend, the neighbourhood kids gathered in the field to play scrub. Lila didn't know the rules, so David explained that you were meant to hit the ball, and run to first base and return before the ball was thrown back. When Lila was the pitcher she hit an older boy with the ball, which was perfectly legal. He got mad and told her she should go live in the poorhouse since she was a dirty mongrel anyway.

David punched him in the mouth.

Annie had never seen her brother hit anyone before. She was impressed. And then he did it again the very next day in the schoolyard.

She and Lila and a few other girls were playing hopscotch in the dirt. They each held a flat piece of brick to throw on the squares they'd traced out with a stick. Annie saw David marching away from a pack of boys. He looked mad.

"Your pa's a stinkin' Red!" one of them yelled at him.

David turned around and ran up to the kid and knocked him to the ground, but his opponent was big and he soon had David on his back. The other boys gathered around and urged them on.

Annie ran to the circle of screaming boys. "Get off him!" One of them pushed her away. She couldn't see what was happening. And then the crowd went instantly quiet and moved off. David had a black eye and a bloody nose. The janitor reached down and grabbed both boys by their collars. "That's enough of that. The rest of you, get back to your own business." He hauled David and his enemy into the school.

Annie and Lila waited for him after school, but when he came out, he didn't even look at them as he hurried past.

"Davy! What happened?"

Annie tried to catch up to him, but Lila held her back. "Leave him alone."

That night, Annie was sent to bed at her usual hour, but she lay awake trying to listen to the murmuring coming from the parlour. Her parents always went there when something was serious, so Annie was sure she was missing something good. She crept out of bed and crouched down at the top of the stairs. If she stayed very still she could just make them out.

"But I don't understand," she heard Davy say.

"I'm opposed to being a Liberal or a Conservative and in this part of the world if you're an anti-capitalist you might as well be a Communist. Being a Red is another name for it. I can tell you quite emphatically that I am not a Communist, but I do believe that everyone deserves a fair shake. I don't think it is right that the big dogs of the world are out to eat the little dogs. This town and surrounding communities are suffering because the men who run the coal mines and the steel mills can't find the moral strength to share their wealth with the people who work for them. I believe that is unfair and wrong. Everyone deserves the same rights, regardless of their station in life."

Annie couldn't understand what her dad was saying except for one part about dogs, so she crept back to bed and snuggled with Squeak.

Mom's sister Muriel ran in the door the next morning while she and Davy were having breakfast. "You're not going to believe it. You know Mrs. Mackinnon up the road, the one who pretends she's such a good housekeeper that she has her washing out on the line at the crack of dawn? Someone saw her putting it out after midnight. Wait till this gets around. The old biddies in church will have a field day!"

Then she ran back out again. Aunt Muriel was always doing things like that.

The trees turned brilliant shades of red, orange, and gold that October. Dad said it was because the nights were cold. Then he asked who would like to go to Round Island to see the autumn colours.

Round Island was about fifteen miles outside of town towards Mira. The Macdonalds had a bungalow there, a small cabin with an outhouse, nestled in a grove of spruce and fir trees. It wasn't very big, but what it lacked in space, it made up for in location. The beach was only a quick run down the path and through the cow pasture by the Dillon farm. Mira Bay was where Annie and David swam and played in the summer months, and it was their favourite place on earth.

David, who was in the porch bringing in some wood for the fire, poked his head around the door. "Are we taking the train?"

"No, I thought I'd borrow Uncle Howard's car."

"Great!"

Annie and Lila were helping Mom cut out cookie dough. "Can Lila come too? I can't wait to show her everything."

"Of course she can come," Dad said. "I'll let Mrs. Butts know we'll be gone for the day."

Annie couldn't think of what occasion warranted a long drive on a chilly October weekend. They usually only went to Round Island in the summer. And to go in Uncle Howard's 1934 Ford Deluxe was beyond exciting.

The drive out to the country went quickly. Annie and David played their favourite game. David explained it to Lila. "If you see a cow, you say 'Have it.' If you see a horse, you say 'Got it.' If you make a mistake you lose all your have its and got its."

When they drove past Port Morien, Mom told Lila the body of water to the left was called Cow Bay. Lila said "Have it!" Annie didn't think that should count, but her mother thought otherwise.

They drove through Black Brook and Homeville and finally Round Island. When Dad turned down the dirt road and parked the car by the bungalow, Annie couldn't contain her excitement. She wanted to get out first and scrambled past her brother onto the car's running board and hopped off into a pile of dead leaves.

The air smelled exactly the same, that wonderful mixture of pine, fir trees, damp earth, and a clean salt breeze.

The shingled white cottage with yellow shutters was cozy, nestled into a grove of very tall spruce trees that kept it hidden from the road. It had a white picket fence around two sides, with a pretty trellised gateway leading to hedges of wild pink roses that bloomed early every summer. Mom always cut them when they were still buds and the roses bloomed in the green glass bowl on the fireplace mantel.

Whenever Annie smelled wild roses, it brought her right back to this place.

The cottage wasn't winterized, so it was very chilly when they opened it to show Lila inside. The kitchen had cupboards and a sink to the right, a wooden table to the left under the window, and a stove on the opposite wall. There was also a compact, cast-iron, cylinder-shaped stove called a Warm Morning. This provided the heat in the early hours. Her parents would shake out the ashes from the tray at the bottom, open the lid, and put in paper, kindling, wood, and finally coal to keep the fire steady.

The main room of the cottage had lots of windows and three small bedrooms off of it, the doorways covered with cloth curtains to the floor. The middle room had bunk beds, and this is where Annie took Lila. They had fun bouncing on the bottom bunk, but didn't stay long because the beach beckoned.

The three friends ran down ahead of the adults, through the cow pasture, and over the creek that meandered down to the beach. They ran up to the edge of the field and saw the endless shoreline that edged Mira Bay. A perfect beach filled with dark, wet sand and then dry, white sand amongst the grasses and vegetation near the top of the field that flanked miles of muted blue, grey, purple, and green rocks.

The water was a steely blue and very choppy. The wind whistled past them and made it hard to hear each other. They held out their arms and the wind kept them upright. Their hair blew every which way. By the time her parents arrived, Annie's ears and nose were cold. But that didn't stop her from flinging herself down past the rocks and to the water's edge. She dodged the waves as she beckoned for Lila to join her. David was already jumping the creek that divided the beach to the right. That creek with its bubbling water provided hours of entertainment for kids in the summer months.

But Lila stayed near Annie's mother. Annie knew that Lila wasn't as adventurous as she was. It was frustrating at times, always trying to push her to do something. Lila liked to have fun, but there was a hesitation before she knew exactly what was expected of her. Mom told her that Lila had a difficult life and that that changes a person. So Annie made up her mind not to get impatient, but it sure was hard.

Finally, Dad whistled for them to come back, and David and Annie raced each other up to the bluff where her parents and Lila stood.

Mom patted her arms with her gloved hands. "Goodness, it's cold."

"Let's go." Dad turned and walked with his long stride towards the cottage.

"I'm hungry," David announced.

"That's good," Dad said. "We've been invited to Mr. and Mrs. Johnson's house for lunch."

The Johnson home was only a minute's drive from the cottage. The kids could race through the fields and woods and get there faster than a car. But they were chilled by now, and it was a relief to crawl into the plush, padded back seats of the Ford.

They returned to the main road, turned left, drove around two turns, and pulled into the Johnsons' tree-lined driveway, passing an open gate. The trees formed a canopy over the laneway, so it was quiet and peaceful, and the air was still, a complete opposite from how it was at the beach.

An emerald-green shingled house with white shutters and a gabled roof came into view. It was surrounded on all sides with glorious trees dotted around the property, but also an enormous yard of grass and shrubbery. A very large rock perfect for sitting on poked out of the ground to the right of the house. There was a pathway lined with pine trees from the front door that went down to the main road, but it looked like no one used it. Instead the car pulled up to the back of the house, under yet another tree. The backyard disappeared into the woods. It was as if the house was all alone in the world, yet it felt protected and safe.

Joe and Eunie Johnson hurried down the back steps to greet them, as if impatient for their company to arrive. They were a little older than Annie's parents and always friendly. Joe was a round man with hair so fine it seemed to float over his head. Eunie was even rounder and a lot shorter than Joe. Forever in a hurry and out of breath, her face was always flushed.

Eunie rushed towards them and herded them towards the house amid the hellos and introductions and hand shaking. Annie noticed how happy Mr. and Mrs. Johnson were to meet Lila. Mrs. Johnson held Lila's hand in hers and kept patting it. Lila smiled up at her.

"May I show Lila the house?" Annie asked.

"Yes, indeed," Eunie said. "I'll get our lunch ready."

So while the adults stayed and chatted, Annie and David took Lila around. Annie loved the Johnson house; it had the same feeling as home. The back porch was clean and organized, and the kitchen was the first room you entered. It had patterned wallpaper on the walls, and the wooden floors and mouldings were a deep mahogany colour.

There were lower cupboards on the left wall and frilly curtains on the window above the sink. A pantry revealed a table, a sideboard, and shelves on every wall filled with dishes, glasses, jars, and such. Bins of flour and sugar were on the floor.

The best part was the little door in the wall facing the back porch. It was beside the kitchen table and used for storage. Annie thought it was a wonderful place to hide. And there was a square in the floor that lifted up so Mr. Johnson could go down in the cellar.

The inside of the house was like a circle. You could go through the right doorway and into the parlour, with a big bedroom off of that, and then continue on to the front hallway and back around into the dining room and out into the kitchen again. There was a small fireplace with an ornate mirrored mantel above in the parlour and exactly the same one on the opposite side of the wall in the dining room. There were windows everywhere and doors panelled with etched glass that opened into the parlour, the hallway, and the dining room. The wood throughout the house was a deep reddish-brown shade that had an almost polished look after years of use.

"But this is the best part." Annie pointed to the door to the left of the parlour's fireplace. David opened it and let Lila go first. There were small, deep, curved steps all the way up to the top floor. You couldn't see the room above until you walked up far enough past the first curve. And then it revealed the open upstairs. It was a sizable room that the stairway railing divided in half. There was a bedroom on each side, but you saw them both as one. The beds were large and so were the bureaus. There were a couple of rocking chairs and chests at the end of the beds for extra bedding. There was a large bookcase filled with books, chairs by the windows, a baby's cradle, a spinning wheel, and a huge old radio.

"What do you think?" Annie laughed. "Isn't this great?"

Lila looked around, speechless. She took in everything and then looked out one of the three windows, where a red maple was close enough to touch the glass.

David went over to the radio and turned the station dial. "I wonder if this works."

"This is the best room I've ever seen," Lila finally said.

They explored for a few more minutes, and then Eunie called up the stairwell to say that lunch was ready. The kids ran down the steep stairs holding on to the walls so they wouldn't fall and were ushered into the dining room.

A luncheon feast was served. The entire centre of the table disappeared under plates filled with dainty sandwiches, trays filled with cheese and cured ham, bowls of potato salad and marinated carrots and macaroni salad, and finally plates of queen's lunch squares and chocolate brownies.

Eunie served the children big glasses of milk and poured copious amounts of tea for the adults. The children were too busy eating to say much, and it wasn't until the last crumb was gone that Eunie spoke to Lila.

"How do you like this house?" she said.

Lila grinned. "I love it. It's the nicest house I've ever seen...except for Annie's house."

"Maybe when Annie and David come out for the summer, they can bring you along and you can come and visit."

"That would be nice."

"What do you like to do, Lila?" Joe asked her.

Annie knew that Lila wasn't used to all this adult attention. She could see her starting to get nervous.

"I like to play and I love to draw."

"Do you like dolls?" Eunie asked.

Lila turned to Annie for help. "She doesn't like dolls. Neither do I."

"Do you like to swim?"

"I...I don't know how."

Annie was surprised. "You don't?"

Lila looked worried, as if she'd said the wrong thing.

"Lots of people don't know how to swim," David said. "I'm not very good either."

Annie knew this was wrong. David swam like a duck. She was about to correct him when Mom placed her hand on Annie's arm under the table, a signal to be quiet.

After a very nice visit and fond goodbyes, the Macdonalds and Lila piled into the car to go home. Eunie came running out with a bag of molasses cookies. She gave them to Lila. "I hear they're your favourite."

Lila took the bag, nodded, and smiled. "Thank you."

"You're very welcome, honey."

Annie thought Mrs. Johnson looked like she was going to cry. She and Mom held hands through the window before Dad started the motor. Then they were off.

After all that food and excitement, it wasn't long before the kids drifted off in the back seat.

CHAPTER THREE

ANNIE HATED SCHOOL—THAT WAS a well-known fact—but she wasn't *afraid* of school.

Lila was.

On this November morning the routine was the same as always. Breakfast with David and then off to school. Mom had bundled them up against the damp cold. David always took off the scarf Mom made him wear and stuffed it in his school bag the minute he was out of sight. Annie never told on him.

As soon as Annie stepped outside, she knew it would snow. The sky had a dark and brooding look, even that early in the morning. David went ahead and Annie waited for Lila. She wasn't coming and Annie knew they were going to be late, so she went up to Mrs. Butts's door and knocked. She heard Mrs. Butts yelling inside for Lila to hurry up.

Lila came to the door and Annie didn't think she looked very good. She was pale and didn't smile.

"Are you okay?" Annie asked.

Lila nodded and fell into step. They didn't say much as they walked to school with other friends from the street. Annie's cousin Dorothy asked Lila if she wanted to go to her house after school, but Lila shook her head no. Dorothy seemed hurt, so Annie went up to her. "Mrs. Butts is making Lila stay in after school today."

"Oh." Dorothy brightened up.

The morning passed by in the usual fashion, and that afternoon Mrs. Coombs had the students come up to the front of the class and recite their compositions. The topic was their families. Annie suddenly wondered what Lila would say.

They went by rows. Annie counted how many would go before Lila. Maybe they would run out of time before they got to her. Annie tried to catch Lila's attention, but Lila was frozen in her seat and wouldn't acknowledge her.

Annie had to go first.

"I am Annie Lucy Macdonald. We spell our last name with a little d, not a big d. My dad says our family was from Scotland, the Isle of North Uist, and we belong to Clanranald. My father works and my mom makes bread. I have an older brother named David and another older brother who died before I was born. I also have a friend named Lila and she is part of our family. The end."

Annie tried to catch Lila's eye when she went back to her desk, but Lila had her head down. Miss Coombs called out Lila's name. When Lila didn't move she called her again. Lila took her exercise book and walked slowly to the front of the class.

"You may start."

She opened her book and stood there.

"Lila, read your composition."

Annie willed Lila to open her mouth. *Just say a few things and it will be over.*

"I'm waiting."

The kids in the class started to fidget nervously. Lila was like a statue. Miss Coombs got out from behind the desk and walked over to her student, but Lila didn't acknowledge her. Annie could tell then that the teacher was mad.

"Lila, look at me."

She didn't.

"You are to read your assignment. Everyone else in the class has done it. Why should you be the exception?"

Lila didn't even blink. She stared at her page and didn't move a muscle.

Miss Coombs bent down close to Lila's ear and hissed, "You spineless jellyfish."

It happened so fast, none of them were prepared for what followed. Lila ripped the page out of her book and threw it in Miss Coombs's face, then another and another until she shredded the entire scribbler. The teacher was horrified; she grabbed Lila by the hair and hauled her out the door. Annie jumped up. "Don't! You're hurting her!"

Miss Coombs turned around and stabbed her finger in the air. "Annie, sit down this instant and don't you dare move, or you'll get the strap."

Annie sat down.

There was a commotion out in the hall, but in only a few moments, Miss Coombs was back in the classroom, her face flushed and her manner agitated. She stormed to her desk and sat down. "Hughie Beaton, read your homework."

Hughie got up carefully and read his assignment as fast as he could. Miss Coombs didn't seem to notice.

There was still an hour of school left. Annie wasn't sure she'd be able to sit through it, but she didn't want to call attention to herself and risk detention. She wanted to get out of the classroom as soon as the bell rang and run to the principal's office and be there for Lila.

It was agonizingly slow, but finally the bell rang and the students were dismissed. Annie ignored Miss Coombs and hurried out. She walked as fast as she could to the office, expecting to see Lila sitting in the chair by the principal's door, but she wasn't there. Was she still in the principal's office? That would be very bad.

As Annie looked around, unsure what to do, the principal's door opened and she walked out with papers in her hand, intent on getting somewhere fast.

"Excuse me. May I see Lila?"

The principal looked down at Annie. "Lila?"

"She got in trouble but she didn't mean it and I'm here to walk home with her."

"Lila Phillips? I haven't seen her all day."

"But where is she?"

"I don't know. Are you sure you have your facts right?"

Annie didn't wait to give her an answer. She ran down the hall and grabbed her jacket and boots. As soon as she opened the door to go outside, a rush of feathery snow came in the door too. The ground was completely white and snow filled the air.

"Davy! Davy!" She leapt off the bottom step into the schoolyard and ran over to where David usually waited for her in bad weather.

That was one of his jobs, to make sure Annie got home safely in the winter months.

He turned around as she ran up to him.

"Lila's not here!"

"What do you mean?"

"She got in trouble and I thought she went to the office, but the principal didn't see Lila all day."

"She probably went home."

"But she doesn't have her coat or boots."

"Let's go."

The siblings ran as fast as they could. As they neared their house, David shouted he'd check with Mom and she should check with Mrs. Butts. Annie ran up to their door and knocked. When nothing happened, she knocked louder with no result. In desperation Annie turned the doorknob, but it was locked. She pounded on the door.

"Just a minute!" Mrs. Butts finally stood there looking like she'd just woken up.

"Is Lila here?"

"Of course Lila's not here. She's in school. You should know that."

Annie turned around and ran down the stairs, just as David and Mom came out of the house, Mom with her coat thrown over her shoulders. "She's not here! Is she over at Mrs. Butts's?"

"No."

Mom looked panicked. "Where could she be?"

"Wait, I know where she is!" Annie started to run through the field and the other two followed her. "Lila! Lila!" She got up to the rock pile and went behind it. There was Lila, curled up in a ball and shaking, her dress and sweater covered with snow.

"Oh my god!" Mom ran to her and covered her with the coat. "It's all right. I've got you." She picked Lila up in her arms and ran back to the house with her, Annie and David at her heels. When they got into the house, Mom started to shout orders. "Annie, get some blankets and wool socks. David, fill up a warm water bottle and there's tea on the stove. Put a few spoonfuls of milk and honey in it."

Annie raced up the stairs and tore the quilts off her bed and opened her sock drawer. Down she ran and found her mother in the parlour with Lila's shivering little body against her. Lila's arms and legs were wrapped around her so tightly that she wouldn't let go.

Mom sat on the sofa and rocked Lila back and forth. "You're fine now. You're safe." Mom gestured for Annie to give her the quilts, so Annie passed them to her mother and she placed them over Lila.

"Take her shoes off and put these socks on her."

David came in the room with a full hot water bottle and a cup of warm sweet tea. Mom placed the water bottle on Lila's back. "Lila, you need to take a sip of this." She held the cup to her mouth and Lila drank a little. The shivering subsided.

Mom gave Lila a warm bath, dressed her in one of Annie's cozy flannel nightgowns, and tucked her into Annie's bed. Then she came up with a tray of hot buttery toast, two boiled eggs, and warm milk. Annie sat at the end of the bed and kept Lila company while she ate, but soon Lila's eyes closed and she was asleep.

At the supper table, Annie retold the story to her father in between bites of corned beef hash, green tomato chow-chow, and cornbread. Dad listened carefully and nodded, sometimes glancing at Mom for confirmation of the facts.

"So I yelled 'Don't! You're hurting her!' but I don't think that was wrong because I was sticking up for an injustice being done to my friend. Lila was being abused."

Everyone stopped eating to look at her.

"Isn't that right, Dad?"

"That's right."

"Miss Coombs should've told the principal that Lila ran out of the building," David said.

"Yeah," Annie said, "she came back in and pretended nothing was wrong."

Mom sighed. "I feel so guilty that I wasn't home. I went to Muriel's for twenty minutes. Why didn't she just open the door and walk in? It wasn't locked. I should've told her that. And God only knows how long she knocked at Bertha's door before she gave up."

Dad didn't say much after that, but Annie heard her parents talking in the bedroom while she was brushing her teeth, and after she slipped into bed beside the sleeping Lila, she heard their low mumbling until she closed her eyes and drifted off.

The next morning Lila stayed in bed. Mom said she wasn't ready to go back to school.

"You're lucky," Annie grumbled as she got dressed. Lila didn't say anything, as if she had no energy to speak. Going out the door, Annie turned back. "I'll see you later, okay?"

"Okay." Lila turned her head to the wall.

Annie and David were in the playground waiting for the bell to ring when they saw their father walk up the road towards the school. They couldn't believe their eyes. Their father was missing work.

He walked by and gave them a quick nod but didn't speak to them. All the rest of the kids looked at him too. It wasn't often that a parent came to school, unless it was for a concert or grading day.

David whistled under his breath. "Miss Doom is going to be in big trouble."

Annie and David never did find out what Dad said to the principal or Miss Coombs, and they knew better than to ask him. All Annie knew was that when Miss Coombs walked into the classroom, she looked as white as a sheet, and she steadfastly refused to look Annie in the eye. Annie knew her father was a quiet man who never lost his temper, so she wouldn't have been a victim of a tongue-lashing, but whatever he said did the trick. Annie never had a problem with Miss Coombs after that.

When Annie and David got home from school, Mom asked David to chop some kindling. While he was doing that, Mom beckoned Annie. She thought they were going to see how Lila was, but Mom directed her into her bedroom instead.

"Sit on the bed, please. I have something to tell you."

"Is Lila okay?"

Mom sat down beside her. "Lila is sick. Not in a physical way, like a cold or the flu, but she's heartsick."

"What does that mean?"

"You know that she's not a very strong little girl."

Annie nodded.

"Well, everything that has happened to her in the last few months has been more than she can bear. She has no father or siblings. She lost her mother and her home. She came to live with Mrs. Butts, who shouldn't be allowed to have a dog, much less a child, and to top it all off, she's deathly afraid of her teacher. When she tore up her book and ran blindly into the snow, that's because she couldn't take anymore. She broke down. She's so tired and sad and missing her mother."

Annie stood up. "That's why she needs to live with us! You can be her mother and I can be her sister and Davy can be her brother. Then she'll be happy. Oh, please!"

"I'm not finished. Sit down."

Annie didn't want to sit down, but she did what she was told.

"Your father and I have given this a great deal of thought. I know you'd like to have Lila live with us. We all love her. We do. But I don't think Lila can handle going back to school here."

"She'll have a new teacher next year. Then it won't be so bad."

"Lila doesn't have the strength to cope with it. I asked her."

"That's not fair! Where is she going to go? You're not sending her back to Mrs. Butts, are you?"

"Heavens, no. Lila and I had a long talk today and she's happy with what we've decided."

"What is it?"

"You know Mr. and Mrs. Johnson in Round Island."

"Yes."

"Well, they've never been able to have children, and they've offered Lila a home with them. She and Boots will live with them in that wonderful bedroom at the top of the stairs and go to a very small school. That way Lila can have a new family, with her own bedroom and backyard to play in."

Annie's lip quivered. "But we won't be together."

"I know you will miss her terribly, but Lila deserves a second chance. It's about what will make her happy, not you."

Annie turned her head away. She sat and stewed and her mother let her. They didn't say anything for quite a while.

"She agreed right away, Annie. I didn't talk her into it. And remember that you and Lila will be able to spend every summer together from now on."

She hadn't thought of that; her best friend on the beach with her in Round Island.

"I'd like that."

"I knew you would."

"But what about Mrs. Butts?"

"Don't worry about her. Your father spoke to her this morning."

Lila went to live with the Johnsons two weeks later. It took her that long to recuperate, or so Mom said. She was probably right; Lila slept a lot. But then Annie thought maybe it was because Mom didn't want to let her go. She ran out and bought Lila a few practical things, like underwear, socks, and pyjamas. Eunie Johnson told Mom that she'd bought enough to clothe two children and begged her not to go overboard. She said she and Joe had fixed up the bedroom and bought lots of toys. Annie wanted to see it.

In the end, they all went with Lila on the journey to her new home. They borrowed Uncle Howard's Ford again, and Mom made a picnic lunch for some reason. Dad didn't think that was necessary, but Mom wouldn't be swayed, because she thought Lila might get hungry before she got there.

For the most part, it was a subdued drive. Lila held Boots and Annie rubbed the cat's head to keep her still. David spent his time looking out the window. Annie was used to her father being quiet, but for her mother not to be gabbing away was strange.

This time, when they pulled up into the Johnson driveway, it looked like a winter wonderland. There was snow on all the trees, which made them look like Christmas trees.

"It's beautiful," Lila smiled.

The Johnsons were at the back door, smiling and waving in the cold. Everyone jumped out of the car and grabbed something to take in, except for Mom. She led Lila and Boots up the stairs into the warm kitchen.

It looked to Annie as if the Johnsons wanted to grab Lila right out of Mom's hands. They hovered and didn't stop welcoming her and the cat to their new home. It was a bit overwhelming for Lila. She leaned against Mom as if to get away.

"I think we should let Lila be for a moment," Mom said quietly.

The Johnsons appeared to get the message, because they instantly turned their attention to everyone else.

"I have a lovely warm lunch for you," Eunie beamed. "You can't come all this way and not have a reward at the end of it." She turned back to Abigail. "Perhaps you and Annie would like to take Lila up to see her new room. I'll join you later."

Once again, they let Lila go up the curved stairwell first. When she got to the top they heard her intake of breath.

The attic room was warm, colourful, and cozy. There were patterned quilts on the beds, hooked rugs on the floor, and toys on a white desk and chair underneath a window. There was a new bureau for all Lila's things and a pretty lamp on the bedside table. There was even a mother-of-pearl brush and comb set with a hand-held mirror beside them.

Three large stuffed animals were at the bottom of one of the beds. Lila walked over and put Boots on the bed before picking up a large brown bear. "Look! It's just like my little bear. This must be the mama bear."

And then she spied the easel, with paintbrushes and paint and lots of paper. "Oh, my!"

As Lila ran from item to item, her face brightened. Even Annie could tell the difference. Lila started to talk more and laughed when she spied a new pair of fluffy slippers on the mat beside her bed. There was a note on the pillow that read, "Welcome to your new home, Lila and Boots."

Lila looked up and smiled. "I have my very own room."

"It's beautiful," Mom said.

"Yeah, it's really nice. Boots sure likes it."

Boots was purring, kneading the soft pillow of the bed.

After another spectacular meal in front of the fire that included fish cakes and beans with cucumber relish and brown bread, it was time to go. Dad put his hand on the top of Lila's head. "Goodbye, dear. We're always here if you need us."

"Thank you, Mr. Macdonald."

"See ya." David waved at her and turned to go, but Lila ran up and hugged him. "I'll miss you."

"You too." David, his face flaming red, left to go outside with his father.

Mom knelt down and held on to Lila's shoulders. "Be a good girl. You're going to be very happy here. Mr. and Mrs. Johnson are fine people, and that you certainly deserve."

Lila wrapped her arms around Mom's neck. "Promise you won't forget me."

"I promise. Never ever." Mom kissed her cheek and then hugged Eunie and Joe and rushed out of the house, dabbing her eyes with tissues.

That left Annie. "I'll see you, then."

Lila started to cry.

Eunie quickly tried to shush her. "Oh dear heart, you'll see each other a lot. We'll come for visits and any time you'd like to come here for the weekend, Annie, you're more than welcome. And before you know it, summer will be here and you'll have two whole months together."

Annie hated crying. She grabbed Lila and hugged her with all her might.

"I love you, Annie."

"I'll write you a letter tonight." Annie ran out the door and into the car. As they pulled away, they saw Eunie, Joe, and Lila at the dining room window, waving goodbye. They waved back.

Annie saw Dad reach over and hold Mom's hand for a few moments. Then they drove back to Glace Bay in complete silence.

It was hard without Lila for the first few days. Annie moped around the house, but her parents didn't say anything to her. They let her be. The first weekend she went to the Savoy with David to watch the movie *Tarzan the Ape Man*. The movie was great, but a boy in the balcony deliberately dropped a piece of chewed gum on her head. She stood up and yelled, "You idiot!" but everyone told her to be quiet because the movie wasn't over. It took a lot of yanking to get the gum out. That was it for Annie and movies for a while.

Mostly she and her cousins Dorothy and Joyce ran wild outside, coasting and making forts before heading to the pond to skate.

The best time was when they skated at night under the stars. It made Annie feel grown up to accompany her brother out for an hour after dinner. If she got too cold, she ran back home and sat on a kitchen chair in front of the open coal stove in her coat and skates, listening to the hiss of water dripping on the door of the oven. The smell of wet wool permeated the kitchen. Mom would hand her some cocoa and she'd sip it slowly, letting the warmth comfort her insides, then out she'd stomp to rejoin her friends.

Bedtime always came too early.

Soon the excitement of Christmas approached. Mom took Annie to do some shopping on a Saturday. There was no bigger thrill than walking down Commercial Street with everyone in a festive mood. The sidewalks were packed with people doing last-minute errands. It sometimes took them an hour to walk the length of the main street because Mom knew so many people.

They went to Woolworth's to get some stockings. Annie had a habit of knocking her knees together and she wore stockings out faster than anyone. Mom let her sit on a stool at the lunch counter and order an ice cream soda, and then it was on to Eaton's, where pretty girls worked selling gloves and scarves. The last stop was the grocer's to pick up a few treats for Christmas—chocolates, ribbon candy, and gumdrops.

Annie's mother had started her Christmas baking at the first of the month. She made white and dark fruitcake to feed those who came visiting between Christmas and New Year's. When the cakes cooled she put halved walnuts and red and green cherries on top, but not the homemade almond paste and white butter frosting that some recipes called for. Mom liked it better plain.

Then she put the pork pies, tarts filled with dates and maple fudge icing, away in tins. Annie thought that was a silly name for tarts. Shortbreads topped with almond frosting and cherries were stacked between layers of wax paper. The gumdrop cake was a favourite with Annie and David, as well as almond cookies, doughnuts, and mince pies.

But of course the best part of all was the night before Christmas. Annie and David walked in front of their parents on their way to church. There was something about Christmas Eve that was magic every year, and Annie's stomach was tight with excitement knowing what was ahead.

Soft snow was falling. Everything was hushed and peaceful, except for the bursts of laughter coming from other children on their way to church. It was cold, with air so crisp and clean that just breathing it in was delicious. There were candles in people's windows and lights decorating some of the houses on the streets.

By the time they got to church, Annie's nose and cheeks were bright red. Walking into the vestibule was a welcome relief, but soon the warmth was too much and Annie took off her hat and scarf. The church pews were filled to overflowing. All the children were dressed in their best, and their faces were happy and expectant. Annie sat next to David and her parents.

She happened to look across the aisle during a hymn and there was a little girl with long curls of reddish gold hair. For a moment she thought it was Lila. She sat back down on the pew and didn't finish the hymn. What was Lila doing tonight? What would it be like for her on this first Christmas Eve without her mother?

When the carol was over, David sat down and leaned in. "What's wrong?"

"I wonder if Lila misses us."

"Stop talking about Lila."

Mom turned around and shushed them.

Christmas Day was filled with fun. Annie and David ran downstairs early in the morning and found their stockings hung by the fireplace, filled with small toys, candy, and an orange. There were gifts under the tree they'd decorated: new skates and a hockey stick for David and a full china tea set for Annie. She was enchanted. Soft green edged the outside, white filled the centre, and a cluster of yellow and orange roses with greenery and berries decorated one side. There was a teapot, sugar bowl with lid, creamer, teacups, saucers, and side plates.

"They were made in Japan," Mom smiled.

That made it ten times better. Imagine coming all the way from Japan!

After their Christmas dinner—goose with all the trimmings—all the aunts, uncles, cousins, and grandparents converged as a unit under one roof. This was Abigail and Kenzie's year, so the entire clan arrived in mid-afternoon and stayed until early evening, the children exchanging gifts and playing outside, the adults sipping tea and laughing together. A big thrill was listening to King George's Christmas message on the radio.

When the sun had gone down and everyone went home, the Macdonalds sat in front of the fire and enjoyed a few minutes together as a family. Annie sat on the rug, carefully taking her china dishes out of the box and assembling a place setting. David was perched on a chair reading *Robinson Crusoe*, one of the books he got for Christmas. Dad was reading the newspaper and smoking his pipe. Annie loved his ashtray with the carved deer on it. Its big antlers held the pipe in place when he wasn't using it. Annie used to pretend that the deer came alive and ran around the house when everyone was asleep. Whenever she heard a bump in the night she knew it was her deer.

It startled them for a moment when the telephone rang, one long and three short rings. Mom got up from her knitting to answer it, then poked her head in the door.

"Annie, you're wanted on the phone."

Annie jumped up. "Me?" It was never for her. She ran to the hall and got up on the chair so she could reach the speaker. She held the heavy receiver to her ear. "Hello?"

"Hi, Annie. It's Lila."

Annie grinned. "Hi, Lila. Did you have a nice Christmas?"

"Yes, I got a puppy!"

"A puppy! You're so lucky!" Annie glanced at her mother who looked very pleased. "What kind?"

"Aunt Eunie says he's a black lab."

"What are you going to call him?"

"Freddy."

"I can't wait to see him."

"Boots has been hitting him on the nose all day, but Freddy doesn't care. I have to run to catch him. What did you get?"

"A china tea set. I can't wait for you to visit so we can make tea."

"That will be so much fun. Maybe we can put real tea in the cups, and we can make tiny sandwiches for the plates."

"Good idea."

"I really miss you, Annie. You're my best friend."

"You're my best friend too. Did you get my letter?"

"Yes, did you get mine? I drew something for you."

"Not yet, but I'll look out for it."

"Aunt Eunie says I should go. Merry Christmas, Annie!"

"Merry Christmas, Lila! Hug Freddy for me!"

Annie hung up the receiver. "That was Lila."

"So I gathered," Mom smiled.

"It sounds like she had a nice Christmas."

"That's the best gift I've had all day."

There weren't quite as many visits between the girls as first planned. Life kept getting in the way, with school and chores, homework and church. Annie did spend a few weekends at the Johnsons' over the winter, once when her father was going out to Mira on the train anyway, and another time when Uncle Joe had to come into town on a Friday, so he drove Annie back to Round Island with him. Annie and Lila spent all their time outside, playing in the snow and running with the puppy. At night they curled up together in one of the beds upstairs.

"This is the best place," Lila said. "It's full of fairies and princesses and ballerinas."

Annie made a face. "No it's not."

"Oh, yes. I'll show you in the summer."

"Why can't you show me now?"

"Because they don't want to be seen yet."

Annie was curious but much too tired to argue. "Promise you'll show me this summer?"

"I promise."

They were asleep as soon as they closed their eyes.

Summer seemed a long time coming, as spring in Cape Breton was often a long, drawn-out affair, prone to sudden snow squalls and cold, windy days. It would be lovely one minute and freezing the next. Flowers could be blooming in Halifax and nowhere to be found on the island.

But then, seemingly in an instant, the first robins showed up and spring peepers started calling out in the night and it was warm enough to take off your sweater. May was, for the most part, bug-free, but it very quickly went downhill with blackflies first, then mosquitoes, then houseflies coming to life inside the window panes and finally the mighty horsefly that could take a chunk of flesh out of you in a painful hurry.

Grading day was the best day of Annie's school year. She ran to school, got her grading certificate from Miss Doom, and happily ran home again to rejoice in the freedom that lay ahead. Two whole months was a lifetime when you were almost eight.

The neighbourhood kids gathered by the rock pile and made plans for the coming weeks. Some of them, Annie and David included, were going out to bungalows in Mira for the summer. That's when Uncle Howard's bakery truck came in mighty handy. The cousins would lie down on the shelves in the back of the van and Uncle Howard could take eight kids to Mira in one run. That was a hoot!

The kids who weren't leaving town made sure to announce the great time they'd have playing and watching baseball games, going to the Savoy or the Russell theatre to watch Westerns, and eating at local diners.

Annie thought David looked wistful as his friends talked about the fun they'd have roaming the town. He was now eleven and Annie could detect a slight change in his enthusiasm for the bungalow. There were friends to play with in Round Island, but by the end of a school year they were often like strangers. And you had to play with whoever was there, even if they wouldn't be your friend in town. It was almost two different worlds they lived in, with their summer friends and their winter friends. Annie had no reservations. Her best friend and Freddy were waiting for her.

By this time, the Macdonalds had a car of their own, a Chevrolet, and so Dad and Mom piled in the supplies they would need for a summer at the bungalow. Dad worked all week and only came out to Round Island on the weekends.

"Poor Dad, he never gets any fun," Annie said.

"I think he enjoys the peace and quiet, so don't worry about him," Mom laughed.

When they arrived all of them hauled things from the car, but after that Mom and Dad said they were free to go. Mom was going to spend all day organizing, making beds, and putting groceries away, and she was happier when they weren't underfoot.

"Just don't go in the water," Mom yelled after them.

"We won't!" David answered as he ran down the hill with Annie. No one wanted to go swimming the very first of July unless June had been exceptionally warm, which it hadn't. The water would still be bone cold.

Down at the beach, they did their customary stop at the bluffs to overlook the entire bay. Mira Gut was to the right and Catalone was in front of them. Scaterie Island was to the far left. The slight rolling hills that made up the horizon directly across from them were something Annie could picture in her head when she closed her eyes, as if that background had been imprinted on her mind.

They both kicked off their shoes and socks and carried them when they realized that the stream was too wide to jump over. The bubbling sound of the water cascading over and around the rolling pebbles was familiar, the water freezing cold and brackish, and a few rocks were slippery with moss. It took great skill not to fall in completely. Their toes were numb, so they stopped in the dry white sand and took the time to put their socks and shoes back on—no easy task when your feet are wet and sandy.

Then they were off to Long Beach, once they navigated the huge boulders that sat on one particular part of the shoreline. It was easy to cross if the tide was low, but pretty difficult when the tide was high, so you had to plan your escape if you wanted to come back the beach way. Fortunately there was easy access to where they wanted to go, just by cutting through the fields and orchards at the back of the Dillon property.

Long Beach was a vast, gently curved stretch of unsullied sand. It took a good three minutes to run across it to the next point, and only if you ran really fast. It was a great beach for writing on with a stick. Your sentence could go on forever.

They headed back onto land and through the woods to get to the edge of the Johnsons' property, following an old pathway. Annie often thought it would be scary if they veered off course, but David taught her to always keep the sound of the waves close so that she knew where the beach was; that way she wouldn't get lost in the thick brush.

They eventually emerged at the back of Joe and Eunie's house. Annie skipped up to the back door first and rapped on it.

"Come on in," cried Aunt Eunie. It sounded like she was in the pantry.

They both entered the house and the smell of baking made Annie's stomach growl. "Hi, Mrs. Johnson."

Eunie appeared in the doorway. "Goodness gracious, call me Aunt Eunie. We're practically family. You've both grown so tall! Lila will be happy to see you. We weren't sure if you were coming today or tomorrow."

"Where is she?" Annie asked.

"Well, she has several places she likes to go. She and Freddy are never indoors."

Just then the sound of a dog barking heralded Lila's arrival. Annie and David ran out the back door as Lila and the dog emerged from the trees.

"Annie! David!"

Lila and Annie ran to each other and hugged tightly. Then Lila let Annie go and she ran and hugged David too. He was a good sport about it.

"Hi, Lila. I like your dog."

"Freddy's the best dog in the whole world." She bent down to give Freddy a quick head rub, as he wiggled in and around the three friends. "Are you here to stay now?"

"We're free!" Annie shouted. "I'm free of Miss Doom and Gloom!"

Just then Aunt Eunie stuck her head out the door. "I've got some bologna sandwiches made and lemonade. Would you like a picnic?"

They all shouted yes and were soon on their way to the beach to sit in the warm sand and eat to their hearts' content. Even Freddy got a sandwich, which he gulped whole. He also finished off the lemon tarts they couldn't eat. Then they lay back in the beach grass and looked at the giant clouds going by. Annie talked and talked and talked and David and Lila listened, or pretended to listen. Lila laughed at David when he'd interrupt his sister to give Lila the real facts of every story Annie told. Annie didn't appreciate it, but it was a happy day so she let it go.

Out of the blue, Lila said, "Do you want to see my ballerina?"

"Sure," said Annie.

David looked confused. "A ballerina?"

"Yes, but you can never tell anyone where she lives. Do you promise?"

They both promised.

Lila led them through the woods, much farther than either of them had ever been. They skirted Long Pond, the body of water beside Long Beach. No one lived here, as it was too swampy, so there were no neighbours or houses nearby. Annie got nervous.

"Do you know where you're going?"

"Of course. I'm a tree fairy, and tree fairies always know exactly where they are."

Annie glanced at David. He looked amused. "You're a tree fairy?"

Lila stopped and turned to face him. "I am a tree fairy, and if you don't believe me, then I won't show you the ballerina."

"Don't get mad. I only asked a question."

"Do you believe me or not?"

"Okay, okay. I believe you."

Only then did Lila turn around. "It's not much farther."

It felt far to Annie, but she could still catch glimpses of the water through the trees, so she wasn't completely lost. After stepping over dead trees and thick branches, Annie was about to say she couldn't go any further when Lila stopped.

"It's just ahead."

How could thick woods suddenly turn into a large clearing? There was this huge empty space in the middle of nowhere. The entire ground was covered with soft green moss and in the centre was a gigantic juniper tree. In fact, Annie soon realized it was three juniper trees all growing together as one, its wispy, unruly branches stretched out as if seeking the sunlight that filtered through the shadowed space. The upper branches looked like the swaying arms of a dancer and the full circle of sloping lower branches appeared to be a ballet skirt made of tulle. It was constantly moving in the wind.

"It does look like a ballet dancer! Do you see it, Davy?"

David had to admit it was true.

"But this is the best part." Lila and Freddy ran towards the tree, so the other two followed. Lila pointed at the base of the trees. "The roots have pulled away from the ground. There's a safe cubby hole in the centre and when you're in it, no one can find you."

"Wow," Annie said. "A secret hideaway."

David crawled in under the maze of roots and disappeared. Annie heard his muffled voice. "This is amazing."

"Let me see!" Annie wriggled her way into the dark. She couldn't see Davy's face, but she felt his body. He was lying on his side. It was surprisingly warm and the smell was earthy and old. "I love it in here. Can you get in too, Lila?"

Lila appeared on all fours and blocked the light completely. There wasn't enough room for her so she withdrew. The other two were silent, except for their breathing. The dog whimpered, wanting them to get out.

"Freddy's worried."

Annie and David crawled back out into the daylight and patted down their clothes, now covered in dirt and small shards of dead wood.

"No one else in the whole world knows about this," Lila said. "It's only for us. Agreed?"

The other two nodded.

"You have to say it out loud."

David looked exasperated. "Do you want to shake on it? That's better than saying it."

Lila nodded.

David spat in his hand and held it out.

"What are you doing?" Lila frowned.

"This is how you know that we won't break our word. You have to spit in your hand and shake it with both of us."

"That's awful."

"No it isn't." Annie spat in her hand.

Reluctantly, Lila spat in her own hand too. They each shook hands with each other. Lila was about to rub her hand on her clothes when David stopped her.

"It has to dry on there or it won't work."

"Boys are crazy," Lila said.

The three of them walked out of their secret cathedral towards the water. The edge of the land was quite high here, too high for jumping down to the beach. They sat and leaned their backs against the trees, their feet dangling off the ledge. Freddy sniffed around before settling by Lila. The sunlight sparkled off the tips of the waves as seagulls cried out from above.

"I love it here," Lila said. "I'm never leaving."

David shook his head. "Not me. I want to see the world."

"I'm going to join the circus," Annie said.

"As what, the bearded lady?"

"I'll be a lion tamer."

"Lions belong in Africa. They're unhappy anywhere else," Lila said.

"Do you talk to many lions?" David teased.

Lila turned her head to speak to him. "There are some creatures on this planet who know where they belong."

David gave her a long look.

"You two belong to your parents. I belong to the ballerina tree and Round Island. I finally have a home."

"I'm glad you showed us," Annie said.

Lila smiled that smile of hers. "I had to. You're my kin."

CHAPTER FOUR

1940

SOMETIMES TWELVE-YEAR-OLD LILA felt like her old life was a dream. Whenever she thought she remembered something it slipped away before she had a chance to grasp it. The only tangible evidence was the picture of her mother holding her as a baby, now framed and hanging on the wall by her bed. Even meeting Annie and David was a blur. Lila's first real memory was driving up to the Johnsons' in the winter with the snow-covered fir trees surrounding the perfect jewel of a house.

Now, five years later, she loved Uncle Joe and Aunt Eunie with all her heart, and the three of them were a content and happy family, contained in their own little world. Aunt Eunie always stayed home, not one for entertaining or gallivanting, and this suited Lila perfectly. Uncle Joe would come home from work and regale them with tales of his employees at the fish plant he managed. Lila had learned over the years to take what Uncle Joe said with a grain of salt. She and Aunt Eunie would exchange knowing looks in the middle of his embellished stories, but they never challenged him because he was always so entertaining.

Lila knew there was a war on, but she tried hard not to think about it. Whenever Uncle Joe listened to the news from overseas on the radio, Lila would go upstairs to her room and read a book or draw a picture. It felt safer not to know.

The one-room schoolhouse, a small wooden structure that housed almost thirty children from grades one to ten, wasn't very far from the Johnsons'. Some of the neighbourhood kids farther along had to get a ride on a horse and sleigh in the winter if the snow was too high. The year they started plowing the roads after a snowstorm was a huge thrill for everyone in their neck of the woods. The feeling of isolation diminished greatly knowing they could get out in an emergency. The other memorable day was when they finally got electricity—no more studying by kerosene lamps.

Lila was close enough to walk to school, but Aunt Eunie had to keep Freddy in the house when she left in the morning or he'd follow her and create a huge fuss when she tried to go inside the building. The dog was finally let out about an hour later and he would still run down to the school, but he was content to lie outside and wait by the door. All the kids knew Freddy by name.

One of the older boys, Ewan, was paid to come and stoke the school's fire at night and early in the morning so it was warm by the time the rest of the students arrived. Lila sometimes wondered when Ewan slept.

Their teacher, Miss MacAuley, was a sweet young woman who spoke softly and was full of encouragement. Lila bloomed under her care. It was a happy day when Lila was given a fountain pen instead of a pencil. She worked hard at her penmanship, but, like Annie, she loathed math. For a girl who was very content to stay in one place, her fascination with geography was a bit odd, but Miss MacAuley made a point of letting Lila take home books that had maps in them. She would pore over them at night upstairs in her room.

Lila didn't have a lot of friends. Other children tried to befriend her, but Lila just preferred to be on her own. The kids knew that Joe and Eunie Johnson weren't her real parents, but who was she, then, and where did she come from? Lila never talked about it.

There were a few girls she liked, but they spent all their time giggling at the boys, and Lila avoided the boys. They looked at her as if they wanted something, and it made her nervous.

One day after school, Lila crunched through the snow with Freddy at her heels. One of her classmates, Archie, ran after her.

"Wait up, Lila. Going home?"

"Yes."

"Want me to carry your books?"

"No, thanks."

Lila hurried along, but he kept up with her.

"I wondered if you wanted to go to the show sometime."

"No, thank you."

"Come on. You can't like being by yourself all the time."

She stopped. "But I do. I do like being by myself. I have to go now."

He reached out and touched one of her curls. "You have beautiful hair."

Lila slapped his hand away and started to run. When she realized he was chasing her, she dropped her school bag in an attempt to go faster, but he was gaining on her.

"Leave me alone!"

And he did. He stopped dead in his tracks. It took a moment before Lila realized why. Ewan, a heavy-set boy, came out from behind a tree and stood in his way. He stared Archie down.

Archie spat. "What do you want, you dumbass?"

"Leave her be."

"Why, you want her for yourself? She won't give you the time of day. You're too stupid."

Lila went up to Ewan and put her arm through his. "I don't want to go to the show with you because Ewan and I are going. Isn't that right, Ewan?"

"Yep."

"You two deserve each other." Archie turned around and walked away.

Ewan picked up Lila's books and gave them to her.

"Thank you."

Ewan nodded.

"I'm sorry I lied, but he had no right to call you stupid. You're one of the smartest people I ever met."

"I am?"

"Yes. The teacher asked us what a group of crows was called and you said a murder of crows. Everyone laughed, but you were right. I think you love animals, like I do."

"I do."

"You're also the nicest boy I've ever met, except for my friend David. He's nice too. Today I'll write in my journal that my hero saved me." When she laughed, Ewan gave her a smile.

"Bye, Ewan! Come on, Freddy."

When Lila got home, she shrugged off her coat and sat at the kitchen table, catching her breath. Aunt Eunie walked in. "Did you run home?"

Lila nodded. "Aunt Eunie, would you please cut off my hair?"

"Why? It's so beautiful."

"I don't want it to be beautiful and I need your help."

"Oh dear, I love your hair."

"You can keep the hair that falls on the floor."

"Gee, thanks."

So Aunt Eunie cut Lila's hair up to the nape of her neck. She sighed when she saw all the soft curls around Lila's feet. "There. Are you happy?"

Lila looked in the mirror and fluffed it with her hands. "Now I look more like Annie, which is a good thing. Thank you. Come on, Freddy." She and the dog bounded up the stairs.

The best time of day for Lila was in the early evening, after the supper dishes had been washed and put away. The family would gather in the parlour and enjoy the crackling fire, Boots spread out in front of the hearth, Aunt Eunie in her rocking chair crocheting trim for her pillow cases, Uncle Joe reading the *Glace Bay Gazette* in his leather armchair, and Lila curled up in one corner of the sofa, reading, with Freddy curled up in the other corner, keeping Lila's feet warm. Sometimes they never said a word to each other, but their contentment was palpable.

Lila made bargains with God that if things could just stay like this, she would be his true servant. She wasn't exactly sure what she would do, but every Sunday the minister mentioned it so she assumed that being a servant was important.

"Did any of the kids in school mention your short hair?" Aunt Eunie asked.

"Yes."

"What did they say?"

"I don't remember."

Aunt Eunie smiled over Lila's head at Uncle Joe, who'd lowered his paper to exchange glances with her. "You must be a very old soul, Lila Jane, because you can't seem to remember anything."

Lila grinned but stayed quiet. That was one of the things she loved most about these two people who'd taken her under their wing. They didn't pry. They knew if Lila said she didn't remember something, it meant that she didn't want to talk about it.

It had taken Annie a long time to catch on to that. She always pressed Lila for answers and sometimes Lila would get exasperated with her, but she had to admit, she did tell Annie things she'd never tell anyone else. She knew that Annie would keep her secrets, even from David.

One evening the phone rang and Lila was the one closest to it, so she picked it up. "Hello?"

"Guess what?" Annie said.

"What?"

"We're moving!"

Lila felt her stomach clench. "Where to?"

"Louisbourg!"

The relief was instant. "That's not so far."

"Dad is in charge of maintaining the ships that come in to the harbour. Now that the war is on, it's really busy."

"Won't you be sad to leave your old house?"

"I'll miss it, but it's exciting to be in a new place."

Lila couldn't fathom that concept. She was a little envious of Annie, always being able to adapt to change. Sometimes Lila wished she was like her. Annie never worried about anything, and Lila never stopped.

"The house we're going to is right on the edge of town and it's pretty big. You'll be able to stay for weekends."

"Or you could come here."

"Lila, there's nothing to do in Round Island, in the winter anyway. There's so much more to do in town. I met my next-door neighbour Erna Jean and she's really nice. I think you'd like her. She was telling me that on Monday nights there's Girl Guides and Tuesday there's Junior Orange Lodge, Wednesday is choir practice, Thursday night is Young People's Fellowship and Friday night is party night."

For the first time, Lila realized that Annie wasn't exclusively hers.

"It sounds very busy. You're giving me a headache."

Annie laughed. "Oh Lila, you never change."

Lila didn't say anything, because she became aware of a cuckoo clock ticking in the background. "I know you're listening, Mrs. Thomas." There was a soft click and the ticking was gone. "That woman listens in on everything."

"Then I'll call you tomorrow and we'll make plans to run away and say we're going to steal money from our parents and hop on the next train out of town."

"Annie, you never change either."

Lila did go to spend the weekend with Annie late in February. Louisbourg had an outdoor rink that had real sides and a clubhouse with a pot-belly stove and music to skate by. Lila knew that Annie couldn't wait to show it to her.

Annie's parents were so pleased to see her. They always made her feel welcome and wanted. They were the only other adults that Lila was attached to.

"Look at your hair!" Annie's mother cried. "I love it."

"Why do I have hair that looks like a fuzz ball and she has hair that looks like *that*?" Annie grumped.

"What you lack in the hair department, you make up for in other ways," her father chuckled.

"In what ways?"

"They're too numerous to count."

Annie showed Lila the new house. It looked a lot like the old one. Annie's bedroom window looked out over the harbour.

"After dinner we'll go skating. I want you to meet all my new friends. There's Erna Jean and Bernice, Edie, and Myrtle."

"You've only been here a couple of weeks," Lila marvelled. "You have that many friends already?"

"You know me. I'm not shy."

Lila sat on the bed and took a deep breath. Annie sat down beside her. "But none of them will be my very best friend. That will always and forever be you."

Annie always knew what to say.

They sat down at the kitchen table and Abigail served them big helpings of corned beef and cabbage. It was delicious. Just as Lila forked in another mouthful, David came in the back door, chucking his skates and hockey stick in the porch. "Am I too late for supper?"

"Look who's here!" Annie cried.

For a moment it looked like he didn't recognize her. "Oh. Hi, Lila."

Lila didn't speak; she had a big lump of meat in her throat and she didn't want to choke. She nodded her head but that was it. David turned his back on her and washed his hands at the kitchen sink. She never would have known him from the back. He'd filled out and was a lot taller than she remembered from last summer. When he sat back down at the table, he didn't say very much, and seemed to concentrate on his dinner. As everyone talked around them, Lila had the feeling that he was annoyed with her for some reason, and that got her back up. So she ignored him right back.

He left as soon as supper was over, and didn't wait to walk with them down to the rink. As they hurried down the main road of Louisbourg, Lila almost had to run to catch up with Annie. Annie had always walked too fast, but lately it was very noticeable as Annie had grown several inches and her legs were the longest thing about her. She seemed older and wiser than Lila, too. When did all these changes happen? Why couldn't people just stay the same? Lila felt her breath become ragged so she stopped for a minute. Annie turned around and saw that she'd fallen behind. She ran back.

"You okay?"

"Why is David mad at me?"

"Mad at you? Why would he be mad at you?"

"I don't know."

Annie dismissed it. "He just thinks he's a big shot now that he's fifteen. All boys are lunatics at that age. You don't know that because you don't have a brother, but trust me. They're completely out to lunch."

Somehow that explanation helped. By the time they got to the rink, Lila had forgotten about David. It was the most exciting thing in the world to skate outdoors at night with music playing, and she didn't want to miss a moment.

Annie introduced Lila to her friends, and she was right. They were nice girls. Lila felt brave enough to talk to them because Annie was there. As her skates slid over the ice with that satisfying whoosh, Lila felt free. She didn't have to think anymore. For the first time ever, she felt she belonged in a crowd. She was in sync with the people around her.

But the moment didn't last. Too soon she found herself bone weary and told the others that she would be in the clubhouse. Going from ice to a wooden floor was jarring. With her skates on, her legs were heavy and she was grateful that there was an empty spot on a bench by the stove, and not by David, who was also warming up. To sit and stretch her legs out was a relief. She leaned against the wall and rested for a while.

Two boys came up and stood in front of her.

"You must be new in town. I'd remember a face like yours," said the first one.

"How old are you? You look old enough to kiss," said the other one.

David answered for her. "She's twelve. Bugger off."

The two boys moved away when David approached them. With his skates on, David looked imposing. Her heart beat a little faster when he came near her. That had never happened before.

He sat down beside her. "Don't let guys talk to you like that."

"How am I supposed to stop them?"

"Growl."

Lila laughed.

"No, the thing you have to do is pretend you're Annie. She dares the boys to say something to her and they keep away."

Lila looked over at her friend screaming with laughter on the ice as her friends whipped her around. "I'll never be like Annie. She's special."

"So are you."

David left her there on the bench and went off with his friends. Lila watched him from the doorway as he crossed his skates over each other around the turns, gaining momentum with that effortless speed and grace that hockey players had.

Lately she was noticing boys more, and she had to admit that David was very good looking. She wondered why she had never realized that before.

That summer the Macdonalds arrived at their bungalow, but David was missing. He wanted to stay in Louisbourg with his dad so he could hang out with his friends. Lila was a little disappointed at first, but Annie was allowed to bring Erna Jean and Bernice as guests and it became the best summer of Lila's life. The four friends swam all day and lay out in the sun. On rainy days they stayed in and made chocolate or brown sugar fudge, eating every bit of it. They even had a taffy pull and made quite a mess, but the cleaning up was fun. While the candy cooled they'd work on jigsaw puzzles and play games.

On the occasional gloomy day, they'd hole up in Lila's upstairs bedroom and have a picnic lunch that Aunt Eunie prepared for them. Lila knew Aunt Eunie loved to have the girls around and hear their laughter and nonsense, so they made sure to spend some time with her.

With the wind howling and the rain hammering against the windows, they'd tell each other ghost stories. Annie would inevitably pinch someone in mid-sentence and the resulting screams from all of them would startle the cat.

"But the strangest thing I ever heard," Annie said, "was about my mom and dad. It was before they were married. Dad and Mom's brother were friends and they sometimes got up before dawn to go fishing. Mom got up and made them breakfast before they left. They told her they were going to take the boat out to Port Morien. Mom went back to bed and she had a dream that she could see both men in the water and Dad was holding up a radio. She got so spooked she called someone she knew in Morien and asked them to go down to the wharf and see if they could see a boat, and sure enough he saw the two of them floundering in the water, my dad with the radio held over his head. He went out and rescued them and they were nearly blue with cold."

"Is that true?" Bernice asked.

"Cross my heart and hope to die. Ask Mom. She'll tell you. She can sometimes sense things."

"I can sense things," Lila said.

"How?" Erna Jean said.

Lila hesitated. "Sometimes I know what a person is going to say before they say it."

"We all do that," Erna Jean said. "It's called being observant."

"And sometimes I see colours around people or animals or things."

"Do you see a colour around me?" Bernice asked.

"I can't do it all the time. It just happens when it happens."

"I believe her," Annie laughed. "She's always been odd."

Lila threw her pillow at her.

The rest of the time they burned their noses and shoulders picking berries on hot August afternoons, and then ran down to the beach and hurled themselves into the cold salty water to cool off. They had a bonfire almost every night, marvelling at the Big Dipper and the Milky Way in the vast and unknowable sky. They lay in the field one night and counted fifteen shooting stars.

Only very gradually did Lila become aware that her energy was starting to wane. She tried to keep up, but more and more often, she'd beg off if Uncle Joe offered to take them to the store for treats, or the girls would head out for a hike around the point. She didn't like letting Annie down, though Annie never showed her disappointment.

The day Annie and her friends were going back to Louisbourg was a low day for Lila. She and Freddy walked across the field, Lila taking time to hug the big tree by the brook that ran past the Dillons' barn. It was a touchstone, a comforting ritual. When she listened hard enough, she could hear the tree's heartbeat.

Annie and Erna Jean and Bernice were helping Annie's mom pack up the car, but when they saw Lila approach, they headed straight for her. The four of them hugged each other, all of them snivelling, except for Annie. She told them to smarten up. They weren't leaving for Timbuktu.

Lila walked back to the cottage with them to say goodbye to Annie's mom. That's when she noticed that David had come with his dad to pick everyone up. He was leaning against the car with a stalk of grass in his mouth and gave her a lazy smile. It made her skin tingle.

"I see Annie Oakley and her deputies haven't killed you yet."

"Not yet."

"What are you going to do when my sister leaves?"

"Miss her."

"Do you ever miss me?"

"Every day."

He laughed at her unexpected answer. Trouble was, ever since that night in Louisbourg, it was true.

After more goodbye hugs, the Macdonalds and friends piled in the car and with a honk of the horn set off for home. Lila ran through the field waving at them. Once they were out of sight, Lila fell to the ground and lay on her back. Freddy came up and licked her face. She rubbed behind his ears, and he sniffed her pockets for treats.

"It's no fun being alone, is it? Maybe we should walk over and help Ewan with his chores."

CHAPTER FIVE

A WEEK LATER EVERYONE WAS back at school and wouldn't you know, Annie got in trouble on the first day after she yanked a skirt off a girl and locked her in the broom closet. "That'll teach you to steal my skirt off my very own clothesline!"

Girls used Annie's antics to come up to David and ask him about her. It was a way of being close to him. David had his share of stolen moments with the girls in school, some more obliging than others, but what made it so damn difficult was that the only girl he wanted was Lila. He tried every which way to stop himself from thinking about her and when he couldn't, he'd get angry and go chop wood or run to the lighthouse and back, anything to get rid of his frustration.

It didn't help that Lila occasionally came to spend the weekend with Annie. When she'd sit across from him at the table he did his best to ignore her, but who was he kidding? He drank in everything about her. The first time she arrived with her hair cut short, it was a jolt. To him, Lila was the lost little girl with golden curls he met on the porch steps, the one he wanted to protect from bullies like Mrs. Butts.

With her hair short, he could see the soft curve of her neck, the wave of her hair behind her small perfect ears, the chin that quivered whenever she was unsure. But he had no business wanting her. She was his sister's friend—though Annie, with her bony everything, still looked like a young girl. Lila was a young woman, completely unaware of her own power.

All he could do was wait. He would be her friend, her protector, her sidekick, until that day sometime in the future when she would be more than that. The only thing in his life that he knew for sure was that he loved her. There was no getting around it, or over it, or under it. This was something he'd have to deal with forever and he wasn't sure if he had the strength.

David was bright, so bright that his teachers almost fawned over him, and he knew that ticked Annie off. All his conversations with teachers usually ended with, "I wonder who your sister takes after?" or "If only your sister was as focused."

David felt like telling them that his sister, despite her foolishness, was better than anyone else he had ever met. There was no one else he'd rather have a heart-to-heart with. She saw things and instinctively knew things before they ever occurred to him. And the thing he loved most about Annie was her loyalty and devotion to Lila. There wasn't anything she wouldn't do for that girl. Which was lucky for Lila; Annie teased her friends and was merciless to her enemies.

One day David waited outside Annie's classroom just before the dismissal bell rang to give her a message from their mother for Annie to go over and pick up a swatch of fabric from Bernice's mother and bring it home.

Annie's teacher, Mr. Hershel, always packed up his belongings to be out the door before his students. His routine never wavered. He'd pick up his briefcase, grab his hat from the coat rack, slip on his shoe rubbers, and leave.

David saw Mr. Hershel pick up his briefcase, grab his hat, and slip on his shoe rubbers. But he didn't move. He just stood there, and then bellowed "Annie!"

She had nailed his rubbers to the floor.

Annie ran out of the classroom lickety-split and grinned at David as she flew by. She was gone before he could stop her. Everyone came pouring out of the classroom in gales of laughter. Mr. Hershel pried his rubbers loose and walked out, closing the door behind him. He saw David and shook his head, a big smirk on his face. "To know her is to love her."

David went to Bernice's house to pick up the fabric. It looked like Bernice was going to faint when she opened the door.

"David! What are you doing here?"

"I came to ask…"

"If I'm free on Saturday night? Yes!"

"Uh…I need to ask your mother something."

Her disappointment was clear. "Oh. Come in."

So David stood in the hall while Bernice's mother arrived, found out what he wanted, and went upstairs to retrieve the fabric.

Bernice regained her composure. "Do you like oatcakes?"

"Sure."

She ran down the hall and appeared a few moments later with a handful of warm and crumbly oatcakes. No bag, just the oatcakes. He wasn't sure if he was supposed to put them in his pocket or eat them on the spot. Bernice looked so enamored that he figured he better eat one, so he took a big bite.

"Mmm."

"I can give you more, if you like."

Bernice looked like she was about to disappear again so he quickly shook his head and tried to talk with a mouthful of dry oatmeal. "No, no. This is good."

Fortunately Bernice's mother showed up and he was free to go. He tucked the cloth under his arm, put his bag over his shoulder, and left with his handful of cookies. Bernice waved goodbye until he disappeared.

The minute he walked in the door at his house, he knew something was wrong. His mother and sister were at the kitchen table and they looked worried.

"What's the matter?"

"Eunie just called. Lila has rheumatic fever."

"Is that serious? It's just a fever, right?"

"The doctor said she can't go back to school for a whole year," Annie said.

David put his satchel on the floor and dropped into the nearest chair. "A year? Why?"

"Rheumatic fever can be dangerous," his mother said. "It can damage the valves of the heart."

The fear that welled up in his throat made it impossible to speak.

"Apparently she had strep throat a while ago, and then this developed." His mother looked distracted. "She's not a strong girl."

"Mom, what can I do?" David asked.

"Pray."

And so he did. Every night while he lay in bed, he asked God to protect her. It wasn't fair. Lila had been through so much already. Why did some people struggle while others waltzed through life unscathed? But he knew that life wasn't fair. He thought of the millions of people who were at war this very night. He would soon be one of them. The minute he finished school, if the war was still on, he'd go overseas and protect the innocent. At least then he'd feel useful.

Mom called Eunie and asked if Lila was well enough for a few visitors. Eunie said Lila would love the company, if only for a few moments. David was unsure if he should accompany his mom and sister. He was afraid his face would somehow give away his feelings.

In the end David went, so as not to raise suspicions. Mom made a special cake, Annie bought Lila some mystery books with her own money, and David went out into the fields near the house and picked daisies. He knew Lila'd like that.

When they arrived at the Johnsons', Eunie was at the door, Freddy wagging his tail beside her.

"How is she today?" asked Mom.

"She's tired," Eunie admitted. "We've put her in our room downstairs, so she can be part of the action. It's too isolating for her to spend every moment upstairs." She walked ahead of them. "Lila, you have some people who'd love to see you."

The three of them crowded into the bedroom doorway. Lila was sitting up in bed, wrapped in a robe, looking pale and drained of energy, but she was smiling. Annie went over and hugged her right away. Mom was next to hold her in a tight embrace. David stood at the end of the bed with his flowers.

"Are those for me?"

David nodded.

"Thank you."

Aunt Eunie took the flowers and came back a few moments later with them in a large Mason jar filled with water. She put them on the table next to Lila.

"I feel like I'm outside now," she said.

"I'm glad," David replied.

Annie took the books she was carrying and put them in Lila's lap. "There. This should keep you busy."

"A good distraction from schoolwork, which I never want to do."

"I'll go slice some cake," Mom said. "I want you to eat a big piece." She and Aunt Eunie went into the kitchen.

As Annie sat beside Lila, David leaned against the window ledge.

"Sit," Lila pointed to the bottom of the bed.

David shook his head. "I'm fine."

"So are you in pain or anything?" Annie wanted to know.

"I get feverish and my joints are swollen and achy, but it's not too bad. I'm just tired all the time."

"You look dreadful."

"You're so diplomatic, Annie," David said.

"Thank goodness. She's the only one who treats me like I'm not sick."

"So who brings up your schoolwork?"

"The teacher, Miss MacAuley, or Ewan Spencer."

"Isn't he the boy who lives on the farm not far from the cottage?" David asked. "He was never allowed to play with us because he was supposed to be helping out at home."

"That's him. His dad died when he was seven and he looks after his mother and two younger brothers."

"So you have a boyfriend."

"You're so diplomatic, David," Annie mocked.

"He's a classmate."

"If he ever tries anything, let me know."

"He's not like that."

"He's a guy, isn't he?"

"The only guy I know is you. Are you like that?"

They all had a slice of cake and then it was time to say goodbye. It was all David could do to not gather Lila in his arms and hold her tight. He gave her a smile and a wave and quickly left.

The drive back to Louisbourg seemed to take forever. Annie told them not to worry because she knew that Lila was going to be just fine. David wanted to believe her, but Mom's silence on the way home suggested otherwise. He wondered what Eunie had said to her in the kitchen.

The minute he got home he said he was going over to a friend's house, but he didn't. He went into the bush and pounded his fist against a tree trunk until he bled.

* * *

Summer, with the arrival of Annie, was a wonderful reprieve from the monotony of Lila's routine, but her weeks of bed rest had taken their toll. Her energy level was low, so she didn't go too far or do too much. Aunt Eunie waited on her hand and foot until Lila got cross with her.

"I'm not a baby. I need to do things for myself."

"Of course you do, pet," Eunie agreed, but nothing changed.

Uncle Joe arrived home one day with a very large package and asked Lila to open it. It was a world atlas that he had ordered from the States. "So you can travel in your imagination."

Lila got up from the couch and hugged him. "I love you." Then she hugged Aunt Eunie, who looked like she needed it. "And I love you, too."

Annie spent her entire summer with Lila. She didn't invite any friends to the cottage. When Lila asked why not, she said she didn't feel like it. But Lila knew it was for her, so they could spend quiet time together. When you put Bernice, Erna Jean, and Edie in one room together it was in danger of combusting, and that kind of energy wasn't helpful to someone in recovery.

They spent a lot of time in the Adirondack chairs at the back of the house, in the shade of the maple trees so Lila wouldn't get too much sun. They'd have lemonade and one of Lila's favourite dishes, a fried cheese sandwich. Annie had never heard of anyone frying cheese in a frying pan, but that's what Aunt Eunie did. She'd place a few slabs of very old cheddar in a pan and fry it until it was bubbly and crispy around the edges. Then she'd slid the gooey mess onto a thick piece of freshly buttered white bread, and they had to eat it hot. Annie said that was one recipe she'd keep in her repertoire.

One day in mid summer, the girls were sitting out in the shade, and Annie had gone so quiet that Lila thought she was dozing. It was easy to drift off in the afternoon heat, listening to the crickets and birdsong all around them, the wind rustling the leaves above their heads. Lila closed her eyes and willed herself to get better, to feel better; to stop the constant anxiety that used up her precious energy and just live.

Out of the blue, Annie—not asleep after all—said, "What do you want to be when you grow up?"

"I just want to grow up."

Annie turned her head and looked at her. "What do you mean? Of course you're going to grow up."

"The doctor says my heart is damaged."

Annie sat bolt upright. "What are you talking about? When was this?"

"He comes pretty regularly to check how I'm doing. He said he heard something with his stethoscope that didn't sound right, like maybe I have a leaky valve."

"So he'll fix it."

"I don't think it's as easy as that."

"I say it is. I say that we'll grow up and find a solution to this problem."

"Okay," Lila laughed.

Annie rubbed her forehead, as if to ease a sudden pain.

"I don't want you to tell anyone. I can't stand the thought of people pitying me. I need to be normal. That's all I ever wanted. Do you swear?"

"Maybe Aunt Eunie already told my mom, but I swear I won't tell David."

Lila spit in her hand and held it out. Annie spit in hers and they shook on it. They sat back in their chairs.

"What do you want to be when you grow up?" Lila asked her.

"Armed with this new information, I'm going to be a nurse and then a doctor. I'll have you as right as rain in no time."

For the third time that week, Lila said "I love you."

Another summer turned to fall, another fall turned to winter. Lila was able to go back to school for grade nine, but most weeks she missed one or two days. Ewan got in the habit of walking her home, just to make sure she got there safely. He was quiet and calm, which was why Lila liked him. He never looked at her like the other boys did. She could be herself.

One day the weather turned milder throughout the afternoon and the crusty ice started to melt. Instead of walking on the snow, Lila was sinking down with every step up to her knees. Before she had a chance to say anything, Ewan picked her up in his big arms and carried her, Freddy dancing around them the entire time.

"I'm too heavy!" she laughed.

"You're as light as a feather."

For the first time she really looked at Ewan. Up close he had nice brown eyes and he needed to shave. His hair was brown, cut shorter than the other boys, and he smelled like hay and horses.

Lila invited him into the house to take a breather, but he said he had to get home to do his chores. He tipped his cap and disappeared into the woods. Lila and Aunt Eunie watched him go.

"Ewan is a dependable young man, and a very hard worker," Aunt Eunie said. "His mother says she'd be lost without him."

"He doesn't have many friends."

Aunt Eunie poured tea into two cups. "He has nothing in common with boys his age. He's been doing a man's work for years now."

A few days later there was a terrible snowstorm. The wind howled and the snow blew from every direction. Needless to say, no one was going anywhere that day, be it school or work. It was strange to have Uncle Joe around for breakfast on a school day.

"Little snow, big snow," Uncle Joe said as he slathered strawberry preserves on his plum loaf.

"What does that mean?" Lila asked.

"It means that when the snowflake itself is very small, you usually get a lot of snow. Big snow, little snow means if the snowflakes are big, you tend to get a little snow.

"The old folk have all kinds of sayings," Uncle Joe continued with his mouth full. "Like a mackerel sky, or a ring around the moon, means bad weather's coming; red sky at night, sailor's delight, red sky in the morning, sailors take warning. Did you know that if wasps build their nests high off the ground we're in for a bad winter?"

"A warm winter means a full graveyard," Aunt Eunie added.

"I never liked that one," Uncle Joe admitted.

Lila, amused at being inundated with Cape Breton wisdom, became aware of Freddy whining at the back door. She got up from the table and tried to open the door without the wind taking it and banging it against the house. "Freddy, just pee and come back in," she hollered as he bolted into the swirling snow.

"I'm sure he heard you," Uncle Joe laughed.

"You watch. He does exactly what I say. He'll be back in a minute."

But he wasn't. Lila shouted out the door until she was hoarse. Aunt Eunie made her come in.

"But where could he be?" she fretted.

"He's a dog," Uncle Joe said. "He likely got the scent of a rabbit and took off after it."

"He's never done this before. He's never this late."

As the afternoon and the storm dragged on, Lila was frantic. So frantic that Uncle Joe and Aunt Eunie bundled up and walked around the yard yelling into the woods. Lila didn't obey them and went out too. She called and called and called Freddy, but there was only silence.

They had to drag her inside; she was wet through. For the first time ever, Aunt Eunie got annoyed with her.

"If you die of pneumonia, how do you think we'd feel? Is it asking too much for you to listen to us for once?"

Lila apologized to them both, and then sat on the rocking chair in the parlour, covered her face with her hands, and burst into tears. They tried to comfort her, but she was distraught.

"Dogs aren't like humans," Uncle Joe reassured her. "They can survive out in the wild. He'll curl up and wait till the storm is over. He can hunt for food. Dogs are very smart; you just see if Freddy doesn't come home soon."

Lila jumped up from the rocking chair. "What's Ewan's number? Maybe Freddy's gone over there."

Aunt Eunie got it for her and Lila dialled the phone. His mother answered.

"Mrs. Spencer, is Ewan there?"

"Who's this?"

"It's Lila Phillips."

"Lila, how are you, dear?"

Ewan must have grabbed the phone from his mother's hand. "What's wrong?"

"It's Freddy!" she cried. "I let him out hours ago and he hasn't come home. You know that's not like him. He always comes when I call. You didn't see him in your yard, did you?"

"I'll go out and look."

"No, don't you dare! But if you see him out the window, could you let me know?"

"I will."

"Thanks, Ewan."

Lila hung up the phone.

Aunt Eunie and Uncle Joe sat in front of the fire and listened to the mantel clock tick off the hours. Lila paced through the house, looking out every window for Freddy to show up. As twilight fell it became unbearable. Just when she was losing hope, Lila spotted Ewan coming through the snow, with Freddy in his arms.

"Ewan's found him!" She ran to the door and held it open. "I told you not to go outside! Is Freddy okay?"

Ewan didn't answer her. His face was bright red with cold, his clothes frozen to his body. He pushed past Lila and went right into the parlour in front of the fire. He put the whimpering Freddy on the rug. "He was caught in a rabbit snare. His paw is pretty bad."

Joe and Eunie quickly ran to get bandages, scissors, hot water, ointment, and blankets. Ewan knelt by the hearth catching his breath. Lila crouched down and nuzzled Freddy's nose. "You're all right now, Freddy." He licked her face.

"That is one smart dog," Ewan said. "He stayed still the entire time it took me to get that snare off him."

Aunt Eunie and Uncle Joe took care of the dog. Lila, still on her knees, reached over and embraced Ewan, wet clothes and all. She held him tight, his frozen cheek against her warm one. He stayed very still, with his arms at his sides. Lila leaned back and held his face in her hands.

"No one else could've saved him. No one. I think you're wonderful!"

She kissed him on the cheek.

Then she focused her attention on her injured dog. Aunt Eunie took her turn kissing Ewan. "You have got to get out of these clothes, or you'll catch your death. I've got some hot soup on the stove. Call your mom and tell her you'll spend the night here."

"I can't leave her alone. The power may go off."

"Are you sure?"

He nodded.

"Well, you're going to have something warm in your stomach before you leave."

Ewan sat at the kitchen table and had two big bowls of Scotch broth with flaky hot biscuits smothered in butter. He drank two cups of tea and said he'd better go. Lila ran to get him a dry woollen hat and scarf and mitts. She wrapped the scarf around his neck.

"Do you need a light to see?" she asked.

For the first time that night, he smiled. "I don't need a light. I know where I'm going."

Aunt Eunie peered out the kitchen window. "It looks like it's letting up."

As Ewan turned to leave, Lila said, "I'll never be able to repay you."

"You don't have to."

"Oh, but I do. Someday I'll pay you back. Call me when you get home so I know you're okay."

❦ ❦ ❦

Walking along the silent white road, as the snow continued to drift thanks to the gusts of wind, Ewan couldn't keep the smile off his face. He was still wet and uncomfortable, but none of that mattered. Lila had kissed him and told him he'd done what no one else could.

For a while he had despaired of ever finding Freddy, but he hadn't given up. Lila loved that dog, and since Ewan loved Lila, he'd known he had to bring Freddy home or die trying.

Lila wasn't like the other girls in school. She was quiet and had a sense of loneliness about her that Ewan recognized. Lila was a kindred spirit.

And when she laughed, she lit up the room. She was the only girl who looked past his old clothes and worn out shoes, and she was the only friend who'd ever come to the farm, wanting to know all about the animals and how he took care of them.

Everyone thought his life was lonely and dull and at times it was, but for the most part he loved the land, the fields that ran down to the rocky beach and the water of Mira Bay constantly moving and changing colour with the weather. He'd be out in the barn before the sun came up, but he'd always go to the door and watch the pink light of the sunrise become gradually golden. Ewan also loved the warmth of the cows' bulk against his face when he milked them. His cows, Daisy and Bossy, were patient and kind, the chickens were funny and energetic, and his two horses, Queenie and Prince, were loyal and hard working. The saucy barn cats, Popeye and Olive Oil and Priscilla and Sylvester, kept the rats and mice down to manageable numbers. And he had a border collie, Scamp. He considered all of them his friends.

Now that his brothers were older, they were helping him, but every time Ewan mentioned buying more livestock, both of them talked about getting away from the farm and getting jobs in town. Ewan knew that one day they would leave and not look back.

His mother, Bess, looked older than her years. She was quiet and not very outgoing. The farm had been her life and she didn't see much beyond it, but the older she got the more she complained of vague aches and pains. Dinner conversation usually revolved around her ailments. Ewan and his brothers always cleaned their plates quickly and left the table with various excuses. She'd sigh and wash up after them.

When he had grabbed the phone from his mother and started to get dressed to go out in the storm, she was upset. "What's going on? Why are you going outside?"

"Lila's dog is missing."

"And she expects you to go out in this?"

"Of course not. I'm just going to have a look around. I'll be fine." He shut the door in her face.

As he approached the farmhouse, he saw that his mother had left the light on for him. The house was plain, but well looked after. Ewan always painted the shingles when the paint started peeling off them. He didn't want any of the neighbours thinking he couldn't do his job.

His mom was at the kitchen table when he walked in the door. She stood up. "I was sick with worry! I almost sent your brothers out to look for you. What's going on?"

"Lila's dog was caught in a rabbit snare. I found him and took him home."

"You could've gotten lost out there in that weather. What were you thinking?"

Ewan started to peel off his outer clothes. "My friend's dog was missing and I wanted to help her."

"You must be starving. I kept your supper in the oven."

"Mrs. Johnson fed me."

"Well, I should hope so. Don't do that again. You have no idea how a mother worries."

Ewan went to the phone and cranked it.

"Who are you calling?"

"Lila. She wanted to know that I got home safely."

"You'll call her, but not me to say you're safe at Eunie's? That's just fine and dandy." His mom went to the stove and opened the oven. She took out his plate and dumped the contents in the dog's dish. Then she left the kitchen.

CHAPTER SIX

THE WAR WAS EVERYWHERE. WHEN Annie and her mother went shopping they had to use coupon books, since sugar, butter, tea, and meat were rationed. The grocer used to regularly slip an extra pound of butter to Annie's mom and sometimes even a jar of strawberry jam.

The first time it happened, Annie asked her about it on their walk home.

"I don't know why he does it. He's just a nice man."

"I think he likes you."

"Maybe he does."

"There were a couple of women behind us who weren't impressed. If looks could kill you'd be dead."

"They should smile more, and scowl less."

Then there were Victory stamps, savings bonds for the war, stickers to turn in for the war effort. Saving aluminum foil was routine, as were the newsreels showing the boys fighting overseas before the start of a film. Aunt Muriel said she could see the convoy ships heading for England from her back porch in Glace Bay. In town they had blackout curtains and an air warden who would knock at the door if so much as a speck of light was seen, but in Louisbourg they only had to keep their shades down if there was a scare.

There were army barracks throughout the local communities, smoke bombs dropped at the Port Morien sandbar as training exercises. And it was quite a thrill for the locals when training planes, the Hurricanes, would zoom right down the Mira River, fly underneath the old car bridge, and instantly soar up and over the train bridge out into the skies of Mira Bay. There were boys training at the airport with Harvard and Hudson bombers, a Canso flying boat, anything that might be useful to them someday.

Every radio newscast had the latest news from the front and the *Glace Bay Gazette* and *Sydney Post Record* routinely showed pictures of the boys from home who'd been killed.

And then one day in 1942 an open truckload of soldiers went right over the bank and the railway track at the end of Horne's Road in Mira Gut because they were going too fast to make the turn. Most of them died on impact after being thrown from the truck.

It was a terrible shock. Everyone talked about it around their supper tables, including the Macdonalds.

Annie's mother was quiet and kept forgetting what she was doing when she got up from the table. She even put a plate of food back in the oven instead of passing it to Annie. Then she sat down and fiddled with her meal rather than eat it.

David didn't notice. He was still talking about the soldiers. "The boys were saying the soldiers were zombies."

"Zombies?" Annie said.

"That's what they call soldiers from Quebec who dress up like soldiers but don't have to go to war."

Before Dad could open his mouth, Mom slammed her hand hard on the table, rattling the dishes.

"Don't you dare speak of them like that! Those boys had families. They had mothers who will never see them again!"

Mom got up from the table and ran upstairs. David looked shocked. "I'm sorry. The guys were only talking."

Their father leaned back in his chair. "Some things should never be repeated."

Annie didn't feel like eating anymore.

"She knows I want to join the air force," David said. "I'll be eligible soon."

"Yes. Your mother is aware of that."

"You went to war, Dad. You trained as a pilot in Texas."

He nodded.

"And your brothers, they fought too."

"What happened to them?" Annie asked.

Her dad was quiet a long time. Annie thought he'd forgotten the question and was about to ask him again when he spoke.

"We lost both my brothers in the same year, one in March of 1919 and one in December. My brother John, we called him Jack, was the youngest Lieutenant Commander in the United States Navy. But he died under mysterious circumstances in Liverpool, England, either murdered or an accidental drowning. They couldn't tell us for sure. They never found his body."

Annie looked at Davy, but he kept his eyes on their father.

"My older brother, Coll, was poisoned with mustard gas in the trenches of France and was hospitalized in England, in Lennon Heath. When we got word, my sister Margaret sailed alone over the Atlantic in a convoy to nurse him, against the wishes of the family, knowing she wouldn't be able to return until after the war. He died the day before she got there. She went on to nurse other wounded soldiers."

Annie bit the inside of her lip.

"I know you're ready to fight for your country, David. I know as a young man you think of it as an adventure and that nothing will happen to you, but your mother and I know different. I want you to be considerate of your mother's feelings and of the people you'll leave behind. We are the ones who will wait for your return."

David got up from the table and went upstairs. Annie heard him knock on the door of their parents' room. The door opened and closed again.

She looked at her father. "Someday I'm going to be as brave as Aunt Margaret."

"I don't doubt that for a second."

❂ ❂ ❂

The following year, David signed up. Lila heard about it almost instantly because Annie called to say he was leaving soon. Lila said she'd come over and say goodbye. Annie would need her.

But she didn't have to go and see him. The sound of a car engine came up the driveway. Lila thought it was Aunt Eunie and Uncle Joe coming home from a day's shopping, but Freddy knew better. He started to bark, so Lila got up and looked out the window. David was getting out of the car. She assumed Annie would be right behind him so she went to the back door to let them in.

But only David was standing there, with his blue eyes and thick brown hair. He seemed much older all of a sudden, and ridiculously cute.

"Hi, David. Annie didn't come?"

"No, she's busy bossing people around. She wants to put on a play and raise money for orphans."

Lila laughed. "Come on in."

David hesitated. "If it's all right with you, I thought we could take a walk, my last look at Round Island before I go."

"I'll get my sweater."

It was a golden September day, but the chill of fall was in the air. The shadows were long as they strolled with Freddy through the woods and then into the field. Leaves on the trees had a yellowy tinge, and some were curled as if to protect themselves against that last gust of wind that would blow them away. Goldenrod speckled the landscape and clumps of purple thistles lined the pathway, along with hidden rosehips in the rose bushes.

They sat on the fallen tree trunk at the edge of the beach and looked out at the water. The sound of the surf was soothing and familiar.

"I'll hear these waves in my mind," David said. "Someday when I'm on the other side of the world I'll close my eyes and this will come back to me."

They watched Freddy run around with a piece of seaweed in his mouth. He tossed it up in the air and chased it.

"Silly dog," Lila smiled.

"Lila, I want to ask you something. Would you write to me while I'm away?"

"Of course, letters from home will make it less lonely."

"I want you to write for a different reason."

She looked at him. "Oh?"

"I'll miss you."

Lila was aware of her heart beating. "You will?"

"Is this a complete surprise to you?"

"I'm..."

David looked away. "I'm an idiot."

"No, you're not. I just never imagined...I've always been the boring friend of your little sister. I assumed you didn't give me a second thought."

He took her hands. "I think of you every day. I'm afraid I might die over there and I couldn't go to my death without letting you know that I think you're wonderful."

And then he kissed her. It was soft and warm. His breath mingled with hers and he tasted sweet and salty all at the same time. When he pulled away, he took her in with his eyes. "I'll miss you so much, Lila. Will you miss me?"

"Kiss me again."

He obliged.

Lila was overwhelmed with the feelings that coursed through her. She wanted him to hold her even closer. Eventually he pulled her up by the hands and put his arms around her to kiss her properly. To be that close to a boy made her giddy. She didn't recognize herself.

Eventually they strolled back to the house, David holding her hand. At the car he hugged her again.

"Wait!" She ran back to the house and went into Aunt Eunie's bedroom. Lila knew Eunie had kept a few locks of Lila's hair in a small jewellery box. She took out a curl and folded it up in a small piece of paper. Then she ran back outside and put it in David's shirt pocket before he had a chance to look at it. She put her arms around his neck.

"Take this with you, it will keep you safe. I'll pray for you every night."

"I'm coming back for you, Lila." Another kiss and then he quickly released her, got in the car, and drove away. He didn't look back.

Lila went up to her room and lay on the bed. Freddy joined her, as her thoughts swirled around her head. She loved David as a friend, as a brother even, but this? To be in love with David was to betray Annie and her parents. They were the special family who had taken her in. Lila felt that they would be disappointed with her somehow, that she was taking advantage of the situation. This was something she had to keep from Annie. She wasn't prepared to lose her best friend over it.

Dawn was almost breaking before Lila fell asleep.

When Annie called and asked if she wanted to come to Louisbourg for the weekend, Lila said she couldn't, that she was helping Aunt

Eunie with the last of the preserves. After she hung up Lila went into the kitchen. Aunt Eunie was at the sink.

"You're helping me with preserves?"

"I'm sorry. I know I lied."

"I'm surprised. Why don't you want to see her?"

She shrugged. "No reason. I'm a little tired and Annie must get sick of me saying that all the time, so I thought up an excuse."

Lila needed to escape that kitchen, but before she got to the door Aunt Eunie said, "If there's anything bothering you, Lila, you know you can talk to me, don't you?"

"Of course."

Lila went upstairs.

It was only a few weeks later that Aunt Eunie found out from Ewan's mother that he had joined up. Because he was a farmer, he didn't have to go to war, but he said he couldn't live with himself if he didn't do his part. His younger brothers were old enough to keep the farm going in his absence, but his mother confessed to Eunie that she would miss him terribly.

When Lila heard the news it didn't surprise her, but she selfishly wished he weren't going. She felt safe knowing that Ewan was just down the road. Sometimes she worried about what she would do if something happened to Uncle Joe and Aunt Eunie.

That night she stayed up late making a gift for her friend. The next day she saw Ewan standing at the edge of the woods, looking at the house. She thought he was going to come to the door, but he turned and walked away. Lila grabbed the card and the first sweater she could find and ran outside.

"Ewan!"

He turned around. He'd had a haircut, which made him look younger, and instead of his overalls he wore a white shirt that was too tight for him, with dark pants and his old boots.

"When do you leave?"

"Tomorrow."

"Everyone will miss you. I'll keep you in my prayers."

"Lila, could you visit my mother from time to time? She gets mighty lonely."

"Of course, I'll be glad to."

He lowered his head. "And would you mind if I wrote to you?

"Not at all."

He looked at her then. "I'll write home, but I won't want to worry my mother and I thought if I had someone to talk to, it wouldn't be so bad."

"I'll write and let you know what Freddy and I are up to."

"Don't let that dog out in a snowstorm," he smiled. "Tie him on a rope to do his business and haul him back in."

"I will. I made something for you to take with you, to remind you of home." She handed him the small card and he opened it. It was a picture of the front of his barn, with all his animals looking out the barn doors. "I even put myself in there. I'm on Queenie in the back."

"Thank you. This is…" He couldn't finish.

"I'll miss you, Ewan. Stay safe."

She gave him a hug and pressed her cheek against his chest. When she let him go, she saw tears in his eyes but pretended she didn't.

Ewan raised his hand in farewell. "Goodbye, Lila."

"Goodbye, Ewan."

He walked into the woods and was gone.

Lila finished grade ten in the Round Island School and then drove into Glace Bay every morning with Uncle Joe to finish high school. Annie had asked if she wanted to stay at her house and commute into Sydney with her, but Lila declined. She felt better coming home to her own bed every night.

A small wooden bridge crossed a stream near the school. Every lunch hour for two years she threw pebbles into the water and said a prayer for Ewan and David that God would see them safely home.

She wrote to both of them faithfully.

David trained in Calgary and Vancouver. His rank was Flying Officer. He went to Bournemouth, England, before picking up a convoy to Northern Scotland, sailing through Gibraltar on a twenty-eight day journey to an area outside of Bombay, India. He was with the 99th Squadron and flew in Liberator airplanes belonging to the RAF in

1945. David would navigate the flight over the ocean, keeping track of the trail and making corrections until they reached the target areas in Siam—oil fields, supply ships in the harbour, and railway lines, to prevent the Japanese troops from retreating. David said the missions were often fourteen hours long, and that they would take off in the dark and land in the dark. It was tricky flying because of an inter-tropical front that snaked along the equator. The Liberator couldn't fly over it so they flew under it, where there were tremendous squalls.

During the last stages of the war, they flew supply drops for the guerilla forces that remained in the jungles north of Singapore. These were particularly dangerous missions because the pilot had to fly low, at close to stalling speed, to look for small flare signals on the ground. Upon seeing the signal, the supplies were immediately tossed out of the plane. The pilot would heave a sigh of relief and pull up, but the Japanese were on to them and would light fires all over the place, to try and get the supplies. There wasn't much time to do the drop before they'd be fired at.

David's squadron completed two missions at the very end of the war, which consisted of dropping supplies to the POW camps. His crew got together and dropped a supply canister, with a note saying, "This is from the Canadians."

Ewan's journey was quite different. He was in the infantry and took part in the Normandy landings at Juno Beach. He was later captured and held in a prisoner-of-war camp for the duration of the war. Lila would try and make sense of his letters, but they were often heavily censored. She did know that the Red Cross gave him books, but he wasn't allowed to receive parcels from home.

She and Aunt Eunie would knit at night, making socks, mitts, and scarves for the Red Cross. They sent David a pair of mitts in a parcel once knowing he would get a great kick out of them, living as he was in the jungle, where the temperature was regularly a hundred degrees.

During those war years, Annie and her Louisbourg friends kept worry at arm's length by having parties every weekend, and Lila did attend quite a few. The gang took turns hosting them. The girls would bring the cookies and cake, the boys, the pop. They'd roll up the rug, push the furniture back, turn the records on, and dance and dance and dance to the hits of the day, the big band standards: "In the Mood," "Jersey Bounce," "Moonlight Serenade," "Moonlight Becomes You," "Smoke Gets In Your Eyes," and a Canadian favourite, "The West, a Nest, and You."

Naturally boys and girls paired off as they walked home. Annie was extremely popular because the boys always had a good time when she was around. She wasn't a delicate flower that they had to be nervous of. Lila knew for a fact that Annie had kissed every boy in Louisbourg at least once, and she had an annoying habit of trying to fix Lila up wherever they went—on weenie roasts and corn boils at Kennelly's Point, when they steamed clams in Barrachois, or even as they sat in straight chairs in the Masonic Hall to watch movies.

"Look at that guy. He likes you. Go talk to him."

"In the middle of the film?"

"Early bird gets the worm."

"Oh, shut up, Annie."

Lila did go out with a few boys, just for something to do. There was a boy named John she spent some time with and he kissed her a few times, but that was as far as she would go, which frustrated the life out of him. He said goodnight after one of their dates and dropped her off at Annie's house. Lila walked through the door as if it were her own. Annie's parents were in the parlour listening to the radio.

"Did you have fun?" Abigail asked.

"Yes."

"Who was that walking you home?"

"John MacLeod."

"Oh, he's a nice lad. His parents are pillars of the community. You could do worse."

From behind his paper, Kenzie said, "Stop trying to marry her off."

"Is Annie back?"

"Yes, she's up in her room. Did you want something to eat before you go to bed?"

"No, thanks. Goodnight."

They both said goodnight.

When Lila opened the door Annie was already in her pyjamas, lying on her bed reading a magazine. "I wish I looked like Vivien Leigh."

Lila flopped on the other twin bed. "I wonder what it would be like to be born with movie star looks."

"Oh, please. You're the spitting image of Rita Hayworth."

"I am not."

"Well, you look more like her than I do Vivien Leigh."

"What would you change about yourself if you could?"

"My hair, obviously. You?"

"My fickle mind."

Annie threw the magazine aside as Lila started to undress. "And what exactly is wrong with your mind, besides the obvious?"

"John wants me to go steady with him."

"He's very picky, so good for you."

"He bores me."

"You don't say."

"I don't really like any of the boys here."

"How scandalous! That means you like girls."

"I don't like you," Lila laughed.

Annie sat up in bed. "And what is wrong with me, may I ask?"

"Besides the hair?"

"Oh, how witty."

Lila walked out of the bedroom and into the bathroom to wash her face and brush her teeth. When she returned Annie was in bed. Lila closed the door and turned out the light. She crawled into her bed on the opposite wall.

"Have you ever liked a boy?" Annie asked in the dark.

"I like my friend Ewan."

"No, I meant as in being attracted to them."

"I guess so."

"You guess so? Don't you know?"

She knew, all right. She just couldn't tell.

"Who's the lucky fellow?"

"Go to sleep, Annie."

CHAPTER SEVEN

1945

THE LOCAL BOYS WERE QUITE jealous of the soldiers coming home, because as everyone knew, girls were suckers for a man in uniform. Everyone else was thrilled to be reunited with loved ones, except of course the people whose loved ones were now buried at sea or under the ground in a far-off land.

It took some adjusting not to be constantly worried or vaguely ill at ease every minute of the day. The whole world seemed to be full of hope instead of dread. It was like starting over.

But it quickly became apparent to families that the boys who went over at the start of the war weren't the same boys who came back. They had become someone else while fighting overseas. It was the making of some of them, but it destroyed a lot of them, too. The ones in the middle of the scale suffered in silence because no one at home would ever believe some of the things they had seen or done. How could anyone in Cape Breton understand what it was like to see children killed or starving to death or have a friend's head blown off right in front of you?

It was a difficult transition for everyone.

David returned in June. Lila was invited to the Macdonalds' for a welcome home party. Lila wanted to have other people around when she first saw him. She was seventeen now and he was twenty. She wondered if he still felt the same way. Not that she had any idea of what she was going to do, and it was damn frustrating not being able to talk about it with Annie.

When David walked in the door, everyone knew that this was someone who wasn't defeated or downhearted but confident and secure with himself and his world. He looked marvellous—tanned and healthy. He held himself like a man.

David's parents embraced him, his mother weeping and his father smiling from ear to ear. As soon as they were done, Annie ran up and jumped on him. He twirled her around and around, both of them laughing. Aunts, uncles, and cousins were next, everyone milling about and talking all at once. The women ran into the kitchen to prepare the feast while the men crowded around him.

Lila saw his eyes sweeping the room as if looking for her. She stayed in the corner, afraid to move in case she jumped on him too. When he finally saw her, his face lit up and he excused himself as he made his way through his many relatives to get to her side.

"It's good to see you, Lila."

"You too."

As he gave her a hug she was aware of the smell of him, the strength in his arms and his broad back. He whispered, "Can I come and see you later?"

Here it was. The moment she'd worried about for two and a half years.

"Not tonight. Your family has arranged this party."

"You're right," he laughed. "I'm just so happy you're here."

Annie came up and put her arms around the both of them. "The three musketeers are back together again. Isn't this great? I'm so deliriously happy."

Abigail poked her head in and announced to everyone that the supper buffet was on the dining-room table. David rubbed his hands together. "Now this is what I've been waiting for." He excused himself and left Annie and Lila standing there.

"Doesn't he look wonderful?" Annie said.

"He does."

"You watch, the girls from here to Halifax will be all over him and I'll have to scratch their eyes out, because no one is good enough for my brother. Now let's get some grub."

Two days later, while Lila was hanging out clothes, David walked towards her from the path in the woods.

"How did you get here?"

"Sorry about that. I left my car at the bungalow and walked over. I don't want to see Eunie and Joe just yet. They'd invite me for supper and I'd have to tell Joe how I single-handedly fought the Japs and won the war."

"That would be boring."

"Would you mind if we took a walk?"

"If you like."

"To the ballerina tree?"

"You remember that?"

"Of course I do," David laughed.

"It's a bit of a walk. Are you sure you want to go there?"

"It would be nice."

So they hiked through the woods and skirted the bay up to the hill where the ballerina tree stood alone amid the forest floor of bright green sphagnum moss. They sat on the grass, leaning against the spruce trees that bordered the cliff, with their feet hanging over the edge. The water in the bay looked indigo blue, with white caps whirling along the tips of the waves.

"I used to dream of this place when I was sweating on the Cocos Islands in the Indian Ocean. I'd picture myself diving into this cold water and remember how fresh and alive I feel coming out of it."

"Where you afraid over there?"

"Sometimes. Once the plane hit a couple of strong down drafts and we were too close to the sea. The pilot thought we might have to ditch the plane in the dark, but he was able to get it under control. And our airstrip was difficult to find, especially at night, during radio silence. It was part of an atoll less than half a mile wide and only five or six miles long. If we missed it, our orders were to fly around as long as we could, ditch the plane in the ocean, and hope we were close enough to swim to the atoll. It was a hell of a system."

"I can't even imagine that."

He looked at her. "One thing kept me going. I was determined to get home to you. Tell me you don't have a boyfriend and that you've waited for me."

"No, I don't have a boyfriend. But David, it's been very difficult keeping the truth about your feelings for me from Annie and your parents. To them I'm practically your sister. I'm ashamed to admit that I care about you."

David took her shoulders and made her face him. "I don't care about what anyone else thinks. I'm ready to tell the world about us."

"But there *is* no us."

"Oh, yes there is."

He pulled her to him and kissed her mouth, her face, her neck. Then he laid her back on the moss and covered her body with his own. "This is what I've been dreaming of. This is real, Lila. Just be with me. I love you."

She surrendered to her body. His hands and his mouth were everywhere and the sensations that enveloped her were something she'd never felt before. Lila was spinning around and around, unaware of what time it was or where she was, or even who she was, but David's voice told her that she was his and his alone.

Once they caught their breath, he stroked her face. "I love you, Lila. Do you love me? Please say you love me."

"I do."

He kissed her again and they held one another before they knew it was time to go. When he sat up, she buttoned her sweater and pulled down her skirt. There was moss in her hair. He rose to his feet and pulled her up off the ground. He held her face in his hands. "I'm going to make you the happiest girl alive. We'll get married and once I finish university and become a lawyer, we'll travel the world. I'll build you the best house and we'll have lots of kids and we'll be able to come back here in the summer. What do you think?"

"Where would we travel?"

"Everywhere."

"I'm not sure I'd like that."

He kissed her cheek. "Of course you will. I'm telling my parents about us tonight."

"No! Don't you dare!"

"Why?"

"It's too soon. This is our business. I'm not ready to share it with anyone. You have to promise."

"What a complicated girl you are. Do you want me to spit on my hand?"

When Lila got home she told her aunt and uncle that she'd strolled over to see Ewan's mom and had supper with her and now she was tired and going to bed. They wished her goodnight. She and Freddy climbed the stairs to her room. When she took off her clothes she looked at her body in the mirror to see if it looked as different as she felt.

She put on her nightgown and got under the blankets. Fred jumped up and assumed his usual position, curled up at the bottom of the bed. When Lila turned out the light, she relived the afternoon over and over, trying to discern whether the fact that she wanted him to do it again meant that she was in love.

Three days later there was a knock at the door, shortly after Uncle Joe and Aunt Eunie left the house to go visit her sister, who wasn't well. Lila hadn't heard a car pull up, so she knew it wasn't David. When she opened the door, Ewan was there.

"Ewan! I'm so glad to see you." She gave him a big hug.

"Hi, Lila."

"Come on in. I just made tea."

As she poured the tea, she glanced sideways at him. He was much thinner and rather pale. She'd only ever known Ewan as the picture of health. It was upsetting to see him so changed.

"Let's sit in the parlour."

They took their cups and sat on either end of the sofa.

"Thank you for visiting my mother. She thinks you're a very special girl."

"I like your mother. She's down to earth."

"She has to be, working on a farm."

"I know she's very glad to have you home."

"She wants to fatten me up."

"You do look thin. Did you get my letters?"

"Yes. I wanted to come by and thank you. They saved my life."

"What do you mean?"

Ewan took a big gulp of tea and set the cup on the side table. "I could picture you and Freddy walking on the beach or that time you wrote and said he got into it with a skunk. It made me smile when I had nothing to smile about."

"Was it awful, Ewan?"

To her horror he put his hands over his face and cried. She'd never seen a man cry before. It broke her heart.

"I'm sorry. I shouldn't have asked you that." She put her arms around him and cradled his head against her chest. It was like he wasn't even aware of her. He continued to sob and gasp for air.

"Shhh, it's all right, Ewan. You're home now. You're safe."

Eventually he quieted down, but still she held him and didn't let go. Her hand swept his brow and she pressed her lips against his temple. When Ewan lifted his head and looked at her, she didn't look away. They kissed and lay back together on the sofa pillows and pressed their bodies against each other. There was no sound, no talking, and no crying out. Lila was safe in his arms. He was gentle and kind. It was as natural as breathing.

After, Ewan stroked her cheek with his thumb. "I thought I was dead."

"You're going to be all right."

"Lila, I swore if I made it home I'd ask you…"

"…don't say anything. Not yet. I'm not ready."

He looked ashamed. "I didn't mean for this to happen. I'm sorry, Lila."

"I'm not."

"I've taken advantage of you, and that's not right."

"No, you haven't. We're friends. Friends help each other."

After they untangled and rearranged their clothes, they sat in awkward silence. Finally Lila said, "Would you like more tea?"

"No, thank you. I best be on my way."

Lila escorted him to the door. "I'm glad you're home, Ewan. Do you still have the card?"

He pulled it out of his shirt pocket. It was bent and dirty and worn from being handled over and over again. "I looked at it every night. It helped me go to sleep."

"I'm glad."

He nodded. "I'll see you around."

"Yes. Soon."

When she shut the door she went in and sat on the sofa, wondering what on earth she was thinking.

❋ ❋ ❋

Ewan walked away in a daze. He wasn't sure what had happened. A part of his brain was processing the fact that he'd made love to the woman of his dreams, and another part of his brain screamed, "You fool. She's paying you back for finding her dog."

Not only that, he had cried in front of her.

He had been so glad to see her. He hadn't believed that he would survive the war, or have the chance to tell her that her letters meant the world to him. He kept them all. Even the scent of her would linger on the paper, keeping him sane when insanity swirled around him.

The only good thing about the war was the friendships he made. He'd never had friends before. He realized there was no one he missed back home except his family, Lila, and his animals. But when most of his new friends died all around him, he became a killing machine. Only Lila's handwriting reminded him he was human. Once he was captured by the Germans, he kept to himself. Making friends was a hazardous game and he didn't have the strength to play it.

As he staggered through the woods, he wondered what she thought of him now. How was he supposed to act around her? Would they ever talk about what had happened, or was she already scrubbing her skin to get rid of his smell?

Ewan didn't go back to the house, where he knew his mother was waiting to hear all about Lila's reaction when he showed up at her door. Instead he went to the barn and climbed up to the hayloft. There he lay until it was dark, alone with his heartache and no one to tell.

❋ ❋ ❋

When Annie finished high school in Sydney, she made the honour roll, which surprised her. Maybe she *was* smart like her brother, who was about to go to Dalhousie University in Halifax, but she'd made a promise to herself a while ago and she was going to keep it.

Annie hopped on the S&L train to go out to Round Island to see Lila. She loved the Sydney–Louisbourg train. They travelled on it to go out to Mira and pick berries, have picnics, or swim at Mira Gut. It brought the mail as well. The train and the telephone were lifelines for residents out in the country, as not everyone had a car.

Lila didn't know she was coming, but Annie knew she'd be home. Now that school was over, Lila didn't go anywhere except to visit Annie on the odd weekend. That was another reason for her coming—to talk about Lila's future.

Annie enjoyed her walk up to the house. It was a perfect July afternoon. No wonder Lila loved the Johnson house so much. It looked like it had been part of the landscape forever. It was nestled perfectly with its back against the woods, and the large leafy trees and fir trees in the front of the property kept it hidden from the road.

Annie rounded the corner of the house and saw Lila sitting in one of the old Adirondack chairs. Her head was back and her eyes were closed. Annie was tempted to say, "Is that all you ever do? Sleep?" but she didn't. She knew Lila didn't have much stamina.

As she passed the screen door, Aunt Eunie called out, "Is that you, Annie?"

Annie poked her head in the door and loudly whispered, "It's me. I'm going to let Lila sleep."

"All right, dear."

Annie sat in the chair next to Lila and settled herself. She watched Lila's chest go up and down as she breathed in and out. That damned fever. What would Lila have been like without this anchor around her neck? She could still see the little girl who had sat on the steps and looked so forlorn the first time they met. Lila had lovely, delicate features, with flawless skin. How Annie envied that skin. Lila had never even had a pimple. It was completely unfair and Annie had often cursed God for his apparent disregard of her nightly prayers.

As she listened to Lila's quiet breathing, Annie closed her eyes. She woke up when Lila shook her.

"You scared me half to death! I thought you were a bear."

"A bear?"

"Well, something dark and hairy in the corner of my eye. Don't ever do that again."

Annie yawned. "Sorry. I'll announce my arrival next time with blowing trumpets."

"What are you doing here?"

"Getting heck from you."

Lila smiled. "Are you spending the night?"

"Probably. What's for dinner?"

"It's Saturday. Baked beans and corn bread."

"I'm definitely staying. Besides, I have something I want to discuss with you." Annie turned her body and tucked her long legs into the chair. Lila turned her head to look at her.

"As I've said, I'm going to be a nurse."

"Are you sure? You don't seem the nurse-y type."

"Great Caesar's ghost! What's a nurse-y type?" Annie shouted.

"Someone who doesn't holler at people."

"I'm going to be one anyway. I'm training at the Glace Bay General and I want you to come too."

Lila made a face. "Me?"

"We can be nurses together. Won't that be fun?"

"No."

Annie threw up her hands. "What are you going to do with the rest of your life?"

"I don't know. Stay here."

"As what?"

"Myself."

Annie jumped out of the chair. "Lila, you're not thinking. What if, God forbid, something happened to Eunie and Joe? How will you look after yourself? How are you going to make money?"

"I could paint."

"As much as I love your paintings, I don't think you'll be able to put food on the table. If we do this together, I'll be with you."

"You really think I should?"

"*Yes*. As wonderful as this place is, you need to get out in the world and experience life. We can graduate together and maybe get jobs at the Halifax Infirmary and we'll be two single gals on the loose in a big city."

"I'm not sure."

"Lila, will you think about it?"

"Okay, I'll think about it."

Uncle Joe stuck his head out the door. "Supper's ready."

Annie loved Aunt Eunie's cooking almost as much as her mother's. She could've eaten the entire basket of corn bread herself.

As Uncle Joe ate his dinner he asked endless questions. "Do you think your parents might move back to the Bay now that the war is over?"

"As a matter of fact, they are. Dad has a new job at a machine shop on South Street, and for him to have to drive from Louisbourg in the winter doesn't make a lot of sense."

"But what about the gang?" Lila asked. "Won't you miss them terribly?"

"None of them are sticking around. Erna Jean wants to be a secretary, Bernice wants to be a primary teacher, and Edie is trying to get into beauty school."

"Edie would be good at that," Aunt Eunie said. "She's the prettiest little thing."

"Pass me the salt, please." Uncle Joe pointed at Annie and she gave it to him.

"I wish you wouldn't eat so much salt, Joe," Aunt Eunie said. "They say it's not good for you."

"Hogwash. Now, Annie, have you decided what you want to do?"

Annie nodded, as her mouth was full of delicious buttery cornbread. When she finally swallowed it down she replied, "I'm going into nurses' training at the Glace Bay General."

"That's a wonderful profession," Uncle Joe declared.

"Oh, it is," Aunt Eunie agreed. "I'm so pleased, Annie."

"Thank you. Lila's coming with me."

Aunt Eunie and Uncle Joe held their cutlery in mid-air. Then they looked at Lila at the same time. "Is this true?" Uncle Joe asked.

"I'm only thinking about it."

Aunt Eunie furrowed her brow, which always made her look ten years older. "But Lila, dear, don't you think that would be too much for you?"

She shrugged. "I guess I'll never know unless I try."

"That's the spirit," Annie grinned.

Everyone went back to eating, but they weren't saying anything. The silence got uncomfortable. Eventually Uncle Joe cleared his throat. "I hear David got a job in Halifax for the summer and will start classes in September."

Annie was puzzled. "How do you know that?"

"Lila gets letters from him all the time."

Lila kept her head down. "Hardly all the time, Uncle Joe. He's only being polite."

If Annie didn't know better, she'd say Lila looked guilty about something, but she was soon distracted when Aunt Eunie asked if she'd like a piece of pecan layer cake.

When Lila and Annie were getting ready for bed, Annie went downstairs to get a glass of water. Aunt Eunie cornered her in the kitchen. "Annie, dear, Joe and I have been discussing this plan of yours. We don't want Lila to go into nursing."

"Why not?"

"Isn't it obvious? She tires easily. Being a nurse is a hard job with long hours."

Annie closed her eyes and took a deep breath. "Lila will never do anything with her life if no one expects anything from her. You're content to have her here forever, but what about her? She needs to stand on her own two feet. Under all this mollycoddling she'll never push herself, but if she's with me she'll feel safe to at least try. And I'm not stupid. I know she might not finish, but at least when she looks back on her life she'll be able to say that she made the attempt."

Aunt Eunie's face crumpled. "You young people today are so smart. I thank God every day that you're Lila's friend. You're a wonderful girl, Annie Lucy Macdonald."

After giving Annie a hug, Eunie went back to her bedroom. Annie got a drink and went back upstairs. She slipped into the bed opposite Lila's and turned the light out. Freddy snorted and grunted at the bottom of Lila's bed.

"Do you really think I could do this?"

"Yes."

"I'll think about it."

"You do that."

Annie stared into the dark. "Can I ask you something?"

"Yeah."

"How often does my brother write to you? He doesn't even write to me."

"Not often. We got in the habit of writing letters during the war."

"Right. Goodnight."

"Goodnight."

❋ ❋ ❋

When Lila wrote to David to tell him she was going into nurses' training, he called her from Halifax.

"You don't have to do that, Lila. I'll take care of us both when the time comes."

"You'll be in school for years. What am I supposed to do in the meantime?"

"Wait for me."

She hung up the phone. He called back, but she didn't answer it.

She received a letter from him a few days later apologizing profusely for being such a jerk and saying he was proud of her for going into nursing and that he would be there to cheer her on at her graduation. It did make her feel better, but she didn't write him back.

It was a relief to have him in Halifax. It would raise suspicion if he were constantly at the house. He said he'd work day and night to put money away before classes started. Lila tried not to think about it.

She and Annie enrolled in the September class of nurses' training at the Glace Bay General. By that time Annie's parents had moved back to town, and it was nice to know they were close by. They would share a room in the nurses' residence. Lila had a hard time saying goodbye to Aunt Eunie, because Eunie wouldn't leave the room. She insisted Lila take three tins filled with baking in case she and Annie got hungry, and then she said she could make the bed and put Lila's clothes away. It was Annie who put her hand on Aunt Eunie's shoulders and said "Go." Uncle Joe put his arm around her and gave the girls a wink. "She'll be okay." He led his sniffling wife out of the building.

Lila couldn't sleep that night. It felt strange and lonely, even with Annie snoring only feet away. She missed Freddy and his comforting body at the bottom of the bed. Real sleep eluded her for the rest of the week, and she kept waking up in the middle of the night and looking at the light from the hall under the door.

The new students wore a blue uniform with a white apron and cuffs. They were in the classroom for the most part, only spending an hour or so on the floors every day, escorted by a nurse, to get the lay of the land.

The director of nursing services, Miss A. J. MacDonald, scared the life out of students. She was strict, stern, and thorough, a tiny woman who held herself straight as a pin. But as much as everyone was afraid of her, she had a reputation for graduating first-class nurses, and everyone respected her for that. If you could survive A. J., you'd be able to handle anything nursing threw at you.

When Lila first heard about A. J. she was worried sick, thinking she'd be even worse than Miss Coombs, but the minute Lila laid eyes on her she knew this woman wasn't mean. She was just damn good at her job.

Nursing students were expected to behave like ladies both in school and out in public. It was easy for Lila to be demure, but Annie was always in the middle of some drama, even if she didn't start it. Once they were eating at the dining-room table and a new student, a big country girl from Inverness, let one go.

"Oops. I made a fart."

Lila thought Annie was going to choke she laughed so hard. Annie was the one who was told to settle down.

One day Annie came running into their room and asked Lila to come with her. Lila followed her down the hall and Annie had her open the door of the bathroom ever so slightly. There were two students who happened to be sisters in the tub together, washing themselves and, while they were at it, all their wet clothes. Lila closed the door and made a face. "That's terrible."

"It's brilliant! Think of the hot water you'd save."

The classes were long and the amount of studying was sometimes overwhelming. Both Lila and Annie regretted not listening more in math class. There were nights when all they did was try to memorize everything they had learned that day, and with Lila's chronic sleepless nights added to the mix she was exhausted, so tired that one day she stayed in bed because she just could not get up. Annie said she'd come and check on her at lunchtime.

As Lila lay there it gave her time to think, something she was good at avoiding. She'd trained her mind long ago to zone out when things became difficult. It's how she got through life. She knew that Aunt Eunie and Uncle Joe found it funny when she said she didn't remember something, but there were events she really couldn't recall. Often things were shadowed and muted, more dream than reality, so to sit still for the first time in weeks without a book in front of her made her realize that she needed to be worried about something.

All the signs were there. Piecing them together didn't take long. There was the vague nausea in the morning and the few extra pounds she'd put on. Her cycles were always irregular but never this long, so she counted off the months. Her last period had been in early June, then nothing in July, August, September, and now October.

The realization made her body go numb. Only bad girls had babies. And worse, who was the father? Only whores wouldn't know who the father was. She was a disgrace to Aunt Eunie and Uncle Joe. Annie's parents would be horrified and maybe not let Annie see her. And what if they found out about David? She'd just ruined everything for their son and his education. And Ewan, poor, broken Ewan who was too young to be a parent.

How was she supposed to tell two boys that they may or may not be a father?

❊ ❊ ❊

Annie sat through class and made copious notes so that she'd have something to give Lila to study. When you missed one class you felt like you'd never catch up, there was so much information. But she was sure that if Lila got some sleep today she'd feel much better tomorrow. Annie was proud of Lila for sticking it out. She had half expected Lila to give up the first week.

When class was over she and the other girls went for lunch in the dining room.

One of the girls said, "I've started to smoke. It's heavenly."

"Is it?" Annie asked. "I must try it sometime. I can put one in a cigarette holder and look like Marlene Dietrich. The boys will fall over themselves."

"They'll fall over laughing!"

Annie stood up and dramatically stuck her nose in the air. "I will not be insulted by the likes of you." She pretended to huff off with the girls hooting with laughter. Quickly she gathered up an egg sandwich, an apple, a piece of pie, and a glass of milk and put them on a tray for Lila. She carried it down to their room and slowly opened the door in case she was sleeping. The lights were off and Lila was in bed, so Annie went to put the tray on the dresser.

That's when she saw the pool of blood.

Annie screamed. The tray crashed to the floor. She pulled down the blanket that covered Lila and saw her slashed wrists and the blood all over the sheets. She grabbed Lila and held her to her chest, taking her fingers and pressing on her neck to see if she had a pulse. She couldn't find one.

"Goddamn you! You better not die on me, Lila!"

Annie tried again and thought she felt a pulse, but it was weak.

"Someone help me!! HELP!! For God's sake! Someone help!!"

All at once everyone was in the room asking what was wrong.

"She's slit her wrists! Get a doctor now!"

Everyone hollered and cried around them. Annie whispered in Lila's ear. "I will never forgive you if you leave me like this. I love you, Lila. Please live."

Two doctors and a matron rushed into the room with a gurney. They ordered everyone out and quickly took Lila from Annie's arms and placed her on the stretcher. Out they went, with Annie running behind them, covered in blood. They had to get out of the building and run over to the hospital only a few hundred feet away, then down into emergency and the case room. That's where the matron stopped Annie. "No further. We'll take care of her." She shut the door and left Annie standing there. One of the nurses came running and took her to another room to sit down. The shock started to set in. The nurse wiped Annie's face and arms to get rid of the blood.

Classmates crowded in the doorway and other nurses tried to calm everyone down.

"Why?" Annie cried. "She didn't want to be here and she didn't tell me because she thought I'd be upset. She tries to please everyone. Why did I bully her? I've killed her."

"Calm down," the nurse said. "It's not your fault. It's nobody's fault."

"Oh, yes it is. I insisted she come here. Oh, God."

Annie cried so hard that another nurse came in and gave her a shot, a sedative to calm her down. They put her on a bed and wrapped her up because she was shivering from head to toe.

From somewhere in the distance Annie heard someone say, "Call the parents."

When Annie came out of her fog, her mother and father were in the room, her mom sitting at the end of the bed and her dad on a visitor's chair. She wondered what they were doing there. Was she at home? And then she remembered. She tried to get up.

"Where is she? Is she dead?"

Her mother put her arms around her. "She's not dead; she's going to be all right. You found her in time."

"I almost killed her."

Her father got up from his chair. "No you didn't, Annie. It's not your fault."

Just then footsteps ran down the hall, Aunt Eunie yelling, "Where is she? Where is she?" and Uncle Joe saying, "It's all right. It's going to be all right!"

Eunie ran into their room. "Is she here?" She looked around in panic. Dad went over to her just as Uncle Joe appeared in the doorway.

"She's down the hall, Eunie."

Aunt Eunie started out the door and then turned around. "I'll never forgive you for this, Annie! She'd never have come here if it wasn't for you!" She ran out and Uncle Joe said, "I'm sorry. She's distraught. She doesn't mean it."

Before they could say anything he was gone.

Annie threw herself on the bed and cried into the mattress. Mom rubbed her back and she heard her father say, "It will get better, Annie. Just give it time."

❖ ❖ ❖

Lila dreamt that she was tucked away safely under the ballerina tree. No one could find her. She was warm and safe and wanted to be left alone with the sound of the waves breaking on the beach and the wind whispering through the leaves. But something or someone was dragging her out of her nest. She didn't want to go.

"Leave me alone. Leave me alone!"

She opened her eyes and didn't know where she was. Aunt Eunie and Uncle Joe stared down at her. Where was Freddy?

"You're all right, Lila. You're going to be fine. Uncle Joe and I are going to take you home when the doctor says you're ready to go. You don't have to stay here."

"Where am I?"

"You're in the hospital, dear. You weren't feeling well, but you'll be right as rain in no time."

"Okay."

Aunt Eunie kissed her forehead. Uncle Joe took her hand and kept it in his own. "We love you so much."

A doctor walked in the room and came over to the bed. "Hello, Lila. I'm glad you're awake. How are you feeling?"

"Tired."

The doctor turned to Uncle Joe and Aunt Eunie. "I wonder if you'd mind if I talked to Lila alone."

They looked at one another but nodded and left the room, shutting the door behind them. The doctor pulled up a chair.

"Do you know what happened to you?"

"No."

"You tried to kill yourself, Lila."

"I did?"

"You slit your wrists."

Lila looked down at her bandaged arms. "I only wanted to go to sleep and I couldn't."

"Why did you want to go to sleep?"

"I can't remember."

"Lila, I need you to be truthful. I know you're pregnant. Have you told anyone else?"

"No."

"Was this a result of…was it consensual?"

She nodded.

"Would you like me to tell your parents?"

"My parents are dead."

"Your guardians, then. Would that make things a little easier for you?"

She nodded again.

The doctor got out of the chair and opened the door, gesturing for Eunie and Joe to come in the room. They approached the bed with worried expressions.

"Is everything all right, Doctor?" Uncle Joe asked.

"There's something that Lila needs to tell you and at this moment she doesn't have the strength to do it. She's going to need your support and your love."

"Anything," Aunt Eunie said.

"Lila is pregnant."

They couldn't hide the look of disbelief from their faces.

Uncle Joe said, "But how's that possible? She's doesn't run the streets. She's a good girl."

"Good girls can get pregnant, Mr. Johnson. It's been happening since the beginning of time and will continue to happen. What Lila needs now is for you to rally around and help her make some important decisions. I can get you in touch with a social worker who can explain your options."

"Of course," he whispered.

"Will what happened today hurt the baby?" Aunt Eunie asked.

"Lila is going to need a lot of rest for the next while. I looked at her medical history and see she has a heart murmur. We have to be extra careful when the mother has heart issues."

Aunt Eunie started to snivel. She reached in her pocket for a tissue.

"Lila will feel a lot better, now that she doesn't have to deal with this by herself."

"Thank you, Doctor," Uncle Joe said. "We want to do the right thing. We'll help Lila in whatever way we can."

The doctor turned his attention to Lila once more. "You're going to stay here for a few days, just to make sure everything is fine. I'll be in to check on you later."

When the doctor left, the three of them looked at each other.

"I'm sorry," Lila said.

"Who's the father?" Uncle Joe asked.

"I'm tired." She turned her face away.

"She's tired, Joe. We should let her get some rest." Aunt Eunie leaned over the bed and kissed her. "Go to sleep, dear."

Lila already was.

❀ ❀ ❀

When Aunt Eunie and Uncle Joe came back into the room, Annie blurted, "Please forgive me."

Her dad jumped up to give Aunt Eunie the chair because she was pale and trembling. Mom went over to her and tried to comfort her.

Uncle Joe fingered the brim of his hat, going round and round, struggling to say something. "There's nothing to forgive, Annie. Lila didn't try to...hurt herself because of training. The doctor told us she's pregnant."

Everyone went dead quiet. Annie couldn't grasp what he was talking about. Lila, pregnant? Surely Lila would've told her. It didn't make any sense.

"She wouldn't tell us who the father is."

"She's in no state to talk about anything right now," Aunt Eunie sniffed. "Oh, my dear little girl. I've failed her."

Mom patted her on the back. "You've always done your best by her."

"You're making it sound like she's a criminal," Annie said. "People have babies all the time."

"The doctor said that if the mother has heart problems, it's more worrisome," Uncle Joe said. "That's why we're upset. Obviously we're going to stand by her. People will talk, but I'm not concerned with other people. I'm concerned about Lila. She's too young to be dealing with this, and that's what makes me sad."

Eventually the Johnsons drove back to Round Island to pick up some of Lila's nighties and toiletries to bring back to the hospital. Annie's parents offered to take Annie home for the night, but she said no. She wanted to be alone.

Their room had been cleaned up while Annie was gone. Lila's small bear was at the end of the bed, but there was a spot of blood on it. Annie took it into the bathroom, washed it off, and then towelled it dry. They weren't letting any visitors see Lila that night, so Annie went back to her room and lay down, staring at the bed where Lila had tried to take her life. She had thought she knew everything about her best friend. The realization that she didn't came as a shock. It was all too much. Annie grabbed the blanket at the end of the bed and pulled it over herself. She needed some peace.

CHAPTER EIGHT

FOR THREE DAYS, LILA WAS allowed no visitors except the Johnsons. Finally, after an endless wait, Annie knocked softly on the door. Lila was dozing. She looked better, thank God. When she approached, Lila opened her eyes.

Annie sat on the bed, reached out, and took Lila's hand. "Why didn't you tell me?"

"I didn't know."

"How could you not know?"

"I'm good at pretending."

Annie squeezed her hand. "You know I'll help you in any way I can. You don't have to go through this alone. Mom and Dad are here for you, as well as the Johnsons."

"Thank you."

"Do you know what you're going to do?"

"It's my baby. I want to keep it."

"I know it's none of my business, but who's the father?"

"There is no father. I didn't have one and neither will this baby."

"Lila..."

"I'm not going to tell you, Annie. I'm not going to tell anyone. It doesn't matter. This is my baby and no one else's."

"If that's what you want, but I hate to see someone being let off the hook. They should at least help you financially."

"Will you promise me you won't tell anyone? I know people will find out eventually, but I need this to be private for now."

"Not even David?"

"He doesn't need to know, does he?"

"You're right. We'll keep this simple for as long as we can."

"The gossips will have me drawn and quartered soon enough."

"If anyone says anything to me, it'll be the last time they open their mouth."

"I'm glad you have my back."

"Always."

When Annie left the room she immediately put on her coat and left the hospital grounds, heading straight for a corner store. There she bought her first package of cigarettes and a book of matches, before heading to a secluded spot near Renwick Brook to light up. Heaven forbid one of the teaching nurses saw her loitering around town. The first time she inhaled, she knew this would be her salvation. At times her nervous energy was almost explosive and she needed to stay calm in the face of what was on the horizon for Lila and those who loved her.

Then she walked for fifteen minutes to get up to Main Street and her parents' new home. It was smaller than the house in Louisbourg, with a large oak tree in the front. Although it was odd walking in the opposite direction to Blackett Street, when she walked in it smelled like home: homemade bread, furniture polish, and lavender soap.

Her mother was in the kitchen, of course. The woman lived in the kitchen.

"Howdy! I'm here for some goodies."

Mom bustled around getting dishes and teacups. "I made pineapple squares and a lemon sponge. Take your pick."

"Both."

They sat down together, enjoying a brief respite.

"So how's training going?"

"Fine, although learning the name of every muscle in the body will be the death of me." She took a bite of pineapple square. "I love these! I'm taking some back with me."

"I'll put them in a tin."

Annie took a sip of tea. "Saw Lila today."

"How does she seem?"

"Resolute."

"In what way?" Mom put a piece of the lemon sponge on Annie's plate.

"She's keeping the baby and she's keeping quiet about who the father is. She says it's her baby, no one else's."

"Eunie was kind of hoping she'd tell you."

"So I could turn around and squeal on Lila? I don't think so. As a matter of fact, she wants to keep this a secret for as long as she can. She told me not to tell David. You didn't tell him, did you?"

"No. It's not my news to tell."

They both took another swig of tea. Mom looked pensive. "Who do you think the father is?"

"Someone she met in school in Glace Bay, I imagine. I don't think it would be Ewan Spencer. He always looks like he's about to faint when a girl talks to him."

"I feel responsible," Mom said.

"Why? Did you get her pregnant?"

"I should've had the talk with her. I might have known Eunie wouldn't do it."

"The train has already left that particular station. Did you ever have the talk with me? I don't remember one."

Mom sat back in her chair. "That's because you came home from school one day and informed me all about it."

"Well, I hope you learned something."

❊ ❊ ❊

Lila watched the snow fall softly out the window. It was December 25 and the Johnsons had a quiet Christmas, exchanging gifts under the tree while the fire crackled in the fireplace. The smell of turkey still lingered in the house. Boots was curled up in a gift box amongst the wrapping paper and Freddy dozed under the dining-room table, while Uncle Joe snored in his chair. Even Aunt Eunie had put her feet up and was now making small blowing noises from between her lips, like she was blowing out a birthday candle every ten seconds.

Lila was content. The last few months had been quiet. She went nowhere and she saw no one. Her whole world was the child inside her, the one thing no one could take from her. This child would want only her.

So far, no one knew about the baby; no one had said a word. She appreciated the support. Not only that, no one would even know she was carrying a baby. She had only a small bump that could be hidden under almost anything. That was something she was counting on, since she didn't have an excuse not to see David over the Christmas holidays. They were invited to the Macdonalds' for a potluck the next day. At least with a crowd of people there would be no alone time.

When they arrived at the Macdonalds' new home, it was festive and decorated inside and out. Cars were parked in the driveway and on the street. Lila stayed close to Aunt Eunie, taking her by the arm and helping her along the pathway to the front door. She saw David in the window and then he disappeared to come to the door and greet them.

"Merry Christmas!" He looked wonderful in a white shirt with a navy blue sweater vest over it. His hair was short and his face clean-shaven. Lila felt an immediate pull to be with him.

David kissed Aunt Eunie and shook hands with Uncle Joe before taking her in his arms and hugging her.

"I've missed you," he whispered in her ear.

"Hi, David."

She withdrew from his embrace as soon as she could and entered the house with everyone rushing to greet them. Annie pushed through the crowd and gave Lila a big hug.

"It's so good to see you."

"Merry Christmas. How are things at the hospital?"

"Horrifying. My brain is about to explode."

Lila saw David out of the corner of her eye. He was trying to attract her attention, but she moved towards Abigail and Kenzie, who both smiled when they saw her.

Abigail took her hands. "You look well."

"I'm fine."

The first hour was taken up with gathering platefuls of food, sweet and sour meatballs, cabbage rolls, lasagna, goulash, coleslaw, and fresh rolls, and then sitting wherever there was space. The laughter and joking was infectious. This first Christmas after the war was a celebration. Life could only get better.

Lila sat down next to Annie's Aunt Muriel on the sofa.

"You're going to eat more than that, I hope?" Aunt Muriel was getting wider with each passing year.

Lila looked down at her two meatballs and buttered roll. "This is good."

"I'm getting hungry just looking at that. I must get some dessert." She got up and David instantly sat down next to her with his plate piled high.

"Are you trying to avoid me?" he smiled.

"Yes."

"You're afraid I'm going to give something away?"

"I don't want to talk about it here."

"Then you're going to have to meet me somewhere, because I can't go back to school without kissing you."

Lila didn't answer him.

"Is something wrong?"

"Excuse me." She got up and placed her plate on the side table and then ran upstairs to hide in the bathroom. He followed her and knocked at the closed door. "Lila, please talk to me."

She leaned against the door. "I can't."

"Why?"

"I'm sorry. I need to be alone."

After a few moments, she heard him leave and walk downstairs. She waited for a few minutes longer and then descended the staircase herself, making a beeline for Annie. She stayed by her side for the rest of the visit, but she need not have worried, because David was nowhere to be found.

She and Annie exchanged gifts up in her room. Lila had made Annie a bright red wool scarf that was so long it had to be wrapped around her neck three times, and a pair of mitts with thick bands of bright primary colours.

"Thank you! This will keep me nice and toasty on those walks to the Forum."

Then Annie passed over her gift. "It's for both of you."

Lila unwrapped a crib-sized white blanket embroidered with colourful baby animals. She held it to her breast. "I love it! Thank you so much." She gave her best friend a hug.

"Honest to God, you'd never know you were having a baby. You're so small."

"The doctor says I'm fine so far."

"How do you pass the time?"

"I read and knit and help Aunt Eunie with things. I'm happy."

Annie flopped back on the bed. "I would go out of my gourd doing that. As much as I complain about the studying, I'm enjoying nursing more than I thought. But damn, some people are ugly."

"Annie!"

"It's true. There are some sorry specimens out there. And old men are the worst. We had this one guy; I swear his nuts were almost to the floor."

Lila made a face. "Stop it! That's not an image I want to carry around with me."

"There was one old man whose toenails were so long they were curly, and on top of that they were green with fungus."

Lila put the pillow over her head so she couldn't hear any more. Thank God she hadn't gone into nursing.

❊ ❊ ❊

David was confused. Lila wrote to him, answered his phone calls, and seemed glad to see him, but the minute he tried to talk to her alone, she bolted.

It was tough for him to be away from her. At university he got plenty of attention from girls and sometimes it was hard not to give in, but he'd take out the picture he kept of Lila and his resolve would last another day.

The whole situation was crazy anyway. He had to hide his feelings from his family, pretend and lie to people. What was she so afraid of? That Annie and his parents would hate her suddenly? They loved her. That was a bonus. But anytime he suggested telling the truth, she would get upset, and so as frustrating as it was, he knew he couldn't cross that line, or he might lose her forever.

The hardest part was trying to see her when he came home for visits. He'd make up stories about seeing old friends and borrow his father's car, but most of the time when he went out to Round Island, the Johnsons' car was in the yard, which meant Eunie and Joe were home. He'd go back to town and try not to appear glum in front of his parents.

A few days after Christmas he drove out to the bungalow and parked the car there, then walked over across the field and through the woods. There was no car in the yard, which was great, but that still didn't mean that Eunie wasn't there. He'd risk it and tell Eunie that he was out for a walk to the beach and thought he'd drop by. Surely he'd get at least a few moments alone with Lila. He needed that before he headed back to Halifax. Something had to change.

He knocked on the door and on cue, Freddy gave his welcoming bark. Lila opened it.

"David! What are you doing here?"

"Are you alone?"

She looked behind her, as if trying to decide what to do. "Yes, but they're coming back soon."

"Would you mind if I came in for a few minutes?"

"All right."

She grabbed a long sweater off the back of one of the kitchen chairs and wrapped it around herself. "Would you like some tea?"

"Sure."

Lila busied herself getting their tea ready and putting out a plate of store-bought cookies.

"Very nice," David smiled. "I keep asking Mom to buy these, but she won't."

She poured the tea and sat down at the table. "Your mother's cookies are much better, that's why."

He took a sip of his tea, as an excuse to look at her longer. She was beautiful, with her hair now shoulder length, and it looked as if she'd gained a few pounds, which suited her. It was hard not to stare at that sweet face.

"Lila, why are you hiding from me?"

"I'm not."

"I thought you cared about me."

"I do…"

"Then why do I get the feeling that you're afraid of me?"

She looked down at her mug of tea, as if looking for the answer to magically appear. "It seems silly to make plans when you have so many years of school left. Why don't we wait and see what happens?"

"I will never change my mind."

"I might." She got up from the table and started to pace, so he rose to his feet and took her in his arms. "I love you." He kissed her and despite what she said, she kissed him back. There was no mistaking that kiss. Even if she never said another word, he was reassured.

"You should go now," she said. "I don't want Aunt Eunie and Uncle Joe to find you here. They aren't stupid."

He tried to hold her close, but she pushed him away. "Go, silly boy."

David grinned and kissed her once more before he slipped out the door and ran back to the bungalow. Those few minutes would see him through the next semester.

❖ ❖ ❖

Annie was the one all the student nurses came to with their problems and concerns; usually because she made them laugh and life would be a bit brighter when she was around. Because she was tall, everyone thought she was older and Annie didn't mind that one bit. She got away with more for some reason.

It was Valentine's Day and the nurses were looking forward to going to the Forum for a skate that evening. It was a great place to be with the gang and size up the boys. Because they were student nurses, they were expected to be ladies and wear skirts in public, but these "ladies" all wore slacks rolled up under their skirts and discarded the skirts when they got to the rink.

It was nearly time to leave the hospital floor when one of the student nurses, a shy girl from Baddeck, came out of a patient's room in tears, holding a basin and an enema bag. The others gathered around her.

"What's wrong?" Annie asked.

"That horrible man keeps trying to touch me and says terrible things while I..." She couldn't finish. One of the other nurses spoke up.

"He did that to me a few days ago. He's a pervert."

"Give that to me," Annie said.

The girl passed over the basin and the full enema bag and Annie marched into the room. The others crowded around the door to listen. The hospital curtain was around his bed, so they didn't get to see anything, but they sure heard it.

"How are we today?" Annie said to him.

"Real good, now that you're here."

"I've been asked to come in and give you an enema."

He grinned. "I can't wait. I hope you enjoy it as much as I will."

"Oh yeah, I'll enjoy it, all right. Get on your side."

He did as he was told and she shoved the tube into him as hard as she could.

"AGGGH!…are you crazy?"

"You could say that. Now, I want you to keep your dirty hands off the nurses and keep your slime-ball comments to yourself."

"Take it out! Take it out! Oh, my stomach! I'm cramping up!"

"Have we got a deal, or do I have to come in here and do this again?"

"Get out! Stop it. I'll stop."

Annie stopped. "Have a good day, asshole."

She emerged from behind the curtain to the delight of the others, who were silently cheering so as not to attract attention.

"He won't be bothering you again," she said to the young nurse, who looked at her with admiration.

Naturally word spread throughout the nurses' residence, and they had quite a few laughs over the whole incident. "Have a good day, asshole" became the rallying cry for anyone breaking up with a jerky boyfriend.

The Valentine's Day skate was a good time. It was like being a kid again. Annie whipped around the ice with her long legs, passing everyone. There was nothing dainty about Annie, which was quite obvious when she plowed into a guy because she was shouting at someone behind her. They both nearly fell to the ice, but managed to save themselves by clinging on to each other's coats and the momentum had them circling each other before they stopped.

"I almost fell head over heels for you," she laughed.

She'd seen this fellow at the hospital once before, and had noticed how nice his suit looked on him, but she didn't know who he was. He had red hair and was at least three inches shorter than she was, but he had a charming smile and dark brown eyes.

"As did I," he smiled. "Now that I've bumped into you, I'm Henry Pratt."

"Ah, Henry Pratfall."

He laughed at her joke. Always a good sign.

"I'm Annie Macdonald."

"Yes, I know."

"You do?"

"Everyone at the hospital knows who you are."

"You don't say. That could be good or bad."

"Only very good."

They started to skate together while they talked.

"What do you do at the hospital?" she asked.

"I'm a doctor."

"Go on!"

"You don't believe me?"

"You look so young."

"I'm thirty, but hopefully that's not over the hill yet."

"Are you from here?"

"Originally. That's why I came back. My mother lives alone and I'm her only son. You know how it goes."

"Oh lordy, a mama's boy. I'm staying away from you."

"I hope not," he smiled.

They skated together the entire time and then bid each other farewell. The girls were eager to get the scoop as Annie untied her skates.

"That was Doctor Pratt, wasn't it?" Irene said. She was one of the girls Annie was close to. "The head nurse says he's very bright and that we're lucky to have him here in the Bay."

"They're lucky to have us, too," Annie said. "Doctors always get the glory, but we're the ones who do the grunt work."

They all snuck a cigarette in the girls' bathroom before exiting the building. It was a blustery evening and Annie was very glad she had on Lila's scarf and mitts. Even in the midst of a group of friends, Annie often thought how much better it would be if Lila was there too. Look how much she was missing, sitting in Round Island waiting for this baby to arrive.

She caught sight of Henry walking home with a few friends. He always had a smile on his face. He happened to look up and catch her eye. When he waved, she waved back.

"I think someone is smitten," Irene said as they walked over the snow-covered sidewalks to the nurses' residence.

"Don't be so foolish," Annie snapped. "He's practically an old man."

"Annie's getting mad at me, girls. I rest my case."

Annie picked up a mitt full of snow and chased Irene down the street with it.

Annie volunteered to go down to the emergency room the next morning to deliver some papers from their instructor to the head nurse. She'd do anything to stretch her legs for a few minutes and get away from the confines of her desk. Sitting for too long still drove her mad.

At the nurses' station she was told to wait, that the head nurse would be with her shortly. That's when an ambulance pulled up to the back door of the hospital. Annie hated to see that. You never knew what you were dealing with. As the attendants wheeled the stretcher down the hall, Annie nearly passed out.

It was Lila.

She ran over to her. "Lila! My God, what's wrong?"

"Annie…"

She grabbed Lila's hand and ran with the stretcher until they got to the largest case room. Annie tried to stay with Lila, but she was pushed aside by one of the nurses. "Clear out. You're in the way."

That's when Annie saw Pratfall. "Henry!"

He looked up.

"She's my best friend! Take care of her!"

He nodded and approached the stretcher. Annie was told to leave. She was in a daze. Lila wasn't due for another month and a half. Then she saw Aunt Eunie and Uncle Joe rush down the corridor. They seemed relieved that Annie was there.

"What happened?"

"She had trouble breathing this morning," Uncle Joe panted.

"I don't think she's been feeling well the last few days, but she wouldn't let on," Aunt Eunie said. "If only I made her see the doctor. I knew something wasn't quite right."

"Don't beat yourself up," Annie said. "I know how stubborn she can be."

"I shouldn't say this," Aunt Eunie sniffed, "but if it comes down to saving Lila or the baby, I want them to save Lila. Is that selfish?"

Annie wrapped her arms around Aunt Eunie. "No, that's not selfish, but I'm sure it won't come to that. There's a new doctor here that they say is very good. I'm sure they'll both be fine."

Lila was admitted to the hospital and only Eunie and Joe were allowed in with her. It was more than frustrating for Annie, who wanted to know exactly what was going on. She'd forgotten all about her class at this point and was relieved when she saw Henry emerge from the casualty room.

"What's wrong with her?"

"I can't discuss it with you."

"Don't give me that bullshit."

Henry looked around to see if anyone was about. "I'm not sure what's wrong."

"It has to do with her heart, though?"

"Or it could be a bad case of the flu. Don't worry, Annie. I'll do my best."

Annie nodded and he walked down the hall. She left the papers with the ward clerk and rushed back to the residence, but only to put on her coat and boots. Then she ran all the way home, like she used to do when she was a kid. She burst in the front door.

"Mom!"

"In here."

Annie paused to take off her boots and then rushed into the kitchen. Mom was doing the ironing.

"Why aren't you in school?"

"Lila's in the hospital."

Mom put the iron back on the coal stove. "Oh God, did she have the baby?"

"No, she had trouble breathing. I'm so frightened."

Her mother hugged her, which was just what she needed. "I know

Lila is fragile, but she has a strong will, and I don't think she'll let anything get in the way of her seeing this baby. All mothers are like that."

"Do you promise?"

"Yes."

Annie knew that was impossible, but it helped to have Mom say it anyway. Then her mother told her to sit down and she'd make her lunch. It was like being seven again. Life was never as scary in her mother's kitchen. A grilled cheese sandwich, a piece of chocolate cake, and a large glass of milk did wonders for Annie's spirits. Of course Lila was going to be all right. Annie couldn't panic. That would only upset Lila, and she needed to stay calm and relaxed.

Then Mom said, "Do you think we should tell David?"

"What can he do in Halifax? Only worry. Let's save him from that for now."

"You're right."

Annie slipped in to see Lila as soon as she could. It reminded her of the awful day when Lila had tried to hurt herself. She looked small and defenceless in the large hospital bed. Thinking she was asleep, Annie backed up and was about to leave when Lila said, "Don't go."

Annie sat on the side of the bed and held her hand. "Are you feeling better?"

Lila shook her head. "They want to keep me here until the baby's born."

"I know that sounds terrible, but this is the best place for you right now. Aunt Eunie and Uncle Joe will be relieved to know you're being cared for around the clock. And I'll come and visit as often as I can."

"Thanks."

"The doctor who's on your case is really good. His name is Henry. I nearly killed him at the Forum."

"Lucky for me you didn't."

"You look tired. Get some rest." She leaned over and kissed Lila on the forehead.

Later in the week, after the Johnsons went home, Annie went into Lila's room before she left for the evening to study. Lila asked her for a drink of water. When Annie came back to the room, Dr. Pratt was in a chair beside Lila's bed. He was inspecting her fingers.

"Hi, Henry." Annie gave Lila a sip of water from the other side of the bed.

"Shouldn't she call you Doctor Pratt?" Lila said.

"She can call me whatever she wants, as long as she calls me."

"How old is that joke?" Annie watched him. "What are you looking for?"

"I'm looking at the colour of her fingertips."

Annie knew better than to ask any more questions in front of Lila.

"Lila, I think I'm going to start giving you penicillin. It will help you."

"But what about the baby?"

"It shouldn't hurt the baby."

"Okay." Lila closed her eyes.

Henry and Annie left the room together. "It's not the flu, is it?"

"I think it might be endocarditis…"

"…inflammation of the inner layer of the heart, or endocardium. Yes, of course! That explains the weight loss and the aching joints, chills, fever…"

"I take it you've been reading up on matters of the heart?"

"Lila's heart matters to me."

One night at the residence, a phone call came in for Annie. She was in her slippers and nightgown with curlers in her hair when she went down the hall to see who it was.

"Hello?"

"Annie, it's me."

"Hi, Davy. Are you coming home for Easter?"

"Probably. Listen, I called Mom and asked her about Lila because I haven't heard from her in a while and she sounded evasive, like she was hiding something from me. Is Lila okay?"

"She had that bug that was going around, and it kind of wiped her out, so she's been staying in bed for now. Doctor's orders, just to play it safe."

"Oh, okay. I was starting to worry. If you see her, tell her to feel better."

"I will. How's school?"

"Lots of work. You?"

"Lots of work."

"I better go. There's a jerk behind me wanting to use the phone… yeah, you heard me, MacIntyre."

"Take care, Davy."

Annie hung up and felt as guilty as hell. This lying to people was for the birds.

CHAPTER NINE

THE LAST MONTH OF LILA'S pregnancy involved her receiving over a hundred shots of penicillin, but still she didn't feel much better. One morning a housekeeper came into the room to mop the floor. She nodded at Lila.

"What's wrong with you, dear, if you don't mind my asking?"

"I'm having a baby."

The housekeeper looked shocked. "What on earth are you having? A mouse?"

Uncle Joe would drop Aunt Eunie off at the hospital on his way to work every morning and she'd stay with Lila for the day.

"I've got everything ready for the nursery," Aunt Eunie reassured her as she sat in the chair and knit a sweater set for the baby. "It's all taken care of, so I don't want you to worry about anything."

"That's nice."

She was dozing off again when she thought of something. "Do you leave Freddy in the house all day? He must get lonely."

"Don't worry about Freddy. He stays with Ewan at the farm during the day."

"I'm glad. What did you tell Ewan?"

"I told him you were a bit run down and that the doctor thought you should rest. I'm not sure if he believed me, but I didn't tell him anything else."

"Everyone will know soon enough."

The days seemed to run together. Lila wasn't sure when it was morning or night. At intervals people would pop into the room to hold her hand and tell her things were going well, but it hardly mattered. It got to the point where she wasn't interested in anything, not even how active the baby was. Dr. Pratt was in every day and she thought how nice he was, but most of the time she just wanted to sleep and wished everyone would go away.

Then one day she opened her eyes and saw the head nurse sitting in the chair beside her bed.

That's when Lila realized she was dying. Head nurses didn't sit with patients unless the situation was dire. She knew that much from the little training she had.

Why hadn't someone told her she was dying? She knew everyone looked at her with sadness in their eyes, but no one said the words. If she died the baby would die. Lila resolved to live.

The baby was born a week early; a little girl. Lila was so sick that she didn't get to hold the baby. A nurse held her up. "She looks like a scrawny chicken," Lila whispered.

Lila heard later that the Johnsons were told she had a boy, and then that the baby had died, before someone came to the rescue and straightened out the facts. That terrible news was for another family. Lila had a girl and she was fine, but only for about two days. One of the off-duty nurses called the hospital and asked them to look in on the Phillips baby, because she was worried about her. They soon discovered the baby had pneumonia. It was touch and go for a while.

Dr. Pratt came in to Lila's room one day while Annie was visiting.

"Lila, you're not going to be able to look after the baby. You're not strong enough."

"I know that. Aunt Eunie and Uncle Joe are going to look after her."

"You'll have to stay in bed for at least six months."

"Six *months*?"

"I'm willing to let you go home in a couple of weeks if you promise me that you will play by the rules. Otherwise, I'll keep you in the hospital, to make sure that you follow my orders."

Annie nodded. "You have to do everything Henry says. That way you'll build up your strength."

"And even then, Lila, you're going to have to go to bed at six o'clock every night for a good year or more. That's the only way you have a chance of recovery. You almost died and that can't be fixed in a hurry. Because of your heart, you'll always have to be careful and rest a lot. But that shouldn't stop you from enjoying your daughter; I know you have friends that will help out. Like this one right here." He nodded his head towards Annie.

"I lost my mother when I was young. I won't let that happen to Caroline."

"Caroline! That's pretty," Annie said.

"It was my mother's name."

Freddy was so happy to see Lila when she finally returned to the house. He was eleven now and had a white muzzle, but he was still frisky enough to dance around the kitchen when he first saw her. It was heaven seeing him again.

Aunt Eunie and Uncle Joe had everything ready for her. She was to stay upstairs, because Aunt Eunie was afraid that Lila would want to help out if she saw what was going on downstairs with the baby. They had put the bassinet and changing table in their room. The whole house was turned upside down for one little five-pound infant.

But Lila didn't mind staying up in her bedroom by herself. She knew she needed the rest. The weariness in her bones was deep, so she needed no convincing that this was the best solution for now. But every day, Aunt Eunie would walk up the stairs when Caroline was peaceful and put her in Lila's arms.

"Isn't she pretty?" Lila touched the baby's face and stroked her tiny fingers.

"She's the most beautiful baby in the world."

"I think so too."

Her favourite thing to do was to breathe in Caroline's soft skin. That heavenly aroma of baby powder, mild soap, and clean and ironed layettes combined to make a scent that Lila knew she'd remember for the rest of her life.

Caroline was a serious baby. She didn't cry much, but looked out at the world as if she knew all about it. Lila was sure Caroline's eyes were going to be brown, but they became more greenish hazel as time went on. As soon as she started to fuss, Aunt Eunie would take her back downstairs and Lila would close her eyes and drift off to sleep.

She'd only been home a few weeks when Aunt Eunie asked if Ewan could come up to see her. Lila knew she couldn't put if off any longer, so she agreed. Ewan's boots thumped up the stairs. He looked even bigger standing at the end of her bed or maybe she was smaller.

"Hi, Ewan."

"Hi, Lila."

"Thank you for taking care of Freddy."

"I didn't mind."

They looked at each other. It was time.

"Is she mine?"

"No."

She knew by the look on his face that she was hurting him, but she had no choice. "I'm sorry, Ewan."

"But...the time fits."

"She's not yours."

"Why didn't you tell me?"

"I didn't tell anyone. You know how people are."

"I know you don't love me, Lila. Is that the reason you don't want me to be the father? You're afraid I'll interfere in your life?"

"I do love you, Ewan. You're my dearest friend, but you're not the baby's father."

He bowed his head and took a deep breath. "Okay."

"Don't be sad."

Ewan looked up at her. "I wanted to do the right thing, that's all."

"You mean marry me?"

"I wanted to look after you and the baby. I still do. I don't care if she's not mine. I don't want to see you go through this alone."

"But I won't be alone, unless you never want to speak to me again," she smiled.

"I can't see that happening."

"I need to get better for Caroline. That's all I can think about right now."

He nodded his head. "Okay. I'm here if you need anything."

"That makes me so happy. Thank you."

Ewan backed up and slowly descended the stairs, but before he disappeared he turned his head to look at her.

"She's a sweet little thing."

"She is, isn't she?"

"As pretty as you are."

"Yes, I look amazing at the moment."

He smiled and when he was gone, Lila took a few deep breaths and closed her eyes. One father down, one more to go.

❄ ❄ ❄

Annie was leaving the residence for Easter weekend. She looked forward to having a few days off and was anxious to see David. There were times when she really missed her big brother, but she'd never tell him that; he might get a swelled head.

Lila had called and asked her to tell David about the baby, instead of him finding out when he went out for a visit. It would give him a chance to absorb the news, as it were. Annie knew he'd be annoyed with them for keeping it a secret, but if that's what Lila wanted, who were they to go against her wishes?

As she went out the door of the residence to walk home, Henry Pratt was coming out of the emergency exit of the hospital. They saw each other at the same time. Henry put up his hand in greeting and came over to her.

"Looking forward to the weekend?" he smiled.

"Yes, indeed. You?"

"My mother will make me look for Easter eggs."

"You have my sympathy."

"Are you in a rush to get home? Would you like to grab a coffee?"

"That would be nice."

They walked down Commercial Street, gabbing like two old friends, before slipping into a local restaurant and ordering two coffees. Henry offered her a cigarette and lit hers before his own.

"If I could smoke in class, I would," she said.

"I have one once in a while."

"Not me. I'd smoke two packs a day if I could."

"I wouldn't. They're starting to talk about the health hazards of smoking."

"Listen, Pratfall, I could walk in front of a bus tomorrow and go splat. Life is uncertain. Why not have fun?"

"I think you have fun all the time."

"Not all the time. I hate dusting."

When Henry smiled at her, Annie felt like she was being rewarded for something. Like the time she and Davy got a trophy for winning the three-legged race at the annual Sunday school picnic.

"So tell me, do you like being a doctor?"

"I do. Although I'm not sure I want to work in the emergency ward forever. I always envisioned myself having a family practice somewhere. I know it sounds ridiculous to say, but I get upset when bad cases come through that door. I'd rather have a steady stream of patients that I could care for over their lifetime. This frantic emergency room drama is crazy one minute and then you may never see the patient again. I always want to know what happened to these people."

"I'm very glad you were on call when Lila first came through that door, and grateful that you took her on."

"How's she doing?"

"She sounds good. She's doing everything you told her to do. And Caroline is putting on weight, I'm told. I'll go and see them this weekend if I get the chance."

"She's lucky to have you."

Annie inhaled her cigarette and blew the smoke up in the air. "I'm lucky to have her."

"Why's that?"

Annie thought about it for a moment. "She has this amazing imagination. Lila once told me she was a tree fairy, and I believed her! And when she loves something she loves it with her whole heart, and she's kind to every living creature on this planet. And you should see her drawings. And she can be quiet for hours on end and not move. I've always admired that."

"She sounds like you, except for the sitting still part."

"She came into my life and made me realize how lucky I was, with two loving parents, a wonderful brother, and a happy home. Lila had none of those things. She had nothing. I can see her yet, on that back step, looking lost and alone. It still breaks my heart to think about it."

She covered the catch in her throat with a sip of coffee.

"You're lovely, Annie."

Annie looked up at him. "I have to say, Pratfall, you're not bad yourself."

He laughed and so did she.

They finished their coffee and headed out to the intersection where they would've parted ways but kept talking instead. They stayed so long that gradually Annie became aware of something in the background. There was a baby crying from the apartment next to them. It was a sobbing cry. It didn't sound right.

"That's not normal," Annie said.

"What?"

"Do you hear that baby?"

Henry listened. "Yes."

"There's something wrong." Annie went up to the door of the apartment and knocked on it. There was no answer. She banged on it again. Nothing happened.

"They're either drunk or they're not there." Annie rattled the door. It was locked.

"We should call the police," Henry said.

"I'm not waiting that long." Annie picked up a rock and smashed the windowpane in the door. She reached in and turned the lock, then went inside with Henry behind her and followed the sound of the baby's cries. She opened the shut bedroom door and nearly died.

A little boy about a year old was in his crib, with a full sagging wet diaper, snot and tears running down his fevered face. He was almost breathless, coughing and choking on his own spit.

"Don't worry, sweetheart. I'm here." Annie picked him up and held him close so he would calm down. "See if there's a phone in here to call the police, or run back to the restaurant and do it from there."

Henry found a phone in the kitchen and placed the call. The police arrived quickly. While they were explaining the situation, the mother came back.

"What the hell are you doing in my house? Was I robbed?"

Annie, still holding the baby, got in her face. "If it were up to me you'd never see this child again. How dare you leave this precious baby alone? You don't know what could've happened to him."

"I was only gone for a minute."

"You're a liar." Annie turned to the cops. "Are you going to call social services? This needs to be investigated. I cannot believe there are mothers who would do such a thing."

The woman grabbed her baby out of Annie's arms. "Who do you think you are, you stuck-up bitch? Do you know what my life is like? You think I don't love my kid? Who's gonna pay for my door? I ain't got that kind of money."

Henry pulled out his wallet and put two twenty dollar bills on the kitchen table. "This should help. Annie, I think we should go and let the police handle this."

Annie turned to the officer. "If you need my testimony for any reason, I'll be happy to give it."

"We'll take it from here," he said.

"Get out of my house! Go preach to someone else, you goddamn snitch."

As Henry tugged on Annie's arm to get her out of the house, she kept her finger pointed at the woman. "I'm going to be watching you. Don't think I won't. I come by here all the time and if I hear one peep out of that child I'm smashing that door again!"

"You heard her! She's threatening me!"

The police officer closed the door to separate the two women. Annie was almost hopping she was so mad. "Can you believe that?"

Henry took her arm and walked beside her as she mouthed off. It took her two blocks before she started to calm down. Finally, she gave a great sigh and pushed her hair out of her eyes. "I'm sorry. I'm going on and on, but gee whiz...."

Henry took both of her hands and stood in front of her. "I think I love you, Annie Macdonald."

She was so surprised, she didn't say anything.

"Do you mind if I kiss you?"

Annie shook her head.

Henry reached up and Annie bent down slightly. It was a great kiss.

"I'd like to take you home to meet my mother," he said.

"Hey, I told you I don't want no mama's boy."

"I'm afraid you're stuck with me, because I have no intention of letting another man sweep you off your feet."

"Is that right?"

"That's right."

"I'll think of you hunting for Easter eggs on Sunday morning. Gotta go. Thanks for the coffee."

"Any time."

They went their separate ways.

Annie arrived at the house the same time as her father. He put his arm around her as they walked to the front door.

"How's my girl?"

"Someone told me they loved me not ten minutes ago."

"How's that possible? You're still thirteen."

"I'll be nineteen soon, Dad. You married Mom when she was eighteen."

"Did I?"

"You know you did."

Dad gave her shoulders a squeeze. "I'm not sure how I feel about some unknown boy taking my best girl away from me."

"He's not a boy. He's a man."

That's when her dad stopped. "What do you mean?"

"He's as old as the hills. He's thirty, a doctor, and brilliant, plus he's shorter than me."

Dad looked away from her for a moment, as if processing the information. "Do you love him?"

"Not yet. He's got to chase me around the block a few more times before I make up my mind."

Her dad kissed the top of her head. "That's my girl."

Over supper at the kitchen table, Annie told them the story of the little boy, and then Dad told Mom about the man who was as old as the hills.

Her mother almost sputtered. "Snag him, for heaven's sake. He's a doctor!"

"What is it with mothers? You don't even know the guy but you want me to marry him because he's a doctor? Dr. Jekyll was a doctor, too."

"Was he the one looking after Lila? Does he have red hair?"

"That's the one. Henry Pratfall."

"Pratfall?"

"That's what I call him. It's a long story. His last name is Pratt."

"Oh, he's sweet," Mom smiled. "I was visiting Lila one day when he was making his rounds. He looks like the salt of the earth."

Annie popped another piece of blueberry cake in her mouth. "He's also the only son of a widow who still makes him hunt for Easter eggs."

Mom deflated. "Oh."

"Exactly. So don't go planning the wedding any time soon."

After dinner Dad went into Sydney to pick up David, who was coming home on the bus from Halifax. Dad asked her if she wanted to go, but Annie declined. She wanted to have a bath and soak her aching feet. They never got to linger in the tub at residence. There was always someone wanting to be next.

She was up in her room lounging on her bed when she heard David's voice come through the door and shout for their mother. She listened to Mom squeal back and then David's voice boomed up the stairs: "Where are you, squirt?"

"I'm too damn tired to come down," she yelled. "You come up here."

"After I have something to eat."

This was always the ritual. The minute David walked in the door, Mom had his favourite dishes ready, a roast chicken dinner with mashed potatoes and gravy, buttery peas and carrots, and banana cream pie for dessert.

It always felt right when she heard her parents and her brother's voice laughing at the table downstairs. She was a kid again, being sent to bed early. Annie scooped up Squeak from the end of the bed and held the cat in her arms. "Remember the first day you arrived?"

Squeak squeaked and wiggled out of her arms and settled back at the bottom of the bed.

"Fine. Be like that."

Lila was just drifting off when David bounded upstairs, threw his duffle bag in his room, and burst into hers.

"I missed you...Squeak!"

David picked up the cat and fell back on the bed. Squeak was now really miffed. She struggled and took a big leap to the floor, scooting out of the room in a hurry. David then smacked Annie on the bottom.

"Don't worry. I missed you too."

Annie rolled on her side and scrunched the pillow under her head. "I don't think so. I'm sure you haven't had time to breathe with all the female attention. Why did you get the good looks in the family?"

David shrugged. "You don't need good looks. Everyone loves you anyway."

She kicked him. "Hey! You're not supposed to agree with me."

He settled his back against the wall. "How's nursing?"

"It's good. You can be bossy while pretending to be nice. I still have two years to go, so who knows. I may hate it this time next year. How's Dal?"

"It's good too, but I feel like it's not moving fast enough. I want to get it over with already and start making big bucks."

"It's all about the money with you, isn't it?"

"What else is there? How's Lila?"

Annie had forgotten all about this particular mission. For a split second she thought she'd leave it till tomorrow, but she knew it might come up in conversation, as it was old news for everyone else. She sat up in bed and looked at him.

"What? You look funny."

"I have something to tell you, and I think you're going to be mad at us."

David stopped leaning on the wall and tensed up. "What's wrong with Lila?"

"She's fine now...well, she's not completely fine...but compared to before..."

David stood up. "What the hell is going on? I knew there was something wrong. I'm so stupid!"

Annie was taken aback. "Wait a minute. Calm down. You don't even know what I'm going to say."

He immediately stopped reacting and looked embarrassed. "Sorry. It's been a long day. You gave me a bit of a fright, is all."

"The only reason we didn't tell you is that Lila asked us not to."

His face went blank. "Okay."

"She had a baby."

He froze.

"I know it's a lot to take in. She had a little girl last month, and quite frankly Lila nearly died having her, but thankfully they're both on the mend. We didn't want to worry you."

"You didn't want to worry me? Am I a member of this family or not? Lila is very dear to me too. What if she had died? What right did you have not to tell me?"

Annie stood up. "David. Listen to me. She asked us not to tell anyone. No one knew but me and Aunt Eunie, Uncle Joe, and Mom and Dad. You know what people are like in a small town. She didn't want to be judged and ridiculed and we needed to protect her. It wasn't a conspiracy against you."

"I'm not a stranger. I'm family." He put his hands up to his head. "Do you mean to tell me she was pregnant at Christmas? She didn't look pregnant."

"To tell you the truth she barely looked pregnant the day before she had Caroline. She developed endocarditis. With her heart trouble…"

"What heart trouble?"

Annie was confused. "Because of her rheumatic fever, her heart valve was damaged. You knew that."

As soon as Annie said it, she remembered her conversation out in the back garden that beautiful summer day, when Lila had asked her not to say anything about her heart.

"Wait a minute. Lila wanted it kept a secret, but I assumed Mom told you at some point over the years."

"No." David's jaw was clenched tight.

"I'm so sorry, David. We just didn't want to worry you."

"I went to war and back, and you didn't think I could handle *this*?" he yelled. "Who do you people think you are?"

Their parents appeared in the doorway, looking concerned.

"What's all the shouting about?"

"It's about discovering I'm a second-class citizen as far as this family goes. I'm not a schoolboy who can't be told that Lila had a baby. This conspiracy of silence makes me feel like a fool."

David rushed past his parents and ran down the stairs, slamming the front door.

"I never even looked at it that way," Annie said. "I didn't think he'd feel shut out."

"Oh dear," Mom fretted. "What should we do, Kenzie?"

"He's allowed to have feelings. Give him some time."

They waited for David to come back in, but it was near midnight before he returned. He stood in the doorway of the parlour, where they'd gathered. He looked chilled.

"Didn't you have a coat?" Mom worried.

"Forget the coat. Everyone, I'm sorry for getting angry. I realize you were put in a difficult situation. But please, the next time something important happens in this family, let me know."

They all murmured their consent. Annie jumped out of her chair to hug him, but David put out his hand to hold her back. "It's been a long day. Goodnight." He bolted up the stairs.

Dad got out of his chair. "It has been a long day. Let's get some sleep."

❋ ❋ ❋

Lila knew David was coming home that weekend, and she prepared herself for his visit. When she heard his car pull in the yard, she sat up straight in bed and held on to the covers with clenched hands. She told herself to relax, but it was impossible. David was higher strung than Ewan, and she couldn't be sure he wouldn't start yelling at her. She heard voices of greeting and the murmur of conversation, as he no doubt took a peek at the new addition to the family. Lila was on pins and needles until she heard the door to the attic stairs open. There were footsteps and then…Annie.

Lila forgot to breathe for a moment. "Annie. I'm glad you're here."

"Your daughter gets cuter and chubbier every time I see her. I have a feeling Aunt Eunie is feeding her evaporated milk." Annie walked over and gave Lila a kiss before she sat on the bed.

"Did you have a nice Easter?" Lila asked.

"It was fine. A bunch of eggs at breakfast and that fruit bread Mom makes every year. I love that stuff toasted. Then church, and all the little girls in their Easter bonnets. That will be Caroline one day. So what did you do?"

Lila gestured at the room with a sweep of her arm. "This."

"It must be hard."

"Whenever I feel low, I remember who I'm doing this for."

"Good plan."

"So did David get home for Easter?"

"Yep. Ate all Mom's cooking and then left."

"He's gone? I thought he might drop by and see the baby."

Annie gave a big sigh. "We had a bit of a brouhaha when I told him about you and Caroline."

Lila's stomach knotted. "What did he say?"

"He wasn't exactly happy that we kept it a secret from him. He blew up and then stormed out of the house. The rest of the weekend, he was pretty quiet. He left this morning to go back to Halifax."

"He's mad at me."

Annie shook her head. "No, he's mad at us from keeping it a secret, and he does have a point. He felt left out."

Lila looked out the window. "He must be angry with me, if he didn't even come to see the baby."

"He'll get over it. Don't be so worried. Let him have his sulk and he'll be fine."

Annie went downstairs to get the baby and bring her up so they could both coo over her. Lila wanted Annie to leave, but she couldn't let on, so she smiled as Annie made silly faces at Caroline. The baby looked at her very solemnly with her big button eyes.

"I don't think she likes me," Annie worried. "She's not smiling. Why aren't you smiling, little girl? I'm your Auntie Annie. Good lord, try and say that three times."

"She's a little shy with people but she loves Freddy. Watch this." Lila looked to the other bed where Freddy was stretched out. "Freddy! Freddy!"

Fred's head popped up. He still looked half asleep.

"Don't bother poor old Fred," Annie said. "I'll take Caroline over to him."

Annie walked over to the dog and knelt down so Caroline and Freddy were eye to eye. Caroline gave him a big smile. Freddy flopped his head back on the mattress as a clear message to leave him alone.

"I see she's going to have her mother's way with animals. Yes you are! Yes you are!" Annie bounced Caroline up and down and Lila was just about to tell her to stop when Caroline spit up all over the front of Annie's blouse.

"Okay, the verdict is in. She does hate me. Excuse me while I give her back to her grandmother."

Lila's heart pounded. It never occurred to her that David would be so angry that he'd disappear from her life for good. As far as he knew, the baby was his—and he wasn't even interested in meeting her.

Lila's motherly instinct to protect her child tripled.

David could go to hell.

CHAPTER TEN

DAVID WAS IN HELL. AS soon as he got back to Halifax, he headed for his apartment and took the stairs two at a time. He didn't bother with a key; his roommate Scott never locked the door. Said it might interfere with women coming to visit.

As usual, the place looked like they'd been robbed. Whenever Scott was left to his own devices, the apartment took a turn for the worse.

David threw his bag onto the floor. Scott was asleep on the couch, or maybe he was in a coma. He stirred when the bag was dropped. "Hey, you're back."

"I'm leaving again, so don't get up."

"Where ya goin'?"

"To get drunk."

Scott leapt off the couch. "Hell yeah. Let's go!"

The two buddies headed to the nearest bar. A lot of their friends were there and it was a grand drunken reunion to celebrate nothing. But often a drinker trying to forget something gets maudlin and feels everyone should know his sorrow.

David had his head propped up at a table in the back.

"Let's go get laid," Scott slurred.

"Can't."

"Why? Did your willy fall off?"

"It's dead."

"Who killed it?"

"It's a secret. She's a secret. All their goddamn secrets are killin' me."

"Forget about her. There are all kinds of women just waiting to resuscitate that dead willy of yours."

They both thought that was hilarious. Eventually they staggered out and sang arm in arm down Spring Garden Road. A few pedestrians gave them a look and scurried out of their way, and a dog chased them for a while, but eventually they made it back to the apartment. Scott resumed his position on the sofa and David fell headlong across his bed with his feet hanging over the side.

His head was hanging over the toilet in the morning. "I'm never drinking again. Do you hear that, Scottie? I'm never drinking again!"

A muffled voice came from the sofa. "Stop yelling. My head's gonna explode."

They didn't make it to class that day and David vowed he'd never do that again. He was too anxious to soak up his education and use it to his advantage on his rise to the top. That was the plan, but that first week, while his body was in class, his head was somewhere else.

His guilt was so vast he couldn't articulate it. He knew if he'd seen Lila and his baby he'd have gone out of his mind. There was only one thing to do: stay away from her until he could figure out a way to ask her forgiveness.

Night after night he'd start to write her a letter, but it never sounded sorry enough, never sounded sincere enough to express his sadness over what he had done to her. She was blameless. He was older, supposedly wiser, and yet he'd taken what he wanted without giving it a second thought. Annie's words kept rattling around in his head. *She nearly died. She nearly died.*

If she had died, he'd have been the one responsible for putting her in the ground.

It made him sick.

He threw up in class one day, much to his horror. Then he did it again on the sidewalk and twice more when he was out with friends. His stomach felt like it was on fire.

Scott, who normally wasn't aware of anything, pointed at him with his spoon one morning. "You look terrible. You should go to the doctor."

"I'm fine."

But he wasn't, so he went to a clinic and found out he had an ulcer. The doctor told him it was caused by stress, among other things.

He gave him some tablets to melt on his tongue and they helped, but clearly the only cure for David was begging Lila's forgiveness.

The trouble was, he couldn't call her on the phone. She'd have to walk downstairs and talk to him with Eunie and Joe listening and that was clearly no good.

The frustration was unbearable, so in the end he shut down. He went to class, he studied, and he made extra money at night working some of the events at the Student Union Building. Basically he was as a freelance bartender who had no trouble avoiding alcohol. Just smelling it sometimes made his stomach turn.

After a while he got to recognize some of the people who attended the fundraisers, the concerts, and the dinners. The university bigwigs were there all the time, and sometimes men in business suits who looked like they had the world by the tail. They'd laugh and joke around with their wives, who looked like movie stars to David. Not that he cared.

There was one night he noticed an older woman staring at him. He looked down at his white shirt and black tie to make sure he hadn't spilled anything. Then he saw her whisper something to another woman and they both glanced at him and laughed. He kept his head down and ignored them.

It was near the end of term when he became aware of a young woman who spent most of her time in the corner, sipping her drink through a straw and following him with her eyes. She had platinum blonde hair to her shoulders, a curvy figure, and a mouth bright with red lipstick. Even David could tell her dresses were expensive. She was the epitome of a rich, classy girl—the kind he knew nothing about.

Until the night she finally approached him instead of the other two bartenders serving with him.

"What can I get you?" he said.

"I'll have a gin and tonic, please."

David reached for a glass and scooped some ice into it before pouring in a shot of gin and filling the glass with tonic. He added a lemon wedge to the side of the glass and handed it to her.

"You're a man of few words."

He nodded and picked up a cloth to wipe up the excess water on the bar.

"Do you know who I am?"

"No."

"My name is Kathleen Hanover, but my daddy calls me Kay. That's him over there in the suit." She pointed to a well-heeled man smoking a cigar. "The woman beside him is my mother."

David glanced up and recognized her as the woman who liked to stare at him.

"She's a bitch."

David didn't react, but wondered in what universe people called their mother a bitch.

"What's your name?"

"David."

"David what?"

"It doesn't matter."

"Don't be like that," Kay pouted. "I'm trying to be friendly. It's such a bore to have to come here night after night and have my father's friends ogle me. He only brings me along to butter up clients."

David couldn't help himself. "What does your father do?"

"He owns…well, just about everything."

"And what do you do?"

"I'm pretending to go to university."

David smiled.

"You see?" She smiled back. "I'm not so awful." She took a sip of her drink and glanced over at her mother. "I'll say this quick because my mother is threatening to come over here and break us up."

"How can you tell?"

"It's her life's work. Would you like to have coffee with me sometime? I live here—in one of the biggest houses in the city, but don't let that put you off."

"I don't think so. Thanks anyway."

David could tell she was disappointed.

"That's okay, maybe another time. Thanks for the drink." She walked back to her parents.

David had a massive headache and couldn't wait to get home.

A week later David ran into Kay again, this time quite by accident. She was leaving a corner store and he was going in. He almost didn't recognize her with her hair back in a ponytail and no makeup on. She still looked lovely, but more approachable.

She gave him a big smile. "Hi, David."

"Hi."

"You know who I am, right?"

"Yeah, I know. I'm surprised that you're shopping at a hole in the wall if your father owns everything in town."

"I try to act like a normal person most of the time."

David held up his hand. "That was rude. I'm sorry."

"Do you know why I look at you when you're tending bar?"

"Why?"

"You're so awfully sad."

"You're right." Feeling like shit had become such a habit he wasn't aware of it anymore. He used to be a happy person. Now it was more energy than he had to put a smile on his face.

"You could use a friend. Why don't we grab a bite somewhere?"

He was about to say no, but he was lonely. "Okay."

They went to a diner and sat in a booth made of imitation red leather and were served by a bored waitress. "What'll it be?"

David waited for Kay to go first.

"I'll have a cheeseburger, fries, and a root beer."

"I'll have a chicken sandwich and a glass of milk."

The waitress moved on.

"That's what my grandmother orders for lunch," Kay smiled.

"I have an ulcer. Fried foods don't help."

"That's too bad. Aren't you kind of young to have an ulcer?"

David shrugged.

"Were you overseas?"

"Yeah."

"Where?"

"Do you mind if I don't talk about it?"

Kay looked sheepish. "I'm sorry. I should know better. My brother never wants to talk about the war either."

"So what are you pretending to major in?"

"English," she smiled. "I thought it would be simple, because even I speak English, but it turns out they want me to read Shakespeare and some guy named Chaucer. Have you ever tried to read Chaucer, let alone understand what he's saying? I've stooped to showing a little leg to my professor, who is now giving me straight A's."

While they ate their lunch, David realized he enjoyed her company. Kay wasn't just a pretty face. She was funny and self-deprecating and she had a great laugh. He insisted on paying for lunch and they left together, walking and talking until they got to campus.

"I have a class at three, so I'd better go," he said.

"Will we do this again?"

He hesitated and then nodded. "Sure."

Kay kissed him lightly on the mouth. "I like you, David."

He watched her as she walked away. There was no doubt she was as spectacular from behind as she was coming towards him, but immediately Lila popped into his head like a splash of cold water. Whatever he did, he couldn't escape her. The sooner he got home the better. He knew he couldn't live like this for much longer.

There was one more event he had to work before he went home to Cape Breton for the summer. His dad had lined up a job for him with the highway department, and the sooner he started the more money he would save.

David saw Mr. Hanover at the dinner. He wondered where Kay was, but it was just as well she wasn't there; he certainly didn't need any more complications in his life. Thankfully it was a relatively short evening and David got to leave around ten-thirty. When he walked out of the building, Kay was sitting on the cement fence that edged the perimeter, dressed casually in slacks and a blue sweater set.

"Hi, David."

He thought about walking right by her, but knew that was unkind, so he stopped. "Hi. Why are you here?"

"To see you."

"It's late. You should be getting your beauty sleep."

"I don't sleep very often. It's a curse."

David put his hands in his pockets. "So, what's new?"

"I'm finished for the year. You?"

"Yeah, I'm leaving for Cape Breton in the morning."

"I've never been to Cape Breton. Is it nice?"

"Very."

"You'll have to show me around sometime."

David nodded but didn't say anything.

Kay jumped off the fence. "I can tell you're annoyed with me. I'll say goodnight." She started to walk away when he pulled her arm back toward him.

"I'm sorry, Kay. I'm always apologizing to you for my awful manners. I'm not usually rude to people."

She looked at her arm and he released it.

"David, do you think I follow men as a rule? I can assure you it's always the other way around. I'm trying to let you know that I think you're special and I'd like to be with you. It's obvious you're having a hard time, but I won't be made to feel as if I'm being a nuisance."

What was he doing? Here was someone who wanted to be with him. Lila might be lost forever and he needed a girl at that very moment to tell him he wasn't a terrible person. David gathered her in his arms and kissed her with everything he had. She responded in kind. He didn't care who was around and neither did she. David only thought how wonderful it felt to have a woman in his arms. At one point they stopped kissing but kept their foreheads together, both of them trying to catch their breath.

"Do you have to go home?" she whispered. "My dad can get you a job anywhere in the city. We can spend the summer together. Wouldn't you like that?"

He kissed her again so she'd stop talking. Reality seeped in nonetheless. He finally pulled away.

"You're a great girl…"

"But…?"

"I have to go home. There's something I need to fix."

"I'm guessing it involves a female." Kay ran her fingers through her hair to try and straighten it a little. "I get the picture. I'm making a fool of myself."

"No, you're not."

"I'm thinking aloud, David. I don't need your opinion. Have a great summer."

She walked away.

When David got home, the first thing his mother said was, "Have you been ill?"

"No. Why?"

"You look terrible."

"Thanks, Mom."

She walked over to him and put her hand on his shoulder. "I know there's something wrong. Don't dismiss me."

"Apparently I have an ulcer."

Now his mother was on a mission, just like the secret missions she'd send him on when he was a kid, like the time he had to go over to Aunt Muriel's kitchen to find out what type of cake she was entering in the Fall Fair, or the time she'd made him take the wine bottles out of the Butts's garbage can so she'd have evidence of their neglect of Lila.

David knew from past experiences that she wouldn't take this mission lightly. She'd find every recipe available that would be easy on his stomach, which was much appreciated—except that he'd then have to hear about where she found it, whose recipe box it originated from, and the life history of the person who gave it to her.

His father also gave him a concerned look at the table, while he and Mom ate fried haddock for supper and David had a plain omelet. "Did you eat a lot of spices when you went to India? Maybe that's what started your ulcer."

"We ate tinned food mostly. Once a month they'd fly in steaks, but we had no refrigeration, so we'd eat it all at once. The first time someone put a rare steak on my plate I thought there was something wrong with it. Mom cooks hers to death."

"Hardly to death, David. I prefer mine well done."

"You like everything well done. When I cut into my fried egg and the yolk seeped out I didn't know what it was. The guys gave me a hard time for weeks."

David could tell his mom wasn't pleased with him—she was known far and wide for her cooking—but he could tell Dad was enjoying the exchange. He made it up to Mom after dinner when he put his arms around her waist while she was washing the dishes and kissed her on the cheek.

"You're the best cook and the best mother in the world."

"Remember that."

David picked up the dishtowel and started to dry the dishes. "How's our Annie?"

"I think she's in love. She denies it, but her face glows when she talks about him."

"Who's this bozo?"

"Henry Pratt. He's a doctor at the Glace Bay General and he's thirty."

"He's a dirty old man! I'm going to have to speak to her."

His mother took her hand out of the soapy water and poked him in the chest. "You'll do no such thing. He's good for her. Annie rides roughshod over anyone younger. Heaven knows I've seen my share of broken hearts in this house, but not one belonged to Annie, just the boys who tried to date her."

David dried all the dishes and put them away. He sat with his parents for a bit, making small talk, and then said he was going to bed.

"Dad, can I borrow the car tomorrow? I thought I'd go out and visit Lila and the baby. I haven't seen them yet."

"Sure."

"Oh, Lila will be pleased," his mom smiled. "That baby is adorable. I feel like a grandmother when I hold her."

David wished them goodnight and took his broken heart up to bed. He lay awake for most of the night, rehearsing a thousand times what he would say to Lila, but he couldn't remember any of it in the morning.

The drive to Round Island was a blur, and he sat in the car outside the house for quite a while before he got out. When he knocked on the door, Eunie answered as expected, and was so pleased to see him. After giving him a big hug she took him by the arm and led him into her bedroom. There in a wooden crib was a little pink baby. She was sucking her thumb in her sleep. He couldn't see her clearly because his eyes filled with tears, but he kept his head down so Eunie wouldn't see.

"She's a little darling," Aunt Eunie boasted. "She's so good to go to sleep, and hardly ever cries."

"What's her name again?"

"Caroline Eunice," Aunt Eunie said proudly. "Wasn't that thoughtful of Lila? I bless the day she came to live with us. She is our daughter in every way."

David wanted to touch Caroline, but didn't dare. He didn't have the right. Not yet, anyway.

"Why don't you go up and see Lila?" Aunt Eunie said. "She gets so lonesome for company. I'm sure Caroline will be up from her nap before you leave. Wait until you hold her!"

David walked to the stairs like he was headed to the gallows. Eunie went ahead of him, opened the door, and called up the stairs. "Lila, there's someone to see you."

This was it. He went up the stairs and stood at the top, then turned to look at her, propped up in bed. He was shocked by how small and frail she looked, dark circles under her eyes and such pronounced cheekbones. If she was doing better now, what state had she been in before? And it was all because of him.

She didn't say anything, just watched him stand there in his misery.

"What must you think of me?"

There was only silence.

"When I found out…it's my fault…all of it. I almost killed you. I don't know how to apologize for that other than to say I'm sorry. I'm sorry for everything. I will regret my actions for the rest of my life, but just now I looked at Caroline and I can't believe that she wasn't meant to be. She's beautiful, Lila. She's as beautiful as you are and I love you both so much. You have to believe me. We can raise her together and watch her grow up. Please forgive me. Please."

"Caroline isn't yours."

The floor tilted and the ceiling came down to greet him. He put his hand out and grabbed the bookcase to stay steady. He tried to formulate a sentence but couldn't speak. The dizziness and nausea he'd become so familiar with rushed through his body, and he bent over to keep it down. Slowly he stood up again and tried to breathe calmly.

"I know you're upset with me, Lila, but don't do this. Don't keep Caroline away from me. We'll present a united front and tell our families the truth about us. Only then can we move forward."

"You're not the father, David. We can't present a united front because there *is* no us. We were together once, and on the grass, no less. Is that a relationship? Neither of our families needs to know anything. You're going to live in Halifax and become a lawyer, and I'm going to stay here and raise my daughter. We'll see each other at the occasional family get-together."

"You're lying."

"I'm lying about what?"

"That child is mine. You're just trying to punish me."

"Think what you like."

David approached her bed. "You made me believe you wanted me at Christmas, and yet the whole time you were hiding the fact that you were having my baby. Do you know how I felt when I discovered everyone knew about it but me? I felt betrayed, Lila, like I'd been stabbed in the back. Not to mention the fact that you never told me about your bad heart. It's like everyone's been privy to your inner world but me."

"Why should you be? Even if you love me to your dying day, I'm under no obligation to love you back."

He shook his head. "Okay, you're doing a great job of making me suffer, and I deserve it. I get that. But this is me, Lila. I've loved you since the first day I saw you. I've wanted to marry you my whole life. I've waited for you my whole life. I declared my love for you before I left to join the air force. I kept your lock of hair with me overseas. When I came back we discussed our future plans..."

"*You* discussed our future plans, not me. You informed me that we would travel the world and come back to Round Island with our children in the summer. But you never asked me what I wanted or if I liked the idea of seeing the world and leaving my home. I'm happy here. I don't want to leave."

"What are you so afraid of? This place isn't going to disappear the minute your back is turned."

"You don't care what I think. It's what you want. You expected me to be here when you got back, as if I have no life other than you, as if I'm here waiting to be told what to do. I know I'm not the fighter Annie is, but I deserve respect."

David was confused. "But you told me you loved me."

"What do I know about love?"

He closed his eyes and tried to get his emotions under control. He didn't want to fall apart in front of her. "I'm sorry. Clearly I've been living in a fantasy world."

Then he opened his eyes and stepped even closer to her. "But I know that child is mine. You can deny it forever, but I know she's mine. And the fact that you won't acknowledge her as such says more about you than it does about me. I hope you can live with yourself when she asks you some day who her daddy is."

He turned around and walked down the stairs. Then he slipped into Eunie and Joe's bedroom and placed his hand on his daughter's back. "I love you, Caroline. Someday you'll know who I am." He hurried into the kitchen, where Eunie had tea poured and a lemon loaf waiting to be sliced.

"Thought you might like a snack," she smiled.

"I hate to disappoint you, but I really have to get back. I'm supposed to start a new job today and I've taken too much time as it is, but it's been wonderful to see you and Lila and Caroline. I'll be busy this summer, so I might not get out as often as I'd like, but I'm sure Mom will keep me informed on the baby front."

"Are you sure you don't want…"

"Positive." He hugged Aunt Eunie before she could say anything else and quickly left. She waved from the door.

"Goodbye, dear. Thanks for stopping in."

David got in the car and drove to the bungalow. He unlocked it, went inside, and sat on the couch, trying to ignore the bile in his throat. His first thought was to leave for Halifax that day and get as far away as possible from Lila and the baby, but he knew he'd be miserable on his own, the campus empty of students during the summer. At that moment he needed his mother's food and her comfort and his dad's reassurance that he was a good person at heart and that he didn't mean to be such a loser and ruin everyone's life. And he needed his sister. Even if he couldn't tell her about Lila and the baby, he wanted to soak up her good cheer and to-hell-with-it attitude.

He was only twenty-one and already weary of life.

❋ ❋ ❋

When David left her, Lila stayed very still. She knew Aunt Eunie would come up and ask why he had left so soon. Eunie soon did, in fact, bring up a tray with tea and a couple of slices of lemon loaf. She put it across Lila's lap.

"Here you are. It's too bad David couldn't stay, but he's starting a new job. He's such a nice boy, and he was obviously moved by our little angel. At one point I thought he was crying. Men are such babies." She cocked an ear. "Is that Caroline?"

"I think so."

"I'll get her bottle ready and you can feed her."

"I'm really tired. I think I'll have a nap, and I can feed her at dinner."

"Fine by me. Do you want me to take the tray away?"

"Please."

Aunt Eunie grabbed the tray and went back downstairs. Lila turned towards the wall and buried her face in the pillow.

She was only eighteen and already weary of life.

CHAPTER ELEVEN

1948

ANNIE REFUSED TO MEET HENRY'S mother for two and a half years. As far as Mrs. Pratt was concerned, Henry was a confirmed bachelor. Now that Annie was nearing her graduation from nursing school at the Glace Bay General, she let down her guard. Annie would never admit it to Henry, but she was conscious of the fact that if Henry's mother had met and hated her, it would have strained the relationship she had with Henry at the hospital. There was enough drama on the wards without a heated argument in the linen cupboard about what his mother did or didn't say.

She also knew that Henry was running out of patience.

"I was born in 1916. During the Great War! We've had a Second World War since then. Just how long do you think I can wait to start a family of my own?"

They sat together on a park bench near the hospital to quickly gulp down a sandwich during their fifteen minutes of free time.

Annie licked a dollop of tuna salad from her finger. "It's entirely your own fault. If you hadn't fallen madly in love with a young ingénue, you could at this very moment be sleeping with a wrinkly old woman in her thirties."

"You are the antithesis of an ingénue, my love."

"Do you want me to meet your mother or not?"

"Come to dinner on Saturday night. I'll pick you up at around seven."

Annie made a face. "Seven? Are you aristocrats? Normal people eat at five."

"I know my mother. When she finds out I'm bringing a girl home, she'll be beside herself. Expect at least six courses."

"Oh, God."

Henry wasn't the only one impatient for something to be decided or announced or at least given consideration. Annie's mom was bugging her to get engaged. That way no one else could steal Henry from under Annie's nose. But as Dad reminded Mom, if anyone attempted to do such a thing, Annie would release the hounds herself.

Annie was more nervous than she cared to admit about meeting Mrs. Pratt. From what Henry had told her, a lot of people withered in her presence. Grown men had been known to avoid her in the street. After trying on three different outfits, she settled for a sleeveless white and navy polka-dotted dress and wore a navy sweater over it in case the weather or Mrs. Pratt got chilly. She also wore heels instead of flats, just to make a point.

It was a nice spring evening and Henry showed up at six forty-five. Mom knocked on Annie's bedroom door to tell her he'd arrived.

"He looks nervous."

"Does he?"

"That's always a good sign. It means he wants his mother to approve of you, and he's terrified that she won't."

"I can't wait for this to be over."

When Annie walked down the stairs, she thought Henry looked rather handsome with his grey pinstriped suit on. He'd shaved and smelled delicious, but he didn't even say hello, just waved her on so he could get her out the door in time. He barely acknowledged her parents in his haste. Annie saw them laughing as they shut the front door. It was all right for them. They got to stay home.

Annie knew where Henry lived, so the house wasn't a surprise. It was nicely maintained in a boring kind of way. She knew his mother planted her flowers in rows, and God help the weed that strayed into the mix.

"Now, don't be nervous." Henry wiped away the sheen of sweat on his upper lip. She'd never seen him this rattled, not even while saving lives at the hospital. Who was this dragon lady?

Mrs. Pratt opened the door and clapped in delight before extending her hand to rush Annie through to the inner sanctum. "It's such a pleasure to meet you, my dear!" She proceeded to kiss both of Annie's cheeks and then hold onto her arms.

"Let me take a look at you! Aren't you the prettiest thing I've ever seen! She's so pretty, Henry! And oh my goodness, so tall! Look how tall you are! And so young!"

Henry's mother talked like there were exclamation points at the end of all her sentences. She scarcely stopped for breath. Annie couldn't get a word in, but she did manage to give the woman the box of chocolates she'd brought.

"Chocolates! I love chocolates! Don't I, Henry! Please make yourself at home! Henry, take Annie into the parlour, because I've made appetizers! Would you like a glass of cranberry cocktail or a stronger beverage!"

Annie was about to tell her when Mrs. Pratt waved her hands in the air. "I'll bring both!"

When she disappeared into the kitchen Annie looked at Henry, who was staring at his shoes.

"Six courses?"

After sampling the tangy cheese spread on crackers, chili sauce dip with celery and carrot sticks, hot chicken-bacon squares, a gourmet crab ring, and liverwurst pâté, Annie was full.

Then Mrs. Pratt, who asked Annie to call her by her given name, Joy, ushered them both into the formal dining room, which glowed with crystal and china. They dined on tomato consommé to start, and then a lettuce and tomato salad, after which the Swiss steak and garlic mashed potatoes smothered in gravy were produced, followed by the happy coincidence of Swiss chocolate cake with fudge icing, ending with a plate of various cheeses and fruit, if desired, with their tea or coffee.

Annie offered to help Joy with the dishes, which produced a hail of compliments.

"You can always tell a well-brought-up girl! Not that I would dream of letting you in the kitchen, but the thought is much appreciated! It's so rare these days to find a young woman like yourself! You've done well, Henry! For goodness' sake, don't let this angel get away!"

After ten minutes of farewells and pledges of undying love, Joy finally closed her front door. Henry was still staring at his shoes as they walked to the car. He opened the door for her and shut it once she was in. Then he got in the driver's side and closed the door behind him.

The silence was orgasmic.

Henry looked at her. "Will you marry me?"

"No."

❋ ❋ ❋

When David heard that Annie and Henry had eloped the day after her graduation, he was disappointed. Apparently his mother was too, but after meeting Joy, she quickly changed her mind. His father was thrilled. No bills, no worries, and no reception with Joy Pratt in the receiving line.

He hated to disappoint his dad, but he and Kay were having the biggest wedding Halifax had seen in a long time. Not that he had anything to do with the decision. It had taken on a life of its own the minute he proposed.

He survived the miserable summer of Lila's rejection by working twelve hours a day, seven days a week. Without even knowing it he put on weight, muscles even, with all the physical activity of pounding asphalt and digging gravel. His mother's ulcer diet brought him much-needed relief, and Annie's nonsense made him laugh when he didn't want to.

Some of his bitterness towards Lila dissipated over the summer, but not all of it. He kept it in check. If he dwelled on it, he'd feel his guts squirm, so he learned to put it on a shelf and ignore it.

School kept him busy. He had a very full course load; he wanted to shave a year off his undergraduate degree and go right into law school at King's as soon as he could. There wasn't much time for a social life, but at least he didn't need a part-time job after making good money all summer with the road crew.

Scott invited him along to a frat-house party that November. The place was jumping, and the smoke in the air was thick. Everyone was swing dancing to the big band sounds of Dizzy Gillespie, Artie Shaw, and Count Basie. It was pretty difficult to stay glum when that music filled the air. Scott immediately left him to go dance with a buxom blonde, so David wandered into the kitchen and grabbed a soda. He stayed on the edges of the group, watching all the fun.

That's when he saw Kay, sitting on a window seat and smoking a cigarette with a couple of fellows by her side. Her hair was combed away from her brow, with soft waves down to her shoulders. Her trademark red lipstick was the same colour as her sweater, and a string of pearls adorned her neck. David had no doubt they were real.

He stayed where he was and watched the guys do their damndest to get her up on the dance floor—or make her smile, laugh, or do anything—but she was content to ignore them. At one point she looked at him, but kept her eyes moving to scan the rest of the crowd. David wondered how long it would take her to realize it was him.

About three seconds.

She looked back at him and slowly smiled, but she didn't move. She took another drag of her cigarette. David put down his bottle and made his way across the room, moving this way and that to get past the laughing girls and drunken guys.

Eventually he stood in front of her and held out his hand. She dropped her cigarette in the drink of the guy on the right and took it. He pulled her up and held her close. While everyone around them did the jitterbug and the lindy hop, he and Kay swayed to their own music.

David didn't meet her parents until the next summer, a weekend getaway to their cottage near Lunenburg. David envisioned barbeques and maybe a bonfire if it was a nice night. Kay picked him up in her silver 1948 Cadillac convertible, honking the horn outside his apartment. Scott looked out the window and shook his head.

"You lucky bastard."

Kay wore a scarf on her head to keep her hair from flying around and a pair of dark sunglasses. Her yellow, checkered shirt tied in the front and white Capris looked very summery, as did the espadrilles she wore on her feet. David threw his bag in the back and jumped into the passenger seat. Kay leaned over for her kiss.

"You look nice."

"Thank you. Before we go, did you bring a suit?"

"A suit? I thought we were going to the cottage."

"We are."

"Then I don't need a suit."

Kay shrugged. "Okay."

The hour's drive along the coast was fun, especially in a convertible. With the wind rushing past, and trees and water flashing by, it felt like he was taxiing down a runway. Kay laughed at him when he put his arm out over the side of the car and pretended to fly. She did the same thing. They soared along the highway together.

"Do you have a cottage?" she shouted against the sound of the wind.

"We have a bungalow. I love it, outhouse and all. I'm sure yours will be a whole lot fancier, judging by your place in the city."

David had seen the Hanover mansion from the outside, but had never gone in. Kay lived in a great apartment near campus and that's where they spent most of their time.

Finally, Kay put on the car's blinker and pulled into a paved driveway in the middle of nowhere. That was David's first clue: It wasn't a dirt road. Then they passed the iron gates and continued on down the landscaped drive until the final clearing, where there was an enormous, rambling house with a circled drive at the front. There must have been twenty cars parked here and there and someone who looked like a bellhop organizing luggage for the guests.

Kay laughed and laughed when she saw the look on his face. "Don't have a heart attack. It's just a bigger cottage with indoor plumbing."

David wished he had brought his suit.

He was given his own room to freshen up, and Kay said she'd meet him down by the pool. David went over to the window and peeked out. There were a lot of people there already, including Kay's mother, lounging in a chair with a two-piece bathing suit on. He tried to imagine his own mother in a two-piece suit, but the thought was ludicrous. Mom would go down to the beach in a rubber bathing cap with flowers on it, and the same old one-piece suit she'd had since he could remember. There she'd splash the water around as she stood up to her knees and quickly run back to her towel five minutes later, declaring it a great swim.

David cupped water on his face and washed his hands. A quick brush through his hair and he was ready to face the mob. The only thing on his mind was what he'd wear for dinner.

He ran into several people on his way to the pool, but hadn't a clue who they were. Everyone smiled and nodded, but they kept moving. Finding a way out to the pool proved a bit of a challenge, but in the end he found the French doors leading out to an enormous patio. Kay spotted him immediately and rushed over to put her arm through his. "Come meet Daddy."

They went over to the bar area, where Mr. Hanover was swilling back a drink, his ever-present cigar in his hand.

"Daddy, this is David Macdonald. David, this is my father Louis Hanover."

"A pleasure to meet you, sir." David held out his hand.

Louis put the cigar in his mouth and shook David's hand. "Well, well. So this is the young man my Kay thinks so highly of. You must be special. She's never brought anyone home before."

"Daddy, don't go telling him that. He'll be impossible now." Kay squeezed him.

Louis was an impressive man, big through the chest and quite tall, but up close David could see the broken veins in his slightly red, bulbous nose and the deep lines around his mouth. He looked tired and much older than David's own father.

"I'll ask all the essential questions. Where are you from and what do you do?"

"I'm from Glace Bay…"

"Coal mining. Is your father a miner?"

"No, sir. He owns a machine shop."

"A man who works with his hands. I admire men like that. What do you do?"

"I'm going to King's for my law degree."

"So you're bright. I'm impressed, Kay. Play your cards right, young man, and I may be able to throw a few job opportunities your way."

David was about to thank him, but Louis turned back towards the bar and signalled for the bartender to fill up his glass. Another man approached and Louis greeted him with great cheer. David's interview was over.

"Now for the hard part." Kay pulled him towards her mother, who was still holding court in her lounge chair.

"Mother, this is David Macdonald, the boy I told you about. David, this is my mother, Virginia."

Her mother leaned forward, her cleavage dangling in front of him. "Welcome to our home." She shook David's hand but didn't let go, pulling him towards her. She put her other hand up to shade her eyes from the glare of the sun.

"Do I know you?"

"No, you don't," Kay answered.

"I'm sure I've seen you somewhere before." Virginia let go of his hand. "I'll think of it. Why don't you two have a swim? Dinner's not for hours yet."

"I hope it's not fried food. David can't eat fried food."

"Talk to the cook about it, not me. I'm sure he'll be happy to rustle up another masterpiece of culinary delight for your new boyfriend."

Kay looked annoyed. "Let's go for a swim." She walked away.

"It was nice to meet you, Mrs. Hanover."

"If you need anything, David, just let me know. I'll arrange it for you, pronto. Anything at all."

David nodded and went after Kay. She took off her robe and dove into the pool without waiting for him, which was too bad, since Kay in a bathing suit was something to see. As David pulled off his shirt, he was aware of Kay's mom watching his every move.

He wasn't in Kansas anymore.

In the end, Kay lent him her older brother's suit. Louis Jr. lived in New York, running a couple of his father's companies. His suit fit David pretty well. Kay dusted off his shoulders and gave him a last look.

"You are a handsome creature."

"Thank you."

"I'm warning you now: don't play my mother's games. She'll turn herself inside out to try to get your attention."

David put his arms around her. "Do you honestly think I could look at anyone else when you're in the room?"

She had to reapply her lipstick before they went downstairs.

There was a cocktail party before dinner, and then the guests were ushered into the dining room. David had never seen a table that long before. Kay's mother patted the chair next to her and asked David to sit down. Kay frowned and sat to the right of her dad.

There were an astonishing four wine glasses at each place setting. Kay need not have worried about David's diet, as everyone was served grilled salmon drizzled with maple dressing. Dessert was a lemon sherbet with chocolate-dipped vanilla wafers on the side. David spent most of the meal nodding at whatever Virginia was bleating on about but keeping his eyes on Kay, who was determined to drive him crazy by licking her cutlery in inappropriate ways when no one was looking.

But while Kay was flirting with him, Virginia was groping him under the table. At first he couldn't believe what she was doing, and assumed she'd reached for her napkin, but the second time it happened it was perfectly clear that her movements were intentional. He reached down with his own hand and took hers away from his crotch, but she just held on to his hand and rubbed it between her thighs.

David choked and pulled his hand away to grab his water glass. Kay asked him if he was all right and he nodded. Virginia patted his back.

"We don't want anyone dying at the table," she laughed.

Thankfully dinner was over then, and he and Kay escaped outside and walked down to the private wharf where the family's boats were kept. Sitting on the dock with their legs hanging over the side and listening to the soft laps of the waves on shore, with the stars twinkling above, was finally something familiar for David. At that moment he missed home.

"Will you ever take me to your bungalow?" Kay asked.

"I'd have a hard time doing that now."

"My father grew up in a company house, and my mother lived in a trailer in Hants County. My dad built his fortune from the ground up. Mom recognized a good thing when she saw it and has been unhappily married to his money ever since." Kay sighed. "All my brother and I ever wanted was to have a happy family, but we have everything else instead. You're underestimating me. I'd never turn my nose up at your bungalow and your fine outhouse."

He put his arms around her and they stayed quiet, listening to the bullfrogs and the call of the loons in the distance. Eventually it got chilly and they headed back up to the house, where the lights shone from every window and the guests milled around, drinks in hand, laughing to kill themselves and talking too loud over the background music. Some of them danced and a few of them staggered. It was like a nightclub.

Kay looked tired, and David suggested they both hit the hay early.

"No midnight visit to my room?"

He laughed. "Your dad knows far too many people who could whack my kneecaps. I think we should wait until we get back to the city."

They kissed each other goodnight. David went into his room and Kay continued to hers. He was taking off his clothes when the adjoining bathroom door opened and Kay's mother walked into the room, twirling a glass full of wine.

"We meet again."

"Uh...I think you have the wrong room, Mrs. Hanover."

"You think I don't know my own house? I have access to all these bedrooms."

"Mrs. Hanover..."

"Stop calling me that. I came to tell you that I remember who you are. You're that lovely sullen boy who was a bartender at the university. My friends and I used to have fantasies about you."

She put the wineglass down on the nearest bureau, walked up to him, and encircled his neck with her arms. "Kiss me."

He backed up, but she took his head and forced him to kiss her, and before he had a chance to get her off him, the door opened.

"I forgot to tell...Mom?"

Virginia turned around. "Oh, darling, David was kissing me goodnight. You really should knock first."

Kay looked like she wanted to cry and her face went beet red. "Why do you embarrass me like this? Why would you embarrass David? It's pathetic."

"I don't think that's a very nice way to talk to your mother in front of a guest."

David removed Virginia's arms from around his neck.

"I'm so sorry, David."

Virginia pointed her finger at her daughter. "Don't you dare apologize for me in my own house. Who do you think you are?"

"I'm not sure yet, Mother, but I thank God every day that I'm not you."

David walked over to Kay and deliberately held both her hands. "You are the most beautiful woman in my world. I'd be so happy if you married me."

Kay burst into tears and then flung herself in his arms. "Yes, yes, I'll marry you." They kissed each other and forgot about her mom standing there until she started to clap.

"What a performance. If you think you've won, Kathleen, you're sadly mistaken. Have a great life with a nobody and his hillbilly family from Cape Breton."

David turned to face her. "I am not a nobody, and I'm very proud to come from Cape Breton. I'm also extremely proud of my family. And can I just say that my mother has more class in her baby finger than you and all of your friends downstairs combined."

Virginia gave him a filthy look. "Don't let the door hit your ass on the way out." She stalked out of the room.

Kay looked at him with adoration. "No one has ever stood up to my mother like that."

"I can't believe your mother, Kay. Get packed. We're leaving tonight."

❋ ❋ ❋

Annie and Henry were deliriously happy in their new house. It was Henry's wedding gift to her, and he made sure it was clear across town from his mother's, so there'd be no unexpected pop-ins. They spent many happy hours together decorating.

The rest of the time, they were in bed. Henry was determined to be a father before his next birthday, and Annie, being Annie, happily obliged.

When David called to say he was engaged and bringing his fiancée home for Christmas to meet everyone, their mother became a cleaning and baking machine. Annie got fed up that every time she was over, Mom was roaring around the house trying to make everything look better.

"Mom, you realize this girl isn't blind. She'll know that the coal stove is a coal stove no matter how many times you polish it."

"What's wrong with making a good impression? She's used to the best, according to David."

"I hate to tell you, but according to David she doesn't know how to cook."

That stopped her in her tracks. Mom gave Annie an incredulous look. "What do you mean she doesn't know how to cook? What about David's ulcer?"

"It'll become gigantic and walk the earth as a terrifying force of evil."

"Stop it. Your brother has a terrible time with his stomach. It's no laughing matter."

Annie reached for a banana and peeled it. "So teach her yourself." She broke off a piece and stuffed it in her mouth. Lately she couldn't get enough bananas.

"When am I supposed to do that? She's only coming for a few days."

"Write all your recipes down in a notebook and give it to her for Christmas."

"That's an excellent idea." Her mom went back to her scrubbing.

"And while you're at it, do one for me, but only include fattening fried things and every dessert you ever made."

Annie called Lila to tell her the good news.

"Give him my best," Lila said tightly.

"You're going to see him, aren't you? We have to be together when we first lay eyes on her, and everyone wants to see Caroline."

"We'll see. It's not much fun to drive into town with a cranky two-year-old."

"She's adorable."

"An adorable crank. Don't make me feel guilty if I can't make it in. I'll do my best."

"Why can't I push you around anymore?"

"I'm a mother. See ya."

David and Kay hoped to be in Glace Bay in the afternoon the day before Christmas Eve, but there were reports of snow squalls between Antigonish and Sydney, which made everyone tense hoping they weren't caught in bad weather. Annie and Henry arrived and Mom wondered if Annie's outfit was fancy enough.

"For cryin' out loud! If my husband likes it, do I give a crap what she thinks?"

"Don't use rough language. It reflects on all of us."

Annie rolled her eyes and reached for a piece of sliced coconut loaf on the coffee table.

"Don't eat that! Wait until they get here."

"Dad!"

Kenzie looked up from his paper. "Dear, let the girl have a piece."

Much to their delight, the Johnson car pulled up. Everyone rushed to the door to usher in Aunt Eunie, Uncle Joe, Lila, and Caroline, nicknamed Cricket, who was looking especially adorable in her new Christmas dress, with her golden-red hair a mass of curls around her face. Henry always grabbed her first and made a big fuss over her. He loved kids. Anyone's kid would do.

They spent a blissful hour watching Caroline run from person to person, handing them candy from a dish and saying "Here go!" to all of them.

"Hey Mom, how come you're not yelling at Cricket for getting sticky fingerprints on all the furniture?

"She's allowed to do whatever she wants." Mom grabbed Cricket from behind and gave her lots of kisses.

Annie thought Lila looked flushed and tired. She went over and sat beside her on the couch. "You okay? Do I need to check your pulse?"

"I'm fine, I have a bit of a headache, that's all."

"Want me to get you something for it?"

That's when Mom, who was constantly at the window, shouted, "They're here!"

Everyone but the Johnsons ran out to greet the happy couple. Eunie and Joe didn't want to interfere, and Cricket was busy tearing up pieces of newspaper on her mother's lap.

When David and Kay came through the door amid shouts of hello and welcome, Annie took one look at her soon to be sister-in-law and whispered to Henry, "He's hit the mother lode."

Kay was dazzling in a winter white coat with a fox-fur collar and cuffs. It was hard for Annie to keep her eyes off her and when she noticed it was hard for Henry as well, she gave him an elbow. Even her father stood a little taller, while Mom beamed at the prospect of gorgeous grandchildren.

David kissed them all and they kissed Kay too, who looked excited and happy to be there. She left red lipstick on the men's cheeks and they grinned like fools. But she was just as nice to Annie and her mom, and Annie knew that she was going to like this girl, even if no one would ever notice Annie again at a family get-together.

Mom ushered them into the living room. "And these are our dear friends, Eunie and Joe Johnson, and their daughter and granddaughter, Lila and Caroline. Lila is like one of the family. She and David and Annie grew up together."

"It's such a pleasure," Kay smiled and walked around to shake all their hands. "What an adorable little girl! Isn't she perfect, David? What's her name again?"

"I call her Cricket," said Lila.

"You are so lucky to have such a beautiful child. David and I would like to start a family as soon as we can, isn't that so, David?"

"Yes, indeed. I'll just go out and get the bags." He left the room and went out the front door. Kay smiled at everyone as she took off her coat. "You have a lovely home, Mrs. Macdonald."

"Thank you. We're happy here, aren't we, Dad?"

Dad agreed.

Henry, Joe, and Dad offered to take Kay's coat. She took off her gloves, unbuttoned her coat, and removed the white cashmere scarf at her neck. "Thank you."

Then they stood around and looked at her like she was an exhibit at a Hollywood movie set. Her silver dress had sparkly snowflakes embroidered on the skirt, and her diamond earrings twinkled when she turned her head.

Cricket got off her mother's lap and reached over to touch Kay's skirt. Kay bent down and let her feel the material. Then David came back in and shouted from the porch that he'd take the bags upstairs. Mom and Dad were finally galvanized to start being proper hosts. Mom asked if Kay would like to go and freshen up. Annie thought she looked plenty fresh already, but Kay humoured her mom and followed her upstairs.

That left the rest of them looking at each other with their mouths open.

"Can you believe her?" Annie said. "Why on earth would she fall for David when she could be the queen of a small country somewhere?"

They were an excited bunch waiting for the couple to come back down. Except for Lila, who got up and took Cricket into the kitchen for a drink.

When everyone came back downstairs, Mom asked Annie for her help in the kitchen, and Dad asked Kay if she'd like a Shirley Temple. She said she would be delighted.

Mom grabbed Annie's hands near the sink. "She's so beautiful."

"I know!"

Lila poured Cricket a small drink of juice. "Anyone can be beautiful if they have money."

"I suppose that's true, but she seems like a lovely girl."

"You've only known her for five minutes."

Annie and Mom looked at each other. It wasn't like Lila to be so negative.

"Did you want an aspirin for your headache?" Annie said carefully.

"Yes, please."

At dinner, Mom served a baked ham crisscrossed with pineapple rings, maraschino cherries, and cloves, and a large casserole dish of creamy scalloped potatoes, with butter rolls, red tomato chow, and sweet peas.

"This is delicious, Mrs. Macdonald. Did you do this all yourself?"

Mom laughed. "Of course, dear. Who else would do it?"

Annie was ravenous and piled as much as she could on her plate. Henry looked at her. "You'd think we had no food at home."

"Shut your gob, Pratfall."

Annie noticed that David hardly touched his meal. He was no doubt too excited to eat. It's a big deal to bring home the girl you want to marry. Lila didn't eat much either, but that's because she was busy keeping Cricket in her chair and cutting up her food.

"So when's the big day?" Mom asked.

"This April," Kay said. "I hope you don't mind that we're having it in Halifax."

"We understand. Your entire family is there and I'm sure your mother is run off her feet organizing everything, but if there's anything I can do, I'd be happy too. I missed the chance with Annie's wedding."

"Mom, are you going to bring that up again?"

"I'm just saying."

"We thought we'd come back in the summer and have a big party out in Round Island, for friends and relatives who can't make it to the wedding," David said.

"What fun!" Mom said. "Won't that be fun, Kenzie?"

Dad didn't even look up. "Indeed."

"I have a great idea," Kay said. "Cricket could be our flower girl. That would be so sweet."

Lila shook her head. "Thank you, but we won't be going to the wedding."

Annie was surprised. "You're not?"

"Cricket gets car sick, and that's a very long drive."

"And Lila has to be careful not to overdo it," Aunt Eunie said. "But we'll be there with bells on for the summer party."

"I was hoping you'd be one of my bridesmaids, Annie."

"You're kidding."

"I'd love to have David's family in the wedding party. I hope you'll say yes."

"Are you sure you want her? She'll be up there crossing her eyes and making faces at me the entire time," David laughed.

"Hey! No I won't...not the *entire* time."

Cricket knocked over her glass of juice on the table and started to cry. Everyone assured her it was fine, but she couldn't be consoled. Lila took her in her arms.

"This little girl is tired. I think we'll say goodnight."

"But she hasn't had dessert," Mom rushed to say. "I made her some rice pudding."

"We'll take it with us."

Aunt Eunie and Uncle Joe looked sorry that they had to go, but they nevertheless got to their feet. Mom got up as well. "I've made a butterscotch pie for us. I'll cut some of that up too, so you can take it with you."

Everyone said it was nice meeting everyone else, and as the Johnsons left with their goodies, all of them shouted Merry Christmas and everyone shouted Merry Christmas back.

Then back to the table to cut up the rest of the butterscotch pie.

Annie looked at her parents, her husband, her brother, and his mate. "So here we are. Our little family unit is growing."

"You're very lucky to have such a wonderful family," Kay said. "You say that Lila grew up with you?"

Annie told her the story, as Mom dished out the pie. David didn't want any, but Mom coaxed him into having a tiny sliver.

"I hope I'm not being nosy, but why did Eunie say that Lila couldn't overdo it?"

"She has heart problems. She nearly died having Caroline. Henry can vouch for that."

Henry nodded. "She was one lucky girl. It was close for both of them."

"Can we talk about something a little less morbid?" David said. "This is supposed to be a celebration."

After dinner, Kay went out to the living room with the men. Annie and her mother cleaned up.

"She's probably never had to do a dish in her life."

"Leave her alone. She's a guest."

"I'm not being mean, it's just an observation."

At that moment, Kay appeared in the doorway. "I wondered where you went. Do you need some help?"

"Oh no, dear," Mom said, "we're fine."

Annie saw that Kay was disappointed. "Don't listen to her. Here's a dishtowel." Annie threw one to her.

"This is so much fun," Kay smiled. "Girl talk in the kitchen. I've always wanted to do this."

"You sure are easy to please," Annie laughed. "You can knock yourself out at my place if you like. I've got a whole sink full of dirty dishes."

Mom rinsed a plate. "What do you mean you have a sink full of dirty dishes? That's not how you were brought up."

"Not every woman in the world is a domestic goddess like you, Mom."

"Amen to that," Kay added.

CHAPTER TWELVE

ON NEW YEAR'S DAY, LILA woke up before sunrise. Something didn't feel right, but she wasn't sure what. It was like something was missing. She sat up in bed and looked around the room. Cricket was fast asleep in her crib and everything looked the same, so what was it?

And then she knew.

She reached down and touched Freddy at the end of her bed. Every morning he would stretch his fourteen-year-old legs and yawn like an old man. Even though she knew she wouldn't hear it, she put her head against his chest and waited for his heart to beat.

"Don't leave me, Freddy. Not now."

She was still holding him when Cricket woke up. She sang to herself for a while and then turned over and saw that her mother was awake. She immediately jumped up and bounced, holding onto the sides of the crib and smiling, her sleepyhead hair every which way.

"Mama. Fweddy."

Lila began to cry, hearing Cricket say his name. Her daughter loved Freddy and he loved her back. He'd put up with a lot—being grabbed by the neck for a hug, or being a horsey, or a handy mat on the floor she could snuggle against.

Seeing her mother cry made Cricket cry, which brought Aunt Eunie running upstairs.

"What's wrong?"

"Freddy's dead."

Aunt Eunie began to cry, which brought Uncle Joe upstairs. When he started to cry, Lila knew they were in big trouble.

Lila wrapped Freddy in his favourite blanket and kept him on the bed. Then she went downstairs to call Ewan.

"Freddy's dead."

"Oh no. What happened?"

"He died in his sleep. I thought you'd want to know because Freddy loved you so much." Her eyes welled up with tears. "I'm sorry, I have to go."

Lila and Uncle Joe got dressed and went outside to pick a spot to bury their special dog. "He needs to be under the maple tree. The leaves brush up against my window and Freddy loved lying under the shade to cool off."

"He also liked it because he was guarding the house," Uncle Joe sniffed.

Lila wasn't surprised when Ewan drove up the driveway in his truck and came towards them carrying a pickaxe and shovel. He looked like he'd been crying too. "Show me where you want him." Lila pointed to the spot and Ewan put the pickaxe up to his shoulder and slammed it into the hard ground. He did it over and over and soon had a hole that Freddy could be snug in.

Aunt Eunie came out with an old throw to line the space, some dog treats, and his favourite ball. Uncle Joe held Caroline, who was delighted to be outside so early in the morning with her snowsuit on. They looked at Ewan.

"I'll go get him."

Ewan went into the house and came back shortly with Freddy's body wrapped in his favourite blanket. While he held him, the family kissed Freddy's white muzzle and told him how much they loved him and thanked him for being the best dog in the whole world.

They were still crying when Ewan lowered Freddy and gently put him in the hole. Lila put in the treats and his ball and then they took the four corners of the blanket and wrapped him up like a special gift.

"You go on in," Ewan said. "I'll cover him up."

"I'll stay with you," Lila said. "Take Cricket into the house."

Aunt Eunie and Uncle Joe took the baby back inside. Lila stood by the grave and watched Ewan shovel the dirt back in and over her beloved pet. He smoothed it and put back the frozen sods before he shovelled some snow over it again so it would look nice.

They stared at the space together. Then Lila's shoulders began to shake and she hid her face against Ewan's heavy flannel jacket. He put his arm around her.

Lila insisted he come in and have breakfast to thank him for his efforts. Whenever Ewan came over, Cricket would crawl up on his knees and make him bounce her up and down like a horse, going slow and then fast and then slow again. Aunt Eunie decided to make buttermilk pancakes with bacon and maple syrup, because those were Freddy's special treats. Lila thought she wouldn't be able to eat, but she had a few bites of pancake.

Aunt Eunie stacked six thick pancakes on a plate and passed them to Ewan. "Does your mother enjoy living in town?"

"It sounds like it. She and my aunt call themselves the merry widows."

"What about your brothers?"

"They finally found an apartment in Sydney. They're moving out soon. One of them has been hired to drive a bus and the other one works at a grocer's."

"So you're going to run the farm by yourself?" Lila said.

"I'll be fine. I've got a man who buys my milk and eggs and all the potatoes I can give him. I don't want for much."

"You'll be lonely down there by yourself."

"I'm used to being alone."

"Then you'll have to come up here more often," Aunt Eunie said. "Come for Sunday dinner. Joe brought home an enormous pork roast yesterday. We can't possibly eat it all."

"Thank you. That would be nice."

Aunt Eunie went out to the kitchen and came back into the dining room with another pile of pancakes for Ewan. "Have some pancakes. They're delicious."

Ewan was too polite to point out he already had a full plate. He took it from her and said, "These look good."

"There's lots of ketchup, so help yourself."

Lila knew her aunt meant maple syrup, that she was just upset about the dog. Uncle Joe was very quiet too.

Cricket picked up a piece of her pancake and yelled, "Fweddy! Fweddy!"

"I hate 1949 already," Lila said.

❋ ❋ ❋

Annie had been keeping her pregnancy a secret from Henry until she passed the three-month mark. She'd seen too many sad faces of young mothers at the hospital. No sense in getting everyone riled up until she knew it was going to happen. She made one last doctor's appointment to be absolutely sure.

As she lay on the examining table, the doctor had his brow furrowed. "Are you sure of your dates?"

"Pretty sure. Why? What's the matter? You're making me nervous."

He took off his rubber gloves and poked around her belly again. "I can't say with total certainty at this stage of the game, but I have a hunch you're having twins."

Annie sat up. "Twins? Twins don't even run in my family."

"Look at it this way, Annie. You get two babies with only one labour."

"You're a genius."

Annie made Henry's favourite, spaghetti and meatballs, for dinner. She lit a few candles, put on some music, and dolled herself up a little. Then she lounged in the chair closest to the table, so Henry would see the entire vignette all at once. She even crossed her legs to the side, like she'd seen Kay do.

She heard the car pull up into the driveway rather quickly and only moments later he burst in the door.

"You're having *twins*?!"

Annie jumped out of the chair. "Why did he tell you? I wanted it to be a surprise!"

Henry came over and tried to take her in his arms, but she kept slapping him away. "Don't blame him. Blame me. I accidentally saw you go into his office today and I choked him until he spilled the beans."

"There was no accident about it. You've been spying on me! Did you already know I was pregnant?"

"Yes! Don't hate me!"

She kept trying to push him away. "How did you know?"

"You've been eating four bunches of bananas a week. You polished off a whole carrot cake by yourself and made me fry cheese in a frying pan."

They both burst out laughing and started to jump up and down with glee. He took her in his arms and held her close.

"You are precious to me, Annie Pratfall. You are my world. I wouldn't be able to live without you."

"Sure you would. It just wouldn't be as much fun."

They filled up on the spaghetti and meatballs before venturing forth to tell the grandparents.

They went to Annie's house first in case Henry's mom had a seizure and had to go to the hospital.

They knocked on the back door and found her parents having tuna noodle casserole at the kitchen table.

"Hi, guys," Annie said.

Her mother jumped up. "You're pregnant!!"

"Oh my god! Did you choke my doctor too?"

"No! I'm looking at Henry's face!"

Mom hugged her. Dad hugged her. Then Mom hugged Henry and Henry hugged Dad. Then Mom hugged her again.

"Wait for it…" Annie said.

"…we're having twins!" Henry shouted.

"I wanted to tell them!"

Mom squealed and Dad chuckled before they got on the phone and called David, who shouted congratulations and passed the phone to Kay, who squealed just like Mom.

Then they called Lila.

She told them about Freddy before Annie had a chance to tell her about the babies, so when she did find out Lila was upset that she'd ruined such happy news with her sad news.

When they walked into Henry's mother's house, Joy jumped up to greet them and immediately fell to the floor in a dead faint.

"Okay, this is ridiculous! How on earth does *she* know?"

Henry rushed over to his mother's side and gently tapped the side of her face. "Mom. Mom. Are you okay?"

She started to come around. "Oh my, what happened?"

"Is your blood sugar low again?"

"Maybe."

"I'm sorry." Annie knelt by her as well. "I thought you'd heard we're having twins."

Joy's face radiated joy before she lost consciousness.

❊ ❊ ❊

It was only a month later that Annie and David's cousin Dorothy was killed in a car accident. She was a passenger in a vehicle that left the road. The man who was driving lived, but she was thrown from the car.

Dorothy had wanted to be a stewardess. She was fun and pretty and Aunt Muriel's only daughter.

When David heard the news, he immediately left Halifax to come home. Kay wanted to come with him, but he said he'd rather go alone. She understood.

The wake at the funeral home was terrible. He and Annie had never been to a wake before. They'd lost three of their grandparents when they were young and hadn't been allowed to go. How Dorothy's parents and older brother stood there by her open coffin and shook hands with a seemingly endless line of people, David didn't know. Annie became very emotional, and Henry asked Lila to take her into the ladies' room, as her parents were standing beside the family.

When the girls finally re-emerged, Henry and David were waiting close by.

"Maybe we should go home," Henry said.

"No." Annie wiped her red and swollen eyes with a wet paper towel. "She was my cousin and I'll do this, but I swear to God, if anything ever happens to me, don't put me in an open casket. I'll come back and haunt you."

Somehow the family made it through the wake and the funeral. Then everyone was asked to come back to the church hall for tea, sandwiches, and sweets. David marvelled at how these small elderly church women had the entire place completely organized for over a hundred people. They even catered to the immediate family, so they wouldn't have to stand in the lineup.

Annie was still visibly upset. "Why don't these people go home? You'd think they were at a wedding reception. Do you see that guy over there? He's gone back for thirds."

Henry patted her knee. "But look at all the people going up to her parents and brother. They're telling them how special their daughter was. They'll appreciate that in the lonely days ahead, when people stop talking about her for fear of hurting them."

When it was time to leave they went back to their parents' house; Annie and David felt they should be there for their mother, who was so upset. But Mom said she needed to lie down and Henry said he should take Annie home too. Dad asked David to take Lila back to Round Island. The Johnsons were taking care of Caroline.

Without saying a word to each other, they got in his car. The tension was palpable, and David knew he was going to lose it if he didn't stop and have it out with her.

He pulled over to the side of the road on the outskirts of Glace Bay.

"Why are we stopping?"

David left the engine running and turned to face her. "I want to know why you felt it was necessary to show up with Caroline the night I brought Kay home to meet my family."

"You want to do this now? After the horrible day we've gone through?"

"I'm not going to get many chances to speak to you alone in the future."

"No, you won't, will you? You'll be a married man."

"And why is that?"

"Because she's rich?"

David resisted the urge to shake her. "I'm marrying someone else because you told me I wasn't the father of my own child. I told you I loved you and wanted to marry you, but you threw me out."

"It didn't take you long to find a replacement."

"Don't bring Kay into it. This is your fault, Lila."

Lila stared straight ahead. "It's my fault that you had your way with me outside, on the ground, the minute you came home from overseas."

"Jesus! You make it sound like I raped you. You enjoyed it, as I remember, or have I got that wrong too?"

"Do you think I wanted to be there the night you brought Kay home? Annie asked me to come and since I'm still pretending to be your little sister, it would've looked odd if I didn't go."

They stopped talking, as if letting the words settle in. David looked out his car window.

"You can't truly love me, David, if you're marrying someone else."

He turned back to her. "That's where you're wrong. What if I call the wedding off? Would you marry me then? Would you let me raise that beautiful little girl? You're the one who holds all the cards here."

Lila gave him a shocked look. "You'd do that to someone who obviously adores you?"

"You did."

She didn't respond.

"Since you find it distasteful to even contemplate marrying me sometime in the future, I have no choice. I want to be married. I want a family. Is that wrong? Isn't that what everyone wants? You're not prepared to give it to me, so I've gone elsewhere. But in your eyes it will still be my fault."

She kept her face turned away. David knew the conversation was over. He put the car in gear and turned the wheels back on the road. They were silent the rest of the drive. When he pulled into the yard, Lila got out of the car and shut the door before he could say anything else. Not that he was going to. He'd said enough already.

❋ ❋ ❋

The wedding took place at Saint George's Round Anglican Church and the reception was at the Lord Nelson hotel. There was a suite of rooms available at the hotel for David and his family, who were driving up the day before the wedding. He paced back and forth waiting for them to arrive.

The hotel room door finally opened and only a round bump could be seen protruding from the side.

"Guess who!"

"Annie!"

Annie appeared, with Henry, Mom, and Dad behind her, as well as his grandmother, Cynthia. David was happy to see them.

"Look at you." He took his sister in his arms and gave her a big hug. "Hi, everyone!"

As they greeted each other, Annie rubbed her belly. "Are you sure Kay still wants me in this wedding? I'll look like a fat cow beside her."

"She said she didn't care if you were as big as a house."

"Can you believe someone that beautiful and that rich is so nice?" Annie said. "You must be the happiest guy alive."

His mom and grandmother approached him with what looked like new cookie tins. "I made some Danish wedding cookies…" his mother said.

"…and I made a light fruitcake. Do you think we should give them to Kay's mom in case she wants them for the reception?"

David loved these two women more at that moment than ever in his life. "Let me handle it. I'll make sure she gets them."

"Your Aunt Muriel and Uncle Howard were going to come, but Muriel didn't feel up to it at the last minute," Dad said. "But everyone else is here. Are we all expected at the rehearsal dinner tonight?"

"No, just the wedding party, and Grandma, of course."

"Is it in this hotel?" Henry asked.

"No, another restaurant downtown."

His tiny grandmother reached up and patted his cheek. "If you don't mind, honey, I won't be going this evening. The drive tuckered me out."

"That's fine, Grandma. Don't worry about it. I'll make sure to order room service before we go."

"What's that?"

"It's great; they make your meal and bring it right to your door."

"What's so great about that? I've been doing that for you fellas for fifty years."

David introduced his family to the Hanovers in the lobby of the Lord Nelson. Louis made a big show of welcoming them to the city, as if they were refugees from another country. Kay's mom kept her cigarette holder glued to her mouth and only nodded at everyone. Kay was happy introducing her brother, Louis, who seemed genuinely pleased to meet them.

Then David introduced his best man, Scott, to his family, along with another school chum who was a groomsman. Kay's maid of honour was her cousin Marion. Marion and Annie became fast friends, both of them giggling over Annie's girth.

They departed for the church and the minister went over the ceremony. It seemed pretty straightforward, so they piled in their cars and hit the restaurant, which was ready and waiting for them. David and his dad walked in together, but when Louis came through the door, Dad asked to speak to him.

Louis stood there with a cigar in his mouth, looking like Winston Churchill.

"What can I do for you, Mr. Macdonald?"

"I'd like to pay for everyone this evening, in accordance with the tradition that the groom's family hosts the rehearsal dinner."

David's stomach started acting up there and then.

"That's extremely generous and kind of you, sir. I will certainly abide by your wishes. Thank you very much."

Louis walked off, but David held his father back. "Dad, you don't understand..."

"I don't understand what?"

"These people don't care what things cost and they drink. It's going to be more than you can afford."

"I have my pride, David. I want to do this for you. You're my only son now and your mother and I want to do our part."

David hung his head. Dad put his arm over his shoulder. "It'll be fine."

It wasn't.

Dad might have been paying for it, but Louis presided over the wine list. "We want three bottles of your best champagne. Nothing's too good for my girl."

David sat next to Annie and whispered, "Dad's paying for this." Annie then whispered to Henry.

The waiter came back with the champagne.

"We'd also like three bottles of your best white wine." Louis turned to Dad. "This restaurant is known for its seafood. White wine goes better with fish, but if you like, we can get red too?"

Dad held up his hand. "We're good."

"Let's have appetizers first," Louis boomed.

"Is this all on one bill?" the waiter asked.

"Yes, it is," Dad said.

Everyone had appetizers except for Henry, Annie, David, and his parents.

Then Louis encouraged everyone to get the lobster, which they did, except for Henry, Annie, David, and his parents, who didn't have the dessert or specialty coffee either.

At one point Dad stood up and cleared his throat. Virginia kept talking until Kay spoke to her under her breath.

Virginia put up her hands in surrender, one of them holding onto a glass of rye and ginger. "No offense meant."

"I'd like to thank everyone for coming this evening. David's mother and I are very proud and happy to welcome Kay into our family. She is obviously a wonderful girl and a credit to her parents. David is a good man, and I know he will take care of your daughter in the years ahead. We wish them all the best."

"Hear, hear!" Louis roared.

Dad held up his glass. "To David and Kay."

Everyone followed suit. "To David and Kay."

David, Annie, Henry, and Mom sat still as the waiter handed Dad the bill. To his everlasting credit, he didn't flinch.

"Excuse me. I'll take care of this at the counter." Dad stood up and walked away. Henry got to his feet and said "Nature calls," before hurrying after Dad. David watched them confer in the corner. He knew that Henry was offering to pay with a cheque and that Dad would have no choice but to accept. He also knew his father would insist on paying him back as soon as he got to a bank.

David was aware that it wouldn't occur to Kay to wonder if there was a problem. She was happy and laughing with her cousin, who was flirting with the best man and the groomsman. Louis Sr. and Louis Jr. were discussing business. Mom stared at her lap, and Annie looked at Henry with such love in her eyes that David had to look away.

There was only one person who noticed everything, and that was Virginia. David saw her sit back in her chair and stare at him with a satisfied look. She even held up her glass and nodded to him.

David had never hated anyone so much in his life.

The first thing David did the morning of his wedding was go downstairs with the cookie tins and speak to the man in charge of the reception.

"I'd like these cookies and this fruitcake to be front and centre on the dessert table. Put them on your best pedestal cake plates, please, and then return the tins to my room."

"Certainly. I'll make sure it happens."

"Thank you."

The rest of the day was a blur. It seemed to be endless waiting, and people running back and forth and cars being arranged and everyone asking him questions, most of which he couldn't answer, since he hadn't planned any of the wedding. He wanted it to be over.

He stood at the altar with his friends beside him and the minister behind him. Most of the guests were crammed into the pews on the bride's side of the church, until it became impossible and the wedding planner started to herd the excess people over to the other side, just for the sake of appearances.

Henry and Dad escorted David's mother and grandmother up to the front of the church. They both had on corsages and new dresses. Not to the floor like Kay's family, but still lovely. When the four of them sat down in the front aisle, David smiled at them. His mother blew him a kiss.

He completely ignored Kay's mother being escorted up the aisle by her son.

Then the music started and everyone stood. The first to appear was Annie, who had a bit of a duck waddle going on. She held her bouquet to hide her belly as best she could. She stuck her tongue out at him when she got to the front. Marion came next and then Kay and her father proceeded down the aisle.

"You lucky bastard," Scott muttered.

Kay had on an ivory, soft silk crepe gown, with a cowl neckline in the front and a low draped back. There was a silk sash to cinch her silhouette and lace cap sleeves at her shoulders. She carried white roses and had a diamond and pearl brooch in her hair.

When Kay looked at David he couldn't believe she wanted him. Why him? She was beautiful. Everything a man would want in a woman. He'd spend the rest of his life trying to make her as happy as she seemed at that moment. He only hoped that someday he'd be happy too.

❊ ❊ ❊

When Annie was finally able to escape the head table, she made a beeline for her family. They sat at three tables in the back corner of the room. Henry had saved her a chair.

"Is it my imagination or is there enough booze and food in here to sink the *Titanic*?"

Her grandmother sniffed. "It's indecent. And the waste! You could feed a village for a week. I saw perfectly good lobster tails that hadn't been touched being scraped off plates, and no doubt thrown in the garbage. I've never seen anything like it."

"I know, Mother," Mom said, "but this is David's reception and we don't need to tell him all about it when he comes over. Let him enjoy the night."

"Well, when this is over, I plan on speaking my mind. I'll talk to him at the wedding brunch in the morning."

Mom sighed.

David and Kay were making the rounds of the tables and eventually came their way. Kay looked even more astonishing up close.

"I want to thank you all for being here. I know it means a lot to David and it means a lot to me, too. I hope you enjoy the dancing later, and the late-night buffet."

Annie got ready to put her hand over Grandma's mouth, but she just murmured, "Wonderful, dear. I'm sure we'll enjoy it."

Kay was called away, but David rubbed his hands together. "I want my three best girls to come and see something." He helped his grandmother out of her chair and Mom and Annie followed. They made their way over to the dessert table. As requested, the cookies and fruitcake were beautifully displayed, front and centre.

"Oh, my," Grandma said. "It looks so nice. How come it doesn't look like that at home?"

"The five-hundred-dollar serving tray probably has something to do with it," Annie said.

Mom kissed David. "Thank you, dear. That means a lot."

Virginia happened to come by with her socialite friends, and they stood in front of the table making their selections. Two other women came running over and pointed at the cookies and the fruitcake. "Oh my God! Did you taste these? I normally hate fruitcake, but this is amazing."

"And those cookies melt in your mouth."

"What did you expect? We only pay for the best."

Annie was about to tell them that they were her family's recipes, but David got there first.

"Actually, you have two talented ladies to thank. My mother, Abigail, and my grandmother Cynthia."

Annie waved. "The talent stopped with my generation."

All the ladies gushed and wondered if they could have the recipes. Annie could tell her mom and grandmother were thrilled. Only one person didn't join in; Kay's mother looked at David with hate and he returned the favour.

Annie grabbed a cookie herself and beat it back to the table. Henry had on his *I'm bored out of my mind* face. "I have something juicy to share."

"Do tell."

"There's some kind of history with David and Kay's mother. I know most men don't like their mother-in-laws, but he's only been married for five minutes, which means something's transpired between them, and I plan on finding out what."

"Right now?"

"Maybe."

"Leave the guy alone."

Annie hit Henry on the arm. "Oh look, here he comes."

David escorted his triumphant relatives back to the table. The grin on his face was ear to ear. Annie waved David over and he knelt down between their chairs.

"Why the mutual hate contest between you and Mrs. Hanover?"

"The first day I met her, she grabbed my balls under the dining-room table."

Henry and Annie exploded with laughter.

"Oh my god, if I have these babies tonight it will be your fault!"

"You asked."

❖ ❖ ❖

The live band played the new hit "Some Enchanted Evening" and David marvelled at how Kay looked in his arms. Next he danced with his mother and Kay danced with her dad. Mom and Dad and Annie and Henry had one dance after that and declared it an evening. Grandma had been taken up to her room earlier.

Most of David's relatives left at the same time. He didn't blame them. Everyone was shouting to be heard over the loud band, and you can only look at drunken wedding guests for so long before it's not funny anymore. But they all went over to thank the bride's parents for the lovely evening.

As everyone else went upstairs, David saw his dad go out the front doors of the hotel, so he followed him. Dad stood against one of the pillars smoking a cigarette.

"Getting some air?"

"Yes, it's a nice evening."

David took a few deep breaths. "Dad, I want to thank you."

"For what?"

"Being here. Paying for that ridiculous meal. For being the person you are…for everything…"

Dad reached over and squeezed the back of his neck. "You're welcome."

David choked up. "I'll never be the man you are."

"I'm sure you will. It takes practice. You have your whole life ahead of you to rehearse."

"Thanks."

"Go inside. Your bride will be wondering where you are."

David nodded and turned to go.

"But David…"

David turned back. "Yes?"

"You're in another world here. Don't lose yourself. Remember where you came from."

CHAPTER THIRTEEN

LILA OPENED HER EYES AND lay on the bed listening to Caroline's soft breathing. She curled up on her side and watched her through the slats of the crib on the far wall. The early morning light made her daughter's hair look more red than it really was. It was always a tangled mess when she woke up, and if she was too warm, her hair would get even curlier.

There was no getting around it. Lila had to get Cricket a new bed. She was too big to be sleeping in a crib, but there was a part of Lila that didn't want to change a thing.

It felt hot out already and it was only six in the morning, which was unusual for mid-June. Annie was calling her every day to bitch that women who were eight months pregnant with twins should not be subjected to a bloody tropical heat wave before it was even summer. Lila finally told her to go stick her head in a bucket of ice cubes. In typical hormonal fashion, Annie took it the wrong way and didn't call her until the afternoon of the next day.

Cricket began to stir. Then, as always, she sang by herself for a while and babbled about nothing. Lila wished she could greet each morning like that, content with her world and happy to be awake. And then it was time to wake mom. Lila sat up and looked over and as soon as she saw her, Cricket's face lit up.

"Hi, Mama."

"Hi, baby."

Cricket was perfectly capable of getting out of the crib herself, but she always waited for her mother to scoop her up and take her into the big bed to snuggle under the blankets.

"I think someone is happy today," Lila smiled.

"I saw a doggy."

"A doggy? Were you dreaming about your puppy dog?"

"Fweddy."

"Freddy. I miss Freddy."

"Sing."

Lila sat up and Caroline made herself comfortable on her mother's lap.

"Mommy loves the button nose,
Mommy loves the button nose,
Mommy loves the button nose
And the little chinny chin chin."

Cricket would point to her nose and her chin at the appropriate moments.

"Mommy loves the button eyes
Mommy loves the button toes
Mommy loves the button nose
And the little chinny chin chin."

"Again."

Then they'd play patty-cake, patty-cake, baker's man, and London Bridge is falling down. Lila would hold on to her hands and let Caroline lean back slowly until her head almost hit the blankets and then pull her up real quick. She loved that one.

"Do you know why Mama calls you Cricket?"

"I love them."

"That's true, but also, they say that if you have a cricket in your house it brings you good luck."

"Luck?"

"And you've brought Mommy the best luck she could ever want. I'm very, very lucky I have you."

"Mama, where's Fweddy?"

"Freddy is a part of the world now. Our bodies die, but our spirit or energy doesn't. So as long as you remember Freddy, he'll stay with you. What do you think?"

"Fweddy's hungry."

"And so are we. Let's go and see what we can rustle up."

It was such a beautiful day that Lila and Cricket took their breakfast outside. They sat on the outdoor chairs and ate cut-up fruit out of their bowls, and then cheese on bread. Uncle Joe came outside to mow the lawn with his push-reel mower. The rhythmic swishing of the blades was soothing somehow.

Aunt Eunie emerged from the house to hang up some towels. "It's going to be a hot one today. I don't envy Abigail and Annie trying to get the food ready for the wedding party."

"That's today?"

"Isn't it?"

"It's next weekend, I think."

"My memory isn't what it used to be." She held up the towels and stood there.

"What's wrong?"

"How do I hang this?"

"What do you mean?"

"How do these stay on?"

"With a clothes peg."

Aunt Eunie lowered her arms and looked at the clothesline. Lila got out of the chair and went over to her. She pointed to them on the clothesline. "You use these."

Aunt Eunie held up the towel and took the clothes peg off the line and then pressed it into the towel, but if fell to the ground.

Cricket giggled. "Nanny Noonie is silly."

Lila felt the hairs on the back of her neck stand on end. "Try it again."

Aunt Eunie took another peg and pressed it harder into the towel, but again, the towel fell to the ground. She was very distressed. "I can't make it work. These pegs are no good. I'll get Joe to buy some more in town."

"Leave the towels with me."

Aunt Eunie went back inside. As Lila hung up the towels, she saw her future stretched out before her. Sometime soon, Lila would have two children in the house.

Ewan's truck came up the driveway. He got out of the cab with a basket of eggs. Cricket jumped up and ran over to him. "Hi, Ooan."

"Hi, Cricket."

She stuck her face in the basket. "Eggs."

Lila took the basket. "Thank you. Come and sit down for a minute."

Cricket ran over to the chairs and spooned grass into her breakfast bowl. "I make soup, Ooan."

"Sounds good."

They sat together under the shade of the trees.

"I need to talk to you about something."

"Okay."

"I'm worried about Aunt Eunie. Lately she's been forgetting things. This morning she couldn't remember how to hang up clothes."

"What does Joe say?"

"That's just it. He's ignoring the problem."

"Now that you mention it, I wondered what she was doing walking down the road by herself the other day. I stopped to pick her up and she said she was out for a stroll, but now I'm not so sure. She had on an apron."

"I'm frightened."

They watched Uncle Joe walk up and down the side lawn with the mower. He waved to them when he got close. Cricket waved back.

"If you need help, I'm here."

Lila reached out her hand and squeezed his. "Thank you."

※ ※ ※

Annie took a kitchen chair and sprawled on it in front of her open fridge, wearing just her underwear. That's how her mother-in-law found her when she arrived unannounced.

"Yoo-hoo! Nana's here! Where are my grandchildren?"

Annie asked all her friends, but none of them had mothers or mothers-in-law who acted like a grandmother before the kid arrived. It drove Annie up the wall, but she tried to stay calm for Henry's sake. She knew there were times when he wanted to strangle his mother. He even mimed it behind Joy's back one day and almost got caught.

Annie closed her bathrobe. "We're in the kitchen!"

Joy fairly danced into the room. "And how are we three today?"

"We three are hot."

"Oh dear, let me fan you."

At first Annie was going to say that wasn't necessary, but it actually was. "Okay."

Joy didn't seem to notice that the fridge was open. She grabbed a newspaper and did a fantastic job waving it.

"I feel like the queen of the Nile," Annie said.

"Your wish is my command."

How could you dislike someone like that? Annie had learned quickly that Joy in small doses was a delight. It was when things progressed to a couple of hours that the fatigue set in. Annie asked Henry how his father died, and he told her to take a guess. Annie didn't want to be mean and say he put his head in the oven, and was briefly horrified when Henry told her that that's what had happened. She felt much better when he told her his dad had been trying to fix the stove when something went terribly wrong. Of course, that was just what his mother had told him as a child. Now that Henry was an adult, he wondered.

"When are your brother and his wife coming?"

"They're in tonight and the party is tomorrow. But to tell you the truth, I've kind of had it with celebrating his wedding. One eighteen-hour ordeal is enough. But if Mom wants to do it, who am I to say anything?"

"I understand how she feels. She wants to be involved with a wedding."

Here it was again. It was thrown in her and Henry's faces at least once a month that neither Joy nor Abigail had had the chance to partake in their wedding.

"What are you up to today, Joy?"

Joy kept fanning. "Nothing, really. I just wanted to see you and the children."

"At the moment the kids are a bit shy."

"Have you thought of any names?"

Annie needed to get up. "Thanks Joy, that's enough fanning. I'm fine now." She carefully got out of the chair and closed the fridge door. "We're going to wait until they're born."

Joy put down the newspaper and rummaged through her purse, taking out a small notepad. "I wrote down some of my family's names, in case there's anything of interest to you."

Annie took the paper. "Asaph, Mehitabel, Jedaiah. I'll have to run these by Henry, but we'll keep them in mind."

"Oh, sorry. The names are on the other side. I wrote those down because they were in the family Bible."

Annie turned it over. "Patience, Hope, Faith, Charity. Interesting."

"My grandmother had eighteen kids. She ran out of names. My mother carried on the tradition with me and my brother, Ernest."

When Joy left, Annie called her mother. "Do we have a family Bible?"

"Yes, it's a huge old thing with a scrolled leather cover about four inches deep. Why?"

"Joy was over and mentioned some family names, and I thought it might be worth a look."

"There were a few Sarahs, Elizabeths, and Janes."

"That's a whole lot better than Mehitabel."

"Good heavens. As long as you don't want to know everyone's date of birth, you're welcome to look through it."

"Isn't that what a family bible is for? To record the date of birth and death?"

"Yes, but Aunt Muriel changed everyone's birthday to make herself seem younger."

Later that evening, Annie was lying on the sofa while Henry rubbed her feet. Their front door opened and David's voice shouted "Anyone home?"

"We're in here," Henry said.

David walked in with Kay. "Greetings! I figured we should come to you. Mom told me you don't go far after supper."

"She's right, so don't mind me if I don't get up. You're looking as fabulous as ever, Kay."

"Thank you," she smiled, "but I think you look beautiful! Pregnancy suits you." She held her hand out. "May I?"

"Sure. Everyone wants to touch my belly. I should charge a fee."

Kay laid her hand carefully on top of Annie's stomach. Annie took her hand and pushed it down on one side. "This one's kicking up a storm tonight."

Kay squealed with delight when one of the twins poked back. "Oh, I can't wait to have a baby!"

Henry pointed at the two armchairs. "Please, sit. Can I get you anything?"

David shook his head and sat down. "If I have one more morsel or drink of anything, I'll explode. You know Mom. I think she's getting worse as she grows older. There must have been four desserts at our disposal."

Kay sat as well. "I've eaten at a lot of restaurants in my life, but your mother's cooking is the best I've ever had."

"Don't tell her. She's already smug as it is."

Henry kept rubbing Annie's feet. "Did you and Kay come alone?"

David nodded. "Yes, everyone's schedule in Kay's family is booked up months in advance."

"David is relieved," Kay laughed. "He had a fit thinking of my mother using an outhouse. I think it's an adventure."

"That opinion will quickly fade the minute you use it," Annie said. "Davy, remember Aunt Muriel?"

"It's hard to forget. She came screaming out of it with her underwear around her ankles being chased by a swarm of wasps. I thought Mom would die laughing."

Annie smiled at the memory.

"Do you have your nursery all ready?" Kay asked. "I'd love to see it."

Henry got up. "I'll take you. I've had it ready for months."

The minute they went upstairs, Annie started the interrogation. "So, what's married life like?"

"We're having fun."

"Do you ever see her mom?"

"Sometimes, but we ignore each other. Kay doesn't care. She can barely tolerate her mother."

Annie turned over on her side. "I wonder what that's like."

"She's never known anything else. How are you getting along with Henry's mother?"

"I'm afraid of what's going to happen when the babies arrive. She'll be camped on our doorstep."

"I'm sure you'll put her straight."

Annie shook her head. "I'd never hurt Henry like that."

"What do you know? Annie's been tamed. I think you love the guy."

"I know I do."

The entire extended family descended on the bungalow the next day, and because it was hot and sunny, the party was outside. They'd borrowed some folding chairs from the church for the older people in the crowd, but mostly they ate and drank on big blankets laid out on the grass, picnic style.

Annie watched David introduce Kay to his friends and the relatives who hadn't made it up for the wedding. They reacted to Kay the same way she had the first time, wondering what the heck someone so sophisticated and glamorous was doing sitting in a hayfield eating sandwiches.

David's friends couldn't help themselves; they did what they could to attract Kay's attention, but her eyes were on David almost the entire time. Annie waited to see David look back at her, but it didn't happen—though, to be fair, David was excited to see his friends and laugh about old times. Annie wondered why she even noticed it. Maybe it was the slightly anxious look on Kay's face.

It was one of those moments that get filed away, and then remembered years later as the beginning of something.

❋ ❋ ❋

That morning Lila and Cricket went to the beach early. Cricket loved to play in the brook with her pail and shovel, and chase after small terns by the water's edge. Lila would lie back and lean on her elbows watching her daughter in the hot sun, and marvel at how this fabulous little creature belonged to her. Now she knew what her mother must have felt holding her, and that was reassuring. Someone had loved her. She wasn't the bad girl Mrs. Butts had constantly said she was. She wasn't a nuisance or a burden or unlovable.

Cricket ran up and plunked the pail in front of her mother. "Wanna help me?"

"What would you like me to do?"

"Make a castle."

They gathered up the dark sand and shaped it as best they could. Lila dug out a moat and Cricket ran to the brook and scooped up water to pour in it. It took five trips before it was full enough. Then they made a wooden drawbridge with sticks and put small rocks all around the castle so no one could miss it.

As they went back up through the field to go home for lunch, Lila heard the party at the Macdonalds'. She stayed at the edge of the field hoping to sneak past, but old eagle-eyes Annie spotted them and shouted for her to come over. Cricket let go of her mother's hand and made a beeline for her. She hugged Annie's knees and Annie bent down as best she could and hugged Cricket back.

"How's my girl?"

Lila knew she was in for it now. Everyone would ask them to stay for the party. Annie's mom would make a huge fuss over Cricket and she'd be stuck there for hours. She saw David look at her and then at Cricket. His eyes followed her daughter around as she flitted from person to person, before she stopped in front of Kay and reached out to touch her dress once again. Kay was delighted to see her.

Lila thought maybe she had had too much sun; she was flushed and dizzy. All she wanted was to be gone. She said so to Annie.

"Get out of the sun. I'll sit with you in the bungalow."

"No, I need to get home."

Annie looked at her with suspicion. "What's wrong?"

"I don't know. I can't stand people around. It's like I want to scream when someone comes up to me."

"I've had days like that. I'll get Henry to drive you home."

"It's only across the way."

"You're not walking in the sun, so stop arguing."

Henry was more than happy to help, so Lila scooped up Cricket, who was too busy eating a cupcake to object and they left without saying farewell.

When they got home they drank some lemonade with Aunt Eunie and Uncle Joe, who said they were going to wander over to the party. Lila told them to have fun, and then took Cricket upstairs for a nap. Lila lay with her on the bed; the two of them snuggled together.

When Lila opened her eyes again, she knew she'd slept too long. Her body was heavy and her mind foggy. Her pillow was wet from her drool and she had no idea what time of day it was, or even where she was. Her eyes swept the room and then automatically looked over at Caroline's crib expecting to see her but she didn't.

Oh, thank goodness, she's in bed with me. Lila put out her hand to rub Cricket's back but there was nothing there. She needed to wake up. There was something going on but she didn't know what it was. The minute she stood up, the realization that Cricket wasn't in the room sent a nauseous wave of fear through her body. Don't panic. She's downstairs with Uncle Joe and Aunt Eunie.

"Cricket!"

Lila ran down the stairs and expected everyone to be in the kitchen or the living room or outside or somewhere. Where was everyone? Why wasn't anyone home? She ran though the house calling for Caroline. She ran upstairs again and looked under both beds in case Cricket was playing hide-and-seek. Then she grabbed the blanket Annie made for her and Freddy the stuffed dog out of the crib and ran downstairs again.

She had no thoughts. There was disbelief and numbness somewhere above her head, but reality was a dream and Lila wasn't sure if she was dead or alive. Her heart hurt her chest every time it beat, and that beat throbbed in her ears. Her mouth was so dry she couldn't swallow. Wake up! Wake up and this will be over.

Her terror sent her running outside in every direction, always expecting Cricket to jump out at her and say, "Surprise, Mama!"

"Cricket! Come to me! I'm not playing now. I want you to come out for Mommy."

She looked under the front porch and over by the cold cellar and in Uncle Joe's shed. Nothing. No one. Nowhere. She turned her head back and forth in the air and shouted, "Caroline! Caroline! Caroline! Baby girl! Come to me!"

She was alone. What was she going to do? And then she heard people laughing in the distance. The party! That's where Caroline had gone. Back to the party to get another cupcake.

Lila ran as fast as she could, still holding onto Cricket's things until she emerged from the woods and ran across the field shouting. No one heard her. She screamed at them. "Listen to me! Listen to me!"

She stumbled in a rut and fell but got right back up and kept running. It was then that Lila saw David and Henry rushing towards her.

"Is she with you?! Is she here?"

They finally got close enough. "What's wrong?" David yelled.

"Is Cricket with you? Please say she's with Eunie and Joe!"

"I haven't seen her."

That's when the stab of agony hit. "Oh my god. I can't find her! She's not in the house. Where is she? Where is she?"

Henry took her by the shoulders. "We'll find her. I want you to calm down and take some deep breaths."

"I need to find my daughter! Annie! Annie!"

She lurched past the men and ran to the party, with Henry and David going after her. Everyone at the picnic was suddenly aware that something was wrong. They all got to their feet. Aunt Eunie and Uncle Joe hurried towards her. All Lila could see was Annie, her arm holding her belly so she could get to her faster.

"I can't find Cricket! Help me! Help me!"

"We'll find her, Lila. Don't you worry. I'm with you."

David shouted at the crowd. "Caroline is missing! The little girl who was here earlier. Everyone fan out and look for her! And someone call the neighbours so they can look too. And go to the beach!"

Lila saw Annie's mother with the same look on her face as the day she found Lila in the snow. That meant everyone was afraid, all of them saying they'd find Cricket but all of them scared too.

Lila pulled on Annie's dress. "What do I do? Tell me what to do!"

"Everyone will look here and we'll go back to the house. I'm sure she can't be far."

"Did I do something wrong? Was I supposed to be home?" Aunt Eunie shouted, but no one answered her. Uncle Joe rushed through the field.

Lila started after him and soon left Annie behind. Henry and David were ahead of her. Kay was in bare feet racing to catch up. Lila wondered where her shoes were. Everyone was calling out Caroline's name. Lila tried to keep shouting for her, but her throat was closed. She couldn't get enough air.

Back at the house, they spread out, searching everywhere. The surrounding trees, the cellar, the bushes, the woodpile. There was nothing.

Lila had to stop running. She couldn't breathe. She heard Henry tell Annie to go and get a blanket and wrap it around her. Why? Was Cricket in bed? Maybe she was under the blankets. In that hot sun, Lila shivered so severely that Annie put the blanket over her and held her in her arms. "It's okay. It'll be fine. She's wandered off, but we'll find her."

David ran out of the woods. "Anything? Has anyone seen her yet?"

No one answered him. They were too busy calling out Caroline's name.

And then Lila saw Ewan's truck tear up the driveway. He jumped out and left the door open as he ran into the yard. Lila threw off the blanket and scrambled to get to him, grabbing at his arms. "Oh my god! I've lost her, Ewan. I've lost her!"

He took her chin in his rough hand and made Lila look at him. "Stay with Annie. I'll get her. She'll come to me."

"Yes, yes."

Annie picked up the blanket once more and put it around her. Lila was able to catch her breath. It was going to be all right. Ewan would bring her home.

❄ ❄ ❄

Ewan knew the woods like the back of his hand. And he was used to seeing things that you might not notice at first, like animal tracks or broken sticks that indicated someone had been there. He had to put his brain on hold. A trick he learned in the war. He had to find Caroline, not imagine where she could be or if she was hurt. He needed to bring her back to Lila.

As he ran though the trees, he was hit over and over again in the face by small stinging branches, and stumbled constantly over rotten logs and downed trees. It wasn't possible for a three-year-old to get around in such a place, so he headed back towards the house. She might be asleep under a bush or watching an anthill. She loved insects, something he and Lila laughed about.

He heard the other voices calling her name over and over, but Ewan wanted to be able to hear her, so he stayed silent as he searched. As time went by he grew increasingly desperate. They had to find her before nightfall. It was chilly and damp on June evenings, despite the sun's strength throughout the day.

To his right he saw the house through the trees and remembered how exciting it was to be small and hide so no one knew where you were. He did it himself as a child. He felt this would be about as far as she would go. She'd feel safe seeing her home, so he kept rooting around and pushing aside dead leaves and branches, inching towards something. What, he didn't know.

Until he saw it.

The old rotten and cracked wood, decaying into the soil, forgotten many years before but now with a small opening. Ewan didn't want to look. He knew it would kill him.

Holding his breath he peered into the dark well. There she was, a lifeless little doll. He rammed his fist in his mouth so he wouldn't cry out. He knew he needed to act fast. The well was shallow, but she might still be out of his reach. Taking his pocketknife, he shoved his work boot under a root on the ground, then slowly lowered his body as far as he could go before reaching out and snagging her dress with his knife. It gave him the moment he needed to grab her leg and hold on tight. Then it was a herculean struggle to pull himself and Cricket out of that hole, but he was determined Lila would never see her daughter like that.

Ewan was gasping for air when he finally emerged. He held Cricket in his arms and wiped the wet hair off her face. He held her close and whispered that Daddy was with her and she was safe now.

And then he got up and took the longest walk of his life.

❋ ❋ ❋

Lila saw Ewan walk out of the woods with Cricket in his arms. Those around her were overjoyed, but Lila fell to her knees. Ewan came towards her with such a look of sadness, that even in that moment she felt terrible for him. It started to sink in with the others that something was wrong. Henry grabbed the blanket now on the ground and took Caroline out of Ewan's arms and laid her on it. He listened for a pulse, and started mouth-to-mouth while everyone howled in the background, everyone but Ewan and Lila. They stared into each other's eyes as Henry did his best to save her, but they knew.

David and Annie were crying in each other's arms. Aunt Eunie and Uncle Joe were in complete shock. Abigail couldn't look. She hid her face in Kenzie's shirt. Kay stood to the side, her hands over her mouth in disbelief.

Others gathered and cries of despair rang out. Henry pushed down on Caroline's chest. He was like a man possessed. It was finally Lila who stopped him.

"Leave her be." She pushed Henry aside and picked up her child, once again holding that precious body next to her heart. She cuddled her with Annie's baby blanket and gave her the toy Freddy. "You're all right. Mommy's here. You're fine. Shh. Shh, sweet girl."

She rocked her back and forth, Henry crying, "I'm sorry. I'm so sorry."

David knelt beside her. "Come in the house, Lila. You can't stay out here with her."

"Go away."

"Please, let me help you..."

Lila needed to get away from these hysterical people. They were scaring her baby. She grabbed the large blanket and wrapped Caroline in it. Instinctively, Ewan reached over and helped her up. She started to walk into the woods with Ewan behind her.

Aunt Eunie's voice went right through her brain. "Stop it, Lila! Where are you taking her? Lila! She's not a dog. She needs to be buried in a churchyard!"

Lila whipped her head around. "You think there's a God?"

David came towards her. "Lila, let Henry take care of things..."

"...so he can pronounce her dead and have an ambulance come and take her away? So a stranger can put her in a box and bury her miles from home? I'm her mother. I brought her into the world and I will see her out." She turned around and kept walking. David started after her, but Ewan stepped in his way and shoved him to the ground, pointing right at him.

"Do that again and I'll kill you." Lila heard Ewan's footsteps behind her on the journey to the ballerina tree. Once he asked if he could carry Cricket for her, but she refused. This was her burden.

When they got to the tree it was mid-afternoon. Lila sat on the moss and cradled her baby. "She belongs to the earth. I know where all the creatures of the earth belong."

"I'm going to get some beach rocks," he said. "I don't want anything to hurt her. I'll be back."

Lila pulled the blanket away from Caroline's face. She looked like she'd just come out of the tub. "When you grow up, we're going to do lots of fun things together. I'm going to teach you how to bake and you'll learn how to sew. You can help me make pretty dresses. And we'll be together at the beach every summer. We'll make sandcastles every day if you want."

Lila was confused. "Wait. We made a castle. It couldn't have been today, because today you're dead. We must have made it weeks ago. But I'm sure that this morning, you were with me. We talked about Freddy. Wasn't that you? Why can't you talk now? I think you should wake up. You scared Mommy, but now I think you should stop. Okay?"

The realization that Caroline would never talk again hit Lila like a lightning bolt splitting her skull open. She had a dead child. This child was dead. This morning Cricket was laughing and now she was cold. Lila's heart exploded into a million pieces, without making a sound.

She didn't know how long Ewan had been back. He had several piles of flat beach rocks ready, but he didn't move or disturb her.

Lila looked at him. "She's dead, isn't she?"

"She's in the next room with Freddy."

"Oh, that's good. That's right, she's with Freddy."

"The sun is going down."

"Okay."

Ewan took the large blanket and fixed it like a sleeping bag in the hollow under the roots of the ballerina tree. Lila swaddled Caroline in her baby blanket and kissed her face. Ewan took her and placed her in between the thick blanket. Lila put toy Freddy next to her and tucked her in like she did every night.

"Goodnight, sweetheart. Mama loves you."

As Ewan slowly layered the rocks that would form a barrier to entomb her child, Lila put her head in her hands and rocked back and forth. Ewan took his time, making the rocks a work of art. Then he set about covering it up with moss and dirt, branches and leaves, so that no one would be able to see anything. The space disappeared before their very eyes.

They sat together and watched the sun set over the water, spreading its pink and purple light onto the ballerina tree itself.

"How am I supposed to live? What do I do? It would be so much easier to be dead. Kill me, Ewan. Please kill me and bury me here."

"I can't do that."

She leaned on him heavily the whole way home.

❋ ❋ ❋

When Ewan pushed David to the ground, everyone was still in shock about what had happened, and having Lila disappear with Cricket in her arms was the final straw. Henry was concerned about Annie, but she refused to sit down. She paced outside, cursing God and everything she had ever believed in. Henry attended Aunt Eunie and Uncle Joe, who were in shock, as well as Annie's parents. Kay tried to console David, but he was having none of it. At one point David bent over and Annie knew he was in distress with his stomach. Kay went up to him and rubbed his back. He straightened up and shrugged her off.

"Will you stay away from me? I can't deal with your sympathy right now. You're smothering me. Go in the house, for God's sake."

Kay glanced at Annie before she left his side. He walked over to his sister and threw his hands in the air. "What are we supposed to do? Just stand here until they feel like coming back? Where are they?"

"You know where she is, and you're never telling anyone. Do you understand me? No one. Lila is suffering enough. Oh God, how am I supposed to have these children when she's lost Caroline? I'm having two."

"Who does that guy think he is, threatening people like that? Who's he to Lila?"

"He's Caroline's father."

David looked at her with incredulity. "What?"

"I can't say for sure, but I always had a hunch it was Ewan. Oh God, I feel so badly for them."

"That backwards numbskull? I don't believe it. Never. And don't you dare feel sorry for him. You should feel sorry for me! I've gone out of my mind all these years and for what? All this didn't have to happen."

Annie needed to sit down, but there was nowhere handy. "Why are you yelling at me? Why should I be sorry for you?"

"Because *I'm* Caroline's father! I'm her father and I lost my little girl today, so who's that guy to tell me I can't see my own child."

Annie felt her stomach contract with a sharp pain. She stared at David. "Yours?"

"Yes! And Lila never let me tell anyone. Why was I the one left out? I loved her and that baby and now the dream is gone."

Annie hauled back and punched David right in the face. He stumbled backwards and almost fell.

"You bastard. Stay away from me and stay away from Lila. Go back to the city and pretend to love your wife. That way we can forget all about you."

Annie rushed back to the house and saw Kay standing inside the screen door. "Get your husband out of here."

"Why? What's the matter?"

Annie saw Ewan walk out of the shadows, now carrying Lila. She hurried over to them. "Come inside. You both need to rest."

David stumbled away in the dark. Kay ran down the porch steps and after him, calling his name.

Ewan carried Lila into the house. Everyone started wailing again. Aunt Eunie jumped off the kitchen chair. "You left her in the woods? Oh my god, Lila, how could you? I'm going to be sick." Uncle Joe hurried after her into the bathroom, where the sound of vomiting went on and on.

"Take her upstairs," Henry told Ewan.

"Can I help?" Mom fretted in the background.

"Take care of Eunie," Henry said.

Ewan carried Lila up the narrow staircase with Henry and Annie on his heels and gently placed Lila on the bed. Then he turned around and ran down the steps as fast as he could. Annie heard his truck start up and saw the headlights back down the driveway. Annie knew he was going home to an empty house, with no one to share his pain.

Henry took Lila's wrist and felt her pulse. "I have something that will help you, Lila." He'd run back to his car at one point and retrieved his medical bag.

"Please kill me, Henry. Please. I beg you."

Annie wept as she held her hand. "Don't say that."

"I want to die. I need to be with her."

Henry gave her a shot. Lila kept whimpering, but soon her eyes were heavy and her head drooped to the side.

"She'll rest now," Henry said.

Annie perched on the side of the bed. "I have to stay with her. I need to be here when she wakes up."

"Okay, lie down." Henry put a quilt over Annie and Lila. "I'll be downstairs with Eunie and Joe."

"Don't let David in here."

"Why?"

"He says he's Caroline's father. I could kill him with my bare hands."

"Never mind all that. He doesn't know what he's talking about. Shock can do that to people."

Annie wasn't going to argue with him. She turned towards Lila and stroked her hair. Henry went downstairs, where Annie heard Eunie still crying out and asking for Caroline. For one brief moment, Annie looked at her pillow. She could use it to smother Lila and put her out of her misery.

She chickened out.

Lila slept through the night. Annie drifted off from time to time, but when she closed her eyes, all she saw was Ewan walking out of the woods with Cricket in her wet clothes. She rubbed her belly, wishing that her babies stayed like this forever. The world was too dangerous for little ones. What on earth would Lila do? How would she go on?

Annie was awake when Lila began to stir at sunrise. When she opened her eyes, she looked at Annie. "What are you doing here?"

Before she could answer, Lila's face changed and she moaned in pain, with a deep sorrow that was unbearable to hear. "My baby, my baby girl."

They were the last words Lila spoke for two years.

CHAPTER FOURTEEN

1952

LILA SPENT MOST OF HER days sitting under the ballerina tree. Uncle Joe gave up trying to persuade her to do anything else; she refused to listen. He retired from his job at the fish plant to take care of his wife, since some days Aunt Eunie would have nothing to do with Lila. With her dementia getting worse, and their collective grief over Caroline, their home held a sadness evident even to strangers.

All Lila knew was that she couldn't breathe in the house and she didn't want to see anyone either. Not even Annie, who now had twin boys and another baby on the way. David and Kay had a daughter themselves. It seemed everyone had children, and they were smart enough to make sure their children were safe, so they were allowed to keep them.

On those quiet days alone in the woods, Lila would wait for a cricket to chirp, a sign that Caroline was all right. The feeling of relief when she did hear one was immediate. It meant her daughter still loved her.

Over the many months, she eventually wore a path to the tree, which made it easier to get there at night. When the moon was full, she'd walk through the woods at midnight and sit with Caroline, overlooking the bay, where the moonlight shone down on the moving water. On darker nights she'd take a light, turning it off when she arrived.

Caroline wasn't tucked in her bed in the circle of Lila's arms, but she was tucked up under the ballerina tree, in the circle of the earth, under a canopy of stars.

This unorthodox burial caused heartache for others, and Lila knew it was selfish, but she didn't regret it. It kept her sane.

When she got back to the house one afternoon, she was surprised to see a car in the yard. No one ever came over except Ewan, who helped Uncle Joe with the occasional chore or brought fresh eggs for breakfast. At first she thought it might be Annie and she panicked, in case she had the boys with her, but she soon recognized it was Abigail, no doubt out to check on Aunt Eunie. She was the only friend who still visited, which made things very difficult and lonely for Uncle Joe.

Lila thought about heading back to the woods, but she was tired and needed to lie down. When she went into the house, the three of them were sitting at the kitchen table having tea and the scones Lila had made that morning for Uncle Joe.

For a moment she was a little girl again, coming into Abigail's kitchen where everything was warm and fragrant and clean. Abigail still got the same big smile on her face when she saw Lila.

"Lila, dear. It's lovely to see you." Abigail got up and gave Lila a hug. Lila nodded and smiled back.

The minute Aunt Eunie turned her head and laid eyes on Lila, she winced. "Get that girl out of here. She stole my baby. I hate you! Go away!"

It was one of Eunie's bad days. Uncle Joe reached over and patted Aunt Eunie's arm. "It's all right, that's Lila, our daughter. You love her."

"No. No I don't."

Lila left the kitchen and went upstairs to sit on her bed. When Aunt Eunie was like that, the only thing to do was disappear. She and Uncle Joe learned that the hard way. It was difficult not to take it personally, but Aunt Eunie had good spells too. The trouble was they came less frequently now. But Lila knew deep down she *had* stolen Caroline away from the woman who single-handedly raised her for the first six months of her life.

Lila didn't blame Aunt Eunie for hating her.

The commotion downstairs continued. The routine was for Uncle Joe to take Aunt Eunie into their bedroom and lie beside her so she'd calm down. If they were lucky she'd stay put for a little while. As the yelling and upset continued, Lila was thankful that Abigail was downstairs to help.

Eventually there was silence, and then a knock on the door, with Abigail peeking through the railing as she climbed the stairs. "I hope you're up for a little company."

Lila gestured towards the end of the bed for her to sit and then hugged a pillow and leaned against the headboard. Abigail settled herself on the soft mattress and bounced a little. "Remember the first time you saw this bed?"

Lila nodded.

"I've come to see how you are. I don't expect you to talk to me, so you can relax."

They smiled at each other.

"Annie got in a fight the other day. I told her it wasn't very ladylike and she said since she has never been and will never be a lady, it didn't matter. It was about you."

Lila went still.

"We were in the grocery store and Joy and I were there to help with our grandsons—not that Joy lets me do anything. She's the nicest woman, but put John or Daniel in front of her and she becomes possessed. Anyway, an old classmate asked Annie if her crazy friend was talking yet and Annie said yes, as a matter of fact she was, and did the classmate want to know what you said? The classmate nodded and then Annie yelled, 'It's none of your goddamn business, you stupid bitch.' The hair pulling started and we were eventually thrown out of the store. You would've laughed."

Annie always had her back. Even though Lila didn't want to meet the twins, her best friend understood and made it okay.

Abigail cleared her throat and took a deep breath. "I want to tell you something, and I don't want to be interrupted."

It was easy to see where Annie got her attitude.

"Lila, you've done nothing wrong. I know you will blame yourself for the rest of your life, because that's how mothers feel when their children die. No matter how they die. We lost a child when he was three. David was a baby at the time. My grandmother had scarlet fever and Coll walked into her bedroom when my back was turned for a minute. He became sick and despite our best efforts, passed away. David almost did too. I felt responsible. It was my fault.

"The only reason I didn't kill myself was because I had to save David. I had another boy who needed me.

"I remember once a teacher told us that the ancient Hawaiians would go up into the cliffs when a loved one died, to smash their teeth out against the rocks, or gouge their eyes out with sticks, and I wondered how anyone could do such a thing. Now I know. They do it to let the pain out."

Abigail stopped then and looked out the window before turning back to face her. "Caroline was your only child. If you needed to lay her to rest in a place that's meaningful to you, you did the right thing. If you don't want to talk for the rest of your life, that's okay too. Everyone has the right to grieve in their own way and in their own time."

Abigail reached for her hand. "Lila, some people tan in the hot sun and some people burn. It's not a choice. It's who you are."

Lila put her hands over her face and began to rock, but she stayed silent. That was something she'd learned to do—cry without making a sound.

It was a relief when Annie's mother stayed quiet as well. Lila appreciated the company. It was lonely up there in the room, staring at Cricket's empty crib night after night. She took the sheets and kept them under her pillow so she could fall asleep, breathing in the lingering scent of her baby.

"There's something else. David confessed to me his role in this story."

Lila looked up, afraid of what would come next.

"Kenzie doesn't know about it, and I won't tell him. He never knew that David loved you like that, but I did. That's why I didn't raise you myself. I didn't think it was fair to either of you to have to live under the same roof. I wasn't sure how it was going to end, but now that David is married to Kay, I assume the infatuation has run its course."

When Lila didn't indicate one way or the other, Abigail pressed her. "It is over?"

"Yes."

Lila was as surprised as Abigail when the word came out of her mouth. It took them both a moment to recover. Lila coughed and cleared her throat. It felt odd and overwhelming to hear her voice again.

"I'd like to ask you something else, then. Was David Caroline's father?"'

"I don't know."

"Do you love Ewan?"

"How did..."

Abigail patted her knee. "I have eyes. That boy lives for you and you alone."

Lila had to get up and move around the room, opening and closing her mouth, almost afraid to keep speaking. She was in control when she was silent. Letting things out could be dangerous, but Abigail waited patiently.

"I love Ewan as a friend. He and Annie are my best friends. But I've never been in love with him."

"What's your definition of 'in love'?"

"I don't know."

"Every girl remembers her first love. David is ambitious and driven. His career is important to him. That's not you, though. Love comes in many ways, Lila, not all of them earth-shattering. Love can be quiet, too. I married a quiet man and Annie married her best friend. Don't dismiss a man just because he's never going to set the world on fire."

Lila struggled to say something, but she couldn't. Abigail understood. She rose from the bed and gave her a hug. "If you ever need to talk about Caroline, you know where to find me."

When Abigail left, Lila collapsed on her bed. Her head pounded, as if her long-lost voice was shouting at her. She didn't dare try to speak again. She was drained, her arms and legs melting into the mattress. What she wouldn't give to go to sleep forever.

❖ ❖ ❖

The only word for Annie and Henry's house was lived-in. Gone were the days of trying to keep up with her mother's standards. Two-year-old twins didn't care about cleanliness, so Annie didn't either. To her credit, her mom never pointed it out, although Annie knew she was probably itching to say something. Instead she'd come over and regale her with stories of when Annie was a baby.

"I remember the time a very proper lady from the church came by and you crawled up beside her on the couch and let out a huge burp right in her face. She laughed, but that only encouraged you, so you continued to burp on purpose. I was mortified."

"You make it sound like I was a brat!"

"You were."

The other major change was the addition they built on the house with a separate entrance so Henry could open his own medical practice and be around to help out in between appointments. That was the plan, anyway, but everyone in town wanted to be his patient, so he was quickly swamped. Annie hoped to one day help out as his nurse, but that was a long way off.

In a flash of genius, Henry asked his mother if she'd like to be his receptionist, to keep her stuck behind a desk and a phone all day and not glued to Annie. Joy was always thrilled to see the patients and practically made them feel like guests. They always mentioned to Henry what a lovely woman she was as he listened with his stethoscope or took their blood pressure. That was at their first appointments. Once they got to know Joy, the compliments seemed to drop off.

It was a warm April Fool's Day, an anomaly in Cape Breton. The kind of day that made Annie look around and think she really did need to spring clean the house—but that urge quickly left. The problem with Henry was that he didn't care if she cleaned the house or not. It was a nice problem to have.

They never needed an alarm clock. One or both boys would wake up before six and shout until someone came to get them. It was Annie's favourite time of day; when she walked in the room first thing in the morning, it was like she'd been away for months. They were delighted to see her.

If there was anything cuter than one little boy with sticking-up red hair, it was two who looked exactly the same, both of them holding onto the railings of their cribs and jumping up and down, drooling.

For awhile Annie had a hard time telling them apart, but soon their own personalities made the difference quite clear. John was curious and always had his nose in something. Daniel was content to sit back and let John do everything first.

That morning, Annie gave the sleeping Henry a push from behind. "Henry! Wake up! My water broke!"

Henry leapt straight up in the air and started to put on his slacks. "I'll call Mom to look after the boys. Stay calm and everything will be fine."

Annie felt bad. "April Fool!"

He turned around, grabbed his pillow and swung it at her. "You brat!"

"Sorry! Sorry! Come back to bed and I'll kiss it better."

"Kiss what better?"

"Your choice."

Henry leapt straight up in the air and crash-landed on the bed beside her. "Well done, Mrs. Pratfall."

But the joke was on Annie. Not two hours later, just when she was up to her eyeballs changing stinky diapers and cooking porridge for the boys, her water did break. She wasn't due for three weeks, so she was a little alarmed, but not panicked—she was only having one baby this time. A piece of cake. She turned off the stove and grabbed two bare-bummed boys and waddled out to Henry's office.

The place was packed and she realized too late that all eyes were on her crummy nightie that should've been thrown out years ago. Joy saw her coming and hung up on whoever was on the phone. "What's wrong?"

"Henry! My water broke!"

His muffled voice came from one of his examining rooms. "I'm not falling for that one again."

"Fine." She put the squirming naked boys down and they ran all over the waiting room, with Joy galloping after them. The shocked looks from some of the older women ticked Annie off.

"Give me a break. Don't tell me you've never seen a pee-pee before." She turned to Joy. "You keep the boys and I'll call Mom. Tell Henry to get to the hospital as soon as he's finished up here."

As it turned out, Henry didn't make it, but by then Annie didn't care. Her body was in control of the situation, she was merely a passenger along for the ride.

When they told her she had another boy, she smiled. The nurse put him in her arms and the first thing she saw was his red hair, just like his brothers.

"Hello, George. What was the hurry?"

❀ ❀ ❀

David's one-year-old daughter, Anne-Frances Macdonald, was his pride and joy, although she was quickly nicknamed Frankie. "Anne-Frances" sounded wonderful when he and Kay had discussed it two hours after she was born, but it quickly became a pain.

"Anne" was after his sister and "Frances" was the name of Kay's beloved aunt, her dad's older sister who'd died five years before. When Frankie's grandmother Virginia heard the name, she rolled her eyes and had another drink. Louis gave out cigars to everyone in Halifax and set up a trust fund for her education, declaring to all who would listen that his granddaughter would be the next tycoon in the family. Frankie's uncle, Louis Jr., admitted defeat to the laughing parents.

David knew that calling his baby Anne was a sneaky trick, but he was desperate for his sister to forgive him. He finally pleaded to Henry to intervene on his behalf. Henry reminded Anne that it takes two people to make a baby and it was none of her business anyway.

When David and Kay made the first trip up to Cape Breton to show off Frankie, Annie was the first one to charge out the door. David held out his arms, but she shoved him aside. "I have to see Annie Junior first!"

They all fell under Frankie's spell. She was a dimpled and chubby angel with flaxen hair and bright blue eyes, wearing a pink silk pleated dress and tiny patent leather shoes with frilly socks. Abigail squealed in delight and Kenzie couldn't wipe off his smile. When John and Daniel tried to touch her with their grubby two-year-old hands and snotty noses, Abigail swooped in and whisked her away. "You come with Grammie."

"Nice one, Grandma. Apparently you boys have been knocked off her list of favourites." Annie turned to Henry, who was holding the newest Pratt in his arms. "Don't take it personally, George. You had your turn being flavour of the month."

It was one of the best moments of David's life, to be home introducing his beautiful daughter to the people he loved. He'd missed Annie terribly. No one made him laugh like she did. He hoped they'd never have another falling out.

The day they were leaving to go back home, Annie approached him. Their mom and Kay had Frankie on a blanket outside and Henry was chasing the boys. David was on the lawn swing and Annie joined him in the fresh air. As usual, she got straight to the point.

"She doesn't look like Caroline. You know that, right?"

David wasn't in the mood to talk about it.

"I see you watch her so intently that it almost frightens me."

David gave her an annoyed glance. "You've never lost your sense of drama."

"I'm telling you, Davy. Don't make Frankie live in Caroline's shadow."

"Okay, now drop it." David couldn't help himself. "How's Lila?"

"Silent."

"Has she seen the boys yet?"

Annie shook her head.

"I hope that someday she has another child."

"I know her. She never will."

David hung his head. "What a fucking nightmare."

Eventually it was time to say farewell. There were kisses and hugs and promises to send lots of pictures. Kay held Frankie in her lap and took her arm to wave back at the family as they headed out. David thought his mother was going to run after the car.

The baby was soon asleep in Kay's arms. Kay too had her head back against the leather upholstery. As they crossed the island, David drank in the highland air and turned his head often to glimpse at the breathtaking look-off views that never staled, no matter how many times he drove past. He'd never noticed them before, but Kay was always enthralled with the wildflowers that grew on the sides of the road. Daisies, buttercups, wild roses, and heather blew with the wind as they sped by.

Like most islanders, he'd taken that small gift of beauty for granted. The first time Kay saw an enormous open field of pink, lavender, and blue lupins, she clapped in excitement. David had laughed at her.

Past the causeway, Kay turned her head to look at him. "It's been over two hours. Why do you never talk to me in the car?"

"Sorry, I thought you were asleep. You have your sunglasses on."

"I don't mean just today. Every time we go somewhere it's like you put up a privacy screen and I feel like I'm intruding when I ask you something."

David gave her a quick look. "I do that?"

"Yes. I used to think it was intriguing, but now it's annoying."

David wasn't sure if he was supposed to respond.

"What were you and Annie talking about on the swing?"

"I don't know. The usual stuff."

Kay put her sunglasses on the top of her head. "It looked serious."

"It wasn't."

"I thought you might be talking about Lila."

"I asked how she is."

"And how is she?"

"How do you think?"

"You have a soft spot for her."

David made a face. "Of course I do. She's family."

Kay put her sunglasses back on and looked out the window.

❉ ❉ ❉

The rain came down in torrents. It splashed against the window by Lila's bed. She watched the maple tree shake its branches in protest. The sound of the rain on the roof used to soothe Lila when she was a girl, but now it only reminded her that Cricket was outside alone. Maybe she was cold.

It was a struggle every day to stop that line of thinking. Cricket was dead, so she wasn't feeling anything. Not hot or cold. But how did anyone know for sure? Where was the proof?

Lila wanted to reach out and choke people who said Caroline was in heaven. No, she wasn't. Caroline had been in heaven with her mother in this room. This was heaven—her crib, her toys, her tiny dresses, her cup and spoon, her mommy singing to her at night.

It amazed Lila how often people said stupid, stupid things to her. *Move on. You'll get married and have another one. Buck up. It happens to everyone, not just you. Don't dwell on sad things. Don't wallow. Don't cry in front of people. Don't bring her up in conversation and make people uncomfortable. Make an effort. Stop feeling sorry for yourself. Death is a part of life.*

Death is a part of life when that life has been lived. When you're eighty-five and looking back on all the wonderful things you did. Not when you're three and drowning in cold brackish water in a dark hole all alone.

At three, you miss everything.

Lila took out a worn piece of paper from her bedside table and unfolded it, a poem she happened to come across a few months after Cricket died.

Maternity
Alice Meynell (1847–1922)

One wept whose only child was dead,
Newborn, ten years ago.
'Weep not; he is in bliss,' they said.
She answered, 'Even so'.

'Ten years ago was born in pain
A child, not now forlorn.
But oh, ten years ago, in vain,
A mother, a mother was born.'

Lila wished Alice was still alive, so she could thank her for being a friend when she needed one.

Even over the rain, Lila could hear Aunt Eunie moving things downstairs. That meant that she was looking for something. It would go on for hours. She'd accuse Lila and Uncle Joe of stealing her money or her wallet, or important papers. They'd find dresser drawers ransacked, but they wouldn't intervene. Eventually she'd forget that she was looking for something and sit on the couch. Then she would look in her knitting bag and take out the balls of wool, slowly unravelling them until the wool was like a plate of spaghetti on her lap. When she got to the end, she'd roll it back up. Lila and Uncle Joe loved that game. It was sometimes the only peace they had all day.

Lila went downstairs in her bathrobe. Aunt Eunie was rummaging through the china cabinet, picking up her Dresden china figurines and making them dance. Lila smiled and patted her shoulder. Aunt Eunie turned around. "Lila. Are you in? I'm not." Then she went back to her dancing.

Lila headed out to the kitchen. Poor Uncle Joe was at the table, staring at the tablecloth, his cup of tea forgotten. He looked old and lost and sad.

"Good morning, Uncle Joe."

"Good morn…" His head went up. "Lila! Oh, Lila, I've missed you!"

He got up from the table. Lila walked right into his arms. "I'm sorry. I didn't mean to hurt you."

"Of course you didn't. I understand. I'm just so happy to have someone to talk to."

Lila cooked them a nice breakfast, scrambling Ewan's brown eggs and frying bacon. Thick slabs of white bread and butter were washed down with a cup of coffee and cream. Aunt Eunie was in good spirits, eating her eggs with her knife.

"Who are you?" she asked Lila.

"I'm Lila. I live here."

"Here?"

"That's right," said Uncle Joe. "We live together. We're a family."

Aunt Eunie smiled. "Isn't that nice?"

The other two laughed and agreed it was very nice.

Since the weather was foul, they stayed in for the day, Lila helping Uncle Joe clean up the house, which had been neglected during her exile upstairs and outdoors. When she saw Uncle Joe smiling as he filled a bucket with soapy water, she was annoyed with herself.

"I've been selfish…"

He held up his hand. "No talking about the past. We're together now and that makes me the happiest man alive."

It was therapeutic to clean away the dust that had gathered for months. Lila gave Aunt Eunie a cloth and told her to wipe everything. She started with her face, but soon got the hang of it. Her dusting was impressive; she spent ten minutes on every object.

Uncle Joe scrubbed the floors and windows. Lila pushed the rug sweeper around and sorted through the pantry. It was a mess. Why hadn't she noticed that before? She gave the kitchen a good going over, cleaning the cupboards and sink. They were at it all day. It was like a renewed energy existed for those few hours and neither one of them wanted to break the spell. By dinnertime they were limp rags, but thoroughly satisfied.

Uncle Joe said he'd be happy with more scrambled eggs for dinner. Lila was grateful, because her under-exercised body was definitely sore. She needed a hot bath. Uncle Joe went to get some of the dishes that were still on the dining-room table waiting to be put back in the clean cupboards. Lila went into the back porch to collect the eggs from the fridge.

And out of nowhere, Aunt Eunie lunged at her with a knife. Pure instinct made Lila grab her arm, but Aunt Eunie wrestled her to the ground and crawled on top of her. "Where's my baby?"

Lila was vaguely aware of Uncle Joe yelling in the background, trying to separate them. Lila couldn't hold her arm off forever—Aunt Eunie was incredibly strong as she slashed at Lila's face. The blade cut through Lila's smock and sliced her shoulder. Blood oozed from the wound. Uncle Joe, in a panic, pushed Aunt Eunie against the back door. The weight of her was too much for the latch and she tumbled backwards down the back steps and onto the wet ground.

Uncle Joe looked horrified. "Eunie!"

Eunie moaned in pain.

"I'm okay," Lila told him. "Go see if she's all right."

He rushed to his wife's side. "I'm sorry. I didn't mean to hurt you."

She lay at an awkward angle, her face pale and her breath quick and shallow. "Get some blankets and cover her," Lila said. "I'll call for an ambulance."

It seemed like forever before the ambulance got there. Eunie couldn't answer their questions.

"My wife…" Uncle Joe stammered, "My wife…"

Lila jumped in, "My aunt has memory loss. It's difficult for her to understand you."

One of the medics felt her hip, causing Aunt Eunie to cry out. "She's no doubt broken something, but we have to get her off the ground. Just to warn you, it's going to hurt."

Uncle Joe looked like he was going to pass out. He kept wiping his forehead with his handkerchief. "It's my fault. I'm to blame."

Aunt Eunie screamed in pain when they laid her on the stretcher. As soon as they put her in the ambulance, Lila said, "Uncle Joe, you go with her. I'll come behind you with the car."

He nodded and scrambled up into the back door. One medic stayed with Aunt Eunie, and the driver shut them in. He looked at Lila again.

"You're bleeding."

"It's nothing."

"Let me see." He pulled her smock away from her shoulder and grimaced. "I'd say you need a few stitches."

"I'll take care of it."

"I don't advise you driving."

"I have a friend who will take me in."

He backed down the driveway slowly, no doubt to keep Aunt Eunie as still as possible. Lila hoped they could give her some pain medication.

Lila held it together while she went back in the house and picked up the knife, washing it under the hot water tap. She called Ewan.

"Hello?"

"Hi."

"Lila?"

"Yes."

"Lila! It's so good to hear your voice. I'm so glad you called."

"I'm happy to speak to you too."

"Are you all right?"

"Yes, I'm all right, but once again I have to ask you a favour. It's ridiculous how often I depend on you and I never get to pay you back…"

"That's what friends are for."

"Aunt Eunie fell and Uncle Joe went with her in the ambulance. I wondered, if you're not busy, could you take me into the hospital?"

"Of course. I'll be right there."

She collected some toiletries for Aunt Eunie, along with a few nighties and a bathrobe. She fed dear old Boots, who at the age of fourteen looked confused and concerned at the commotion. Then she went upstairs to get a sweater and her purse. Ewan was in the doorway when she got downstairs.

"Thank you for coming…"

"…you're bleeding."

"It's fine."

"No. Sit down. Do you have a first aid kit?"

"There's some stuff under the bathroom sink, but I'll get a doctor to look at it."

"Stay there."

He came back with a box of items. He gave her an aspirin, then took her sleeve and cut the bloody cloth away. He cleaned it and placed gauze over the wound to protect it.

"Have you been taking lessons from Henry?"

"I look after my animals, remember."

He helped her into her sweater, took her things, and escorted her out to his truck. It was a relief to sit back and stay still after her incredibly tiring day. She closed her eyes and the truck's motion almost rocked her to sleep.

"How did you get the cut?"

"I tripped when I went to help Aunt Eunie."

"What happened?"

"She fell out the door and down the porch steps. It was awful."

"I know I shouldn't be happy at the moment, but it's great to hear your voice again. Why did you decide to talk?"

"Annie's mom made me feel better. She lost a three-year-old too, so she understands. That's important to me."

At the hospital it was a long and tiring wait. While they assessed Aunt Eunie, Lila received five stitches. The doctor asked how it had happened. Lila said she fell.

"Your skin looks like it's been sliced open." He was an older doctor who looked like he'd seen it all. "Did your aunt do this to you?"

She couldn't believe he guessed.

"Your aunt has obvious signs of senility. Violent outbursts are not unusual for someone in that condition."

"My uncle and I can look after her. I don't want anyone putting her somewhere. She'd die if that happened."

"I'm afraid she'll be in the hospital for awhile. Her hip is broken and may need to be replaced."

"Poor Aunt Eunie."

The doctor looked at her kindly, but his tone was firm. "At some point this situation will become unbearable. You and your uncle have to look after yourselves too."

Lila went back out into the waiting room and sat down beside Ewan. "Aunt Eunie's hip is broken. She'll be in the hospital for awhile."

"I'm sorry to hear that." He paused. "But if you don't mind my saying so, I think you and Joe need some rest from all this. You both look like you've been dragged through a knothole."

"Does Uncle Joe look bad to you?"

"He looks a lot older."

"That's my fault. He's put up with so much from me. I've only been thinking of myself. I didn't even consider what my silence was doing to him. All these terrible things happen to the people I love. And it's my fault."

"It's not your fault. It's called life."

She rested her head against his arm.

Eventually Uncle Joe came out, and Ewan was right. He looked like death. Lila jumped up. "Let's get you home."

She led her uncle out of the hospital as Ewan went to get the truck. They put him in and he didn't say a word all the way home. Lila knew he was exhausted. When they pulled into the yard, Ewan got out and went to the passenger door and helped Lila get Uncle Joe in the house.

"I'll fix you some tea," she said.

"No. I want to lie down."

"Okay. Shout if you need anything."

Uncle Joe nodded and shuffled out of the kitchen, but before he disappeared altogether he stopped and turned his head toward Ewan. "I don't know what we'd do without you, big guy."

"Anything for you, Joe."

When Joe left the room, Lila asked Ewan if he wanted a cup of tea. He shook his head. "You need to get to bed too. I'll bank the fire before I go."

She reached out to give him a hug, but a stab of pain from her shoulder stopped her.

He pointed at the door. "Go."

Up the stairs she went. She didn't hear him leave.

Now Uncle Joe's job was driving into Glace Bay and sitting with his wife all day. Sometimes Lila joined him, but not often, because it upset Aunt Eunie too much. So Lila would make sure that she had a delicious supper for him when he came home at night, like stuffed halibut or breaded smelts.

She spent the entire month of May cleaning the house from top to bottom. It was now as pristine as it had been dirty. It kept her hands busy, if nothing else. Lila also called Annie a lot. The first time Annie heard her voice over the phone after such a long absence, she sobbed, which is not something Annie did often. She also rambled that she was sorry she had kids and would Lila like to share the boys with her. Lila told her that wasn't necessary. Sometimes in the middle of a conversation there would be a crash and one of the twins would start crying. "Did you hit your brother? Just a minute, Lila." Lila would wait and wait, but Annie would forget to come back.

The realization that Aunt Eunie wouldn't be coming home was slow and difficult. The anesthetic from the operation to replace her hip had made her fragile state of mind even worse. Everyone said what a tragedy it was. Aunt Eunie was only sixty-five. Lila heard Uncle Joe crying at night sometimes. The walls of their house were seeped in sorrow.

One of the worst days of the year for Lila was Mother's Day. When the first Mother's Day after Cricket died rolled around, Lila stayed under the covers of her bed the entire day. When the second one came, she realized how mean she had been not to visit Cricket the year before, so she spent the entire day on the moss beside the tree. She fell asleep and when she woke up there were three deer standing not far away, eating the grass. She watched them until they wandered off.

On this Mother's Day, she stepped outside to go to the ballerina tree and found a bouquet of mayflowers on the bottom step.

Ewan.

She smiled as she walked to the tree, holding the flowers, their delicate scent lingering in the air. These would be perfect for Caroline, but there was a bouquet of mayflowers under the tree already. Lila stared at it for a long time.

She patted a kiss into the ground, as always. Whispered words to tell Cricket she loved her and was grateful to be her mother, even if their time together on earth had been too short.

Then she turned around and walked with her flowers back to the house. Ewan was squatting in the yard, sharpening Uncle Joe's lawn mower. "The grass needs mowing, shouldn't take me long."

"You don't have to do that."

He watched her walking towards him. "You look like a bride."

She smiled. "Do I look like your bride, Ewan?"

He dropped the file and slowly rose to his feet. "Yes. Yes, you do."

CHAPTER FIFTEEN

THE FIRST PERSON LILA WANTED to tell after Uncle Joe was Annie. That meant she had to go to Annie's house, which now had three little boys in it—boys that Lila still hadn't met. Lila practiced in the mirror what she would say and how she would act, but really she had no idea what she was going to feel when she saw Annie's children.

Uncle Joe took her to town to drop her off on his way to see Aunt Eunie. Ewan said he'd have supper for them when they got home. Lila made a couple of loaves of bread and some cookies for Annie and put the baked goods in a basket, along with a few jars of last year's strawberry jam. She imagined baking with three small boys would be impossible.

When Uncle Joe left her at the curb and drove away, Lila wanted to run. She worried that she should have called first. Taking a deep breath, she approached the front door and rang the bell.

"It's open!" Annie hollered from inside.

Lila unlatched the door and walked into the front porch. You couldn't see the floor for the shoes and toys. "It's only me."

Annie appeared at the doorway into the kitchen, wearing a full-length apron over her dress, a kerchief on her head, and bare feet, holding the baby against her shoulder and trying to shake off the twins, who had their arms around her shins. The look on her face was priceless.

"Holy shit! It's so good to see you!"

"You, too."

"Get in here! I can't move."

Lila approached Annie gingerly. She breathed in to stay calm and kissed her dear friend, before putting the basket of goodies on the untidy kitchen table. The twins stopped hanging off their mother's legs when the smell of the cookies permeated the air. They stood in front of Lila as if waiting for her to offer them some. Annie never said a word as Lila gazed at their dirty faces.

But she didn't see Caroline when she looked at them. They were just little boys, alien creatures not even remotely like her daughter. The relief was exhilarating. She grinned at them and they grinned back. "Would you like a cookie?"

"Just give them the bag. That'll keep them out of our hair for a while."

"Are you sure? It might ruin their dinner."

"What dinner? I haven't even had time to make lunch."

So Lila gave them the bag of cookies and they raced down the hall to eat them under the telephone table. She turned to Annie. "I'll make you some tea, shall I?"

Annie fell into the nearest chair with baby George. "I could kiss your feet."

Lila got up and rooted around for mugs and the kettle and tea bags. Annie watched her every move. "My god, it's good to see you."

"I'll make us a sandwich, too."

"I only have peanut butter, but make sure you put it on this heavenly bread."

After putting the cups of tea and sandwiches on the table, Lila sat down. "I've missed you. I'm sorry I've…"

"…don't even say it."

Lila took a sip of tea. "It's good to be somewhere else. I think my refuge became my prison for a while."

"Strange. That's how I feel about this place."

They laughed together. It felt like old times.

Lila looked at baby George. "Your children are sweet."

"Sweet is the last word I'd use, but I love them."

"It must be hard with three little ones."

Annie looked down. "Whenever I get to the point of screaming, I think of you. That cheers me up in a hurry. I'm so sorry, Lila. I miss her. I miss her so much."

"I know you do. You were one of her favourite people."

"And not many people say that."

Lila took a deep breath. "Ewan and I are getting married."

Annie's head popped up. "Get out! He finally wore you down."

"It was my idea."

"Don't kid yourself," Annie laughed. "That boy's been asking you to love him for more than fifteen years."

"Your mother said the same thing."

"Well, as far as I'm concerned, you couldn't have picked a better husband."

"Why did you marry Henry, then?" Lila joked.

"He couldn't keep his hands to himself. I got tired of fighting him off."

George decided he'd had enough girl talk and let his mother know that he was tired and cranky. Annie excused herself to go upstairs and change him before she put him down for a nap. While she was gone, Lila began to clean up the kitchen. She'd totally forgotten about the twins until she turned around from the sink and saw them holding out the empty bag filled with crumbs. She took it from them.

"Thank you."

They burped in unison.

Lila and Annie eventually drifted out to the living room and chatted while the boys played with their blocks on the rug. Then they too nodded off where they lay. Annie grabbed two towels from a nearby laundry basket and covered them up. "Don't be scandalized. If I tried to put them in their cribs, they'd wake up and have a fit. This is easier, but I don't do it in front of the grandmothers, so you're sworn to secrecy."

"I'm good with secrets."

Annie settled back on the sofa. "Yes, you are."

Just the way she said it, Lila knew what she was referring to. "I thought you'd hate me if I told you about David."

"Why?"

Lila shrugged. "It's complicated. I didn't want to disappoint your family. Anyway, it's over and done with. He's married to someone else and has a daughter. He's not thinking about me anymore."

Annie looked down and brushed some crumbs off the sofa. "David passed his bar exam. He's officially a lawyer now. Kay's father has hired him, naturally. He's got it made."

Lila nodded but didn't comment.

"So where is the wedding going to be?"

"We're getting married in the courthouse in a couple of weeks. Uncle Joe and Ewan's mother and brothers are our witnesses, but I wondered if you'd like to come."

"Of course! I'll get the dynamic grandma duo to come and hold down the fort. I'm really happy for you, Lila. You must be excited."

Lila shook her head. "I don't feel like I can be excited about anything. I always think I'm betraying Caroline. It's ridiculous, maybe, but I can't help it. Ewan is a good man and my best friend. I can't imagine my life without him. I want him to be happy, and right now he's very happy."

❋ ❋ ❋

Annie and Henry were in bed.

"She never said a thing about loving him, only that she was marrying her best friend like I did. I didn't want to point out that I also wanted you to tear off my clothes."

Henry removed his reading glasses and put them on the bedside table. "People marry for a lot of reasons."

"I want her to have the kind of happiness I have."

Henry turned off the light. "Stop trying to orchestrate Lila's life. You're becoming a meddlesome old woman."

Annie turned her back to him. "My happiness meter just went down a notch."

"Go to sleep, my love."

❋ ❋ ❋

Ewan whistled everywhere he went and his jaws ached from smiling. Even his animals knew there was a change. They looked happy for him.

"Or maybe living alone has made me crazy," he said out loud. Dawn was breaking as he sat and milked the cows. The rhythmic pull of his hands made a steady stream of milk fill the bucket at his feet. There was nothing like milking a cow to ease the mind and soothe the soul.

When the sun rose now, it was as if it rose just for him. The dew from the early morning left tiny droplets on spider webs in the tall grass, creating lace doilies all over the field. The mist was low to the ground and the fog bank lifted as the sun rose over the still water in the bay.

He'd just started on the second bucket when he happened to look up and see Lila walking down his laneway through the haze. She wasn't in any hurry, just chewing a piece of grass and looking at the birds chirping in the trees. Everything about her was lovely. Her golden hair was longer now and curled around her face and shoulders, the front held back with combs. Her worn gingham dress and out-of-shape sweater hung on her small frame, but Ewan knew he'd never forget how she looked at this very moment.

She saw him lift his hand and waved back. "Morning."

He continued to milk. "Why are you up so early?"

"I couldn't sleep."

"What's wrong?"

She leaned against a couple of bales of hay. "I don't want to tell you."

Ewan smiled at her. "You obviously do. You're here at the crack of dawn. I don't recall that ever happening before."

"It's something I've been thinking about and I'm not sure if you'll agree and that's okay because it matters to the both of us and we're going to be a team from now on…"

"Spit it out."

"I'd rather not move here. I know it's only down the road, but Uncle Joe will be alone, and I have to visit Cricket most days and Freddy is buried under the tree. There are so many pieces of me there that I would never be whole here. I know it sounds silly, but it's how I feel."

She was calling it off. He stood up, knocking the milk bucket over.

"What's wrong?"

When he didn't answer, she looked confused for a moment and then put her hand up to his face. "I still want to marry you."

The relief that rushed through his body made him dizzy. He reached out and took her in his arms. "Don't ever do that to me again."

"I'm sorry. I only wanted to discuss what we might do."

Ewan let out a deep breath. "Let me finish milking Bessie and I'll make us some coffee."

After talking over all the different scenarios, Ewan's suggestion made the most sense, but they had to get Uncle Joe on board first. Lila told him to come for supper and they'd discuss it then.

Her kiss goodbye kept him smiling for the rest of the day.

As the three of them sat down together in Lila's kitchen and ate flaky chicken pot pie, Ewan spelled it out for Uncle Joe.

"If I sell my farm—"

"—sell the farm? What does your family think of that?"

"They'd be happy. None of them want the responsibility of it and we'd split the money between us. I think my brothers would be relieved. They could use some cash to start their lives. Mom says she's never setting foot in the place again. She's having too much fun in town."

"Who would buy it?"

"I've had someone who's approached me a few times. It won't be hard to sell. But if I came here to live with you, I would want to bring my animals with me. I could build a barn and a chicken coop here, and still sell my eggs and milk. That is if you don't mind me taking some of the back trees down. It wouldn't be anywhere near the house. I could tuck it out of sight. And then I could plant a garden and sell my vegetables in town. Everything I do at home, I could do here, but I'd have a nest egg in my pocket to support Lila, and I know she doesn't want to leave you alone here."

Uncle Joe's eyes lit up. "I could help you build the barn! I was a good carpenter in my younger years. Yes, indeed. We'd get it up lickety-split."

"I take it you like the idea, Uncle Joe?"

"Like it?" He tried to continue, but he choked up for a moment. "I don't mind telling you both that I wasn't looking forward to living alone."

"So that's that," Ewan smiled.

The future looked bright.

It was only a few days later that Ewan went to see his friend about buying the property. They shook hands on a price and it was all done but the paperwork. As they walked down to his friend's barn to look at some seed he'd picked up, Ewan thought he was seeing things. In the dog pen was a black lab who'd had a litter of puppies a month before. Through the fence, they looked like a swarm of pure energy and happiness.

"Good lord," Ewan said. "How many are there?"

"Banner had eighteen pups. Can you believe it? I'm giving them away. Help yourself."

The perfect wedding gift for Lila, right in front of him.

A week later they were married in the courthouse with a judge and six witnesses.ABigail, who told Annie she'd have to find another babysitter; Annie herself; Uncle Joe; and Ewan's mother and two brothers. Ewan and Lila said goodbye to each other the night before their wedding. Lila told him it was bad luck to see the bride on her wedding day.

When she stepped out of the car that morning she had on a long double-breasted grey jacket and skirt, with a pretty white blouse underneath, a white beret-style hat that framed her face, and a white corsage on her lapel. She carried white gloves and even had red lipstick on. The sweetest bride Ewan could have imagined.

The ceremony was over before Ewan even registered they were there. He didn't remember a word he said, just how it felt to put the thin yellow and white gold band on her finger. When they were pronounced man and wife, everyone clapped for them.

They went out for lunch to a nice restaurant and were presented with a specially made cake that Ewan's mom had asked the restaurant to bake. It had their initials entwined on the top. Annie regaled everyone with Lila stories and made them laugh so hard people at the surrounding tables glared at them.

Then it was time to go. Annie was driving her mother and Uncle Joe back to Abigail's for the weekend so the happy couple could be alone for at least two nights. They elected not to have a honeymoon because the cows had to be milked. One of Ewan's brothers took off with his mother tearfully waving goodbye; Ewan opened the door of Uncle Joe's car for Lila and spotted his youngest brother come out of the restaurant and look around.

"Where'd everyone go?"

So that's how Ewan and Lila started their married life; with someone else in the back seat. But they dropped him off as quickly as possible and headed to their new home.

Ewan carried Lila over the threshold and put her down in the kitchen. "Okay, get those clothes off."

Lila stood there. "You're romantic. Can I pee first?"

"I'm almost that desperate," he chuckled, "but I have a surprise wedding gift and I don't want your nice suit to get ruined. I'll be back in fifteen minutes."

"You're a madman."

Ewan got in his truck and drove to his friend's farm. He picked up the gift and drove it back in a box that he had papered earlier—though the bow wouldn't stay on with all the nonsense going on inside the box. He quickly drove home, picked up the squirming carton and hollered from the door. "You have to come now or it will be ruined!"

Downstairs she came. "What's this?"

"For God's sake, open it quick."

She did as she was told and two black lab puppies jumped up and down with excitement to see her.

"Two Freddies!" she squealed, and cried and hugged him, and raced around to pick up both the puppies at the same time, and they were so excited, they dribbled pee down her shirt. As she hugged them close to her heart, Ewan was filled with gladness. He'd missed that smile. He thought it had disappeared for good, but here it was and he was the one who had put it there.

"Where did you get them?"

"Bill, the guy who's buying the farm. His dog had eighteen puppies and he wouldn't let me take just one. He's desperate to find homes for them."

Lila kissed them over and over again. "This one looks exactly like Freddy. Do you mind if I call him Fred?"

"They're your dogs."

"And this one looks like a Willy. Fred and Willy. Welcome home, you beautiful creatures!" She put them down and they scrambled on top of each other and jumped up on their legs, but Lila was too busy kissing Ewan to notice.

"Thank you."

"You're welcome."

Lila stepped back and looked Ewan steadily in the eye for a moment. "I love you."

There it was. The three words he'd waited most of his life to hear.

But the joy of that moment lessened somewhat after they stayed up all night trying to comfort two puppies missing their mother. He should've thought his idea through. Lila was completely distracted trying to comfort both dogs, and in the end, he fell asleep with Lila running in and out of the house, trying to get them to pee on the lawn or at least on newspaper on the floor.

That was their first night as a married couple.

The next night was shaping up to be more of the same, so for the first time in his life, Ewan put his foot down. He closed off the dogs in the kitchen, put on some music to drown out their whimpering, picked up his wife, and threw her on the bed.

"They'll be lonely," she fretted.

"I'm lonely!"

Lila giggled. "There's no need to shout."

That summer and fall were the happiest of Ewan's life. His brothers helped in dismantling the farmhouse, everyone taking something of use. There wasn't any room in Uncle Joe's house for Ewan to bring large furniture back, but the one item he did want was an old writing desk. He remembered opening it up when he was a boy and being fascinated with all the cubbyholes inside and the narrow drawer with a lock where his mother hid important papers.

Once that was done, he and Uncle Joe started to build the large barn that would house the cows and horses. Ewan hoped the cats would like the new barn and the chickens wouldn't be too upset by this change in their routine. He knew Lila was excited for the animals to come.

Lila spent her days training Fred and Willy, who were troublemakers of the first order. Poor old Boots spent most of her time upstairs on a bed to get away from the pesky critters, but every so often she'd cuff them in the face with her claws to remind them who was boss. Two puppies were ten times more work than one, but Lila thrived on it. The three of them were inseparable. The days she spent outdoors running with them brought colour to her cheeks, and Ewan was pleased to see that Lila put on a little weight. Even her dull, pain-filled eyes seemed to sparkle again.

She still had her moments, especially in the evening when all was quiet, but Ewan never interfered, resisting the urge to jolly her along. She was still processing Cricket's death, and it would take years for Lila to understand her new reality of life without her child.

They were both learning to live with Cricket's death, but neither of them would ever get over it. When he was alone, Ewan often cried for the little girl who used to run to him with her happy smile, shouting "Ooan." The hardest part was keeping the image of her in the well out of his head.

In October, the leaves turned scarlet, orange, yellow, and gold before falling into crispy piles on the ground, perfect for striding through, and then being swept along with the nippy wind that chilled the bone and heralded the coming of winter.

And then at last it was moving day.

Annie and Henry came out with the kids to see the procession of animals walk from the farm to their new digs. It was much easier to walk them up the road than drive them, though of course the cats and chickens would come later via the truck.

The little boys were thrilled to see the animals come up the driveway, Ewan in the lead with the horses, and Lila and Uncle Joe bringing up the rear with the cows. Fred and Willy were left in the house so as not to ruin the parade, and they weren't shy about letting everyone know they were upset.

The entire gang walked with the animals to the new barn, where everything was ready—their stalls, the hay, the bags of feed, bridles, and the plow. They took pictures of the kids on the horses' backs and patting the cows. Then Ewan let his animals loose to wander in their new paddock. This new grass seemed to be to their taste, as they nibbled on it right away. The only hiccup in the whole day was when Ewan and Uncle Joe arrived with the chickens in two pens and the cats in another. John opened the door when his mother wasn't looking and the dogs ran into the yard barking up a storm. The cats became furballs and the chickens had a fit, feathers flying everywhere.

Eventually the dogs were corralled and the chickens clucked their displeasure in the new coop. The cats smelled around the barn and then ventured out. Ewan put down some food so they'd be lured back when they had finished the inspection of their new home.

Lila had egg salad sandwiches for the crowd and a large chocolate cake. Naturally it was a zoo inside; the twins ran amok chasing the dogs, the baby cried endlessly, and Uncle Joe told his larger-than-life stories of barn building.

As Ewan watched from the vantage point of the kitchen door, he silently thanked God for his beautiful wife, his good friends, and his healthy animals. If he died tomorrow, he'd die happy.

❀ ❀ ❀

As the Pratts set off for home, Lila ran out to their car holding up a bag of molasses cookies for the boys. Annie rolled down the window and Lila passed them to her.

"My god," Annie said. "Do you remember Aunt Eunie running out to the car with molasses cookies for you?"

"Yes! I'd forgotten it."

"I also remember my nose being out of joint because she made them just for you."

"Well then, eat these and don't tell the kids."

Annie smiled. "Thank you for the lovely day. Ewan looks so happy."

Lila leaned down lower to look at Henry behind the steering wheel. "Thank you for coming. It means a lot to both of us."

Then John hit Daniel, which made Daniel yell, which made Annie yell, which startled George, which made him cry, and the conversation was over. The noisy family waved and left in a hurry.

Lila went back into the house to straighten up and wash the dishes. Uncle Joe and Ewan were getting the animals into their new stalls. Anything that wasn't nailed down, the twins had moved, so it took Lila a while to get things in order.

When she reached down to plug a light fixture back in, she noticed the edge of a bowl under the sofa. She pulled it out.

It was one of Cricket's little bowls that she liked to fill with grass, only now the grass was dead. Missing Caroline hit her like a punch in the face. Lila hugged it to her chest and cried so hard she couldn't breathe, so hard she frightened Fred and Willy, who hid their heads in the corner; so hard that when Ewan and Uncle Joe came running she didn't know they were there.

CHAPTER SIXTEEN

1954

NEARLY THREE YEARS AFTER FRANKIE was born, her little sister Colleen came into the world. Both David and Kay were expecting another beautiful baby doll. What a surprise they had when Colleen screamed from morning till night. She was as dark as her sister was blonde, and when her face screwed up, wailing for hours, it became bright red. Her grandmother Virginia said she looked like the devil.

David wanted to punch his mother-in-law's lights out. He and Kay had moved into a very nice house in the South End of Halifax. Kay's father insisted he buy it for them as a belated wedding gift. He didn't want his granddaughters living in an apartment. David didn't like to point out that they were too young to know where they lived, so he decided to shut up about it and take the gift.

He was becoming more and more accustomed to the high life, but he never let on to Kay's mother. He knew that she was waiting for him to screw up, and that she'd wait forever if she had to.

David worked for the Hanover empire as a lawyer in the office that dealt with the shipyards and granaries down by the docks. He knew he had to start somewhere and that he wasn't ready for a big corporate office just yet, but that was his future goal. He wanted to make his father proud.

It was hard to believe that David's dad, a pilot and mathematician in the First World War, a master machinist who ran the naval shipyards in the Second World War, only had a grade six education. His love of reading had taught him about the world and everything in it. David took after him. Kay was always complaining that he had his nose in a book and he told her that at least he wasn't at a bar downtown every night, like some his colleagues.

Life in the fifties was a complete turnaround from the forties.

There was hope, optimism, and money to be spent. More and more people had cars, and luxury items for the home. Not having a wringer washer was a huge deal, and more and more people had dryers and dishwashers, miracle machines for busy moms everywhere.

Naturally, Kay had only the best of everything. She loved to shop and she did it brilliantly, especially for Frankie. The child always looked like she was in an advertisement. It wasn't as easy with Colleen. She inevitably threw up on her clothes or twisted about in them until they were a wrinkled mess.

One evening, David came home to Kay crying in the kitchen while she bounced Colleen up and down in her arms.

"What's the matter?"

"Your daughter has cried all afternoon. I'm going out of my mind. I don't even like her anymore."

David couldn't help laughing. There was Frankie, as good as gold on the floor, moving pots and pans around while giving him a sweet grin. Colleen looked at him and screeched.

"Give her to me."

Kay was more than happy to pass her over. "There is something wrong with the child besides colic. The doctor pats me on the head and says she'll grow out of it. I feel like a failure!" She sat on one of the kitchen chairs and held a dishtowel to her face to mop up her tears.

David went over and patted her on the back. "You're a wonderful mother. There's no one better."

"I'm never having another one. Do you hear me? Never!"

David dismissed her. "Don't be ridiculous. She'll soon settle down."

But she didn't. By ten that night, Kay had escaped into Frankie's bedroom and refused to come out, and David was ready to rip his hair out. He dressed Colleen and took her for a walk in the cold night air, but that didn't help. He drove her in the car around the block a few times. Again, nothing changed.

At eleven, both he and his cranky daughter were exhausted. Colleen lay limp in his arms, still *sup-supping*, with her voice almost gone. She looked up at him at one point and he swore he saw pain in her eyes. He couldn't stand it anymore. He called Annie.

"I was sound asleep," she moaned. "If you're not dying, hang up."

"We can't get Colleen to stop crying. The doctor says it's colic, but I think there's something else going on."

"Here's Henry."

Henry's sleepy voice came on the phone. David poured out his tale of woe.

"It sounds to me like she could have lactose intolerance or a milk allergy."

"Isn't that the same thing?"

"Yes and no. It's too late to explain it now. Go to your doctor and demand she be tested."

"Thanks, Henry."

"Good luck."

David covered Colleen with a baby blanket and laid her on his chest. They fell asleep on the living room couch and snored together until morning. Then the weary parents left Frankie with her grandmother, something neither of them liked doing, and took Colleen to the doctor.

Once they were in his office, the doctor listened carefully to what David had to say.

"I told you these symptoms the last two times I was here, but now you're concerned because my husband is with me?"

The appointment went downhill from there.

Once the tests were done and it was discovered that Colleen did have a milk allergy, they felt dreadful that they hadn't done something sooner. With a new formula Colleen was a different baby in a matter of weeks, but as she grew it was evident she was still high-strung and much more sensitive than her sister. If anyone looked at her the wrong way, she hid her face in her mother's skirts, which meant her grandmother Virginia never saw her. David didn't blame Colleen for hiding from the wicked witch.

Virginia made a point of paying more attention to Frankie, constantly saying that she looked like Kay as a baby. She often wondered aloud where on earth Colleen had come from. "Perhaps she's a throwback from your side of the family, David. All those savage Scotsmen running around in kilts."

"I'm sure she'd rather be a proud Scot than belong to the German house of Hanover."

When Virginia stormed out the door, Kay was annoyed with him. "I swear you do that on purpose."

"Of course I do it on purpose. Who does she think she is? And why do you let her talk about Colleen that way?" David loosened his tie and sat at the kitchen table. Frankie held up her arms. "Up. Up." He picked her up and played horsey, as Colleen watched them with her big brown eyes from her high chair.

Kay was at the stove cooking potatoes. "I don't talk because it only encourages her. She knows how to get under your skin. The best thing you can do is ignore her."

"I won't let your mother say anything about my girls."

Kay poked at the potatoes with a fork. "Does that include me?"

"Have you forgotten that I proposed to you in front of her?"

"I sometimes wonder if you did that more for your sake than mine."

David sighed. "What have I done now?"

"Nothing."

Once it was time for bed, David went into the girls' rooms and watched them sleeping in their cribs. He still looked for traces of Caroline, but he never saw any resemblance. He reluctantly admitted to himself that Ewan must have been Cricket's father, which made him sad. He couldn't explain why. It was a wound he carried around, but no one else knew.

When he got into bed, Kay had her back to him. Her silk pyjamas shimmered in the light of his table lamp. He turned it off and scooted over to put his arm around her. "I love you."

"So you say."

It was going to be one of those nights.

"Kay, I have no idea what I'm doing to piss you off."

"You're not pissing me off. I'm tired."

"Too tired to make another baby?"

Kay turned around to face him. "That's all I am to you, isn't it? You want baby after baby and you don't care how I feel about it."

"You said you wanted a big family."

"I've changed my mind."

David sat up. "How can you change your mind without consulting me?"

Kay sat up too. "You do it all the time."

"I do?"

Kay groaned and flopped back on her pillow. "You always seem so surprised when I point out your behaviour. I can't figure out if you're very stupid or very clever."

David crawled on top of her. "I must be a very clever man—I married you, didn't I? I can't help it if I love you and want your babies. They're so darn cute."

Kay smirked. "Oh, here it comes. You'll charm me into submission."

David kissed her neck and nuzzled her ear. "Is it working?"

She put her arms around him. "You do love me, don't you?"

"What a ridiculous question."

❊ ❊ ❊

September of 1954 saw the Pratt twins start school. John and Daniel were happy to go to primary. They told George how much he was going to miss, but in typical two-year-old fashion, George didn't care. Annie did. Little did her sons know the horrors that lay in wait for them.

Annie couldn't sleep the night before their first day, and Henry couldn't either; she was up and down like a yo-yo.

"What are you so nervous about? They'll be fine."

"They're bigger than most five-year-olds. The teacher will be harder on them, you watch. And you know what they're like. John will push someone and Daniel will join in. It's going to be a disaster."

Henry rubbed his eyes. "Every kid in the history of the world has survived their year in primary. I'm sure ours will too."

"Spoken like a true man."

"Thank you."

"That wasn't a compliment."

"Did you have a bad experience in school or something? You're anticipating the worst before they've even darkened the door of the classroom."

"I hated school."

Henry fluffed his pillow and turned away from her. "Don't let the boys know that."

Annie sighed and laid down in the dark. "Do we have any bananas downstairs?"

"Uh-oh."

"Can't I have a banana for bananas' sake?"

"Nothing is that simple with you."

The boys were up at six and working themselves into a lather of excitement. Annie had given them both a bath the night before, but she scrubbed their faces, necks, and hands anyway. On went their new plaid shirts and sweater vests, ironed pants, and shiny shoes. Annie never dressed them alike. She preferred to see them as two separate entities and not as halves of a whole.

Henry gave them their breakfast as Annie got herself and George dressed for the procession to school. Both grandmothers were insisting on coming too. Joy would have her enormous camera and make everyone stand still for minutes on end while she fussed with it.

Joy and Mom walked in the back door just as Annie made it downstairs with George on her hip. Henry put the boys' school bags on their backs and handed them their Lone Ranger lunch boxes. Then Annie made the boys take off their school bags and put down their Lone Ranger lunch boxes to go upstairs and brush their teeth.

Finally they were on their way. Henry waved them goodbye before he went into his office. It was a lovely day, perfect for walking, or for running up and down the sidewalk. Annie had George in the large bouncy stroller. It could be converted back into a pram if she needed it. Maybe she did need it. Was there a banana sale anywhere? All these silly thoughts to chase away the fact that her first-born sons were now going to spend most of their days in a stuffy building with germy kids. Annie felt slightly sick.

There were plenty of other first-time moms hanging about the school yard, waving goodbye to their offspring. As Annie had predicted, Joy made the boys stand still so she could take a picture. Then she wanted a picture of herself with the boys. Annie grabbed the camera and took the stupid picture. Joy suggested Annie and her mother might like to be in one, but Annie had had enough.

"They have to go. Say goodbye."

Both grandmothers knelt down and said goodbye to their little men, telling them to have a great time and make lots of new friends. Then Annie took them by the hands and walked with them over to the school steps. She could do this. They weren't going to Siberia. They would be home this afternoon. It would be all right.

No, it wouldn't.

The minute Annie leaned over and gave them both a kiss; they hung onto her legs and cried their hearts out.

"I don't want to go, Mommy!" Daniel wailed. "I want to stay with you."

"I don't like this place," John sobbed. "I have a tummy ache."

Oh God. The mothers of boys gave Annie sympathetic looks. The mothers of girls looked smug. Their little angels were so ready for school they had their pencil cases and rulers out.

Both grandmothers were wringing their hands and looking distressed. Even George seemed worried. They were no bloody help. What she needed was someone to slap her and/or the boys. She took a deep breath and knelt between them.

"I want the two of you to stop this nonsense right now. You're going to have a great time and Mommy will be here to pick you up after school. Do you understand?"

They shook their heads. "No, Mommy. Don't go!" they cried in unison.

Annie wanted to pick them up and run home. Instead she took them by the hands and literally dragged them into the school, all the while telling them what fun it was going to be. Annie was surprised a bolt of lightning didn't strike her dead for lying to her children.

The primary teacher had the look of someone who'd been through the wars. She was no-nonsense and took in Annie's situation with a quick glance.

"For goodness' sake! We have twins this year. How exciting! The children will be very happy to see you boys. You come with me and we'll have a jolly time."

Both boys were still wailing as she shut the classroom door. Annie ran out of the building and burst into tears. That's when she knew for sure Henry had knocked her up. She marched over to her entourage and sniffed, "I have to buy some bananas."

❖ ❖ ❖

In the two years since Ewan and Lila married, their family had expanded too. There were now three goats, a couple of sheep, a donkey, and two terrifying geese who thought they owned the joint. The horses and cows enjoyed the company, but the chickens were miffed about the geese. So were the cats, but good old Fred and Willy loved everybody.

So did Uncle Joe. Lila had never seen him so happy. He whistled from morning until night, feeding the critters and mucking out the barn. She and Ewan and Uncle Joe were always bone weary at the end of the day, but it was a good tired.

Much worse was going in to see Aunt Eunie, which Lila did more frequently now that Eunie didn't recognize anyone. Lila's stomach always turned a little when she walked into the nursing home. The smell of urine and feces was never quite erased, no matter how clean the place was, and the air felt thick. The patients' pain and loneliness seemed to seep out of them and waft down the halls. It was difficult to see the old men and women sitting in wheelchairs with their mouths agape, their lunch splattered down the front of their bathrobes or blouses, and even harder to cope with the hostile looks from some of the residents, as if she were responsible for putting them there.

Aunt Eunie was confined to her bed. She was wasting away and didn't look like Aunt Eunie anymore. Lila was sure Eunie would be horrified if she knew what was happening to her. She'd always been so dignified and kind-hearted. Lila missed her.

One Sunday Lila came in with some flowers from the garden. She put them in the vase she'd left on the windowsill and filled it with water. After she placed them on the side table so her aunt could see them, she whispered, "It's me, Aunt Eunie. I've come to see how you are today."

Aunt Eunie was usually asleep and didn't respond, but today her eyes opened. They looked glassy and vague, but when she reached out her bony hand Lila took it, whereupon Aunt Eunie began to shake it. Lila couldn't believe the strength in a hand that was nothing but sinew and bone.

"It's good to see you," Lila said.

Aunt Eunie moaned and tried to talk, her mouth opening and closing like a guppy. Tears ran down from her eyes. Lila didn't know what to do.

Luckily a nurse came in to check on her.

"She's crying."

The nurse smiled. "That's a good thing, isn't it, Eunie? That means she knows you're here."

"But…"

"Crying often means happy. She knows you're here and she's responding to you. That means she's having a good day. Don't worry." The nurse left.

It didn't feel like Aunt Eunie was having a good day, but Lila put on a brave face. "I love you, Aunt Eunie. Uncle Joe will be in tomorrow and Ewan will be in the day after. We're very busy with the farm and the animals. You'd love it there. I'm making goat milk soap and selling it at the market, and I've been spinning wool from our sheep. Ewan sells his vegetables and milk. Uncle Joe is an expert with the chickens. They love him. They always lay more when he's around. And you'll be happy to know that I've taken up quilting and rug hooking but I still love drawing the best. Ewan wants to fix up the front porch so I can sell my work to tourists. He's already painted a sign to put up at the end of the driveway. I'm thinking of selling homemade jam. The blackberry and raspberry bushes are full this year. We've also had a lot of blueberries and strawberries. I know you'd love to be in the kitchen with me. I wish you were."

Lila had to try and extract her hand from Eunie's grip because her fingers were white. Where was this strength coming from? It was as if Aunt Eunie wanted her to know there was still a spark of Eunice somewhere inside her dying body and diseased mind.

Aunt Eunie finally closed her eyes and slept. Lila stayed for another hour, just so she wouldn't be alone, but she sucked in great gulps of fresh air in relief on her way to the car.

She needed to talk to someone living. She stopped in at Annie's before heading home, which was like walking from a funeral parlour into a three-ring circus. The boys were running wild all over the house, every burner on the stove was on, and the phone didn't stop ringing. Annie was in the middle of the mayhem, seemingly unperturbed.

"Can I just say that you seem to be carrying this baby differently? I bet it's a girl."

"It's another boy. Want some tea?"

Lila sank into the kitchen chair. "Yes, please. I'm wiped."

Annie stuck a box of animal crackers under her chin and grabbed the tea and some mugs. "I know that look. You've been in to see Aunt Eunie."

"Is it awful to say you wish someone was dead?"

"No. Not when the only life they have is a beating heart."

Lila took a big gulp of hot tea. "I know everyone says this, but I really mean it. If I ever end up like that, please take me out and shoot me."

"If I shoot you, who's going to shoot me?"

"I'll get Ewan to do it."

"Deal."

Lila took her cookie and dunked it in her tea. "How are the boys coping with school?"

"John loves it, but Daniel isn't sure. He came home after his first day and plunked himself down on the chair and said, 'There. That's done.' You should've seen the look he gave me when I told him he had to go back the next day."

"They're so cute."

Annie sipped from her mug. "I think I already know the answer, but..."

"I don't want another baby. It's too scary. Besides, Ewan won't let me because of my heart. He says I can have as many dogs as I want, though."

"I love Ewan. If I wasn't married to Henry, Ewan would be my man."

"Don't tell him that. He's afraid of you."

"Me?"

"A lot of people are afraid of you, Annie. Didn't you know that?"

"You're the biggest chicken of all, and you're here."

"That's just because I know there's a gigantic marshmallow heart behind that big mouth of yours."

"Phooey."

It turned out Annie was right.

Henry managed to make it to the birth of his fourth son. Robert Ewan Pratt was quickly nicknamed Robbie, and Ewan stopped being afraid of Annie from that day on. All of Robbie's red-headed brothers came to the hospital to visit him. They gathered around the bed.

"Mom, I don't think he's cooked yet," John said.

"What?"

"His hair isn't done."

"He's blonde." Annie passed Robbie over to a waiting Henry. "How the heck did I end up with three redheads and a blonde when my hair is brown? You're stomping all over my genes, Pratfall."

"The next one will be a brunette. I promise."

"The next one? I hope you're having it. This shop is closed for business."

Henry smiled down at Robbie. "She says that every time."

"I do not."

"Oh yes, she does. She says that every time, Robbie, so don't listen to her."

For every life there's a death. Aunt Eunie finally went to her resting place, and while it wasn't unexpected it still hurt like hell. The next morning, Uncle Joe went to town to make the funeral arrangements. He insisted on going alone. It was late in the afternoon when Lila heard his car pull up in the driveway. She was ironing the clothes she'd washed earlier, the ones they would wear to Aunt Eunie's funeral.

When he didn't come right in, Lila assumed Uncle Joe had gone to the barn to speak to Ewan, but surely he'd change his clothes first. She ironed for ten minutes more and then decided to look for herself. Rounding the corner of the house, she saw him lying on the ground beside the open car door. There was a box from Aunt Muriel's bakery beside him, held together with string.

"Oh my God. Ewan! Come quick!" Lila fell to her knees in the dirt driveway and listened for a heartbeat. Ewan raced over and got down with her. "Is he breathing?"

She looked at Uncle Joe's face. "He's gone. He didn't want to live without her." Lila reached down and hugged Uncle Joe where he lay. She didn't cry. She had nothing left.

When word got out about the awful news, it spread like wildfire. It was a romantic and tragic end to a marriage between two wonderful people who had spent their lives giving of themselves. Friends and neighbours worried that Lila would have another breakdown, but she knew nothing in her whole life would ever be as bad as losing Caroline.

Ewan, though, had a much harder time. Uncle Joe had been like a father to him, and more than once Lila found Ewan sitting on a bale of hay in the barn and staring out at nothing. She tried to talk to him but he said there was nothing wrong.

All the Macdonalds were there for the funeral. David and Kay came up from Halifax without the girls, as they were only staying for the night. After the funeral everyone was going to Abigail and Kenzie's for supper.

Aunt Eunie and Uncle Joe were buried together in the Mira Gut cemetery. It was a small green space fenced off from the road, but the view was of Mira Bay in all its glory. It pleased Lila to know her aunt and uncle would be close by. When she looked out over the water from the cemetery, she could see the woods where Cricket was, which meant that Uncle Joe and Aunt Eunie could watch over her too.

It was a grey and blustery September day, with mist in the air that threatened to turn to rain. Annie and Ewan arranged for the minister to give his service at the graveside instead of in a church, so everyone was gathered around the grave when Lila and Ewan pulled up behind the hearse. The number of cars lined up on both sides of the highway took Lila by surprise. Perhaps she should've arranged a tea for everyone after the service, since that was the customary thing to do on the island, but it was too late now. The only people she cared about, she'd see at dinner in Glace Bay.

Ewan and Uncle Joe's friends and co-workers carried the casket to the edge of the dug hole. As the ceremony commenced, Lila's attention wandered. She didn't have to listen, since God never listened to her. Annie and Henry stood side by side, giving her loving and sympathetic looks. So did Abigail and Kenzie, which was reassuring. She didn't notice David at first because she was too busy looking at the soft pink tweed suit Kay had on.

Who wears pink to a funeral? She stuck out like a sore thumb. Lila knew that Kay was doing it because she hated Lila. She was always pleasant and chatty, but Lila knew. It was something she never discussed with anyone, and Lila was pretty sure Kay didn't let on to anyone in her life either. It was a silent battle simmering just below the surface.

Every time Lila glanced his way, David was looking at her. His dark blue suit fit him perfectly and he'd filled out in the last few years. He had always been good looking, but now he had the classic features of a confident and sexy man. Even the women at the funeral were looking at him from under their eyelashes, no doubt wishing that they were on his arm, but who would be able to compete with Kay?

Lila would.

She had what Kay wanted: David's love.

Lila wondered how much it hurt Kay to know that even with her beauty, her style, her money, she wasn't enough. Her husband was fixated on a woman who was wearing a faded shirtdress and knitted sweater.

A wave of longing washed over Lila as she stood there. Kay was going home to two beautiful daughters. David had given Kay babies who didn't die. Lila couldn't stand it anymore. When she walked away from the graveside no one went after her, knowing how upset she was, but she didn't go to the truck. She crossed the road, scrambled down the bank by the water's edge, and screamed her lungs out on the beach.

She didn't care. Everyone thought she was crazy anyway. She was the crazy lady who lived on a farm in the middle of nowhere. The great bastard in the sky was making sure that she'd suffer forever because she was a bad, bad mother. Where was she when Caroline was crying out for her? Who lets their child die alone?

Caroline wasn't ever coming back. Aunt Eunie and Uncle Joe weren't ever coming back. Her mother and father were never coming back. The handsome man, who just a minute ago looked at her with hunger in his eyes, was lost forever. There was only one thing to do. Calling for Caroline, she ran into the cold water until she couldn't feel her legs. The water pulled at her as she tried to push through it. Her dress and sweater weighed her down. She needed to get the water over her head and find peace.

But just as the water was reaching her shoulders, a hand grabbed her arm and pulled her back with such force it nearly took her arm out of its socket.

"Let me go!"

Now an arm held her tight and started to drag her out of the water. She struggled against it. "I want to die! Let me die!"

"I'm not going to let you die," David shouted at her. "Stop struggling or I swear to God I'm going to hit you."

Lila opened her eyes. David was up to his chest in water. There were people all over the beach shouting and gesturing. Ewan was coming, too. When the water was at their waists, David picked her up as if he was carrying her over the threshold. She slapped at his head and neck.

"Why did you leave me?"

Water dripped down David's face. "You made me go."

Suddenly Ewan was upon them and he grabbed her from David's arms and headed into shore. His face was set in stone.

"I'm sorry, Ewan," she whispered.

"We're going home now."

"Yes, take me home."

She was aware of the shocked faces that lined the beach, and of Annie and her mother hurrying after Ewan.

And the pink lady who looked only at her bedraggled husband walking out of the water in his expensive suit.

❊ ❊ ❊

Annie was thankful she and Henry had gone to the funeral in their own car. God knows what was happening in her parent's car, with a sopping wet David and Kay in the back seat.

"What was he thinking?"

"I imagine he wanted to save her."

"He got to her before her own husband did. That says it all. I could honestly wring his neck. Poor Kay."

Henry kept glancing at her as they drove back to Glace Bay. "Annie, you need to keep your mouth shut. Nothing good will come of you getting in the middle of all this."

"Excuse me, but I'm supposed to stand aside while my brother makes a laughingstock of his wife?"

"No one at that funeral knows anything about David and Lila. As far as they were concerned her brother got to her first, with her husband close behind. No one is thinking anything except that Lila is a deeply troubled young woman."

"You know I don't blame Lila for this. She's had so much grief in her life, I think she snapped today. But poor Kay has been nothing but wonderful to David."

Henry abruptly pulled over to the side of the road and looked her square in the face. "Your brother's marriage is none of your concern. They have two children together. You don't know what Kay is thinking. She's stood by him through everything. That says a lot. So if you go into your mother's house and start giving David hell, I know for a fact that Kay won't thank you for it. It's between a husband and wife. Have you got that?"

Annie crossed her arms and looked out the window, so Henry pulled the car back on the road. She knew he was right but it ticked her off. "Sometimes you treat me like a father instead of a husband."

"When you act like a child, I do."

Annie took her gloves and swatted him on the arm. "I should've married some young stud with no brains. Then I could be superior."

"You are superior in every way, my love."

"You are so corny."

When they got back to her mother's house, Kay and David were nowhere to be seen. Henry and Dad went out into the garage to look at a new table saw her father had bought, which left Annie and her mother alone in the kitchen.

Abigail frowned as she looked in the oven. "I have this huge ham and no one is going to eat it."

"What are we? Chopped liver?"

"I made a cherry pie too."

"Where are Kay and David?"

"Kay said she had a headache and needed to lie down. Your brother is changing his clothes."

They were both aware of raised voices up in the bedroom. Mom pointed at the ceiling. "I'm worried about those two. Is there something I should know?"

Annie heard Henry's voice in her head and was, for once, discreet. "All couples fight. They're fine. I'm worried about Lila."

Abigail stared out the kitchen window. "Oh Annie, what's going to become of that girl? I feel like I've failed her."

"Lila was broken when we found her."

"She was, wasn't she? I'm not sure Ewan can fix her."

"Ewan loves her. That's all she needs."

They heard footsteps on the stairs and then David poked his head in the kitchen. He looked dreadful. He made a point of not looking at her.

"Mom, Kay wants to go home tonight."

"But what about your dinner?"

"I'm sorry we've ruined your plans. Would you be able to make us a couple of sandwiches for the road?"

It was a quick goodbye and it was obvious that Kay was uncomfortable, but she made sure she kissed Annie and her mother goodbye and apologized for the inconvenience, saying she knew it was silly but she was lonely for her girls. Mom said she understood.

A week later David called Annie. She was in the middle of changing Robbie's diaper, with George standing next to her passing her the safety pins.

"I was called into Louis's office this morning."

"Oh?"

"He's sending me to Montreal. It's a big promotion."

Annie heard the sorrow in his voice.

"What does Kay think?"

"She's happy about it."

"I'll miss you terribly, but this might be just what you need, Davy."

They both knew what she was talking about.

CHAPTER SEVENTEEN

1961

COLLEEN'S BREATH WAS HOT AGAINST her hands as she covered her face and kept her eyes tightly shut. She leaned against the brick at the back of the house while counting to one hundred. It wasn't easy. A housefly kept buzzing around her head and the back of her checkered dress was sticky with sweat, she'd been standing so long in the noonday sun.

"Ready or not, here I come!"

Colleen opened her eyes and had to squint. The very large garden at the back of their house in Westmount was perfect for hiding in. The hedges and large flowering shrubs were so thick you couldn't see behind them. There was also a rock garden and massive oak trees along the edge of the property. Colleen had names for all of them, but she didn't tell Frankie in case she thought it was silly.

When she and her sister played here it didn't feel like they lived in the city. The beautiful old trees that grew on Mount Royal kept the noise of the city below at a minimum. The neighbourhood consisted of winding streets filled with old stone mansions and large homes, well back from the sidewalks, with the front gardens filled with flowers, bushes, and cedars among the common wrought-iron fencing and gates. Their house wasn't as big as the rest, but it was still very nice. Colleen's mom said the houses mostly belonged to people with old money, but Colleen wasn't sure what that meant.

Colleen had just celebrated her eighth birthday and one of her gifts was a note from Frankie saying she owed her one game of hide-and-seek. It was thrilling because her sister didn't like to play outdoors very much, which was too bad really since there was a lot to discover. Like the toads that lived under the rocks in the koi pond or the family of chipmunks that burrowed into a hole at the back of the gardening shed.

After hunting for almost twenty minutes, Colleen was out of ideas about where to look. Frankie had to be the world's best hider, which was surprising since she didn't have a lot of practice. Colleen was thirsty and decided to run into the house and get a drink before venturing out again.

Elena, the cook, was in their sizable kitchen stirring a bowl of something. She did that every day.

"Can I have a drink of water?"

Elena had dark hair and eyes, and a bit of a mustache that Colleen was fascinated with, but the best thing about Elena was that she was nice. Colleen liked her better than Grandmother Hanover.

Elena put down the bowl and turned on the kitchen tap. "Would you like lemonade instead?"

"Water first. Then lemonade. Please."

Elena produced a glass of each and Colleen downed them. She wiped her dirty hands across her upper lip to wipe away the sweat. "It's too hot."

"You're flushed. You should come inside now."

"I can't. I'm looking for Frankie."

"She's up in her room."

Colleen couldn't believe it. This was supposed to be her birthday gift. She stomped out of the kitchen and down the hall before climbing the broad stairs to the second level. Frankie's room was the first one to the right and her door was closed. Colleen opened it without knocking. Frankie was on her canopied bed listening to the radio and cutting dresses to put on her paper dolls.

"Why aren't you playing hide-and-seek?"

"I am. You just found me. It took you long enough."

"That's because I was looking for you outside. That's how you play the game."

"Sorry, you should've told me."

"Every kid in the whole world knows how to play hide-and-seek."

Her sister made a sad face. "Honestly, Colleen, I thought you meant we could hide anywhere. I figured this would be the last place you'd look…and I was right."

Colleen stormed out of the room and down to her own bedroom, where she slammed the door before flinging herself on her own unmade bed. How was it possible that instead of Frankie saying she was sorry, her sister had made it seem like it was Colleen's fault for not explaining the rules?

It happened all the time. Colleen was secretly envious of this ability and tried it a few times but it never worked. She crawled over to the bedside table and took her diary out of the drawer. It was pink with a picture of a garden on it. A pencil was sharpened and ready, stuck between the pages and the clasp. The best part was when she took the tiny metal key, stuck it in the lock, and turned it to the right. Open sesame.

Frankie never plays with me. She's mean!!!!!!!

Colleen closed the diary and locked it up again before putting it back in the drawer. She wondered if Frankie ever tried to look in it. Probably not.

The house was too quiet. Colleen went downstairs to be with Elena. "I'm hungry."

"What about your dinner?"

"Mom said I could have some cookies before supper."

"I don't think I believe you, but it will be our little secret." She smiled and placed a glass of orange juice and a plate of cookies on the table in front of Colleen.

"Thank you."

"It's too bad you can't drink milk. Cookies are much better with milk."

"Yuck." Colleen polished off the entire plate while Elena asked her questions about school.

"My teacher has a brace on her leg. It's really loud when she walks on the wooden floors. It makes me nervous."

"Why?"

Colleen shrugged.

"I think lots of things make you nervous."

"I hate it when planes fly overhead. I always think they're going to fall out of the sky and land on me."

Elena laughed while she got up to take the roast out of the oven. "Of all the people in the world, why would that plane land on you?"

Colleen spoke immediately. "Because I'm bad."

Elena turned around. "Why would you say such a thing?"

"Frankie's the good one."

"Who told you that?"

"Grandmother Hanover."

"She may be your grandmother, but she doesn't know what she's talking about."

That had never occurred to Colleen. Adults were always right, weren't they? Just then the front door opened and her mother called out, "I'm home!"

Colleen shoved the kitchen chair back and ran out to greet her mom, who put her purse and parcels on the foyer side table. "Hi, Mommy! What took you so long?" She put her arms around her mother's waist. Mom kissed the top of her head.

"I was out to lunch with friends. We got to talking, you know how it is."

"No."

"Someday you will." Mom took Colleen's dirty hands away from her light blue dress and looked at them. "Just as I thought. What on earth do you do after school? Build tunnels?"

Colleen laughed. "I'm making a tunnel to Daddy's office."

"Go wash your hands before dinner."

Frankie appeared at the top of the stairs. "Hi, Mom. Did you go shopping?"

"As a matter of fact, I did. For both of you." Mom reached into one of the bags and pulled out a very pretty dress with a daisy collar and hem, and a crinoline underneath. Frankie ran down the stairs.

"I love it! Thanks, Mom. I'm going to try it on." She raced back up the stairs and disappeared.

Colleen didn't want a dress with a crinoline, but, just her luck, her mother produced one.

"After you wash your hands, you can try it on. I'll bring it upstairs."

"That's too itchy."

Her mom grabbed her purse and parcels and headed up the stairs. "There's always a price to pay for beauty."

Sometimes her mom made no sense.

Colleen washed her hands in the small bathroom off her bedroom. She loved it in there. It was small and only had a sink and toilet in it, but she loved the fat porcelain handles on the chrome taps in the sink that said *Hot* and *Cold*. Before she could read she didn't know what the black marks meant, and was amazed when in first grade she read the words out loud one night and realized it meant hot water from this tap and cold water from that tap. It was like discovering a new world.

Colleen struggled into the new dress her mother left on the bed and had the familiar feeling of being disappointed. It was too tight. They were always too tight. The pretty ones, anyway. She wanted to get out of it, but she couldn't get it over her head. Frankie came into her room wearing her dress, which fit perfectly, and saw Colleen's dilemma.

"Here, put your arms up."

Their mother walked in on them. "Oh, Frankie! I love it. Wait; let me see yours Colleen."

Colleen put her arms down and stood there feeling big.

"Well, perhaps if I move the buttons..."

"I hate dresses!" Colleen marched into her bathroom, shut the door, and locked it. Her mother and sister made soothing noises on the other side of the door.

"Go away!"

They left her alone. She eventually got out of the dress herself and threw it on the floor. Then she sat on the toilet, even though she didn't have to go, but that got boring after awhile. Eventually she heard her father come home and her mom yell up the stairs to come for supper. She got back in her play dress and ran down the stairs.

Her father was sitting at the head of the table in the dining room and smiled when he saw her. "Hey, Coll the doll, how was school today?"

Colleen walked over and gave her dad a kiss before she sat at the table. Frankie still had her new dress on and looked very pleased with herself. Now that Frankie was ten, a lot of people said how much she looked like her mother, and Colleen knew that people thought her mother was beautiful.

No one said she looked like Mom.

"School is dumb."

Dad laughed out loud as Mom passed him the gravy. "You remind me of your Aunt Annie."

Colleen loved to make her father laugh. "I do?"

"She hated school."

"Why, Daddy?" Frankie asked. "Didn't she have any friends?"

"Your Aunt Annie had more friends than you could shake a stick at. She just hated to sit still. When the school bell rang, she was the first one out the door." Dad took a forkful of potatoes and pointed them at Colleen. "She still runs around today."

Mom put peas on Colleen's plate before she picked up her wine glass. "With four boys, she'd have to."

"That's right, but the difference is she's running around with her sons. What time did you get home today?" Dad asked.

Her mother took a sip of wine. "I have no idea."

"When I was a kid, my mother was always home for us after school."

Mom put down her wineglass. "My childhood was different, and I don't think I turned out half bad. Let's drop it, shall we?"

Colleen hated it when her parents talked without looking at each other. It gave her a stomachache, but by the end of dinner, they were looking at each other again, so Colleen could relax. Mom brought out the tea and the cake that Elena had made that afternoon.

"This looks good," Dad said.

"I whipped it up myself," Mom said.

Frankie and Colleen both shouted, "No, you didn't!"

"Who did, then?"

"Elena!" they laughed.

Mom shook her head. "I could've sworn it was me." She set about cutting the cake and served the first piece to Dad and then one to Frankie and Colleen and the last piece for herself.

Colleen looked at everyone else's plates. Her piece was smaller, and she didn't think that was fair. She always finished first because she didn't get as much.

"Can I have some more, please?"

Mom shook her head. "That's enough for tonight."

Frankie didn't finish hers. Neither did Mom. How could they leave half a slice of cake on the plate?

When Colleen was ready for bed, her mom came in and sat on the edge of the mattress. She brushed Colleen's hair off her face. "Did you have a good day?"

"No. Frankie was supposed to play hide-and-seek with me and she says she did but she didn't. She was just in her room. That doesn't count."

"Big sisters can be a pain sometimes."

They smiled at each other.

"Did you wish you had a sister?" Colleen asked.

"Yes. You're very lucky to have one."

"I guess she's okay."

Mom leaned over and kissed her cheek. "I love you."

"Goodnight, Mommy."

❀ ❀ ❀

David and Kay always agreed on one thing. Their sex life was superb. In the early days of moving to Montreal when they knew no one, their evenings were filled with each other, once the girls were in bed. It was as if Kay was rewarding him. She was relaxed and fun and adventurous. He had it all with this beautiful woman who turned heads everywhere she went. He knew how lucky he was. And he did love her. He did. She was the mother of his children.

Thoughts of Lila slowly faded into the background. Everyone said their first love was memorable, he wasn't the only one, and he was grateful to Ewan for being so good for Lila.

David was always out the door to work before the girls left for school. They'd come down for breakfast just as he knocked back the last of his coffee. Elena didn't arrive until ten in the morning, so it was left to Kay to organize the first meal of the day, and she was pretty good at it. Of course the girls only wanted cereal and he was fine with toast, but still, things had improved. Now she cut up bananas on top of the cereal and had either jam or honey on the table.

David kissed his daughters' heads as they sat in their chairs.

"Isn't that the same dress you had on last night, Frankie?"

"Yes, Mom bought it for me yesterday. I want to wear it to school."

"It looks very nice. Where's yours, Coll?"

"I hate mine."

"You hate everything. Be good today."

"Bye, Daddy," they said in tandem.

He crossed the floor and came up behind Kay, who was at the sink. His hand disappeared under her robe to cup her breast as he kissed her on the ear. "See you tonight."

"Stop that," she whispered, "the girls."

He picked up his briefcase and car keys before leaving the house. His Studebaker was behind Kay's red convertible. He joined the rest of the men in the neighbourhood who backed their cars into the street at the same time every morning to try and beat the downtown traffic. Luckily, David didn't have far to go. His office was on the ground floor of the Linton on Sherbrooke St. W., an impressive Beaux-Arts apartment building built before the First World War. It was mostly for residents, but one of the first-floor apartments had been renovated as an office for David and two other lawyers who worked for Hanover Industries. The original woodwork and crown molding was throughout the seven rooms, with nine-and-a-half-foot ceilings and enormous windows looking out over one of Montreal's most famous streets.

David's office was the largest, so his desk had to be massive to fill the space. He placed it in the middle of the room, and when the girls were very little they loved to come in and crawl back and forth underneath.

David often walked down the street on his lunch hour, perusing the many art galleries along the way. He developed a taste for oil paintings and collected quite a few over the years. They graced the walls of this office, as well as his home. Sometimes Kay met him for lunch and they'd look together, but she was always drawn to Holt Renfrew. Kay had her own money, so he didn't concern himself with how much she spent on clothes for herself or the girls, but he insisted on paying for everything else. He made sure he paid his father-in-law back for the money he'd lent them to buy the Montreal house.

David made a damn good wage, but not so high that he felt like Louis's puppet. He earned what he made. There would be no looking at himself in the mirror if he did otherwise. He'd never shame his dad like that.

Every so often, mostly in the late afternoon when he started to wind down for the day, David looked out the window at the people hurrying past on the concrete sidewalks and the cars honking their horns, everyone trying to get somewhere. He'd think of his dad walking home from work alone, with his long stride down the dirt road, wearing work pants and a flannel shirt, carrying a tin lunch box with hands black with grease.

David would hear him whistle from down the street and he'd run up to keep him company. Dad's face would look tired but satisfied. He'd ask David what Mom was making for supper and hoped it would include a lemon meringue pie. It usually did.

Then David would watch as his father stood at the sink and washed his hands with abrasive soap to take all the black away. Dad would turn around and wipe his hands and arms dry up to his elbows, asking Mom about her day. That's how he liked to remember his dad, with that towel in his hands.

The phone rang and startled him. How long he'd been at the window, David didn't know. He pushed his chair back to the desk and picked up the receiver. "David Macdonald."

"Listen to ya. Can't say hello like the rest of us peasants?"

David grinned. "Annie! It's good to hear your voice."

"You too, Davy."

"That's odd. I was just thinking about Dad. Remember when he came home from work?"

"He'd pretend to chase me with his dirty hands."

"I'd forgotten that. So, how's the family?"

"They're boys. All they do is fart and burp."

"How old are the twins now?"

"Twelve. George is nine and Robbie's six. You're their uncle; you need to know things like that."

"It's seems a long time since I've seen them."

David and his family hadn't been back to Cape Breton at all. They did go to Halifax twice, where Annie, Henry, and the boys met them at Kay's family cottage while her parents were in Europe. They'd had two glorious weeks together each time. Annie was convinced it was heaven, what with the pool and a chef, but the best part was seeing their children get to know each other. David's parents had also come up to Montreal a few times to visit, but never for more than a week. That was the time it took for Dad to do all the odd jobs around the house. After that he was like a caged lion. He even offered to mow the neighbour's yard once when their gardener didn't show up.

"Well, you may be seeing them sooner than you think."

"Oh?"

"Mom didn't want to call you, but I said I wasn't making that mistake again."

"Call me about what?" A shiver of unease ran through him.

"It's Dad. He has TB."

"Tuberculosis? Isn't that serious?"

"It can be. The doctor wants him to go to the sanatorium in North Sydney for rest and drug therapy. He may be in there for a few months or more."

"Dad in a bed for two months? You might as well kill him now."

"He needs rest and he knows it. He doesn't have the energy to do much anyway. I plan on raiding the local library. He can read to his heart's content."

David's mind wandered and he only half caught what Annie said. "...Mom thinks you're too busy with work and what can you do anyway..."

"Screw that, I want to see him. The girls finish school in a few days. We can be packed and on the road by the weekend. Hell, I'll put things on hold and we'll come for the whole summer."

The relief in Annie's voice made it clear that she needed him there. When was the last time Annie had asked him for anything?

He told Kay and the girls at dinnertime that they were going to Cape Breton for the summer.

"Oh, goody!" Colleen clapped her hands and jumped up and down in her seat. "We'll see Grampy and Grammie and Aunt Annie and Uncle Henry!"

"Do I have to play with those boys?" Frankie asked. "They put a worm in my drink last time."

Kay's face had gone completely white. "You didn't think to discuss it with me?"

"Annie called. Dad has TB. He's going into a sanatorium."

"Oh, I'm sorry to hear that."

"What's TB?" Colleen asked.

He looked at his youngest. "I'm talking to your mother." David took a roll and broke it open before buttering it. "I want to help Mom. It's the right thing to do, and I'd like to see my Dad. He's not getting any younger."

"Of course. That means we'll stay in Glace Bay?"

"I want to go to Daddy's bungalow. I've never seen it," Colleen shouted.

Frankie made a face. "Are there bugs there?"

"We'll stay in Glace Bay, I imagine, but I do want to take the girls to the cottage on weekends. I want them to see where I spent my summers."

Kay nodded and excused herself from the table. She went upstairs.

"Where's Mommy going?"

"She's finished her dinner." David knew what the rest of his evening would entail.

"Can I have her potatoes? Dad, can I have her potatoes?"

"No, you don't eat off other people's plates. Now, you and Frankie clear the table and get ready for bed."

"Awww…"

"Now, Colleen. You too, Frankie."

David kissed them goodnight once they brushed their teeth. Their mother was missing in action. She'd be in the tub, with the bathroom door locked. David closed the door to their room and was in bed for a good hour before Kay decided to grace him with her presence.

Her hair was in a knot at the top of her head, still damp. David knew she was furious; she'd covered herself completely with a long nightie, and ignored him as she sat at her makeup table applying night cream.

"Kay."

She didn't answer.

"Do you expect me to never cross the causeway again? My family lives in Cape Breton. My relatives are getting older. My loved ones are going to die. Am I going to sit here in Montreal while all that happens and never go home again because you're afraid of Lila?"

She looked at him in the mirror but didn't say a word.

David pressed his fingers into the corners his eyes to ease his headache. "How can you be this insecure? You've been my wife for twelve years now. We live in this big house that we own together and are raising our children here. Me seeing Lila is not going to end our marriage. I love you. She's been married to Ewan for nine years. She loves him. It's ancient history!"

Kay got to her feet and swung around to face him. "My problem is trying to forget the look on your face when you went after her in the water. If I remember correctly, we were married when that little drama unfolded."

"And you forget that Lila grew up with Annie and me. I was afraid she'd drown in front of my mother, who thinks of Lila as one of her own. That's what you saw, Kay! Fear."

Kay hesitated and looked away. He got up off the bed and took her in his arms. "You are my wife. I want you with me on this trip. I'm going to need you. I don't know how serious this is with my dad. It scares me. Please, Kay. I love you."

He knew as soon as she kissed him and dropped her nightie to the floor that the crisis was over.

This was one time that being related to the big boss came in handy. Louis told him to take all the time he needed to be with his father.

There was a mad dash in the household over the next three days. The girls barely had time to put their report cards away before David and Kay had them packing up for the big trip. As usual, Frankie did everything quietly and efficiently, without asking them a hundred questions. Colleen came back and forth into their bedroom with endless queries.

"Dad, should I bring my winter coat? You said it was cold in the evening down by the beach."

"Not that cold. A couple of sweaters should do."

"Take your old red one and the new blue one," Kay said as she opened drawers and considered what to bring herself. Colleen was back only a few minutes later.

"What about shoes?"

"You don't have to bring any," David smiled. "We never wore shoes in Round Island."

Colleen's face lit up, but Kay squelched that idea in a hurry. "Bring your sneakers and sandals. And a good pair in case we go to church."

Out she went. David looked at his watch. "Let's time her."

Forty-five seconds later she was back. "We can't go!"

"Why?" her parents said together.

"What about Bear and Tigger and Charlotte? We can't leave them behind."

"The dog and cats are coming with us," said David.

"The cats too?" Kay cried.

"Yay! Wait till I tell them!" Colleen zoomed off.

Kay stood there with her hand on her hip. "I thought we'd put the cats in a kennel."

"For two months? Let the poor little bastards have a romp in a real field and catch a country mouse."

"You're nuts."

Elena packed a picnic basket for them and said she would make sure everything was locked up after they left. David could tell she was looking forward to this unexpected vacation too. It took him close to an hour to get everything packed into the car. They were so laden down their car scraped the asphalt when they backed out of the driveway. They waved at Elena as she stood by the front door yelling, "Have a good time!"

Bear was a small fluffy stray dog they'd found the year before. He was nervous to be outside. Loud noises scared him, no doubt because of some traumatizing event in his past, but he was as good as gold in the car. Kay and the girls took turns holding him. The only fly in the ointment was that he shed everywhere. They were covered in fur whenever they got out at a gas station or a rest stop.

The cats were still howling in their cages between the girls in the back seat as they passed Quebec City. After several snide glances from his wife, David laughed, "Okay! I was wrong! We should've put them in a kennel."

"They better catch the biggest mouse out there," Kay said.

"They better catch Mickey Mouse," Colleen laughed.

"Mickey Mouse is in Florida," Frankie sighed as she looked out the window.

"Maybe he goes on vacation in Round Island."

"Don't be stupid, Colleen."

"Frankie, apologize to your sister, please."

"I'm sorry I called you stupid."

David looked in the rearview mirror and saw Frankie stick her tongue out at her sister. Colleen returned the favour.

He couldn't wait to see Annie.

❋ ❋ ❋

Annie couldn't wait to see Davy and his family either. She loved her nieces. They were fascinating creatures, though the two of them were like chalk and cheese. Frankie was a lady. Colleen was Annie Junior, but without the confidence. Maybe a couple of months of roughhousing with the boys would toughen her up.

Annie and Henry now lived in a bigger house. The trouble with boys was that they accumulated sports equipment. The day Annie tripped and twisted her ankle on the skates and hockey sticks strewn all over the back porch was the last straw; they put the house on the market a week later.

Their new house was near the end of South Street, back in her old haunting ground. It had five bedrooms and three bathrooms and a huge yard where all the neighbourhood kids gathered. Annie overheard one of Robbie's friends say that was because Mrs. Pratt liked dirt.

Henry had his office on Commercial Street. His mother was still his receptionist; he didn't have the heart to fire her. Annie stayed out of it. It kept Joy out of her hair and into the hair of all Henry's patients. Joy knew everything about everybody. Her circle of friends grew and grew, as other widows invited her over for lunch or supper to get caught up on the latest gossip but she swore to Henry on her life that she never said anything confidential, just the stories she overheard in the waiting room.

If Henry spent as much time in his waiting room as Joy did, he'd know that people loved to talk about their ailments, and those of their friends and families.

Because Annie was so busy with her brood, she often phoned her parents instead of visiting, and so it had been at least a month between visits to their house. When she saw her dad sitting on the couch in the middle of the afternoon, she knew something was wrong. They had a nice chat before he said he thought he'd lie down. Annie rushed into the kitchen so Mom could fill her in.

That was at least a month ago, and several doctors' appointments later, the diagnosis was announced. As much as Annie and her mom told each other Dad would be fine, they both looked forward to David reassuring them too.

Kenzie went into the sanatorium before David and his family arrived. Henry didn't let the boys see their grandfather at all, just to err on the side of caution. Annie and her mother cried when they left Dad lying on his bed covered in a white sheet, one of several patients in the same room. Dad was the one who comforted them, assuring them he'd be fine and thanking Annie again for all the books.

Annie didn't want to drop her mom off at an empty house, but Mom insisted she wanted to be in her own home. Annie didn't blame her. The boys would've been all over her.

Annie didn't announce she was back at her house that day. The kitchen was empty and she heard Henry upstairs with the gang. She made herself a cup of tea and sat looking out the window. It was the first time she let herself think that someday her parents would die. What would her world be like without them? How would she stop being their child and needing their comfort? It didn't matter that she had children of her own.

And for the first time she realized the enormity of Lila's loss. If at the age of thirty-three Annie was terrified of losing her parents, what horror did seven-year-old Lila go through when her mother died?

Thinking about Lila made Annie worry about something else. Should she tell her that David was coming or not?

She heard Henry come down the stairs, saying, "I'll be right back. I have some more glue in the garage." That meant the boys were busy making models, all except for Robbie, who only liked to play with the glue.

Henry came into the kitchen. "I didn't hear you come in. How did it go?"

"I need a hug." Annie stood up and Henry obliged.

"Let me make you a cup of tea," he said after she sat back down.

"I just had some. Sit with me."

Henry obliged once more and reached across the table to clasp her hand. "I know your dad will be fine. They caught it in time. And soon David will be here and he'll be able to help you with the visiting part of it."

"I know. Should I call Lila to tell her David is coming home?"

"Lila? You don't honestly think there's going to be a problem? That's old news."

Annie reached over to pat Henry's cheek. "You men are such simple creatures."

"And you females make life more complicated."

Annie paused. "I'd better call."

Henry got up for the table. "I'll be in the garage gluing my mouth shut."

❖ ❖ ❖

Lila said all the right things to Annie, like she was glad David was coming home to see his dad. She told Annie not to worry, it was a lifetime ago, and made sure to mention that she was up to her eyeballs in work and probably wouldn't have a chance to even see David's family when they came out to Round Island the odd time. But when she got off the phone, she immediately went outside and sat in one of the old Adirondack chairs, a favourite thinking spot.

She could hear banging in the distance, Ewan hammering the new enclosure for the sheep he was planning to buy. Lila couldn't wait to have little lambs come spring. There was no chance they would become lamb chops. Ewan wanted the sheep to keep the grass down on their very large property, now that he had cleared more trees at the back of the house.

Lila and Ewan painted the barn red and the hen house a bright yellow, and this new building was going to be blue. It looked like a little animal farm from a picture book and that gave Lila the idea that she and Ewan could have a petting zoo and charge families a few dollars to come see the critters. That's what they did anyway when the neighbourhood kids dropped by. The donkey, goat, and two miniature horses were very popular. They might as well charge something to keep their menagerie well fed.

Ewan's colourful sign at the bottom of the driveway enticed lots of folks to come up to the house. Their enclosed front veranda had become a little shop, just as Ewan had planned. She sold her quilts, hooked rugs, and preserves, all the recipes that Eunie had taught her over the years. She had honey from their bees and even gathered driftwood and sea glass from the beach that tourists loved to buy. Her watercolours of the animals and views of Mira Bay were also snapped up.

She and Ewan were content. They made good money and loved what they did. They wanted nothing more.

And now David was coming to bugger it up.

She wouldn't let it happen. Lila got out of the chair and wandered over to the new sheep pen. Ewan saw her coming and gave her a smile. His face always shone when he saw her.

"How's it going?" she asked.

Ewan wiped the sweat off his brow with the sleeve of his flannel shirt. "Good. Should be done by suppertime, and then I can go get them."

"What do we call these new kids?"

"I was thinking *Lamb*ert and *Ram*sey."

"What about *Ewen*?"

They both laughed.

"I'll leave you be." Lila started to go but turned back. "David and his family are coming home for the summer because of Kenzie. They're staying in Glace Bay and I imagine they'll be out to Round Island occasionally, but I don't think our paths will cross. There's no need to see them, so don't worry about anything."

He gave her a long look. "Why would I worry, Lila?"

Lila felt unexpected frustration rising. "No reason. I thought you'd want to know, that's all. Don't read anything into it. God!"

"Why are you angry?"

"I'm not! Annie happened to call and I'm letting you know what she said."

"All right."

Annie walked away. David wasn't even here yet and he was already making a mess. She vowed to stay on this side of the field until he went back to Montreal where he belonged.

❖ ❖ ❖

Colleen was thrilled to be at her grandmother's house for the first time. The best part was that she let Colleen eat as much as she wanted. Of course, Colleen made sure her mother wasn't around when she asked. Grammie didn't know there was a problem.

"It's so wonderful to have a little girl around this table again," Grammie smiled as she put a big piece of pie in front of her. "I wish you lived closer. Then you could come every day."

"I'd like that," Colleen said with her mouth full.

"Where's your sister? Maybe she'd like a piece of pie too."

"She went with Mommy and Daddy to the grocery store."

Grammie poured herself a cup of tea and sat at the kitchen table. "So tell me what you've been doing since I saw you last. Are you still friends with the little girl across the street?"

"No. She decided she didn't want to be friends anymore."

Her grandmother frowned. "That's not very nice."

"She didn't invite me to her birthday party, either, but I didn't care."

"If she behaves like that, she doesn't deserve your friendship. Good riddance to her."

"That's what Daddy said. Oh wait, I almost forgot." Colleen put down her fork and picked up the bag she brought with her, filled with things she thought her grandmother might like. "I have some pictures of the ballet recital."

"Oh, wonderful."

Colleen passed them over and continued to eat. "There were a lot of people there."

"Frankie looks sweet in her blue tutu."

"I know. I wish I got to wear one."

Grammie looked up. "I thought you were in the recital too."

"I was. I was the Pied Piper. I had to wear black pants and a red-and-white striped shirt. I was the only one who didn't get to wear a dress."

"That's too bad. Well, I bet you were the best Pied Piper ever."

Colleen smiled. "Thanks, Grammie."

That night her family went over to Aunt Annie's. The kids were told to go outside and play until they were called in for supper. Frankie spent most of the time swinging on the swing. She didn't want to play cowboys and Indians.

"Is she always stuck up?" John asked Colleen.

"I guess so. She's pretty boring."

They were up in the tree house waiting for the Indians to raid their compound. Daniel and George were hiding behind the garage. They sent Robbie out with a message. He had to take the sucker out of his mouth to deliver it.

"There will be no peace treat."

John hollered from the tree. "What?"

Daniel shouted from behind the garage. "Peace *treaty*, dumdum!"

"Peace treaty," Robbie repeated.

"Then prepare for war!" John yelled.

"Yeah! We don't need your stupid peace treaty," Colleen added.

"Do you know how ridiculous you sound?" Frankie said.

"Who asked you?" John answered back. "You better duck or their arrows will poke your eyes out."

Frankie jumped off the swing. "I hope you're all killed by dinnertime." She went back into the house.

John shook his head. "She may be the pretty one, but her attitude stinks. Come on, pick up your gun and follow me."

Colleen's cheeks felt hot. They always did when someone mentioned Frankie's looks. No one ever said that about her, which was mean and unfair, but she did as she was told and followed John's orders to the letter. They snuck down the tree and ran to the back porch at the same time that Daniel and George ran to the gardening shed.

Robbie galloped around the yard with his horse on a stick pretending to shoot everything with his index finger. John told Colleen to stand on a small folding chair to see if the enemy was on the left or right side of the shed. When she did, the chair broke and she fell to the ground on her knees. It was only when she saw they were bleeding that she started to cry.

"You'll be all right, my dad's a doctor." John helped her to brush the gravel away from her skin. Daniel and George came running to see what the fuss was about.

"That's my chair!" Robbie trotted over and shot her right between the eyes. "Why are you so fat?"

"Robbie!"

Aunt Annie was on the porch. She hurried down the steps and ran over to her.

"Are you all right, sweetheart?"

Colleen needed to cry all over again. It wasn't only her knees that hurt.

"Boys, take her inside and let your dad look at it." Aunt Annie then stood up and marched over to Robbie, who ran away when he saw her face.

"I didn't do nothin'!"

"Get over here, mister. Stop! And I mean *now*."

The last glimpse Colleen had of Robbie was Aunt Annie holding him by the elbow and smacking him on the bum, while he tried to get away. The more he did, the more she smacked. Now he was crying too. Good.

The next day, Colleen and the boys piled into the back of Uncle Henry's big station wagon. Uncle Henry, Aunt Annie, and Grammie were in the front. Frankie sat between Mom and Dad in the back seat. They were off to see Grampy. Not that any of the kids were allowed in the sanatorium, but they planned on waving to him from the parking lot while Grampy stood in the window.

It was a hot and sticky summer day and all the windows were open in the car. Frankie and Mom complained that their hair would be ruined. Dad laughed at them and mussed their hair up even more. Mom laughed, but Colleen could tell Frankie was annoyed.

Her cousins spent most of the time pushing each other out of the way so they could make faces at the cars behind them. Daniel had the worst face. He pushed his nose up with his thumb so that his nostrils were huge.

"Yuck!" Colleen closed her eyes.

Once they knew that made her squeamish, they started making some really revolting faces, until their father saw them from the rear-view mirror. "Boys! Knock it off."

They were allowed to go to the corner store and buy a pop, a chocolate bar, and a bag of chips, as well as one comic book. That would keep them occupied while the adults went to see Grampy. Frankie and Colleen got Archie comics and the boys got Superman.

They all piled out of the car and John and Daniel were put in charge of the kids. Frankie said she didn't need looking after. The adults had been gone for what seemed like forever when suddenly the curtains moved on the second-floor window and there was Grampy, wearing his bathrobe. He waved at them and someone opened the window for him. They heard a faint, "Hello!"

They yelled, "Hi, Grampy!" and waved like mad. He waved back.

Colleen missed him. For the second time in as many days, she cried.

"What's the matter with you?" George asked.

Frankie put her arm around Colleen's shoulder. "There's nothing wrong with her." She opened the car door and told Colleen to get in, then closed it on the boys.

"It's okay."

Colleen wiped her eyes. "They're lucky. They get to see Grampy all the time. It's not fair."

"I know. Remember the night he and Grammie were babysitting and there was a thunder and lightning storm?"

"Yeah, he let us stay up and rocked us in his lap."

"I like these grandparents best," Frankie confessed. "Don't tell Mom."

"I won't."

Frankie told her to read her comic and they ate their snacks. Frankie didn't want all of her chocolate bar so she gave it to Colleen. Sometimes she was really nice.

A few days later, they went out to Round Island for the first time. Straight away, Colleen felt like she was home. She belonged to the big field and the tall trees and the blue water shining in the distance. The sky and the clouds and the wind that bent the daisies and buttercups were all hers.

There were bumblebees and salamanders, toads and chipmunks, rabbits and seagulls. Her father showed her the eagles and the ospreys, the terns and the hawks. On the third night he took her outside to hear the owl hooting from the very top of a gigantic fir tree. It swooped down towards them with its wings spread six feet across.

The next evening a bat got into the cottage and Frankie and Mom screamed blue murder and hid their heads under the covers along with Bear. Colleen and Dad were the only ones brave enough to shoo it out with a broom, and poor Frankie almost fainted the night after that when a flying squirrel looked through the cottage window with its huge brown eyes.

"That's it!" she screamed. "This place is terrible! There's nothing but mosquitoes, blackflies, horseflies, houseflies, and every other fly in the world!"

"But there's also butterflies and fireflies," Colleen argued.

"And I think I just saw a mouse! Weren't these cats supposed to catch them?"

"That was the idea," Dad said. "Looks like they've been city cats too long."

Charlotte and Tigger both purr-meowed from up in the rafters. They were having too much fun inside.

The beach was another source of delight for Colleen. Finding crabs and starfish and sand dollars occupied her for hours. She'd wander to the rocky part of the beach when the tide was low and pick up snails, hermit crabs, and minnows to put in her bucket. She even liked the jellyfish, but didn't touch them.

Sitting on the beach in a damp bathing suit, with sand and salt drying on her body in the hot sun, she'd stay perfectly still, holding the hermit crab under the water to see if it would come out of its shell. Once one came out so far it started to crawl up her arm, but it disappeared in a flash when Colleen moved.

After they'd been at the cottage for a couple of weeks, her dad took her snorkelling. He taught her how to spit in her mask so it wouldn't fog up. He pointed to a flat fish hiding in the sand and she dove to see it better, only to get water up her nose and have her mask fill up. She spent a lot of energy trying to get her equipment to work, but when Dad chased her through the waves with his flippers on, it was all worth it. She started snorkelling as much as she could after that.

She would yell from the water at Frankie and Mom, tanning in the sun.

"Mommy! Watch me! Mom! Watch me!"

"I'm watching!" she'd yell back.

Colleen would do a somersault in the water and come up brushing her wet hair from her face. "Did you see it?"

"Great!"

"Come in the water, Frankie!"

"That's okay. I will another time."

But she never did.

The really fun days were when Aunt Annie and Uncle Henry brought the boys out for the day. The boys knew the summer kids in Round Island and ran with them as a pack. As long as her cousins were there, Colleen would play with the summer kids, but on her own, she was too shy.

On rainy weekends, they'd play cards and Monopoly and make fudge. The only problem Colleen had was trying to sneak more than her share of the fudge, but she was pretty clever in that regard, thanks to all the practice she'd had. She could open anything without anyone hearing, or she knew how to cough at the right moment to cover the sound of cellophane. Only occasionally did she get sloppy and take too much.

"Who ate the brownies?" her mother asked once. "I was saving them for supper."

"Not me," Colleen said.

"Not me," Frankie said.

"Don't look at me," Dad said. "Perhaps the boys had some this afternoon before they left."

The best time was when Grammie came out for supper too, with Aunt Annie, Uncle Henry, and the boys. After dark, Dad and Uncle Henry made a bonfire on the beach, where a trillion stars hung above them in the black night. When the waves rolled in, Colleen saw the white foam approach and then recede back to the inky bay.

Dad began to tell them ghost stories. Colleen and Frankie shivered under the same blanket. The boys poked at the fire with sticks and tried to burn their marshmallows while they listened. Mom sipped her wine and Aunt Annie's cigarette glowed as they giggled together in the firelight. Grammie was the only one in a folding chair, bundled up in a blanket. The rosy fire made her face look young.

"They say," Dad said, "that the old man woke up out of a sound sleep. He sat up in bed. "Who's there?" It felt like someone was in the house but he lived alone. And then a key on the downstairs piano began to play. The same key over and over. 'What do you want?' the old man cried. The piano key got louder and louder. It sounded like it was coming up the stairs. Now it was outside his room…a deafening sound pulsing…"

George stood straight up and pointed into the night. "There it is!"

Coming down the beach was a gauzy apparition that shone brighter and brighter as it approached. It was floating three feet in the air!

Colleen screamed and so did all the other kids. They jumped up and ran around the fire, escaping in different directions into the night, scared out of their brains.

Only after they stopped screaming did they realize the adults were killing themselves laughing. Uncle Henry approached the fire holding a balloon draped in a sheet, a flashlight shining behind it.

❊ ❊ ❊

Lila sometimes heard children's voices on the wind from across the woods, and she would wonder if they were David's children, but every time it crossed her mind, she busied herself with her chores and helped Ewan with the farm.

One day in late August Ewan went to town to stock up on feed and other necessities, and Lila almost went with him, but she had three loads of wash to finish, so she begged off. Hanging clothes was a pleasure on a hot, dry day, the kind of day when the first pillowcase she hung out would be dry by the time she got to the end of the line. On days like this, she put out her tablecloths and napkins to let the sun fade the brown spots.

The dogs barking alerted her to a visitor, a visitor who shouted, "Go! Go!" Lila left the line and hurried through the trees. A little girl held a small dog out of reach of her two rascals, who were happy to greet the new dog despite his refusal to return the sentiment.

"Fred! Willy! Stop it at once."

The labs stood still as they wagged their tails and panted with their pink tongues hanging out and big smiles on their faces.

"It's all right," Lila said. "They won't hurt you."

"My dog was frightened, I wasn't. He's a city dog. He doesn't know any better."

Lila reached over and patted the dog's head. "What's his name?"

"Bear. He's not Papa Bear or Mama Bear. He's Baby Bear."

"I can see that. You must be David's youngest girl, Colleen."

The girl's eyes got big. "How did you know?"

"I grew up with your dad. Your Aunt Annie and I are best friends."

"How come you haven't come over, then? She's been here every weekend."

"I'm busy looking after my animals."

"You have animals? I love animals."

"Why don't you put Bear down and I'll show them to you."

Once Bear was on the ground, he quickly joined the other two dogs in their sniffing ritual. All ill will was forgotten.

As Lila led the very excited Colleen around the stables and barns, she snuck peeks at her, looking for any resemblance. Once she looked up and grinned while holding a chick and for a second Lila thought she saw Caroline, but quickly dismissed the glimpse as wishful thinking.

Colleen was delightful company. She talked the entire time they roamed around the farm. Lila learned that she wasn't as pretty as her sister Frankie and that her mother preferred white wine to red and that her dad seemed really happy to be back in Cape Breton. Colleen talked about Elena who gave her treats and the mean girl next door who called her Fatty Fatty Two by Four.

"You're not fat."

"I'm not?"

"No. You're you."

Colleen seemed content with that.

In the distance Lila heard David and Kay calling for their daughter, and the sound panicked her. "You better go now. Your parents will be worried."

"I have to find Bear." With that Colleen ran off to round up her dog. Lila wasn't sure what to do, but she wanted David to stop calling. She ran towards their voices.

"She's fine! She's here! Colleen's here!"

Kay and David hurried towards her.

Lila hated to see parents as worried as she'd been, no matter who they were. "I'm sorry. It's my fault. I was showing her the animals. I didn't think."

Kay looked furious. "Where is she?"

Lila pointed. "She's getting Bear out of the barn. The dogs frightened him, you see…"

Kay didn't stay to let her finish. She ran over to the barn and disappeared inside it. That left Lila and David standing there alone.

"I didn't mean…"

"I know you didn't," he said. "It's all right."

It had been years, but he still looked like the David Lila had always known. He had a few more laugh lines, slightly deeper shadows under his eyes, but he was still her David. She took a deep breath and raked her fingers through her hair. No doubt she looked a mess, and that bothered her. It was hard to look him in the eyes, so she turned towards the barn. "She's lovely. Colleen, I mean."

"She is."

"You're lucky," Lila said gently.

"Yes."

Kay came out of the barn, clutching Bear under her arm and

pulling Colleen by the hand. "Don't ever do that again. You must always let us know where you're going."

"I had to get Bear," Colleen said.

"I'm sorry she bothered you," Kay said. "It won't happen again."

"She was no bother…"

"Are you coming, David?"

David stood there. Lila knew that look. He was embarrassed.

"It was nice to see you, Lila."

"You too. Goodbye, Colleen."

"Thank you for showing me your animals. Can I come back sometime?"

"Anytime," Lila said, smiling.

"You can't," Kay said. "We're leaving in a couple of days." She walked away, holding onto a struggling dog and a mutinous child.

"When you see your dad, give him my love," Lila said.

"Will do. Take care of yourself."

David gave her a look that went through her body and out the other side. Then he turned around and followed his wife.

Lila went back to the clothesline and folded the dry laundry into her wicker basket. Then she hung the folded dry clothes back on the line before she disappeared into the house.

CHAPTER EIGHTEEN

1967

EXPO 67 WAS A HUGE deal for Montreal—and all of Canada, for that matter. Maritimers in Montreal who usually went home every summer suddenly had an influx of visitors for the first time in years. Relatives they'd never heard of called and asked if there was a spare bed going.

The Macdonald family was no different, but in their case, the family also wanted to be in Montreal because after recovering from TB, Kenzie now had emphysema brought on by years of smoking, and David had him flown up to Montreal to see the best specialist he could find. His mom stayed with them while Kenzie was in the hospital, so she could visit him every day. Annie and her family were coming as soon as the boys finished school. The twins were graduating that year and had their prom and parties to look forward to.

There was also a special someone who was coming to Montreal for the first time—Henry and Annie's two-year-old daughter, Leelee. Her name was officially Lila, but by the time they took her home the boys had changed it to Leelee and she was Leelee forever more. Annie was relieved in a way because it only occurred to her afterwards that it might upset Kay when she heard her name, but as Henry said, she was allowed to name her daughter after her best friend, feelings be damned.

Lila cried buckets when she held her namesake for the first time. Annie and Henry cried too, with joy and with sorrow. Leelee had the sweetest little face, dark hair, and almond shaped eyes—the face of a child with Down syndrome. They weren't sad because of that. They were sad because more than a few people had suggested she go into a home to make their lives easier. Henry had to restrain Annie from killing her hospital roommate, whom Annie overheard telling her husband they were so lucky their baby wasn't retarded.

Leelee's brothers loved her. They took her everywhere—on their backs, on their shoulders, and in their arms. Henry was surprised his daughter learned how to walk since she was always being carried.

Annie would often take Leelee out to visit her Aunt Lila and Uncle Ewan. They'd make a huge fuss over her and then Uncle Ewan would take her out to see the animals, while Annie and Lila sat in their weathered chairs on the lawn to catch up on their news. Lila gave Leelee fifty kisses when they said goodbye to see her through until she came back. Ewan patted her head with his big hand. They always waved goodbye until Annie's car was out of sight.

And now Leelee was coming to Montreal.

Both Colleen and Frankie were excited to see her. It had been a year since they'd last laid eyes on her in Cape Breton, and of course they'd seen pictures in the meantime, but now she'd be able to run around, which was much more fun. Colleen used one of the pictures to put on a poster she made and taped to the house. "Welcome Leelee and Everyone!! Xoxoxox"

Colleen had moved into Frankie's room so Grammie could have her room. The boys would bunk in the family room downstairs, and her aunt and uncle would be in the spare room. Colleen had hoped Leelee could sleep with them, but Mom said she wasn't a doll.

Being in Frankie's room was a real eye-opener for thirteen-year-old Colleen. She hadn't realized how much time her sister spent getting ready in the morning. The first time her alarm went off at six, Colleen threw a pillow over her head. She woke up two hours later and Frankie was still fiddling around with lotions and potions.

"It never occurred to me that you *bought* the face you present to the world. I thought you were a natural beauty."

"Ha, ha. You know, it wouldn't be such a bad idea if you took the time to pluck your eyebrows and cover your pimples."

Colleen had a big stretch before she answered. "Nope. Doesn't matter. No one looks at me anyway. Not with this stunning body."

"I can help you if you like."

"I said no."

Frankie turned around on her stool. "Colleen, your trouble is that you constantly whine about things but never do anything about them.

If you think you're overweight, then stop eating so much and you'll lose it. You're as pretty as I am. I just try harder."

You're as pretty as I am echoed through Colleen's head.

"Do you mean it?"

"Do I mean what?"

"That you'd help me?"

"Sure. We'll start with your eyebrows."

Colleen yelled so loud and made such a fuss every time the tweezers came near her, Frankie gave up. "You're impossible!"

Colleen grabbed her arm. "No, don't go. I'll be good."

Frankie started again and Colleen writhed on the bed howling. Frankie threw the tweezers at her. "Be my guest." Then she picked up her purse and left the room.

Colleen called after her, "Wait a minute! I'll be better this time, I promise!"

Frankie didn't come back.

This world of beauty was a bitch. She went downstairs and raided the fridge when no one was looking.

When Leelee arrived dressed in a sundress and sandals, the first person she ran to was her Grammie, who picked her up and twirled her around. Colleen, her sister, and her parents barely said hello to the rest of the gang, in their rush to hold Leelee first. It was pandemonium for the first five minutes out in the driveway. Even the neighbours peered over to see what was going on.

Colleen fell in love with her all over again. "She never stops smiling!"

Aunt Annie put her arm around her. "She has her moments, but I can tell she loves you."

"I wonder why?"

"Don't be daft!" Aunt Annie said. "Who wouldn't love you?"

The next month was a family reunion like no other. The days they visited Grampy were sad but also nice; everyone shared their memories of him over the dinner table when they got home. The boys remembered when Grampy would take them to Morien to go fishing. He'd tie them to the wharf so they wouldn't fall in. Aunt Annie talked about him making porridge every evening before bed and told the kids about her dad's deer ashtray that she swore came alive at night. Colleen and Frankie told their cousins about the night of the thunderstorm.

"Annie, remember when Dad came to school and we couldn't believe he was missing work?" her father laughed.

"Why did he go to the school?" Mom asked.

Dad hesitated and Aunt Annie jumped in. "The teacher was crazy and I was always in trouble. He set her straight."

On other days they would take the Metro to the Île Ste.-Hélène station and follow the crowds to Île Notre-Dame. Colleen had never seen so many people in her life. Frankie and the twins, and sometimes George, would wander off on their own after they got their instructions about where and when they would rendezvous. They usually headed for La Ronde, the big amusement park on the other side of the man-made island. They never asked Colleen if she wanted to come along, but she didn't want to anyway. She had too much fun with the others. Dad and Uncle Henry would stay behind with Grammie to take her to the hospital. On other days it was Mom and Aunt Annie who stayed behind.

Colleen felt like she was touring the world, going into the US Pavilion shaped like a globe and the USSR Pavilion with its soaring roof, but she also loved the souvenir shops, where she picked up candy, a Mexican sombrero, small woven baskets, and a soft leather coin purse with a fringe. There was even a pavilion that gave out candy while you waited in line. You'd suck on it for awhile and then the taste would change, and then change again.

Colleen wore a bright red raincoat with a blue tote bag over her shoulder to collect her treasures. She thought she was the epitome of style, since the coat hid her stomach.

It seemed to Colleen as if the sun shone every day that summer. It was only after Grampy died that the storms moved in.

Once, just after he died, her mother asked her to take fresh towels to Aunt Annie's room. Colleen was outside the door with her hand ready to knock when she heard her aunt sobbing, "Oh, Daddy. Oh, Daddy."

It was the first time she'd ever heard an adult cry. She backed away and put the towels on the chair in the hallway, before going outside to the garden shed to bawl her eyes out. There was nowhere else to go. Every room she went in had sad, heartsick people in them.

And then she cried when her parents decided it would be better if she and Frankie didn't go to the funeral in Cape Breton. There was no discussion about it. It was decided and everyone left. Frankie went to stay at a friend's house and a friend of their mom's came to stay with Colleen.

The night of the day her grandfather was buried, Colleen couldn't sleep. She went over to the window and looked at the moon and wondered if her family was looking at it too. Perhaps Grampy could see it from the other side now. It was bad enough that she couldn't be with her family in Cape Breton, but to not be with Frankie was terrible. She'd never been so lonely in her life.

When her parents came home, she yelled at them for being horrible. She was so upset that both of them came up to her room and told her they were sorry. That it had been a mistake not to take her or Frankie. Her sister confessed to Colleen later that she didn't have a very good time at her friend's house either and wished Colleen was with her.

That made Colleen feel better, but she wasn't ready to forgive anyone. She went downstairs that night and took a jar of peanut butter and a loaf of bread back to her room. She finished them off before going to sleep.

❖ ❖ ❖

Standing beside his mother and sister in the receiving line of his father's wake was an ordeal for David. Not only because his father was dead, but because every friend and neighbour who shook his hand had a memory or story attached to them. His best friend in elementary school was there. Even the guy who beat him up in the schoolyard came to pay his respects. Everyone said how good it was to see him, how much he was missed.

These were his people. This is where he grew up. Why was he living his life in a city that meant nothing to him? Why was he apart from his sister and his mother? If he'd lived closer, he could've seen his dad more often. Now it was too late. Was he going to go back to Quebec and let his mother miss him and the girls once more?

He shook hands with his father's friends, his second cousins, his third cousins, his fourth cousins, his mother's auxiliary group, every doctor and nurse in town, people he'd never met who said they loved his dad. How he always helped the needy, spent time fixing up back sheds and such for elderly neighbours, or shovelled walks in the winter. Those hands of his, always busy, always black from work.

He wasn't going to break down in front of his mother or Annie. They needed him. He cleared his throat and shook his head a little to gather his wits about him. That's when he saw Lila and Ewan. Kay tensed beside him.

"Stop it," he said under his breath.

It didn't seem like Lila had come so much as Ewan had brought her. He had his arm around her, holding her up as they moved down the line. He'd heard Annie tell Lila on the phone that she didn't have to come, that she and Mom would come out to the farm and they could have their moment there, but she knew people would talk if she didn't attend; the downside of living in a small community.

Lila shook Kay's hand and then David's, but she didn't look at him or say anything. Ewan nodded and said he was sorry for their loss. Lila kissed Henry, but when she got to Annie, they grabbed each other. Mom joined in and they softly cried in each other's arms before they had to part, as there was a still a line-up out the door. Ewan guided Lila to the closed casket, where she paused to lay her hand on the polished wood before they left without a backward glance.

Jesus Christ. This was only the afternoon wake. They still had to live through the evening wake and then the funeral tomorrow.

When they finally closed the door on the last mourner the next afternoon, they all collapsed into the closest chair. The boys went home to relieve Leelee's babysitter. The quiet was a blessing. After talking and shaking hands with every adult for miles, they were worn out. They were too tired to even change their clothes.

"Your father would be pleased," Mom said. "He always told me he wanted a closed coffin so the old biddies in Glace Bay wouldn't have a chance to take a peek at him. I know there were a few who were disappointed."

"I've already told everyone I want a closed coffin," Annie said.

Mom frowned at her. "Don't talk about dying, please. I have enough to contend with at the moment."

"I need a drink," Kay said. "Can I get anyone anything?"

They all declined.

"More for you," David said under his breath as she left the room.

He saw his mother and sister look at him. Henry slapped his knees and rose to his feet. "I'm going home to be with the kids." He went out the front door and shut it behind him.

"Don't look at me like that, Annie," David said defensively. "She drinks all the time. I never see her without a glass in her hand. She's turned into her mother, for Christ's sake."

"We're all upset," Mom said. "Just leave it alone. This is not the time."

"When's a good time, Mom? Frankie is sixteen now. Is that the kind of behaviour I want her emulating? Guzzling wine with her friends?"

"It's not that bad," Annie said.

"How do you know? I live in Quebec. You're not at my house every day, so don't tell me it's not that bad. Colleen found empty wine bottles under the bathroom sink. She's not stupid."

Kay leaned on the living-room door frame, twirling her wineglass. "I turn my back for one minute and you're telling tales. Perhaps they'd like to know why I drink."

David stood up and pointed his finger at his wife. "That's enough! I'm not going to be blamed for something I haven't done. I was with Lila once when we were teenagers. *Once*! And you've fixated on it our entire married life! I even moved away from my home so you would be happy. Well, lady, things are going to change. I don't give a shit anymore. Since you don't believe me anyway, I'm taking my children and I'm moving back home, so I can be near my mother, my sister, my niece, and my nephews. I refuse to hide anymore. Why should I? I don't get credit for good behaviour. You can move in with your family or stay in Montreal and drink yourself into a stupor. I don't care. Your father can stuff his job. I'm going out on my own. I don't need you and I don't need him. If it wasn't for you, I'd have been with my dad all these years."

At this point all three women were standing in front of him in shock. He grabbed his car keys and slammed the door. He jumped into his car and drove as far away from them as possible.

It seemed only minutes later he was parking the car at the bungalow. He knew he stuck out like a sore thumb with his suit on. He avoided the people playing on the beach, edging his way through the trees and followed the path worn smooth by another.

He fell to his knees under the ballerina tree. "Dad. Dad. What am I going to do?"

The branches of the tree hid him from view. He leaned against it and rubbed the earth with his hands. Caroline was buried here somewhere. The only thing that made him feel better was thinking that maybe his dad was with her now. Even if Ewan was Caroline's father, she was Lila's child and David loved and missed her still.

The afternoon sun blazed over the water. He loved to swim on days like this. Instead he was hiding from his family, hiding from himself…lost.

A twig broke behind him and he turned around. There she was.

"I knew you'd come," she said.

He reached out his arms and she dropped to the ground and held him while he grieved. As he cried, he felt all of the barriers he'd built up around him melting away, and by the time his tears had subsided, he felt as close to Lila as he had the last time they'd been together by the ballerina tree.

Eventually she spoke. "I loved your dad."

"He was the best."

"So are you," she said softly.

David shook his head. "I've made a mess of everything. I ruined your life. I've ruined Kay's life. I didn't mean for any of this to happen."

She pressed his fist against her heart. "You didn't ruin my life. You gave me my life. My daughter. What if she'd never been born? What if I'd never met her? I have you to thank."

"Do you think she was mine?"

"My heart says yes. That's all that matters. *I* ruined things, not you. I gave you up. I still can't explain why."

"Ewan's a better man. You were always going to be better off with him."

"Ewan is a good man, but David, I loved you first."

Years of longing exploded then and there. It was as if they were in a breathless race against time. Someone might see, someone might know, but it couldn't be stopped now. They wrestled on the ground, pulling and tugging to get rid of the clothes that kept them apart. They cried out in that shaded spot, whispering against each other's lips, moving together like the tide against the rocks on the shore. The ballerina tree danced above them, the moss gave way below them; the sun warmed their bodies while the wind made them shiver.

David kissed her as if his life depended on it. Now she lay in front of him, for him, giving to him and receiving in return. He had no doubt now. She loved him. She had always loved him.

How do you leave one another when the hunger still burns? They stayed as long as they dared and made plans to meet at the crack of dawn. Lila planned to tell Ewan she needed to rest after such a traumatic day. She often slept upstairs when her mood was low. Ewan would never disturb her and so wouldn't know she was gone so early. David was going to spend the night at the cottage but be at the tree before the sun came up.

He couldn't stop kissing her. She finally had to push him. "Go!"

He weaved his way along the path in a stupor before locking himself in the bungalow. He fell into the nearest bed and sleep rushed up to meet him.

Lila was there when he returned the next morning, the sun still below the horizon. They never said a word to each other. She put her arms around his neck and he picked her up and buried his face in her hair. They collapsed on the ground and spent the entire morning holding each other tight. It was as if he wasn't David and she wasn't Lila. They were strangers, a one-night stand turned on its ear. They had no homes, no families, and no responsibilities. Tomorrow wouldn't come. Nothing would reach out and touch them here. This was their world and no one was allowed in it.

When David came back to his mother's house from the bungalow that afternoon, his mom and Kay were in the back garden and no one else was around. It was a lucky break. He quickly went upstairs and had a shower, then shaved and changed his clothes. He glanced at himself in the mirror and thought he saw his father's face. Out in those woods there were no consequences. Now he was back in the real world and his guts tightened.

When he went back downstairs Kay was alone at the kitchen table looking miserable. The minute she saw him she jumped up and ran over to him.

"You're right! I'm sorry. I've been so stupid, making our lives miserable because of my jealousy when I had nothing to be jealous about. Will you forgive me? I'll stop drinking and we'll move back here and our families will be together. It's what your father would have wanted. I love you, David. I'm never going to make that mistake again. I talked to your mother and sister and they assure me that Lila is happy with Ewan and her life. I see that now. I've been a fool."

She reached up and kissed him, holding him close. Her familiar scent moved him like it always did, but his heart shut down.

A few hours ago he hadn't been a villain. Now he was fucked.

❊ ❊ ❊

Lila watched Ewan sleep. He always worked so hard during the day that when he slept, he never moved. She always thought he had nice lips, not thin lines like some men had, but full, soft lips that touched her with tenderness. She moved over closer to him and kissed his mouth. He didn't respond, just the same even breath in and out. She kissed him again, very quietly, with her lips pressed gently against his, as if testing the waters. How many times could she do this without him waking up?

Only twice more. He stirred and rolled her on her back, his body a familiar weight. Their lovemaking was always quiet and slow; as if he was afraid her heart would race too fast. She tried to speed things along, but he didn't notice. Before he left the bed he stroked her face. "I love you."

"You too."

When he left the bedroom, Lila felt that Ewan had failed her test—her unfair, underhanded test.

She went to the ballerina tree for the next two days, but David didn't show up. She knew he was leaving for Montreal soon, and that made things worse. Finally on the third day, he was there. They ran to each other and held on tight.

"I was afraid you'd gone back without saying goodbye."

"I couldn't get away. I had to help Mom with Dad's estate, such as it is. I'm leaving tomorrow."

Lila let him go and wrung her hands, pacing back and forth. "You never said what we'd do. How do we do this? How can I not see you for years?"

"I'm moving back home."

She stopped in her tracks, eyes wide. "You are?"

Before she said anything else, he took her by the hands. "Kay's agreed to move back here with me. She wants to start over, but I can't think about that. The only thing I want to do is move here to be close to you. That's all I can offer right now. I have to resettle my family before I can make any final decisions. You do understand that, don't you?"

Lila looked away.

"I know this is a terrible dilemma. It's tearing me up inside. My dad's dead, everything is a complete mess."

She placed her cheek against his chest. "Not everything. You'll be here and we'll be able to see each other from time to time. Just knowing that you're on the island and that you love me will keep me going."

Once more the talking stopped as they breathed each other in. They were frantic, knowing it would be awhile until they saw each other again. There was no time for niceties. In a matter of moments, David had his hands in her hair, pulling her down beside him.

He passed her test with flying colours.

❊ ❊ ❊

Colleen had never seen her sister so angry.

"Are you joking?!"

Mom and Dad sat on the sofa together, a united front. Frankie leapt up from the armchair and, for the first time in her life, couldn't contain herself.

"You expect me to move to Cape Breton and leave my school, all my friends, and not to mention my boyfriend—"

"—since when do you have a boyfriend?" Dad asked.

Frankie turned on him. "You don't have a clue about my life. You breeze in, you breeze out. You're only thinking of yourself. What about Mom and the friends she'll leave behind? And what about this house? Our hamsters are buried in the yard! We feel about this place what you feel for Glace Bay. Have you considered that?"

Colleen wanted to speak up and say she was absolutely delighted with the news, but she didn't dare open her mouth.

"I want to move too, Frankie," Mom said. "Don't forget my family is in Nova Scotia too. When you get older you want to be near the people you love."

"That's crap!" Frankie yelled. "You don't love your parents! You love Uncle Louis, but he lives in New York. Should we move there instead?"

Dad stood up. "I think you should calm down."

"Why should I listen to you? You never listen to me! I hate you both!"

Frankie ran out of the room and slammed the front door behind her. They watched as she ran up the street.

Dad took a deep breath. "That went well."

Despite Frankie's objections, the move proceeded with unseemly haste. While everyone else packed up, Frankie lay on her bed and refused to get up. By the third day, Dad got mad and made her take the stuff out of her closet. Colleen offered to help.

"No, thank you. I know you can't wait to get out of here, you little traitor."

Colleen sought refuge in the kitchen with Elena, who spent most of her time snivelling into a tissue as she made Colleen's favourite dishes.

"I wish you could come too, Elena."

"I don't think my kids would be happy if I did that." She placed a plate of warm tea biscuits topped with butter in front of Colleen, along with her juice, before she sat and patted Colleen's arm.

"I need you to promise me something."

"Sure," Colleen said with her mouth full.

"Always be proud of who you are—right this minute. Not someday or one day, but right this minute. You are a wonderful girl just the way you are."

"Thanks, Elena."

Mom's high heels announced her arrival. She had a stack of wrapping paper and an empty box in her hands. "Colleen, we just had lunch not an hour ago. Is this really necessary?"

Colleen felt brave because Elena was there. "Yes, it is necessary. This is the last time I'll taste Elena's baking and it makes me feel better."

"Fine. Just don't complain when you can't get your zipper up. Elena, I'm looking for scissors."

"They're in the cutlery drawer."

"Ah, yes." Mom got the scissors and left the room. Colleen watched Elena's face as her mother disappeared. Wow. Elena didn't like her. That was interesting.

The drive to Cape Breton was a bit of a nightmare. Frankie never opened her mouth or stopped looking out the window. At one stop Dad asked if she'd like an ice cream cone, but Frankie pretended to be asleep. Mom said, "Ignore her."

Waiting in the store for Dad to pay for two large and one small ice cream cone, Colleen saw Frankie watch them from the car. For the first time in her life, Colleen felt sorry for her.

Moving from a large home in Westmount into their grandmother's house was quite an adjustment. Not that they were going to stay there forever. Dad wanted to buy Mom a house she'd be happy with, and it took the rest of the summer to find one. In the end it was three streets away from Henry and Annie.

Everyone was thrilled, especially Grammie, who confessed to Colleen that having her whole family around made missing Grampy bearable. It was also Grammie, with her obsession for feeding people, who noticed that Frankie wasn't eating.

"Should I say something to your mother? I don't want to worry her."

"Frankie's in a snit. She'll be fine."

But she wasn't. When she fainted at the supper table at Aunt Annie's one night, Uncle Henry took her in his office and shut the door. They didn't come out for quite awhile. When she did, Aunt Annie took care of her while Uncle Henry asked to speak to Mom and Dad. Colleen never did find out what he said to them, but whatever it was, it worked.

That night, Colleen peeked down the hall of their new house and saw her parents on Frankie's bed, talking quietly to her. Frankie was crying but calm.

Colleen was glad. It made life so much easier when everyone was happy.

CHAPTER NINETEEN

1970

DAVID RAISED A GLASS ON New Year's Eve to celebrate the new decade. Everyone was gathered at their house for the celebration. Even his in-laws.

"The past ten years have been a difficult time in the world. Three great men assassinated, the Vietnam War, the Manson killings…"

Kay made a face. "Don't bring that up! It's too horrifying."

"Sorry, you're right." He cleared his throat. "For us personally as a family, the death of our patriarch is still difficult. We miss him every day. But there have also been hopeful times, like the thrill of men landing on the moon, and best of all…the birth of Leelee!"

"To Leelee!" everyone cheered. The five-year-old clapped her hands and jumped up and down yelling, "Meemee! Meemee!"

"So raise your glasses and let's hope that the seventies bring us happiness and most of all peace. To peace in our world."

Everyone joined the toast. "To peace in our world."

There was hardly room to breathe in the house. Annie's boys had brought their girlfriends. Technically, fifteen-year-old Robbie didn't have a girlfriend, but the friend he brought just happened to be a girl. His older brothers gave him a hard time, while his girl friend blushed.

"Knock it off, you knuckleheads, or I start telling the girls your dirty secrets!" Annie warned them.

"You wouldn't dare!" Daniel laughed.

Henry shook his head. "They never learn."

Annie jumped up from the coffee table where she'd been perched, cigarette in hand, and pointed at Henry. "Remember the time Daniel said he wanted to be a girl because his pee-pee wasn't as big as John's?"

The hooting that followed was deafening. David needed a breather. He went back into the kitchen with empty glasses. Colleen was by the counter with her back to him. He knew in an instant what she was doing: hovering over the pineapple squares Annie brought. No doubt she had one in her mouth now, which was why she wasn't turning around. He never said anything to her about her weight because he always thought Kay said too much. There was no way of broaching the subject without Colleen flying off the handle. It was a topic that simmered under the surface. Perhaps if he talked to her, he could help.

When he put his hand on her shoulder she jumped and quickly wiped the crumbs from her mouth. "You scared me! I'm cutting these up for Aunt Annie. Do you know where Mom keeps the serving trays?"

"No."

"She doesn't even know where she puts them."

"Are you okay, Princess?"

Colleen averted his eyes. "What do you mean?"

"You look unhappy most of the time. You can always talk to me."

Colleen laughed. "Are you kidding? You're never here." She turned away from him and busied herself getting a glass of water from the tap.

"That's not true."

Colleen turned off the tap and gave him an incredulous look. "No one is ever here! Frankie's at Dal with all her new best friends and her endless boyfriends who all think she's fabulous, you're always out the door the minute you get home, and Mom's here but she's not because she's too busy lying down or having a headache. Do you have any idea what it's like to live here? I miss the few friends I did have. I haven't made any friends here and I never get invited out. Oh yeah, and I'm fat. Is there anything else you want to talk about?"

David was numb. Was this her life? Why hadn't he noticed?

"Look honey, all teenagers go through difficult times…"

"The only time I'm happy is when I'm out in Round Island but you and Mom are always too busy to go! I don't count! Now I know how Frankie felt when we moved. *Not listened to!*"

She grabbed her coat off the hook and yanked the back door open, leaving it to bang shut.

David tried to gather his wits. He needed to talk to Kay. Did she know this was going on? He turned around and there was his mother-in-law, Virginia, leaning against the dining-room door.

"Your family appears to be going down the toilet."

"What do you know about it? How can you see through that haze of booze?"

"I may be a drinker, pretty boy, but I'm not blind. This is going to blow up in your face, and I'll be here to take Kay home when it does."

"What are you talking about?"

Virginia uncrossed her arms and came towards him. "It takes one to know one, David. I visit—what, three times a year at the most, and I can smell it the minute I walk in the door. I see your guilty looks and I hear your excuses. You're not fooling me."

"Why don't you tell Kay, then, if you're so smart?"

She pointed at him. "Because you forget one thing: even a bad mother will protect her child. I love Kay and there's no way in a million years I'd tell her about you. She doesn't trust me. She'll have to find out for herself."

Kay and Annie walked into the kitchen still laughing. Annie looked at them and scrunched up her face. "Jesus, what have you two been up to? Lighten up! It's 1970! The next ten years will be the best of our lives!"

❊ ❊ ❊

When it all came tumbling down a few months later, it happened so quickly that no one had a chance to stop it. It was almost effortless.

David told Kay he had a meeting in North Sydney. Lila told Ewan she was taking the truck to North Sydney to meet the owner of a craft store who was interested in selling her braided rugs. Kay's friend Linda asked Kay to keep her company while she drove to North Sydney to pick up her sister-in-law's enormous tea urn. She needed it for her daughter's baby shower.

Poor old Linda was oblivious to the couple walking towards the motel room with a key. She was watching the road. Poor old Kay did a double take before she sat back, frozen in her seat. She stayed in the car while Linda ran her errand but had one request when Linda started for home.

"Let's go for a drink."

❋ ❋ ❋

When David got home, Colleen met him at the door with a tear-streaked face.

"She's drunk! She promised me she wouldn't do it again but obviously booze means more to her than I do."

David knew he was caught. He put his hand on Colleen's shoulder. "Your mother and I love you more than life itself. Believe me when I say that this has nothing to do with you. I want you to take the car and go over to Aunt Annie's, please. I need to be alone with your mom."

"Don't you go anywhere!" Kay slurred.

David and Colleen turned around at the sound of her voice.

"You see!" Colleen cried. "I hate her like this! Stop it, Mom!"

"I think you mean stop it, Dad. Stop fucking the crazy lady who lives on a farm."

"Why are you doing this, Mom? Stop swearing. You're hurting me."

Kay emptied her wineglass. "I don't hurt you. That's Daddy's job. He hurts people all the time. He's hurt me for years and what do I do? I believe him when he tells me there's nothing going on. What a dope! What a stupid fool! My husband spends his days in bed with another woman and then comes home for dinner like it never happened. Who *does* that?!" She threw the wineglass at him and narrowly missed hitting Colleen before it broke on the wall behind her.

Colleen looked at him. "That's not true."

He couldn't do it anymore. He couldn't protect her. "It's true."

The look on his daughter's face told him what a bastard he was. Never in a million years would his father have done that to Annie. Colleen took the car keys and walked out the door. He knew she'd be safe with his sister. He turned to look back at Kay.

"I'm sorry. It's my fault. You did nothing wrong, Kay. You fell in love with a guy who doesn't deserve you."

She walked up to him and slapped him across the face. "Do you have any idea what it's like to make love to a man who never stops thinking about another woman? Even when he begs you to believe him and you want to believe him but you know. You *know.* You crawl into bed every night so he can love your body but not you. I'm your whore, David."

"Don't say such awful things. You're not a whore."

She poked him hard in the chest. "I *feel* like one, and that's your fault."

* * *

Colleen had to go somewhere before she went to Aunt Annie's. The roads were slick and she wasn't used to driving at night, especially on such dark roads. She skidded a few times, which gave her a fright, but she didn't slow down. It's not like anyone would notice if she ran into a ditch.

She missed the driveway and had to turn around, which wasn't easy because she couldn't see the edge of the road in her father's car. Luckily another car wasn't coming the other way. She fishtailed into the farmer's driveway and gunned the engine up the hill, nearly smashing into the back of their truck.

Dogs started to bark and she saw a shadow look out the window. Colleen wasn't sure which door to use, but it didn't matter. She wasn't going to knock.

The back door opened just as she got there and a man stood peering out into the night with two border collies at his feet.

"Can I help you? Did your car break down?"

"My car didn't break down. My whole life did."

"Who is it, Ewan?"

Colleen pushed past Ewan and walked into the living room where Aunt Annie's best friend sat with her knitting. A look of fright crossed her face.

"Excuse me," Ewan said. "What are you doing?"

Colleen had a hard time catching her breath. She wanted to yell at this woman, but she kept gulping for air and no sound came. Her heart was beating too fast, so she turned around and tried to run out of the kitchen. Both the farmer and the farmer's wife told her to sit down and breathe slowly. They pulled up a chair and sat her in it. The woman—she couldn't remember her name—poured her a glass of water. She didn't want it. What was she doing here? Where was she? She needed to get home but then she remembered what was going on at home and got too hot. Her fingers clawed at her neck. The woman helped her open her coat and unbutton the top of her blouse.

"You're going to be fine, Colleen. I know it feels like it but you're not going to die. You're not having a heart attack. It's a panic attack and it will subside in a minute."

Colleen didn't want this woman to be nice, but her words helped. She wasn't going to suffocate in a stranger's house after all.

"I need to go," she croaked. Colleen felt tears roll down her face, but it didn't seem like she was crying.

"Is this David and Kay's daughter Colleen?" Ewan asked. "What are you doing driving out here alone at night?"

Colleen looked at the woman. The woman answered.

"She's come to tell you that David and I are having an affair. She's come to tell you that she hates me and she hates her dad. She's come to tell you that her mother is hurting and she's hurting and she wants you to hurt too. Have I got that right, Colleen?"

Colleen nodded.

The man didn't say anything. The only sound was the clock ticking.

"I think this little girl has been through enough tonight," he said. "I'll drive her home in her car and you follow me in the truck."

And that's what happened.

He didn't say anything on the way back, other than to ask if she was cold and would she like him to turn up the heat. She nodded at that. Colleen turned around and looked at the truck's headlights glaring behind them. The man was calm and that made her calm.

She asked to be dropped off at her Aunt Annie's. When they arrived, he took the car keys out of the ignition and gave them to her.

"I'm sorry you've had such a bad day, Colleen. I hope tomorrow is better."

"You've had a bad day too."

He smiled sadly and got out of the car. Then he went to the truck and got into the driver's seat as the woman slid over to the passenger side. Colleen watched their headlights disappear in the dark.

Through the door she saw Aunt Annie sitting at the kitchen table with curlers in her hair, flipping though a magazine. She licked her fingers and then picked up another sugar doughnut. When Colleen opened the door she looked up, startled.

"Hi, honey," she mumbled before she swallowed her mouthful. "I didn't know you were coming. Would you like a doughnut?"

Colleen couldn't hold it in any longer. She covered her face with her mitts and wept. Aunt Annie hurried over and held her in her arms. "There, there, pet. Whatever it is, it's going to be all right."

Colleen shook her head. Nothing was going to be all right ever again.

❊ ❊ ❊

Henry said he'd sit with Colleen while Annie went over to David's. She didn't take the car, choosing instead to walk over and try to let off steam, completely forgetting she had a head full of curlers. She was so angry at David and Lila that she wanted to spit. So she did, right in the street. She didn't realize she was marching up the middle of the road until a car honked at her to get out of the way. She moved aside but gave the driver the finger as he went by.

She barged into the house without knocking and threw her coat on the floor. "Kay! I'm here, Kay!"

On her right was her brother, sitting on the living room sofa, his hands at his sides, looking at nothing. He didn't seem to notice her so she walked across the rug and shoved his shoulder so he'd look at her.

"Hey there! How are ya, you no-good, dirty rat? If you're worried about Colleen, she's bawling her eyes out at my house. Apparently she drove to Lila's, by herself, in the dark, on icy roads, because her father destroyed her family. And good old Ewan…kind, trusting, wonderful man that he is, drove his wife's lover's daughter home because he wanted to know she was safe. I'm wondering if you're picking up on what I'm trying to tell ya here. You, on the one hand, are a selfish bastard, while Lila's husband is a prince. I hope he walks out on her and never comes back. In the meantime, I'm going to take the mother of your children with me so she doesn't have to see your stinkin' face, and I will do everything in my power to get her and Colleen packed up and moved out of Glace Bay before the end of the week. Have fun sitting here by yourself, you goddamn loser."

"Oh, Annie," Kay cried.

Annie hadn't realized her sister-in-law was in the room. She hurried over, picked up her coat off the floor, and put it around Kay's shoulders. "I'm here. You're going to be fine. Where are the car keys?"

Kay was crying too hard to talk, but pointed to David's keys on the side table.

Annie took Kay by the hand. "We're getting the hell out of here."

She slammed the door shut and for good measure, opened it and slammed it again. She bundled Kay into the car and then drove her to her mother's house. When they walked in, Mom was in the living room watching television. She stood up. "What's wrong?"

"Mom, this woman needs looking after. I want you to take her upstairs and get her in the tub, then put her in pyjamas and give her some strong tea and a hearty sandwich. I'm going back to my place to pick up Colleen and we'll do the same thing for her. Once they're taken care of, I'll tell you all about it."

Mom immediately took the sobbing Kay and started to lead her up the stairs.

"That's what I love about you, Mom. You listen the first time."

When Annie got home, Henry was giving Colleen a bowl of cereal, while Robbie, holding a sleepy Leelee, gave her a *what's going on* look. "Do you know you have curlers in your hair?"

Colleen glanced at her with reddened and swollen eyes.

"Finish your cereal, honey, and then you and I are going over to Grammie's house for the night. Your mother is already there having a bath. You'll be feeling better in no time. That's a promise."

"I love you, Aunt Annie."

"Of course you do. I demand it of all my relatives."

In the end, Annie didn't have to tell her mother anything, between Kay's garbled tale of woe and Colleen's tearful description of the night's events. She and Mom finally got Kay and Colleen into Annie's old bedroom, where mother and daughter held onto each other for comfort.

Annie and her mom collapsed onto either end of the sofa and looked at each other.

"What's going to happen?" Mom asked.

"We're going to call Virginia and Louis tomorrow and they'll come and take Kay and Colleen back to Halifax with them for the time being. Frankie's there and they need each other right now. The movers will do the rest."

"They could stay here with me."

"Mom. I know you mean well, but they don't want to be within a hundred miles of David right now."

"Do you think this is the end of their marriage? Those poor girls. I can't imagine anything more horrible than your family breaking up."

"I don't know what's going to happen."

Mom turned her head away and when she did, she absentmindedly rubbed the deer antlers on Dad's ashtray with her hand. "I can't believe I'm saying it, but I'm glad your dad isn't here to see this. It would've broken his heart. I can't understand it. David was brought up better than that. Do you think I did something—"

Annie put her hand out to stop her dead. "Don't even say it. The blame is his and his alone."

"And Lila's, I suppose, but she never was a stable girl."

"We've been giving her the benefit of the doubt her whole life. It's time she grew up. Now let's go to bed before we pass out."

Kay, Colleen, and Mom were still sleeping at five-thirty in the morning, but Annie was wide awake. And she knew that Ewan would be awake too. She called their number and he answered the phone.

"I've been thinking of you all night."

"I knew you'd call, Annie."

"I can't tell you—"

"—don't feel sorry for me. I'm a grown man."

"As well as the nicest man. I wanted to thank you for taking care of my niece. It was beyond the call of duty. You should've called us to come and get her."

"No, I think it helped to sit for a while with someone who understood."

"If you ever need a place to go, Ewan, our door is always open."
"Thank you."
"I've had words with David. I can't face her yet, but I think I need to say something to her over the phone."
"I'll get her."
Annie waited and waited.
Her soft voice was barely audible. "Hello, Annie."
"You've betrayed us, Lila. You know that, don't you?"
"Yes."
"How you could do this to me? Never mind hurting Ewan and Kay and my nieces and Mom. How could you do it to *me*?"
"I wasn't thinking about you."
"Exactly. You're so wrapped up in your own misery you've forgotten how to think about anyone else."
"Annie—"
"I have to go, Lila. I've been up all night dealing with heartbroken people, myself included."
She hung up the phone.

❊ ❊ ❊

If Ewan wanted to make her suffer, he was doing a good job. He didn't scream, or yell, or even talk.

He completely ignored her. And he kept it up. It had been six weeks since that terrible night and he didn't even open his mouth when she was around. He'd talk to his animals, and the neighbours, and the families who came to their petting zoo, but not her. He wasn't cross or impatient; he didn't make faces if she came near him. He slept in their bed beside her as usual, but it was as if she wasn't there.

Of course, she deserved it, and accepted that this was his way of working things out, but as the months went by, the isolation made her crazy. This must have been how everyone else felt when she stopped talking after Cricket's death.

She sent them all letters of apology, even though she was sure Kay and her daughters would tear them up. It was hard to bear the lack of communication from Abigail, but it was Annie's silence that hurt the most, and she was desperate to see Leelee again.

One day she showed up at Henry's office. His mother frowned when she saw her, and Joy *never* frowned.

"Hi, Joy. I wondered if I could see Henry."

"You'll have to see him outside office hours. He's much too busy."

Henry came out and called the name of his next patient before he saw her at the desk.

"I told her, Henry. I said you were much too busy—"

"That's okay, Mom. I'll handle it. Come in, Lila."

There were a few annoyed glances from his patients before she disappeared down the hall with Henry leading the way. He gestured to one of his examining rooms and said, "I'll be with you in a minute," before he entered another one and said, "How are we today, Mr. Cathcart?"

Anyone who didn't know Henry thought he was a hen-pecked husband because Annie had centre stage. But Lila knew that Henry was Annie's rock and that Annie relied on him to pull her back when she spun out of control. He was calm and wise and strong.

Lila needed some of that.

The longer he kept her waiting, the more nervous she became. She didn't want to get into trouble and was afraid of what he might say. This was probably a stupid idea, but she had no one else.

Entering the room with his white coat on and stethoscope around his neck, Henry appeared taller than he really was. He almost frightened her, but when he sat on the stool beside the examining table he smiled. "How are you, Lila?"

Immediately the waterworks started. He reached over and gave her a box of tissues. It all came out in a rush.

"Everyone hates me and I hate myself and no one is speaking to me—not that I blame them—but it's almost October now and Ewan hasn't said two words since this whole thing happened, and I miss Annie and Leelee!"

"You don't miss me?"

She waved her tissue around. "Of course I miss you and the boys when they're home and especially Annie's mom. I'm so ashamed and I know she hates me. She's been like a mother to me and I miss her. I don't know where David is. It's like I'm all alone in the world and I know I did a bad thing but I didn't mean to hurt anyone. It was separate. It was private. It was nobody's business and now everyone and his dog know how horrible I am…"

Henry held his hand up. "Okay. I think I get the picture. First of all, no one hates you. We all love you, as a matter of fact. And we love David. People make mistakes. You made a mistake. You've apologized and done as much as you can."

"But no one is listening! No one is calling!"

Henry looked away as if to gather his thoughts. "I seem to remember someone who didn't talk to us for two years. And we all understood. Lila, you're going to have to be patient and let people come to you when they feel like it. I'm not suggesting that the two situations are even remotely similar; I'm saying that you need to believe that all these people that you miss so much will come back to you. But in their own time."

Lila gave a big sigh and blew her nose. "You're right. I'm selfish…"

"I didn't say that. You're lonely, that's all."

She blubbered once more, "I miss Annie!"

Henry waited for her to calm down. "And Annie misses you."

She grabbed onto that glimmer of hope. "She does?"

"Of course she does."

"Will you tell her I love her and I'm sorry?"

"I'll tell her." He rose off the stool and gave her a hug. It was the first human contact she'd had in four months. She didn't let him go as he patted her back. "I better get out there or there will be a revolt in the waiting room."

"Thank you, Henry."

"Take care of yourself, Lila."

❋ ❋ ❋

Annie washed her face and brushed her teeth, then gave herself a close look in the mirror. Some sprouts of grey hair, a few wrinkles, especially around her mouth, which Henry said was from smoking, and a few small age spots, but all in all she didn't look bad for forty-two. Her skin was still tight and she still had her slim body. As a matter of fact, she sometimes worried about being too bony.

She shut the bathroom light off and sat with her back to Henry on her side of the bed. He was still mired in hospital reports, his reading glasses at the end his nose. Annie gave the bottle on her bedside table a few pumps and began to rub the lotion onto her elbows.

"I'm taking Lee to the hearing clinic tomorrow. There's another test they want to do."

"Okay."

"Next it will be the eye doctor. I practically live in that office."

"Okay."

"I was talking to Mom and David is coming home soon."

"Okay."

David had sold the house in Glace Bay soon after that awful night and given the money to Kay and the girls. Then he'd left the country to do some "soul-searching," as he called it.

"Apparently he's going to live with Mom when he gets home."

"Okay."

Annie turned around. "Are you listening to me?"

"No, I'm reading."

"I don't want to see David when he comes home."

Henry took off his glasses. "Don't be ridiculous. Are you never going over to your mom's house again? It's time to let this go…speaking of which, Lila came to my office today to cry her eyes out and she wanted me to tell you that she loves you and she's sorry."

"I love her too, and she *should* be sorry." Annie paused. "Don't worry. I'll be in touch when I stop this round of medical appointments with baby girl."

"You've been not talking to your brother long enough. I wish I had a brother I could talk to."

"That's over and done with. The reason I don't want to see him, if you want to know the truth, is that I was a little hard on him the night I went over to get Kay."

"Oh, *now* I get it. You didn't just get Kay and leave."

"No."

Henry sighed. "What did you say?"

Annie plumped her pillow before she got into bed and then pulled the covers over her head before she spoke.

"I called him a no-good, dirty rat, a selfish bastard, and a god-damn loser. I also said I didn't want to see his stinkin' face."

"Oh, Annie."

"Well, at least I didn't call him an asshole."

Annie and Leelee stopped into Mom's the following week to get her large cake plate. The twins, who now worked in Halifax, were coming home for their twenty-first birthdays, and Annie and Henry were having a big barbeque in their backyard.

There was an unfamiliar car in the driveway. David was home.

Annie didn't usually get nervous, but once a younger sister, always a younger sister. She wondered what he'd say, so she let Lee in the door first. As usual she ran straight for her grandmother, who bent down to give her kisses. "How's my big girl?"

"I gots a sucker." Lee pulled out the lollipop from her mouth and showed her grandmother her red tongue.

Annie put her purse on the table. "I swear that eye doctor has a deal with the dentist in that building. He's forever giving her candy."

Mom straightened up. "David's home."

"I see that. Where is he?"

"In his room. I'm making him a sandwich."

"Didn't take him long to make himself at home."

"Don't be like that. Go see him; I'll keep Lee with me."

Up the stairs she went, almost reluctantly, because it was going to be awkward and she had too many things to do before the boys arrived. His bedroom door was open and he was lying on the bed reading. She went as far as the door frame.

"Hey, you."

He put down his book and smiled at her. She had to admit, he looked ten times better than the last time she saw him. He looked rested and the constant worried expression on his face was gone.

"Hi, Annie."

"So, where the heck did you go? I could use some of that relaxation."

"To hell and back. Sit down."

She sat on the end of the bed. His big feet were only inches away, which reminded her of the time he'd made her smell his feet as punishment for taking his baseball glove without permission.

"I'm sorry I let you down—let the whole family down. I realize the mistakes I've made and I'll be spending the rest of my life trying to get my daughters to love me again."

"They still love you; they're just really pissed at you. Like I was the night I took Kay back to Mom's."

"Were you there?"

Whew.

"Only for a minute. So Mom says you're going to be staying with her."

"I didn't expect it. I was going to get an apartment in Sydney, but she said she was lonely here and felt safe with me around."

"That's rubbish. She wants someone to feed. Do you have a job?"

"I've been hired as a legal aid attorney."

"Going to help the little guy."

"Going to try."

They looked at each other and Annie knew what he wanted to ask, but he was unsure if he should bring it up.

"No, I haven't seen Lila. Henry did and she was a bit of a mess, saying she missed everyone. I needed time to forget the look on Colleen's face before I talked to her again. I know you didn't want to hurt your kids, but the fact is you did. And Lila did. But life is short and I will no doubt wander out to Round Island at some point and she and I will go for a walk on the beach and pick up where we left off."

"I'm glad. Is she alone?"

"She's married to Ewan. What do *you* think?"

"I think he's a better man than I'll ever be."

"I think you're right. So what are you and Kay going to do?"

"She wants a divorce, so that's that."

"Have you seen the girls?"

He nodded. "I met them at a coffee shop. Frankie was cool and detached as always. I felt about two feet tall when she looked at me. Colleen tried to be cool like her sister but you know Colleen. She got a lot off her chest. It's a good thing we were in public. I'd hate to think what she would've said to me in private."

"God love her." Annie slapped her knees with the palms of her hands. "Okay. So we're good?"

"We're good."

She looked at her watch. "Geez, I gotta go." She stood up and ran down the stairs. "We're having a barbeque for the twins tonight. Come over whenever."

❊ ❊ ❊

Lila finally snapped. It's not like she was an axe murderer. She marched out to the barn at dawn one morning while Ewan was feeding the animals, walked right up to him, and pushed him. He didn't move, of course; he was too big. But that didn't stop her from doing it again and again.

"I'm here, Ewan! I'm here! Don't pretend you can't see me. I want you look at me. Look at me, goddamn it!" She punched his arms and kicked him in the shin.

He looked at her.

"I know what I did was wrong. If I could go back and change it I would. But I can't do that, so I'm begging you to forgive me. I can't take this anymore. I'm here but I'm not here. I feel invisible."

"I know how that feels."

His voice startled her. She couldn't believe it had worked. She grabbed at his sleeves and tore the feed bucket out of his hand. "Hold me and say you'll forgive me. I need you." She tried to snuggle against his chest, but he kept his arms at his sides.

"You always need me, Lila."

"You see? I do! I do!"

"You need me to find dogs and bury dogs and take care of you when I'm grieving for Joe. And worst of all Lila, worst of all, you needed me to find that sweet child and bury her for you. I am haunted every day of my life by the image of Caroline floating in that well. You're not the only one who suffers."

"Oh no, no, no…"

"What did David ever do for you? Was he here after you had the baby and almost died? Did he stick around to help when Caroline was growing up? Did he shovel your driveway or take you to the hospital or fix your roof or dig your potatoes?"

"You're right. But I'm trying to explain. He was my first love. We were kids and we never had a chance to know what that meant."

"Well, did it mean anything? Because it's sure taken you long enough to figure it out."

Lila hesitated and then gave him a look. "Did you know about David and I before Colleen arrived at our door?"

He looked away.

She started to hit him again. "What man lets another man take his wife and does nothing about it?"

"A man who knows that a wild filly comes back to the barn in her own good time."

"Oh my god! How long did you know?"

"It doesn't matter."

"Why didn't you *fight* for me, Ewan? Why didn't you tell him you'd kill him if he touched me? You never get angry. I never know where I stand. I know you love me, but you never show it. You handle me with kid gloves."

Ewan took her by the arms and shook her. "I may not be the most passionate man you'll ever meet, but how dare you say I never show it? What have I been doing my entire life but show you? Every goddamn day. David wasn't here, and yet he's the one you dream of. I hate him for it and I hate you too!"

She was crying so much she could hardly breathe. "I'm sorry. I'm sorry. It was such a stupid thing to do."

"Yes, it was."

Ewan walked away from her and picked up the feed bucket once more. Lila hurried over to him and put her arms around his waist, pressing her cheek into his back. "I need to tell you something. Please listen to me. I love David because he gave me Caroline. I truly believe that. But you were Caroline's dad. That was you. David was never with her, but you were. You're the lucky one. We had three wonderful years with her. And if it wasn't for you we may never have found her. You were the one I needed that day. We buried her together. I wanted no one else there. That's love too. And our life here, this beautiful life is nothing but love. I had a girlhood fantasy about a boy I thought I loved once upon a time. But he was a boy. You were always the man in my life. All this time without you has been hell, absolute hell, and I know now more than ever that you are the only man for me. And I will always be very sorry for taking so long to realize it."

He went very still and then put his big rough hand over hers and pressed it against his heart.

The early sun shone its rays through the open barn door, giving the interior a golden light.

That same sun was high in the sky when they walked back to the house arm in arm, bits of straw still clinging to their hair.

CHAPTER TWENTY

1975

COLLEEN AND FRANKIE LIVED WITH their mother in a luxurious apartment in the South End of Halifax. Their mother and Frankie were thriving. They spent weekends shopping and going for lunch, hosting parties, and hobnobbing with other rich people.

"It's like people with money sniff everyone's ass until they find another rich person they can breed with."

Colleen and her friend Nancy were lazing on her bed in scruffy jeans and t-shirts, their hair long and parted down the middle. Colleen knew her hairstyle drove her mother nuts. That's why she had it.

Nancy chewed the straw as she sipped her soda from a can. "So when did your sister get engaged?"

"A week ago. They've already picked out their china."

"Is he nice?"

Colleen loved to make things sound worse than they were, but she actually liked Edward Roth. "He's okay. He's weird looking in a romantic kind of way. Dark and brooding."

"What does he do?"

"Who knows? Don't most of them just manage their trust funds?"

"You're the only rich person I know, so I couldn't tell you."

"It's all a facade. I live off my grandfather. I don't have a penny to my name."

Colleen had disappointed her dad when she opted not to go to university. Everyone knew that Frankie was never going to go, so Colleen was the last hope. Instead she worked downtown at an old bookshop. It was there she met the few friends she had, all of them eccentric, or hippies, as her mother called them. Colleen said she was about a decade too late. Hippies had lived and loved in the sixties.

The seventies were sort of boring by comparison, unless you went to rock concerts and got high, but no one really famous ever came to Halifax and she wasn't the sort to fly off to attend a concert in Toronto.

Colleen made a point of leaving little bags of marijuana all over the house, hoping her mother would find them and think she led an interesting life, but Mom never seemed to notice. Or when she did she'd say, "Why does that new cook insist on keeping herbal tea around the house?"

Colleen was never cut out to be a drug addict anyway. The only thing she did when she smoked a joint was sit in a dark corner, alternately giggling and shouting, "Who's there?!"

When Nancy left, Colleen got on the phone and called her Aunt Annie.

"Hey babe...what's goin' on?"

"Frankie's getting married."

"I know, she told me."

"Frankie calls you?"

"Don't sound so surprised. You're not the only one who thinks I'm great."

"How's Lee?"

"Getting big. Sweet as always."

"Have you seen Dad?"

"He's working very hard. That's all he does really. I keep telling him to have some fun, but he never listens to me."

There was a knock at her bedroom door. "Who is it?"

"Me."

"Sorry, Aunt Annie, the amazing Frankie wants to talk to me."

"Ciao, babe." Her aunt hung up.

"Come in."

Frankie looked like a slob, her version of a slob anyway. Her jeans were old and she had on a sweater that was slightly too big. Her crowning glory was up in a ponytail. She sprawled on the end of Colleen's bed.

"Mom's got a date tonight."

"Oh, goody. My forty-nine-year-old mother is having more sex than I am."

"I keep telling you I can fix you up, but you're never interested. Are you a lesbian?"

Colleen sat back against her headboard. "Geez, I never thought of that. Maybe I am."

"If you like both sexes your chances of meeting someone doubles."

"You're a genius. I'll get right on that."

Frankie suddenly sat up and looked serious. "I need to talk to you."

Colleen knew what was coming. "You don't want me to be your maid of honour because I'm too big and I'll ruin your wedding pictures."

Frankie gave her a horrified look. "Don't be ridiculous. Of course you're my maid of honour."

Colleen wanted to hug her but Frankie was saying something else.

"What I should do about Dad? Do I let him walk me down the aisle? Do you think that would make Mom mad? I don't want to bring it up with her because I'm afraid of what she might say."

"Do you want him to walk you down the aisle?"

"Yes."

"Then it's simple. It's your day and you can do what you want. Mom got to do what she wanted on her wedding day. I'm sure I'll never have a wedding day."

"You will, don't worry. Thanks for the advice." She got up to leave.

"Where are you going?"

"My power walk."

"Can I come? Hey! Get that incredulous look off your face."

Frankie was getting married next year. Surely to God Colleen would be able to lose ten pounds by then. Wedding pictures lasted forever, and she wanted to look as good as possible.

She'd seen the other bridesmaids.

❖ ❖ ❖

Annie drove out to the farm to pick up Lee, who'd spent the weekend with her Aunt Lila and Uncle Ewan. Both of them assured Annie that Lee was no problem, but Annie knew how tiring it was to be on guard every minute of the day. Lee loved the animals and she'd help Ewan feed them, but he had to watch how much she was giving them and make sure she remembered to lock the gates behind her.

Now that Lee was ten, she wanted to do more things on her own, but that wasn't always possible, which was frustrating for her. Sometimes at night when Annie couldn't sleep she'd worry about Lee's future. She'd turn over and snuggle up to Henry's back, and even in his sleep he'd take her hand and hold it.

Then there were the nights she'd lie awake and think how lonely it must be for David, going home to an empty bed every night and living away from his children. At least he spent time with them now. He'd head to Halifax every month or so and take them to dinner or out to a movie. The girls weren't kids anymore and didn't come to Cape Breton as often, what with jobs and relationships. She and Kay stayed in touch. She'd always liked Kay and was glad she was able to stop drinking. Too bad her mother couldn't quit. The last time Annie saw Virginia she had looked like Cruella de Vil. Louis didn't look so hot either. She was grateful that she and Henry had only as much money as they needed. There was a time when she'd hoped to work after Robbie was old enough, but Lee came along and that ended that.

Annie got a kick out of going to the farm now. She had started to think that Lila's affair was the best thing that could have happened to Ewan and Lila. Before the whole mess, Annie sometimes felt that Lila treated Ewan more like the hired man than her husband, but now she saw how happy they were together. Lila would stroke Ewan's cheek when she'd leave the table to bring dessert, or button his sweater to make sure he wouldn't get cold. It had taken them long enough, but she guessed some people were slow learners.

It was a lovely spring day and as soon as she pulled up in the car, Lee and Ewan saw her and waved. Lee wasted no time running over to her, her thick glasses askew. "Mommy, there's babies!"

Lila came out of the house wiping her hands on a tea towel. "Hi, did you get a little sleep?"

"I stayed in bed the entire weekend. It was bliss. Thank you."

Lee grabbed her hand and made her go over to the first fence. "Two lambs."

Annie smiled at the sight of the dear little creatures, following close behind their mother. "What are their names?"

"Lester and Bobby."

Annie made a face at Ewan and Lila. They shrugged.

"Well, Lester and Bobby are very lucky to have you to watch over them."

Ewan held out his hand. "Come on, Lee. We still have to clean out the horse stall." Off they went while Annie and Lila headed to their chairs that sank into the ground more and more with every passing year.

"Is it just me, or is it harder to get in and out of these babies?"

"We're old, Annie."

The two lifelong friends sat back and enjoyed the sunshine. When Annie glanced over at Lila it was as if they were back on those hot lazy afternoons when the only thing they wanted to do was sit and drink lemonade. Aunt Eunie always made the best lemonade.

"You and I should take a trip somewhere," Annie said.

Lila turned her head to look at her. "Where to?"

"I don't know. Norway? Chile? I should go to Scotland and visit the Isle of North Uist. That's where our people are from."

"I wish I knew where my people came from." After a moment she reached out her hand. "Of course you and your family are my people now."

Annie took her hand and squeezed it. "Well, we had to do something. Can you imagine Bertha Butts being your people?!"

Lila laughed. "I wonder what happened to her."

"She went to that great settee in the sky."

"You're terrible."

"Oh, my god! I can't believe I didn't tell you first thing...John's wife is having a baby! I'm going to be a grandmother."

"What's wonderful! Are you really old enough to be a grandmother? Where did the years go?"

"I suspect Daniel's wife will be pregnant soon if she isn't already. Those boys always were competitive."

"Henry must be so excited."

"Not as excited as his mother!"

"She doesn't still work for him, surely. She must be almost eighty."

"I've told you this three times now. Her job ended when she called up that nun and told her she was pregnant."

Lila playfully slapped Annie on the arm. "That's right! Oh my, I'm getting like Aunt Eunie."

They stayed out and talked long into the afternoon.

❋ ❋ ❋

David couldn't keep saying no, so on the Victoria Day weekend, when the boys and their families were home, he went along with Annie and Henry to a family picnic at their friend's cottage in Mira. It belonged to a doctor, a specialist who had a lot more money and toys than Henry did. Apparently there were speedboats and sailboats, canoes and tubes—everything to keep people amused all day.

David tended to steer clear of parties where people gathered with their children and grandchildren. It made him uncomfortable. His loved ones lived away and he was the reason. Not that he thought about it all the time. Lots of people got divorced and had their kids living elsewhere.

If anyone were to ask him, he'd say he was happy. He enjoyed his job and even enjoyed living with his mother. She never hovered. Now that Aunt Muriel's husband was gone, the two of them were quite the pair, visiting family in Hingham, near Boston, and the Miramichi in New Brunswick as well as friends in Montreal.

He even had a love life, but he kept that private because he knew he'd never marry again, so there was no sense in introducing anyone to the family. He never went out with a woman for long. His lady friends would start to hint about settling down and when he didn't budge, they'd give up. Then it was on to the next one.

The picnic turned out to be a nicer time than he'd anticipated. David enjoyed his nephews very much now that they were young men with wives and girlfriends of their own. He never missed having a son; he always felt he had four already. To sit and laugh together while having a beer and a hamburger was a real treat and he was glad he'd made the effort to come.

Lee also sought him out for their usual reading time. She crawled up onto his lap like always, and they sat together reading her favourite Roald Dahl books. She always had them handy in the book bag she carried. Then they'd colour together. It was fun when she was little, but now that she was a hefty weight, it had become a little more uncomfortable.

His niece eventually wandered off to get a drink. He closed his eyes and put his hands behind his head, as he settled into his deck chair. The heat of the spring sun felt good against his skin. The laughter, banging of the cottage door, and sounds of the motorboats slowly drifted into the background. He was back on the beach in Round Island, laying on the hot spot, as the kids called it—the white sand that absorbed all the heat from the sun. Sometimes it was so hot you couldn't walk on it and were forced to run across it on your heels shouting, "Ow, ow, ow."

He was just drifting off when Annie came up behind him and put her cold hands over his eyes. "Guess who!"

David batted her hands away. "You miserable creep. I was enjoying my nap."

Annie perched herself on the arm of his chair. "You're fifty, not a hundred. You can nap when you're dead."

"You'll be dead in a minute if you don't get lost."

"Come in the canoe with me."

"No, I'm fine here."

"It's got a motor on it if we get lazy. Come on, you never do anything with me."

"Jesus, you sound like you're seven."

Annie got up. "All right, I'll go by myself."

He watched her go down to the dock and then onto the sand where the canoe was beached. She tried to push it into the water, but it wouldn't move.

David stood up and shouted, "For God's sake, let me do that." He got to the water's edge, where she stood there grinning.

"You knew I'd come down here, didn't you?" He pushed the boat into the water.

"I know you better than you know yourself."

"Where are the life jackets?"

"They're back at the cottage. Let's just jump in and go. We'll be back in five minutes."

"I don't like going…"

Annie jumped in the canoe. "Where's your sense of adventure?"

The damn canoe floated away faster than either of them anticipated, so David ran up to it and almost tipped it trying to get in so she wouldn't be on her own.

"Yahoo!" She grabbed the oar and started paddling before he was even settled in his seat.

"Damn it, Annie. Just a minute."

"You're such a grump."

Finally the canoe righted itself and David grabbed the other oar. He would've preferred to be in the back to steer the canoe, but it was too late now. "All right, I'll start on my right; you start on your left."

"Aye, aye, captain," she laughed behind him.

The water was calm when they started, but got a little choppy as they paddled out of sight of the cottage.

"I don't want to go too far," he said.

"Honest to God, you're like an old woman. When did you turn into Mom?"

"Shut it, squirt."

They paddled along the shore and listened to the birds.

"I love it when the leaves are new," she said. "The green is so delicious."

The sun went behind the clouds and the temperature dropped considerably.

"Brr...I should've brought a sweater and put something on over these shorts."

David wasn't listening. He was worried that the prevailing winds were taking them farther and farther from shore. If he'd been with Henry or the boys they could've powered their way home, but Annie didn't have as much strength.

"Annie, I think we should head back," he shouted behind him.

"That's what I was thinking."

They turned around and paddled quickly, but now the current was against them and made it much tougher.

"I don't think we're making any headway," she said.

"It would be a good idea to start that engine behind you."

"How do I do that?"

Shit. If only he'd been in the back. He tried to explain it and she followed his instructions, but every time she pulled the cord, the engine stalled.

"I can't do it! Change seats." Her teeth were chattering and she was covered in goose bumps.

"That's a bad idea. We don't want to tip this thing over while we're trying to switch spots." He took off his shirt and threw it at her. "Put that on. I'm sure someone will notice we're missing and get in the speedboat and we'll be home before you know it."

She put on the shirt. "Pratfall's gonna kill me."

"Does the shirt help?"

She nodded.

"Let's keep paddling to keep warm."

She nodded again.

David had never paddled so hard in his life, or for so long. He kept looking back at Annie and thinking how thin she was. Why hadn't he noticed that before? Annie wasn't fragile, she was larger than life, but now her scrawny arms stuck out of his shirtsleeves like two toothpicks.

"I think we're making progress," she said slowly.

David knew they weren't. And he didn't like the sound of Annie's voice. The waves got choppier and the wind picked up. The canoe was now moving from side to side. They mustn't tip over. The water in May was still ice-cold. All these thoughts were going round and round in his head. He was so angry with her.

"You should've listened to me!"

"Sorry, Davy."

He didn't know what to do. If he could get the engine going they'd be all right. "Okay, now do what I tell you. You're going to have to lie down if you can, so we can keep it steady."

She wasn't listening.

"Annie!"

He startled her, and that sudden small movement caused her to lean too far. The water poured into the left side of the canoe and in only a few seconds they were swamped, the canoe now bobbing upside down in the ocean.

The shock of cold was the first thing that hit him. He thought he saw Annie's legs kicking before they disappeared behind the other side of the canoe. He treaded water, waves splashing in his face with the overturned hull like a whale between them.

"Annie! Annie!"

He heard a small voice. "I'm here!"

David swam over to her side of the boat. She was clinging to the side but kept slipping. "Davy, help me!"

He grabbed her around the waist and on pure adrenalin alone heaved her up as far as he could so she could hang on with most of her body out of the water.

"The engine is weighing down the boat.. I'm going to try and take it off."

"No! Don't leave me!"

"It's okay. You'll be all right. You sing 'Onward Christian Soldiers' until I come back up."

He dove back under the canoe hoping there'd be an air pocket, but as he suspected the engine kept that from happening. David popped up to the surface again and heard Annie singing before he took another deep breath and went down again, trying to feel where the screws were in the murky water. He twisted with all his might but they wouldn't budge.

Back up to the surface and this time Annie's voice was slurred, "Don't leave me here alone. Stay with me."

"I'll go to the other side and grab your hands around the hull. It will make it easier for us to hold on."

He swam under the canoe and when he got to the other side, he pulled himself up by the fingernails to reach Annie's hands on the first go. He took one hand and then the other and pulled her up so that they could see each other.

The waves and the wind made it difficult to hear. "We're going to be okay. Someone will be along shortly to take us back. You make sure you hang onto me until they get here."

"I'm scared, Davy."

"There's no need to be. I've got you!"

David didn't know how long they floated there, but every time he looked at her the mottled blue around her mouth had spread wider.

Whenever it seemed that her head lolled to one side, he'd shout at her to wake up.

"Don't do this to me, Annie! Don't leave me! Open your eyes!" He'd try and shake her hands but he was too frozen to move. "We're going to be all right! I'm here with you."

A wave hit him in the face and he coughed up water. "Don't die! Don't die, Annie! Can you hear me?"

In the distance was the buzz of a motorboat. He looked up and saw it rushing towards them.

"Annie! They're here! They're here! You're safe now!"

Annie's head drooped so far back he knew she was gone.

He screamed into the wind.

❊ ❊ ❊

The shock was so severe that it took four days to organize Annie's funeral. No one was capable of doing anything. The entire family didn't eat, they didn't sleep, and they couldn't talk without bawling their eyes out. It seemed the whole of Glace Bay was at Henry's and Abigail's doors with trays of food that went unwrapped, flowers that went unseen, and cards that went unread.

Kay brought the girls home by airplane. The three of them collapsed into David's arms and they wept as a family.

"It was my fault," David cried. "I knew better. I should've protected her."

Kay tried to look into his face, as he rocked on the chair with his head in his hands. "It wasn't your fault. You held on to her. You kept her from drowning. She's not on the bottom of the ocean somewhere."

David stood up and began to pace. "I should never have let her get in that damned canoe in the first place. I could've picked her up and dragged her out. Why didn't I?"

Round and round and round he went with guilt and anger and sorrow. He held on to his girls and wept on their young shoulders.

Annie's mother stayed in her room with her Bible. She didn't want to see or be with anyone.

Henry was so broken he couldn't stand up straight. He was only fifty-six and was hunched over like a very old man. The twins, with the help of their wives, were the ones who helped their younger brothers and made sure that Lee was taken care of. Henry couldn't bear it when she asked, "Where's Mommy?" over and over again.

Henry had to deal with the funeral home director who asked if he wanted a top-of-the-line casket for his dear departed wife.

"No. A pine box will do."

When the director glanced up at him, Henry shrugged. "That's what she said. And she wants it nailed shut."

"Well, then…"

"…what she really said was that she didn't want to lie in some stupid casket that reminded her of her grandmother's parlour. She hated to dust that parlour."

"Right. Now for the wake…"

"No wake."

"No wake?"

"That's what she said."

"Are you having a church service?"

"Yes. She said her mother would kill her if she didn't."

❋ ❋ ❋

When Annie's son John called Lila and told her that Annie had died of hypothermia she went out to their chairs and sat all afternoon staring at nothing. It was only at sunset, when she noticed Ewan crying as he tried to feed his critters, that she sprang out of the chair and ran to him, holding him tight. "It's okay, Ewan, I'm here."

The funeral was at the Baptist church in Glace Bay and she would be buried beside her dad at the Forest Haven cemetery on Grand Lake Road.

The church was packed and stifling hot and the minute Annie's draped pine box was brought into the church, everyone cried. There was a small bouquet of mayflowers placed on top. Her sons had taken Leelee out to Round Island that morning and picked them. Leelee said they smelled best of all.

The service seemed endless, the minister droning on, liking the sound of his own voice. He read scripture after scripture that meant nothing to any of them on this day. That used to bug the hell out of

Annie. As Lila sat beside Ewan she remembered the first day she met Annie, and how glad she was that Annie held her hand in church. She also remembered her fidgeting and rolling her eyes for the minister to get on with it. Lila felt Annie's warm hand in hers and a voice in her head said, "Shut him up, for God's sake."

She stood up. Ewan took her hand. "Do you want to go outside?"

"No."

She pushed passed everyone in her row and walked up to the front of the church. Leelee was in Henry's lap and he had his arm around his tiny mother. All the boys looked at her with such misery. Then she saw David, who looked twenty years older, holding up his mother, with Kay and girls beside them. All of Annie's loved ones. They needed to get out of here.

She walked right up to the pulpit and the minister had no choice but to move aside, whispering that perhaps she could save this for later. Lila ignored him.

"Annie would always get mad at me because I was such a scared little thing growing up. She'd kick me in the behind every so often and say, 'You've got to live, Lila.'

"Annie didn't travel the world or climb mountains or do great deeds, but she *lived* every day of her life. She got more pleasure out of a plate of cornbread than anyone I know. If she beat you at Rummoli, she'd cackle while she dragged all the pennies out of the kitty. She thought heaven was going to a movie with Henry.

"And she loved as hard as she lived. *She loved us.* And I know one thing for sure. If we don't pick ourselves up and dust ourselves off and live our lives, she'll be very cross. Yes, we'll miss her desperately and yes, we'll be sad for a long time, but I want her legacy to be that we walk out of this church today and do her proud."

Lila looked down. Annie's family was smiling. Time to get out of here. She left the altar and walked straight down the church aisle and out the door.

❊ ❊ ❊

When Annie's first granddaughter was born she was christened Annie Lila Pratt.

CHAPTER TWENTY-ONE

1976

THE ENTIRE FIRST HALF OF 1976 was taken up with Frankie's June 26 wedding. Nothing happened in the universe that wasn't related to bridal dresses, hairstyles, flower arrangements, and guest lists. That's the way it seemed to Colleen, anyway.

But to tell the truth, she was kind of glad to be distracted and living in Halifax. She knew how much suffering was still going on in Cape Breton, where a year later, everyone was still trying to deal with their huge loss. It was harder for the relatives who had to live where Aunt Annie lived. The presence of her absence was everywhere.

Lila and Ewan were stepping in to take care of Lee whenever Henry was having a bad week, which was apparently often. Abigail was being remarkably stoic, relying on her faith in God to see her through. Aunt Muriel spent a lot of time with her, as she knew firsthand what it was like to lose a beloved daughter in a horrible accident. Her dad told her that for the first time Grammie understood what her mother-in-law went through when she lost two sons in the same year during the Great War.

Colleen had managed to lose thirty pounds by the time the wedding rolled around. Her mother was thrilled.

"Oh, Colleen, you look wonderful!"

Colleen wasn't used to this sort of attention from her mother. It felt nice.

"But if you could only lose twenty more you'd be perfect!"

"Why don't you lop off my head, then? How's that for being perfect?" Colleen headed up the stairs but then turned around. "Just once, Mother, I'd love it if you ended your sentences before your inevitable big *but!*"

It was Frankie who talked her into cutting her hair to her shoulders. Colleen had to admit it looked nice. When she walked down the street now she occasionally saw boys look at her, which was refreshing. Then came the day when she ran into an old friend from the bookstore. He seemed shocked when he saw her and asked her out on a date. They went out for a couple of weeks and he was constantly asking her to *do it* with him. How long did one wait? She didn't want to ask Frankie because having to ask made her even more pathetic. So one night she did it and Colleen never saw him again, a sad fact she was taking to her grave.

There was another distraction that Frankie refused to talk about because she was too focused on her future life with Edward. That or if she should cover her face with a veil.

The distraction was their mother's new boyfriend, Derek.

He wore a thick gold chain around his neck. That was all Colleen needed to know. Derek was *so* not her father, and she hated the way her mother giggled around him. She was fifty, for goodness' sake.

Derek tried to be her friend, like she was a ten-year-old or something, always asking if she'd like to go to dinner with them or the movies. She'd grimace and her mother would distract him long enough to give her the evil eye and tap her on the head with her clutch.

He was harmless, she supposed, but like every child whose parents split up, she'd always had a tiny glimmer of hope that her mom and dad would get back together. At least they were friendly now. Aunt Annie's death had made everything else seem not so terrible. Colleen even changed her mind about Lila. Just the way she helped her that winter night by saying what she wasn't able to say and then the way she spoke in the church at the funeral. Colleen had had chills when that happened. It was as if Aunt Annie's words were coming out of Lila's mouth. And it had had a profound effect on her father. He didn't seem quite so helpless after that.

❖ ❖ ❖

The whole family drove down for the wedding, and once again a suite of rooms were at their disposal. Kay told David to stop making a fuss about the expense. She was paying for it…theoretically. It was déjà vu when he insisted he pay for the rehearsal dinner.

He sat back at the table and looked at all the faces that had also been there on the night of his rehearsal dinner. Louis Sr. was hunched over, skin sagging, his nose more bulbous than ever, but you could still hear his voice booming throughout the restaurant. When David looked at Virginia it wasn't with hate but with pity. She was a shell of her former self, a woman in her seventies who still applied makeup like a teenager.

Henry and his mother tried to look happy, but were watered-down versions of themselves, missing the loves of their life on this night. David and Annie's grandmother Cynthia was also missing, having died in her sleep shortly after Frankie was born.

David wasn't sure how he was going to get through the wedding, thinking of Annie, big as a cow, coming up the aisle and sticking out her tongue at him before she moved off to the side. He prayed to Annie and asked that she help him the next day, to be by his side.

And there was Kay, lovely as always, excited about tomorrow, chatting and laughing with her new beau. David didn't think much of him, but he doted on Kay and David knew she needed that. His guilt about Kay was like a sore tooth, always there in the background. Kay must have sensed him watching her, because she looked up and held his gaze. Her face softened and she gave him a genuine smile, then she pointed at the girls and put her hand over her heart, as if to say "We did a good job."

Frankie was exquisite, the picture of her mother, sitting with her soon-to-be husband. David liked Edward. He was intelligent and sincere. He'd take care of her.

The biggest surprise was Colleen with her new figure. She still had the sweetest face. Annie had always said that Colleen was the prettier of the two girls. He agreed. She had more bubbling under the surface, but her anxiety and moodiness often got the better of her. She was her own worst enemy.

In the morning, he put on his tuxedo and heard Annie in his head saying he looked like a penguin, which made him smile. Then he took his small gift and went down the hall to knock on Frankie's door and asked if he could come in. A bunch of women shouted, "Not yet!"

So he waited patiently, rubbing at his tight collar a few times. Then he looked at his watch and thought they'd better get a move on. He was about to knock again when the door opened. Kay and Colleen and the bridesmaids were in their yellow and peach finery.

"You ladies look lovely."

They smiled and looked back into the room. There was Frankie, standing in her wedding gown, looking excited and happy. Her dress was soft and flowing, with long, draping sleeves; her hair was up and her veil reached the floor.

Like all dads he had a quick movie in his head of how excited they'd been when she was born and all the birthdays and milestones after that. He felt his eyes well up with tears and knew if he started crying, he'd never stop, so he cleared his throat. "You're the most beautiful bride I've ever seen, Frankie…apart from your mother."

He looked at Kay and she touched a tissue to the corner of her eyes.

"Thanks, Dad."

He went forward and gave her a kiss, careful not to muss her hair. "I have something for you."

"Oh, Dad, you didn't—"

"—it's not expensive and you don't have to wear it today, but it means a great deal to me."

He passed over the small box and she opened it. Inside was a Clan Macdonald of Clanranald crest kilt pin.

Frankie picked it up. "Thank you."

"You can wear it as a brooch. The motto describes what I feel about you. *My hope is constant in thee.* As my father said to me on my wedding day, I want you to remember where you come from and who you belong to—a long line of Macdonalds who were good, God-fearing, hard-working people, who fought for their country and looked after their families. Be as proud of them as we are of you."

Frankie gave him a real hug, which meant a lot. And then she surprised him when she opened the clasp and pinned it to her wedding dress.

Kay pointed at it. "Perhaps you should put in on your waistband, so it doesn't spoil—"

Frankie gave her mother a look. "I want it where I can see it."

He looked over at Colleen, who was a mess. Her mascara was running as she blew her nose. "Gee whiz, Dad, you could've warned me you were going to say all that."

❀ ❀ ❀

Champagne flowed, the meal was spectacular, and the band was spot on. Everyone was on the dance floor and Colleen was feeling no pain. As a matter of fact, she was having a great time. All the groomsmen danced with her at one point or another. Her new brother-in-law dragged her out of her seat and they cut a rug to the Bee Gees song "You Should Be Dancing," and Elton John's hit, "Don't Go Breaking My Heart."

Colleen came back from one of her many trips to the ladies room and found a guy sitting in her chair. He looked up at her. "Oh, is this your chair?"

"Yes. I carry it everywhere."

He laughed and laughed and he wasn't half-bad looking, either, although at this point even the hotel doorman looked good to her. He stood up and put out his hand.

"I'm Arthur Brown. My friends call me Artie, and since you are definitely going to be a friend of mine, I hope that's what you'll call me."

"Arty the Smarty! I always wanted to meet you!"

"Who's Arty the Smarty?"

"Don't tell me you didn't read the book? It's a classic by Faith McNulty. About a little fish who wants to make a big splash. I need to get another glass of champagne, I'm parched."

"No need. I brought my own bottle." He produced an open bottle of bubbly and two glasses.

"What did you do? Knock the barman out?"

"Let's just say I have my methods."

They drank the bottle and hit the dance floor. He was taller than she was and when they danced to the slow songs, he held her tightly. Almost too tightly, but it was nice to feel his warmth across her breasts. He kissed her neck and nibbled at her ears before he covered her mouth as they swayed to the music.

"You're staying here tonight, right?" he whispered.

"How did you know?"

"You're the bride's sister, aren't you? Louis Hanover's granddaughter?"

"You should be a spy."

"I do my homework when I see a beautiful woman, and you are one beautiful woman. Let's go upstairs and make our own music."

Colleen felt like she was in the movies, wearing a long gown, dancing with a nice-looking guy, about to go up to a hotel room. She was just as sophisticated as her sister. So there.

"Come on, let's get dirty." He kissed her again.

"I don't like dirt." This was her attempt at being coy.

"Then we can have a shower together and I'll make sure you're very, very clean."

She didn't remember how they got up to her room and she didn't remember much about what they did in the room either, other than he liked to say "Oh yeah" a lot.

When she opened her eyes the next morning, they felt like two pissholes in the snow. It was hard to believe her maternal grandparents drank booze night after night. What were they made of? Cast iron?

She tried to move her head. That didn't go very well, so she stayed still and watched the ceiling fan go round and round, but that was also a stupid move. She whispered "Help!" but no one came.

She glanced to the right without moving her head to see what time it was and there was a note leaning against the clock. She walked her fingers over the sheet slowly to see if that would have any repercussions. As long as she did it slowly she was all right. After repeating the move, she brought the note close to her face.

"Good morning, beautiful. I LOVED last night and I want to do it again tonight. I'll pick you up and we can go to dinner first. Don't worry, I know where you live. Artie."

Uh…that was nice, but she didn't think she'd be able to walk until next week. The trouble was she had no way of getting a hold of him.

Her mother knocked on the door and came in. Colleen crumpled the note in her hand.

"What in the name of God happened in here?" She inspected the room as if she were the maid, heading for the bathroom next. "What's your dress doing in the bathtub?! It's soaked!"

"Mother, don't shout."

Mom came over to the bed and made the mistake of sitting on it. "You had too much to drink."

"Since you're the expert in this area, what should I do?"

"Stop insulting your mother, for one thing. Who was the man you were dancing with last night? He was a little too smooth for my taste. And he was all over you."

"That's what people do at weddings. They get drunk and fondle each other."

Mom looked around the room again. "Oh God. He didn't come up here with you, did he?"

"That is none of your business. And for your information I'm a consenting adult, not a delicate flower. My maidenhood was snatched ages ago."

Her mother got off the bed. "Honestly, Colleen. You'd try the patience of a saint. Drink a bottle of cola and take a few painkillers. We're leaving after the brunch."

Out she went.

Artie *was* a smarty. He called Colleen non-stop, paid her compliments, and bought her dinner and flowers for weeks. Whenever she wasn't at work, she was with him. She told her mom she was out with friends, which technically wasn't a lie.

They went to the drive-in a lot but never watched the movie. He said he wore condoms. She felt positively wanton. And then it occurred to her one day that she'd never been to his place.

"It's a mess," he said. "I'm in the middle of renovations."

"What are you renovating for?"

He took her in his arms and rubbed himself ever so softly against her thighs. "I'm looking to settle down. I just have to find the right woman. And I think you're it."

Before she could even process this, he had his hand down her blouse.

One night she asked him what he did for a living. They were at a nice restaurant, but she ended up paying because he forgot his wallet.

"I'm an investor. That's why I was interested in your grandfather's business. I'd like to get in on the ground floor of one of his companies. It's always smart to learn from the best."

"I'll have to introduce you to him."

He reached out to touch her hand. "Tomorrow?"

She was taken aback. "I don't think tomorrow, but I can ask him."

"Oh yes, babe. You're the best." He kissed her palm and then put her pinky finger in his mouth and sucked on it.

She pulled her hand back. "Not here!"

"Speaking of family, when am I going to meet your parents?"

"My father lives away and my mother is out a lot."

"That's too bad. I was hoping to meet your father. There's something I might want to ask him."

Colleen felt her cheeks get hot. If she didn't know any better, Artie was going to propose to her! She'd be like her sister, properly married with a home of her own. Artie was smart and ambitious and it was obvious he adored her. He never took his hands off her. She felt sexy for the first time in her life. He always said he loved her when they were doing it.

"Do you have any family?"

"My parents are dead and I'm an only child."

"That must be terrible."

"It's lonely, which is why I want to spend every minute with you."

Colleen called her grandfather and asked him if he'd meet Artie. He agreed and set a date for him to come to his office in a week.

"Not sooner?" Artie looked disappointed.

They were at the mall in the food court, eating fries. "There are people who have to wait months to see my grandfather, and they own companies. He's doing me a big favour."

"I suppose."

"Geez, don't thank me or anything."

The day of Artie's meeting with her grandfather came and went. She didn't hear from him, even though she waited all day. That wasn't like him and she got worried. She called but he didn't answer, and since she didn't know where he lived, she was stuck. It was ridiculous that she didn't know where Artie lived after all this time, and she intended to remedy that as soon as possible.

That night her mother asked to speak to her in the living room.

"Why am I being summoned in my own house?" She plunked down on the sofa and put her feet up.

"Your grandfather called me."

Colleen sat back up. "He did?"

"Apparently he met a friend of yours today, an Arthur Brown. I believe he's the one you met at Frankie's wedding. I didn't realize you were so close."

"We're dating, that's all. What did Grandfather say?" Her mother hesitated, which made Colleen nervous. "Artie hasn't called me. Did Grandfather say something to him?"

"I don't think he was very impressed with him."

Colleen stood up. "I don't care if he's not impressed with him. I am. So I guess that means he's not going to help him get ahead. All he wanted was a chance to try and learn from him, which I think is admirable."

"I'm just telling you what your grandfather said. He's worried that Artie is a little too fascinated with money."

Colleen couldn't stay still. She walked around the living room like it was a boxing ring. "Who's more fascinated with money than Grandfather? Since when is liking money a bad thing? That should be the Hanover family motto... *Your money or your life*!"

Her mother was surprisingly quiet. She looked almost uncomfortable.

That's when it hit Colleen. "You think he likes me for my family's money? Is that it? That there's no way on earth anyone would love me?"

Mom stood up and shouted at her. "That's not true, Colleen. Stop putting words in my mouth. Of course someone is going to love you someday, but Dad is a bit worried that it seemed to be the only thing on Artie's mind. Your grandfather wanted to hear him say something about you, but he didn't, and he found that odd. He phoned because he was concerned. He loves you, Colleen, and he doesn't want anyone hurting you."

"I've got to get out of here." Colleen went into her room and got a poncho before she left the apartment. She stared at the ground as she walked down the sidewalk. Everything smelled musty and rotten, with the decay of leaves accumulating in the gutters. It was wet and dreary out. It matched her mood. Before she realized it, she was in front of Frankie and Edward's apartment. Her hands were cold, so she pressed the buzzer. The speaker crackled.

"Yes?"

"It's me. The loser in the family."

Frankie buzzed her up. They lived on the third floor, and there was no elevator. Talk about dumb. Frankie had left the door open slightly, so Colleen walked in, kicked off her shoes, and headed for the kitchen, but Frankie said, "I'm in the living room."

Colleen followed her voice. Her sister was curled up on the couch with a blanket over her. She didn't look that great.

"Where's Edward?"

"I've sent him for supplies."

"You look like shit."

"That's what happens when you're going to be a mother."

Colleen jumped right out of her chair. "Get out! Already?"

"These things can happen on your honeymoon."

"Am I the first to know?"

"Yep."

That made Colleen feel important. "I'm going to be an aunt!"

"You can be my kid's crazy Aunt Annie."

"I'll do my best. Wow. I'm really happy for you both." She sat back down next to her sister and gave her a hug.

Frankie said, "I hope it's a girl. I can't wait to dress her up!"

"What if it's a boy?"

"Boys are great, but I'd like a daughter."

"Good luck with that. When are you going to tell Mom?"

"Edward's parents are out of the country at the moment. We'll let everyone know when they get back. Why are you out and about?"

"Everyone is shitting on my boyfriend."

"You have a boyfriend?"

"Why is everyone so surprised to hear that? Am I that hideous?"

Frankie rolled her eyes. "Knock it off. I'm surprised because you never said anything. Most people talk about their boyfriends."

That was true. Why didn't she talk about Artie?

When Colleen got home her mother was gone, no doubt with Derek. She had a boyfriend that Colleen didn't like very much. Talk about a double standard.

Just as she was getting ready for bed, the phone rang, and it was Artie. He sounded drunk and asked her to come and get him, which she did. She even got to see where he lived, which was pretty run down. She helped him onto his sofa and he pulled her down too. He was maudlin.

"I don't think your grandfather liked me."

"Never mind about him."

"All I wanted was an in."

He got one. A week later Colleen found out she was pregnant.

There was really only one thing that Colleen remembered from before she walked down the aisle. Her mother took her aside as they were leaving for the church. "The photographer said if you lost thirty pounds, you could be a model."

Her wedding had a different atmosphere, as it was a hurried affair and much smaller because of Artie's lack of relatives. Dad did all the things he'd done with Frankie, even if his face wore an anxious expression, and he seemed to hug her a lot. Her mother cried and so did her sister.

The only thing she remembered about her wedding night was that Arthur got so drunk he passed out.

Her mother rented them an apartment in her building, which Colleen didn't agree with, but Artie was thrilled. He made a list of what they needed and gave it to her. "That's for your mother."

Colleen looked at it. "You expect my mother to pay for all this stuff? Isn't that what the husband usually does?"

"I have to find a job first. Does she expect us to live on air? Your paycheque won't even keep us in groceries."

"What about your investments?"

"You should ask your grandfather again if he can get me a job. Louis Hanover's great-grandson needs to be looked after."

He got the job and he got the furnishings, because every time her mother came down to the apartment she looked distressed about what they didn't have, and more would show up a few days later. Her dad would come to town and ask her for lunch, quizzing her on married life and how she was feeling and how she was doing and if she needed anything.

The only thing she needed was to be loved, but Artie wasn't as affectionate as he used to be. Now the sex was over in five minutes. He said he was fast for her sake, because they had to be careful about the baby. Then he said it was because she was getting too fat.

As time went by, Colleen occupied herself with making the nursery as nice as possible. She and her sister would go shopping and they both said how much fun it would be to have the babies grow up together. They were expecting within a month of each other, and Colleen felt very close to her sister. It was the first time they'd had anything in common.

When Colleen was fourteen weeks along, she fell down the stairwell on her way to her mother's apartment, and Kay found her an hour later, unconscious and bleeding. At the hospital they told her the baby was dead and she'd have to have a D and C. She didn't know what that was. All she remembered before she went under were the masked nurses putting her legs in big slings that were hanging from the ceiling.

When she finally crawled up to the surface of her conscious mind, she cried for her baby. The doctor told her that something had gone wrong during the procedure and she was bleeding so badly they had had to take her uterus. She couldn't have any more children. She cried even harder.

Once she got home, the first thing Artie did was give her a black eye.

"You stupid bitch. Any idiot can push out a kid and you go and fuck it up. That's it for my bloodline joining the Hanovers. You're useless. I want a divorce and I expect to be well compensated."

When Frankie and Edward's son Mark was born that winter, Colleen was in Aunt Annie's old room in Glace Bay. Her grandmother made her nice things to eat and her dad said they were thrilled that she wanted to live with them.

Artie was long gone, his cheque in hand, with a warning to stay away from Colleen.

His parting shot: "My pleasure."

CHAPTER TWENTY-TWO

1978

DAVID WAS VERY WORRIED ABOUT Colleen. It had been more than a year since she'd moved in with him and his mother, and unfortunately the news that Frankie was pregnant again had worsened her mood. At the ripe old age of twenty-four, Colleen didn't have a job, the thirty pounds she'd lost had come back, and she spent most of her time watching television in her room.

At first David did mollycoddle her; he felt terrible about what had happened. But with no one expecting anything from her, she wasn't trying to move on at all. He wasn't sure how to proceed. Kay thought he should talk to Henry.

Henry's advice was just common sense: get her outside and active. Get her interested in something else. And if none of that worked, then maybe it was time to see a doctor about depression. This time of year was difficult anyway, since Cape Breton winters always seemed to last forever. A few times David made her come downstairs to help him shovel, but her efforts were half-hearted at best. She'd fall dramatically into a fresh expanse of snow and stay there. She didn't even bother to make an angel. Then he tried to get her to go skating, remembering how much fun it was when he and Annie were kids. She said she didn't want to break her ankle as well as her heart.

And then, just by chance, he met Lila at the post office one day. She looked happy and content and he was glad for her, though his heart always paused for a moment when he saw her face. They were kind to each other in the months following Annie's death, but David didn't come out to the house now out of respect for Ewan. A little too late, but better than never.

On a whim he asked if she'd like a coffee, and to his surprise, she said yes. They ended up at Tim Horton's, sitting opposite each other at a small table with two coffees between them. He spilled his guts about Colleen. It felt good to be able to talk to someone about it other than Kay. She'd get too emotional, or when she'd come to visit Colleen, Derek would have to take her home a day early because she'd be so upset about the whole mess.

"I have a suggestion that might help," Lila said.

"I'll take anything."

"Get her a dog, a mutt from the pound; another soul that's been through a hard time."

He sat back in his seat. "You're brilliant."

"No. I just know it helped me."

David smiled sadly.

"And didn't you tell me that she loves to be out in Round Island? When she's there this summer, perhaps she'll walk over and I can show her the animals. She could even help. We're always looking for extra hands. An animal makes no demands of you; they don't ask you to talk about your feelings."

"Thank you, Lila. I'm grateful."

David could hardly wait to get home. He told his mother what Lila had suggested and her face lit up. "Of course! That'll do the trick."

He bounded up the stairs and knocked on the closed door. "May I come in?"

"At your peril."

Colleen was where she usually was, on the bed eating peanuts. The television was loud.

"May I?" Her father shut the TV off.

"Hey! I was watching *Laverne and Shirley*."

"How about we get a dog?"

"No. Turn the television back on."

He couldn't believe it. "Why not?"

"I know what you're trying to do and it's not going to work. The TV, please."

David turned on the television and left. He went down to the kitchen where his mother was stirring lemon curd with a wooden spoon. "Was she excited?"

"No. She doesn't want one."

Mom knocked the spoon against the pot and turned off the heat. "Get one anyway."

David went to the SPCA the next morning and looked through the cages of barking dogs. There were so many. For a minute he thought about taking them all home. One of the employees came with him and pointed out some of the obvious favourites, the younger and cuter dogs who jumped and tried to lick his hands. He almost didn't see the last cage, where a quiet black dog sat at the back of his kennel and didn't join in with the ruckus.

"Can you tell me about this dog?"

"He's been here for a while. His time is almost up. It's a known fact that most people don't like black dogs, that's why he hasn't been chosen."

"I thought black labs were popular."

"That's the exception. But when you get the mutts like him, most people don't want them. And he's older, too. The vet said maybe three years."

"Do I want to know his story?"

"No, you don't."

"Could you open the cage?"

The young man unlocked the door and opened it, but the dog didn't move. David squatted down and held out his hand. "Here, boy."

The dog looked at him with sad brown eyes. David was patient. He knelt there for quite some time and talked softly. Eventually, the dog took a hesitant step forward, but when David stood up to meet him halfway he backed up, so David got down on his haunches again. David told the young man, "You can go. This might take awhile."

The more he looked at the dog's face, the more he wanted him. He was there for a good twenty minutes before the dog slowly came to sniff his hand. He cowered when David put out his hand to pat him, so David did it very slowly and was soon rubbing his head.

"I have someone I want you to meet."

❋ ❋ ❋

When Frankie's second son, Adam, was born, Colleen and Lucky were at the bungalow in Round Island. Her mother called with the news. There was just the teensiest part of Colleen that was glad it was another boy, and not the daughter Frankie so desperately wanted. Sometimes you don't get what you want.

She and Lucky were out earlier than most of the summer residents, and she liked it that way—fewer people to nose around in her business. Lucky's favourite thing to do was fetch sticks from the water. Every time she picked up a piece of driftwood on the beach, he'd be on alert. He'd crouch on his front paws, tail in the air, and wait for the smallest move to tell him it was going to happen. One time she pretended to throw it, but he bounded out into the waves and looked so earnest that she couldn't do it to him again.

The flies were bad in the evening, so the two of them would snuggle on the couch. She'd eat popcorn and he'd have his rawhide treat.

"We're like an old married couple, Lucky," she said. "Actually, I wish I'd married you instead of…" She never said his name anymore. She didn't want any part of him to contaminate her life.

The phone rang again. It was her father. "I have a job for you."

Colleen knew she couldn't live like this forever, but inside, she knew she wasn't quite ready to move on. People hurrying her only made her more anxious and she felt like she was doing something wrong all the time. If only people would leave her alone.

"What kind of job?"

"I want you to look after your grandmother and Aunt Muriel. They've decided they'd like to be at the cottage for the whole summer, just for kicks. You'll be there to drive them around and stay with them overnight. I won't let them go otherwise. They're standing here waiting for your answer."

"Pack 'em up, move 'em out, rawhide." Lucky barked. "No, not your rawhide."

Colleen wasn't stupid—not as stupid as she used to be. She knew that her father was trying everything he could to make her part of the world again. But two months with her Grammie and Aunt Muriel would either make her or break her. They'd soon see.

Dad delivered the girls the next day. Colleen heard Aunt Muriel's voice through the car door. Aunt Muriel was a big woman with a large laugh, the type who drowned out anyone around her. She opened the door with her usual enthusiasm and never heard a word Colleen said because she was too busy shouting at Dad that she couldn't find her small overnight case and don't forget the bag of shoes in the trunk and who owned the mangy mutt.

Grammie got out of the back seat and kissed Colleen on the cheek. "I wonder if we'll survive."

They soon had a routine.

Every morning, Grammie would get up at the crack of dawn and turn on the valve of the oil stove. She'd wander off, mumbling about how cold it was, to get a piece of newspaper to light. By the time she found a match, lit the thing, and threw it in, the oil pooled at the bottom of the stove resulted in a fireball roaring up the chimney. Colleen would shout that she was going to burn the place down while Aunt Muriel snored away in blissful ignorance. She never got out of bed until the place was toasty.

Meals were an ordeal. Aunt Muriel liked steak every night. Grammie didn't.

"How about a chicken leg?"

"A chicken leg? How's that supposed to feed a body?"

"What about haddock?"

"I know. Let's have steak."

Colleen would take them grocery shopping and they'd each buy their own items. They insisted everything be put in different bags so they wouldn't get them mixed up.

"They're going to the same kitchen," Colleen pleaded. "It doesn't matter what bags they're in."

Apparently it did.

They wanted their hair washed once a week and said Colleen could do it. First she washed their hair in the kitchen sink, and then the two of them sat on either side of the old table with their identical bags of small grey metal rollers, and their pink plastic hairpins that were held in old Sucrets tins. Colleen would roll up their hair as best she could and they always said she did a great job, but the well water was soft and an hour after taking the rollers out, the tops of their heads would be flat.

But the biggest challenge Colleen had was trying to convince them that she could take their wash into town and do it there. No, no, no.

They didn't want to inconvenience her. They'd go to a laundromat. So Colleen would take them to the one in Louisbourg and she'd have to sit there with them on the hottest days of the summer. They insisted on using separate machines in case they got their underwear mixed up. The fact that Aunt Muriel's were large and Grammie's were small was irrelevant. She begged them to let her take the laundry back to the cottage and hang it up on the line, but they said that was a lot of work. They'd dry it here. Another hour in the sweltering heat would go by.

The other thing they did that drove Colleen up the wall was watch television. They loved detective series. *Hawaii Five-O* was a big favourite. But just as the plot twist was about to be revealed, a car's headlights would drive by and the two of them would pop out of their chairs like gophers and wonder who it could be. While they wondered, they talked right over the best bit of the show. Finally Colleen had enough.

"It's either the Spencers or the Scotts or the Morrisons or the O'Neills, or the Caldwells or the Kerrs or the Fergusons or the Bruckswaigers or the Dillons. That's it! There's nobody else who comes down this road. Geez!"

The other thing that Grammie did was push out her top dentures a little. Then she'd chatter them while she tsked about the kissing part in the show. She also ate copious amounts of candy, which she kept in her apron pocket. Colleen went to put her clean nightgown away one day and in her top bureau drawers was a stash of pink peppermints, scotch mints, liquorice all-sorts, hum-bugs, chicken bones, and gumdrops.

"Why don't you weigh three hundred pounds?" Colleen griped.

But as much as they drove her crazy that summer, she had never laughed so hard in her life. Like the night the bat got in. Aunt Muriel sat in bed hollering with the covers over her head.

"Oh shut up, Muriel!" Grammie chased the bat with a broom to shoo it outside while Colleen kept the door open. Lucky ran back and forth on the furniture in a frenzy trying to jump up and get it as it flew by.

And the two old birds constantly traded stories back and forth. Aunt Muriel told her about a friend who ran a boarding house. She walked in the bathroom and found her husband naked, bent over with his back to her, one leg up on the bathtub as he dried himself. She couldn't resist. She put her hand between his legs, grabbed his willy, and said, "Ding-dong! Avon calling." When the boarder turned around, she screamed, and in her panic, slipped on the floor and broke her leg.

The funniest part was watching Aunt Muriel act it out. She laughed so hard, you couldn't make out what she was saying. She clapped her hands and then slapped the table in delight, Grammie snickering the whole time. The thought that her Grammie and Aunt Muriel even knew what a penis was startled Colleen, but eventually she stopped seeing them as elderly relatives and saw them as women. They certainly were her best friends that summer.

But there were still times when she felt lost. She'd take Lucky and stop to see some of the regulars on the lane and get their news, or go visit the fudge lady.

While her roommates read their Harlequin romances, Colleen took a walk up to Lila and Ewan's farm one sunny day in mid-August. It felt a little awkward, but her mother and Lila did speak to each other now.

There was something about Lila that felt familiar, and Ewan was a sweetheart. She couldn't imagine anyone not liking him.

Their dogs barked at Lucky and came running over. Lucky was a little defensive at first, but the happy creatures soon put him at ease as they chased each other around the yard. Ewan poked his head around one of the sheds.

"Hi, Colleen."

"Hi, Ewan. Everyone's told me about how this place has grown. I thought maybe I could look around."

"I'll give you a tour."

"I'd like that."

Colleen was fascinated with how each animal had its own routine and its own home. The pens, sheds, coops, and barn were all clean and well organized. Everything was painted in bright primary colours. All the different animals were delightful, and because they were used to people, they'd let you come right up to them. Ewan handed her a bucket with oats in it and asked her if she'd feed the miniature horses for him. She was so enthralled with their soft muzzles munching away she forgot everything else.

Lila eventually walked over and asked if she'd like a cup of tea and something to eat. Colleen declined, but Lila insisted.

"You'd be doing me a favour. It's fun to talk to a woman instead of a man or a critter."

So Colleen followed her into the house. Lila had cucumber and tomato sandwiches on the table along with a pot of tea and a plate of chocolate brownies for dessert.

Lila told her about their farm, how over the years it had turned into this special place, and how the petting zoo earned them enough money to keep everything in operation. Then she spoke about her craft store, which fascinated Colleen.

"I'd love to be able to hook or knit or quilt. I've just never had anyone who could teach me."

"I'd be glad to."

"Do you mean it?"

"Of course."

So that became part of Colleen's routine as well. She spent a few hours with Lila every day, learning how to sew, braid rugs, hook rugs, and quilt a pillow cover to start with. She practised at night in the cottage while the ladies watched *The Rockford Files*.

Once the cottage became too cold for the old dolls, Colleen took them back to town, their summer adventure over. She was sorry to see them go but also relieved, because that meant she and Lucky could spend even more time at the farm. Lila had her help with canning, making jams and pickles and chow-chow. Ewan would come in for lunch and they'd sit around the kitchen table and feast on salmon sandwiches and hot tea with Apple Betty.

Ewan told her about his Uncle Gaya from Mira who taught music many years before. He was a marvellous violinist and in the evening when he'd sit on his porch and play the Minuet in G, a big buck with enormous antlers would walk out of the woods and come up to the house to listen to him play. It was only when Gaya stopped that the buck would disappear.

"And people say animals are dumb beasts?" Ewan shook his head. "We could all learn a lesson about living on this planet from the species we share it with."

When Ewan went back outside Colleen said, "Ewan is a wise soul, isn't he?"

Lila smiled. "Yes."

It was while Lila was showing her how to cast off a pair of mitts that Colleen blurted, "I lost a baby, you know."

"I heard. I'm so sorry, Colleen."

"And I can't have any more."

Lila put down the ball of wool. "I lost a baby and I was told not to have any more because of my heart."

Colleen couldn't believe it. "Is that true?"

Lila nodded.

"How old was your baby?"

"Three. Her name was Caroline."

"That's so sad. Was she sick?"

"She drowned in a well."

Colleen burst into tears. Lila reached over and held her while she wept. "I want you to cry your heart out, sweetheart. It will feel better."

❀ ❀ ❀

Lila was at the window the next morning when Colleen arrived with her dog. Ewan waved and she ran over to him. He handed her one of his baskets and they walked together through the grass to collect the morning eggs, Lucky wagging his tail behind them.

David's little girl was back in her life.

❀ ❀ ❀

It seems everything happens in threes. Colleen's mom was getting married to Derek; Frankie was having another baby; and Grandmother Hanover died.

Not that Colleen was ever close to her, but the way she died was horrible. She was drinking late at night on their yacht. Grandfather was in the cabin below. For some reason she decided to leave the boat and tried to get up the ladder to the wharf, but slipped back into the water and got mired in the ropes. They found her the next morning.

After the funeral, Colleen's dad went back to Cape Breton. Colleen stayed on in Halifax, because her mother's wedding was supposed to take place two weeks later, but now the girls weren't sure if it was going to happen because their mother had gone to pieces. She couldn't get out of bed, she didn't want to see anyone, and she cried all the time.

Her daughters were at a loss. They'd always thought she hated her mother.

Colleen went over to Frankie's house, a new one large enough for a growing family, and spent her evenings there. She was ashamed of herself for having resented Frankie's children in the past. The boys were adorable, and she realized that she could love her sister's children too. Everyone did need a wacky aunt around the house.

"I'm not sure what's going on," Frankie said. "Mom bitched about her constantly. You'd think she'd be happy now that she's gone. She didn't even want Grandmother to come to the wedding."

"But she was her mother, and the way she died was awful."

"They say mother and daughter relationships are difficult anyway. I sure hope I get to find out."

"And when this baby's a boy?"

"I'm not stopping until I get a girl."

Her sister always did want her own way. "Does your husband know this?"

"He'll be informed when the time comes."

"Oh, brother."

When she got back to her mom's apartment, Derek was in the hallway wringing his hands. "I don't know what to do! I keep telling her it's all right and we don't have to get married if she doesn't want to, but it's like she's not listening. I feel helpless. What should I do? How can I make her feel better?"

It was amazing how the passage of time had changed Colleen's perspective. Derek, his gold chain notwithstanding, was actually a nice guy. He really was only concerned with her mother. She thought it must be nice to be loved like that.

"I'll try and talk to her. Why don't you make her some cocoa?"

"How do I do that?"

"Why don't you run to Tim Horton's and get her a hot chocolate. And one for me, too."

His face brightened. He had a task. "I'll get us some Timbits, too, shall I?"

Colleen knocked on her mother's bedroom door and walked in. Mom looked sad and worn out. She sat on the side of the bed and took her mom's hand.

"I know what's wrong, but what's wrong?"

"I never had a relationship with my mother the way I have with you girls, and now I never will."

Colleen loved her mother dearly, but there were times when she wanted to wring her neck. Her mother was capable of hurting her without even noticing, which made Colleen resent her intensely sometimes. But it seemed Kay's view of their relationship was a tad rosier.

"What was *her* mother like?"

"Awful, apparently. She never kissed her, not once in her life."

"Now, that's lousy parenting. Your mother did better than that, and you did better than your mother, and Frankie is at this very moment doing a much better job than you ever did."

Her mother burst out laughing. "Oh, Colleen, I love you. You always were the funniest little thing. You were Aunt Annie's favourite, you know."

Colleen sat up a little straighter. "Did she tell you that?"

"Not in so many words, but I could tell. Frankie was standoffish, but you were only happy when you were in someone's arms. Annie used to carry you all day when we'd come up for the summer."

"If Aunt Annie were sitting here today, what do you think she'd say to you?"

"Stop your bellyaching, get off your ass, and marry the guy."

"You heard the woman."

The wedding went ahead.

❋ ❋ ❋

Frankie's daughter Hilary was born on July 13, 1981, at 5:20 A.M., just as the sun was coming up. They put her in Frankie's arms and Hilary looked at her mother with big, brown eyes.

"Hello, sweetheart. I've been waiting for you.

❂ ❂ ❂

When her Aunt Colleen and Grampy Macdonald came down to Halifax to meet the first granddaughter in the family, Hilary was asleep in her crib. Frankie wanted them to wait until she woke up, but Grampy asked for just one little peek. When he bent over the crib, Hilary had her thumb in her mouth.

David's heart stopped.

She looked like Caroline.

CHAPTER TWENTY-THREE

1991

HILARY'S BREATH WAS HOT AGAINST her hands as she covered her face and kept her eyes tightly shut. She leaned against the garage door at the back of the house while counting to one hundred. It wasn't easy. A housefly kept buzzing around her head and the back of her checkered shirt was sticky with sweat, she'd been standing so long in the noonday sun.

"Ready or not, here I come!"

Adam was always hard to find. When Mark used to play with them, before he got all cool and everything, he was even harder.

There were lots of great places in their backyard for hiding. There was the multi-level deck, the gazebo, Dad's baby barn, the pool's dressing rooms, the mega-bushes their gardener had brought in fully grown. There was even a bicycle shed at the very back of the property. Mom wanted a bush planted in front of that as well, to hide the unsightly thing. Dad wouldn't take it down because there were about forty-two bikes of every size in it. Mom said she was going to plant lots of ivy beside it and hopefully it would grow up the side of the wall. Dad didn't care if she did that. It saved him from painting it.

Hilary's mother opened the sliding door. "Come in for lunch, please."

Hilary took off. "Can't…gotta find Adam."

Her mother stepped out even further. "Get back here now, Hilary Anne!"

When her mother said her middle name, you couldn't argue with her. Hilary turned around and stomped up the stairs. "Lunch is stupid."

"Stupid seems to be your favourite word, but looking for someone who isn't here isn't very bright either."

"What do you mean, not here?"

"I sent him to the store."

Hilary sulked. "Thanks a lot, Mom. He finally plays with me and you mess it up."

Mom reached over and took her daughter's baseball hat off. "Wash your hands."

Washing her hands was also stupid. Her mother had an obsession with cleanliness.

Once at the table, she realized she was pretty hungry. Her usual, a bowl of canned ravioli, was on the glass table. Their tiny dog, Precious, lay down under the table and stared at her. It was like being watched by a hairy rat. Precious was her mother's dog. Hilary wanted a real one, but so far the answer was no.

Her mother emptied the dishwasher while watching *The Price Is Right* on the small TV sitting on the kitchen counter. Her fifteen-year-old brother, Mark, was practicing in the family room on his drums with his so-called band. Her father was on his computer in the study.

Hilary hated the weekends. They were lonely.

She didn't have a lot of friends. Girls were stupid. The only things they cared about were dolls and boys and clothes. The day before Hilary had asked some of the girls on the street to come over and play volleyball and they did, for about ten minutes, and then complained it was too hot and asked if they could go in her pool. They chased each other around screaming at the top of their lungs, and acted as if a splash of water was acid burning their skin. All of them went into hysterics when Mark and his buddies came in through the back way to go practice.

Hilary sat at the top of the stairs, watching the mayhem. Her father had come outside to supervise and sat with her.

"Don't feel like going in?"

"Would you?"

"Can't say I would."

"As Grampy says, I rest my case."

Shopping with her mom was also stupid.

"Please, Hilary! This is gorgeous." She'd hold up stupid dresses again and again and then get mad when Hilary didn't want to try them on. Mom also got annoyed when she told the hairdresser she wanted her hair cut short.

"Don't cut it too short, honey. You'll look like a boy."

"Exactly."

Sometimes her mom watched her as if she'd done something wrong.

"What are you looking at?"

"Nothing."

Hilary knew she was looking at something. Or for something.

The only thing she looked forward to was her summer with her Aunt Colleen and Grampy. The boys didn't care for Round Island, saying there was nobody around, but of course they didn't see anyone. They just sat inside playing video games all day.

At last the big day arrived and her mother helped her pack, sneaking in a few girly t-shirts when she thought Hilary wasn't looking. Some of them were okay so Hilary let it pass.

Then it was goodbye to her brothers, who grabbed her around the neck and gave her a noogie each.

"Have fun, squirt," Adam said.

Mark gave her a ten-dollar bill. "Don't spend it all in one place."

She did love her brothers…sometimes.

Then it was off to the airport because Mom and Dad were super busy and couldn't spare the two days it would take to drive her up to Cape Breton and drive back home. Hilary didn't mind. She had a nice flight attendant who let her sit near the front. It was a small Dash 8 and it only took about fifty minutes to get to Sydney.

Aunt Colleen and Grampy were at the airport window, waving like crazy. She waved back and ran into the terminal. They had a race to see who could grab her first. Grampy won.

Back in Glace Bay the three of them sat at the kitchen table and ate their chicken casserole with homemade scones, coleslaw, crispy sweet pickles, and candied carrots. They feasted on chocolate cake that Aunt Colleen made from her Grammie's recipe book. They listened to every word Hilary said and wanted to know all about what she did, and how she felt.

Grampy smiled at her. "What would you like to do while you're here?"

"This."

❋ ❋ ❋

Colleen missed her grandmother very much. Abigail died in 1985 after a series of small strokes, her sister Muriel soon afterward. Grammie's last year she was in the old folks' home just down the street, because Colleen and her dad couldn't cope. As small as her grandmother was, she was a dead weight when Colleen tried to get her in the tub. She was incontinent as well. It broke Colleen's heart to have her Grammie look up at her from her hospital bed and say, "Where am I? I want to go home."

Her dad would go visit during the day, as he had retired by then, and he'd read to his mother from the books he inherited from his father. The sound of his voice soothed her. Colleen would go for an hour or so in the evenings, after she came home from the farm. She worked there full-time, managing Lila's craft store and helping Ewan with the animals. She'd stay at the cottage with Lucky the Second, a black mutt, naturally, from May until October, and then come back home with her dad in the winter months. The original Lucky was buried near the cottage. Ewan had helped her dig the hole. It was a terrible day.

As a way of remembering her grandmother, Colleen typed out her recipes. They were in black hard-covered scribblers and most were written in pencil, and after years of use, the writing was disappearing. Splatters, drops of vanilla, and even the feel of dusty flour covered a lot of the pages, and Colleen could always use these signs to tell which ones were the family favourites. The hardest part was interpreting the directions. Grammie knew what she was doing. She often wrote down, for example, "1 baking soda," knowing it wouldn't be a tablespoon. Instructions were just as vague. *Place in a warm oven* means what? *Until done.* How done?

She made copies for her sister and all her cousins so they could pass it down to their children. Uncle Henry was thrilled when she gave him a copy. He said Annie would've loved that, because no one enjoyed her mother's food more than she had. Leelee kept it in her room. Then Colleen gave one to her cousin John, who was a sales rep in Cape Breton with two boys and one girl. His wife was a bit of a scatterbrain, but harmless. Colleen loved their kids and they loved her, probably because she saw them more often than the others and took them to McDonald's to let them eat crap.

She went up to Baddeck to hand one over to John's twin brother, Daniel. He was a fisheries officer and his wife was a teacher who was always as busy as a blue-ass fly. They had three sons, all of them full of piss and vinegar.

Then she mailed a copy to George, who was a banker living in Ottawa. His wife was a nurse at the Heart Institute and they had two daughters who were sophisticated city girls.

When Colleen went down to Halifax to visit her mom, she gave one to her cousin Robbie, a great machinist like his grandfather. He had a daughter from his first marriage and three girls and a boy from the second. Colleen always thought of the old woman who lived in a shoe when she pulled into his yard.

Lastly she handed one to Frankie. She wouldn't use it, since she made dinner with food that came from frozen food containers, jars and cans, but maybe Hilary would someday.

The three musketeers, as they called themselves, settled into the bungalow for a long and glorious summer. Dad would swing on the hammock, his straw hat over his face. Colleen and Hilary would go for a swim with Lucky before heading to the farm.

"This is what heaven looks like," Hilary told Ewan.

"You are absolutely right," he smiled.

Colleen and Lila got a kick out of Hilary because she wanted to do everything at once. She was almost hopping. They watched her climb over the fence into the pigpen. "You'd think she was your daughter, Colleen."

Colleen nodded. "She might as well be. I love her with all my heart."

"She reminds me of another little girl."

"Who?"

Lila smiled. "Just a child I knew a long time ago."

A truck came up into the yard with a load of hay in the back. It was Duncan, the son of the man who bought Ewan's property. He worked almost full-time on the farm, as well as helping his dad with his place.

He was always joking around with Colleen, in a good friend sort of way. He certainly knew about animals and running the operation, so he was a great source of information when Ewan wasn't around.

After a long day she and Hilary crossed the field and smelled Dad's barbecue going. He had pork chops for supper with boiled new potatoes and steamed spinach with butter. Hilary hoed into her food. "I don't know why, but when I come here everything tastes delicious."

"There's nothing like hunger to make food taste good," Dad said. "I hear you put in a full day's work up at Ewan's."

"I love it there. When I grow up I'm going to work there."

Dad pointed at her. "You're going to university first, young lady."

"Yes, sir."

They had fresh raspberries and cream for dessert. Out of nowhere, Hilary said, "That man likes you, Aunt Colleen."

"What man?"

"The hay guy."

Colleen made a face. "Duncan? He's a friend."

"He likes you."

Colleen felt herself blushing. "Eat your dessert, you saucy brat."

❦ ❦ ❦

One day when Aunt Colleen had to go to town to get groceries, Hilary's Grampy said they should go for a walk. They started up the beach, with Lucky leading the way, his nose to the ground, sniffing everything in sight. Once they got to Long Beach he took her up through the woods and onto a long path that snaked through the trees. She saw glimpses of Mira Bay every so often and then they came to a clearing, where there was the biggest tree she'd ever seen in her life.

"Wow! How old is this tree?"

"I'm guessing pretty old. Someone once told me that it looked like a ballerina. What do you think?"

Hilary considered it. "Yes, it does, but it also looks like mommy when she tries to put me in a dress."

Her grandfather laughed. "That's true. That's how she used to look when I told her she couldn't go out on a school night."

They sat together on the edge of the bluff and looked out at Mira Bay, Lucky beside them.

"This is a special place. I used to come here when I was a kid."

"Does anyone else know about this place?"

"My sister, Annie, who you would've loved. You remind me of her."

That made Hilary feel good for some reason. "Was she nice?"

Grampy looked out over the water. "She was the best."

Grampy looked sad, so she put her arm through his and leaned her head against him. He patted her cheek.

"I have it on good authority that a tree fairy comes here."

Hilary wasn't easily fooled. "You're making that up."

"Cross my heart, it's true. There's also a very special cricket that hides here."

"A cricket?"

"If you listen for it you'll hear it."

Hilary listened but she only heard the water below.

"I hope you remember this place, Hilary."

"Oh, I will."

"Promise?"

"Promise."

"Then spit in your hand and we'll shake on it."

It was a done deal.

"We should head home," he said. She helped him up. "Thank you, dear. Now, do you think you could handle a secret mission?"

"A secret mission? Oh boy!"

"I'll tell you about it as we walk back."

He wanted her to find out more about Duncan. Was he nice? Was he a hard worker? What was he like around the farm? He said that Aunt Colleen never told him anything. He knew he was being nosy, but he was interested. Hilary asked him why he didn't go up to the farm himself and check Duncan out. He said it was more fun this way.

Hilary took a notebook with her the next day and snuck around when no one was looking, peeking at Duncan from behind the barn. She followed him as he and Ewan unloaded bags of feed from the truck. At one point he turned around quickly and she had to run and hide ramrod straight behind a rather skinny tree. She worried that he saw her but he didn't seem to notice, though he did wink at Ewan for some reason.

She gathered her observations in the notebook and put it in her pocket, before heading out to find Aunt Colleen. There was only one place to look, the little store in the screened-in porch. She was forever fiddling and placing things so that it looked nice. Hilary loved to go in there because it was so chock full of neat things, like knitted throws and quilts, Lila's paintings, jars of pickles and preserves, bowls of sea glass, old bottles, and tin signs.

Aunt Colleen said she could stay as long as she didn't interrupt anyone. A big car pulled up and two elderly couples emerged wearing fanny packs and sun visors. Aunt Colleen greeted them and they said they were thrilled to be here in Cape Breton, wasn't the weather beautiful and they couldn't get over how friendly everyone was. Her aunt asked them where they were from and they said Columbus, Ohio. Hilary thought their accents sounded different.

They smiled at Hilary and said how cute she was. Hilary didn't like being called cute but she never let on. Then the two ladies went nuts over the quilts and especially the hooked coasters and table runners. The handmade rag dolls they adored. They'd never see anything more beautiful and were enthralled when Colleen said she'd made them herself. The two men said they knew they shouldn't have stopped in. Everyone laughed. The men went to sit on the new Adirondack chairs that were placed outside on the lawn for just such a purpose. Aunt Colleen said she'd learned over the years that if men were comfortable, their wives shopped longer. She sent Hilary out with some lemonade for them and you'd think she'd given them gold. They couldn't get over it.

The two ladies bought every one of the dolls because they said they had six granddaughters between them. Hilary wondered why older people always thought girls would like dolls.

Then they picked up two table runners, two sets of hooked coasters, an embroidered tablecloth, painted rocks, a piece of driftwood that looked like a loon, bars and bars of homemade goat milk soap, and four jars of honey.

By the time they left Aunt Colleen knew their life history and called them by name. "Thank you, Deborah. Thank you, Dana. Have a great time around the trail!"

After they left Hilary looked at the handful of cash in Aunt Colleen's hand. "Holy moly. Do you sell this much every day?"

"During the summer. That's why I pay some of the local women to hook and sew and quilt for me. Lila and I would never be able to make all these things on our own. Our business has grown."

"And then you get the families who pay to let their kids pet our pets. I wonder if I could do that with Precious. Probably not. He's too cranky."

Aunt Colleen set about replenishing her inventory, so Hilary went into the house and found Lila at the kitchen table making a list. She went over and looked at it. Lila put her arm around her waist.

"Anything I can do for you?" Hilary asked.

"Yes, you can keep me company while I do this."

"That's not very important."

"It's terribly important to me to have a little girl sit at my kitchen table. Would you mind?"

"Sure."

"Before you sit, go into the pantry and get us some molasses cookies. I made them this morning. And get two glasses of milk."

Hilary set about getting their snack and when she was done she sat. Lila gave her a big smile. She picked up a cookie and held it in the air, gesturing for Hilary to do the same.

"To us!"

"To us!" Hilary repeated.

They knocked their cookies together and dunked them in the milk.

To Hilary's delight, Ewan's parrot, Polly, was awake and feisty that day. Lila told her that someone had given the bird to Ewan because they knew he would take care of it. Polly was over thirty years old and they didn't know much about her other than she could swear like a trooper. She was forever hollering for people to "Come in!" when someone knocked on the door. More than once Lila said she found people standing in her back porch looking confused.

So while Hilary and Lila ate their cookies, Polly was on her perch eyeing the cat, who was eating a dish of food on the counter, away from the dogs. The cat's tail swished back and forth. Polly reached over and bit the end of it. The cat turned around and swatted Polly so hard she landed on the floor.

It all happened so fast, Hilary and Lila didn't have time to react. Polly flew back on her perch and screeched, "You son of a bitch!"

The two of them fell into fits of laughter and made such a commotion that Polly turned on them. "Drop dead!"

Hilary eventually went back to the cottage ahead of Colleen so that she could report in to Grampy. He was in the kitchen preparing supper.

"Hi Grampy! My secret mission is complete."

"Wonderful. What did you find out?"

Hilary took out her notebook out and looked at it. She sat on a chair and jumped right back up again. "Ow!!"

"What's wrong?"

"I sat on that!"

It was the electric frying pan he'd placed on a chair because there were so few outlets at the cottage you had to make do. There were sausages in it. Fortunately it was on low.

Grampy looked upset. "Did you get a burn?"

Hilary wiped her greasy jogging pants. I don't think so."

"Don't tell Aunt Colleen. She'll kill me."

"I won't."

She changed her pants before she stood and delivered her report. Grampy sat on the sofa with a glass of sherry.

"Our suspect's name is Duncan something. I don't know his last name because people only call him Duncan and I didn't want to raise suspicions if I asked Ewan or Lila."

Grampy nodded approvingly. "Quite right."

"But I can check his mailbox at the top of the road if you like."

Grampy put his hand out. "No! Don't do that. Never go up to the highway by yourself. The cars drive by too fast up there. Do you promise me?"

"I promise. Okay, so Duncan has brown hair but sometimes it looks lighter. He has blue eyes I think. He's taller than Ewan but not as thick. He was at work before I got there, so he must come early.

He helped Ewan unload bags of seed, he cleaned out the horse stalls, fed the goats and donkey, and put a splint on the wing of one of the ducks. The duck wasn't happy.

"I casually asked Ewan what his favourite colour was and he said blue. Duncan was standing right there so he said green, like the trees and the grass.

"Then he helped Ewan fix a fence, he milked the cows, and he took some people around to show them the animals. He made them laugh a lot. When Aunt Colleen came out to ask him something, he made her laugh too. She told him he was being silly and he said what's wrong with that? He watched her go back into the house and then he put his gloves back on and shovelled cow poop.

"I conclude that Duncan is a hard-working, funny, nice man, who likes Aunt Colleen and the colour green. The end."

Grampy put down his glass and clapped. "An excellent report, Miss Roth. You make a superb spy and I will use your services at a future date, if that's convenient."

"Very."

When Aunt Colleen came home for supper, she asked Grampy to pass her the plate of sausages. He did, and then turned to Hilary. "In my day, they were called bum warmers."

Aunt Colleen couldn't figure out what was so funny.

CHAPTER TWENTY-FOUR

1995

COLLEEN'S GRANDFATHER LOUIS HANOVER DIED at the age of ninety-five. He'd been sick for years, but when you have money death can sometimes be delayed for a while. He left his empire to his son, Louis Jr., and daughter, Kay, with endowments to many charities and foundations that were close to his heart.

Louis and his partner, Stephens, still lived in New York City. They flew in on a private jet for the funeral. The church was packed and the reception afterwards was catered. If Colleen hadn't known better, she would have said it was a cocktail party for the movers and shakers of the business world. Her grandfather's body was placed in the family crypt at a local cemetery. Colleen didn't know they had a family crypt. It sounded creepy. Her sister said it was on the better side of the cemetery.

"You mean he's on the side that's deader than dead?"

Their mother told them their grandfather had left them both a letter that was to be read in private. Colleen was intrigued. Naturally Frankie ran off and came back about a minute later. "He said I was a beautiful girl and he loved me. He gave me a cheque for fifty thousand dollars and told me to spend it on shoes!"

While Frankie celebrated, Colleen went into her old room. She opened up the letter.

Dear Colleen,
Your mother has kept me up to date with the work you've done on the farm in Cape Breton, and how the craft store has now hired more people in your rural area. You have a nose for business, my dear. Maybe you're even a chip off the old block. I know you haven't had it easy, but in the end that's what will make you stronger. You're a beautiful girl and I love you.
Grandfather.

Colleen felt like crying. She hadn't really known her grandfather, and now, seeing his shaky handwriting, she realized that that was an opportunity lost. You think these people are going to be around forever. He practically *was* around forever, and they had never spent any time together. Why was that? It was a shame.

Her cheque was for fifty thousand dollars too. Then she looked again. There was another zero. A half a million dollars? What on earth was she going to do with this? She didn't deserve it. The little voice inside (the one everyone in the family called Aunt Annie) said, "Put it away until you can think." That's what she'd do. She'd deposit it at the Credit Union when she got back to Cape Breton. She could only think on the beach with Lucky beside her.

Colleen tucked the cheque into her wallet, put the wallet in her purse, put her purse in her suitcase, and zipped and locked the suitcase. She almost put the key down the front of her bra, a consequence of having watched too many cowboy movies.

She joined her mother and sister.

"Well," Frankie asked, still grinning from ear to ear.

"He said I was a beautiful girl and that he loved me. My cheque is for fifty thousand dollars too!"

"Did he tell you what to spend it on?"

"Candy."

"Oh, he did not. Daddy always was a generous man," Mom sniffled. "I'll miss him."

Dad came down for the funeral of course. He and her grandfather had respected each other. At seventy, Dad looked pretty good for his age, but Colleen knew he suffered with his stomach. She could always tell when he was in pain. His eyes looked duller.

He was taking her and Frankie out for dinner and asked Mom if she and Derek would like to come along. Mom said that would be nice, but when she met them at the restaurant she was alone. Dad pulled out her chair for her.

"Where's Derek?"

"Something came up. He had to go out of town at the last minute."

Just the way she said it, Colleen knew something was wrong, but her mother arranged her face into a polite mask. "This is nice, isn't it?

Just the four of us."

Colleen did think it was nice. It reminded her of when they used to sit at the table in Montreal. "I wonder what ever happened to Elena?"

Frankie took a sip of water. "She always liked you better than she liked me."

"She hated me too, Frankie, so don't worry about it." Mom picked up the menu and stared at it.

Dad looked confused. "Who are we talking about? Who hated who?"

"It doesn't matter…it was our cook in Montreal."

"Why would she hate you?"

"She always thought I was too hard on Colleen about her eating habits."

"You were."

Colleen silently cheered.

"I don't want to ruin the evening. Let's drop it."

Colleen looked at her mother. "You never want to talk about it. Does that mean you feel guilty, please, God?"

The waiter picked that moment to come and take their orders for drinks. Colleen was surprised when Mom ordered a glass of white wine. She and her father and sister gave each other covert glances. Mom didn't look up from the menu. "Mind your own business."

Colleen had been planning on having a nice piece of baked salmon, but reconsidered.

The waiter came back with their drinks and asked if they were ready to order. Dad looked around. "Does anyone want appetizers first? I don't."

Both Mom and Frankie said no.

"I'll have the large sampler platter and for dinner I'll have the fettuccine carbonara," Colleen said calmly.

Her mother glared at her.

Colleen glared back. "Mind your own business."

Dad ordered a steak and baked potato. Frankie wanted fish and chips, and mom said she'd have a piece of grilled chicken with steamed vegetables.

When the waiter put the sampler platter in front of Colleen, it was so big she had to move her cutlery and glass out of the way. It was piled high with onion rings, mozzarella sticks, chicken fingers, potato skins, and Buffalo wings.

She looked at her mother's face. Dad and Frankie were killing themselves in the background.

"Would you like some, Mother?"

Mom grabbed an onion ring. "You think you're funny, don't you?"

They damn near ate all of it.

Before they went back to Cape Breton, Colleen and her dad invited Frankie's kids to go out for lunch. The boys declined, which was too bad. Colleen didn't know her nephews as well, now that they were growing up. That would hopefully change when they got older.

The person they really wanted to take to lunch was Hilary. Both Colleen and her dad nearly died when they arrived for the funeral. She had pink hair, a nose ring, and so much eyeliner on she looked like a raccoon. Her face brightened when she saw them, and Colleen could still make out the little girl they adored, but the minute her mother walked in the room, the smile was replaced with a sullen demeanor. It was like a light had switched off.

They took her to a Thai restaurant she liked. Colleen knew her father wouldn't be able to eat anything, but he was a trooper. He ordered some sort of plain noodle concoction and fiddled with it.

"So, how goes the war?" Dad asked her.

"Which one? The one at home, the one at school, or the one being waged on our planet by gas-guzzling freaks who drive their kids a block to school in their shiny SUVs?"

Colleen figured she'd better pick one. "The one at home."

Hilary ate her pad Thai with chopsticks. "Mom spends her life at the gym or the spa or the mall. Dad travels every week so he's never home and when he does come home he lives on the cell phone. If you ask me he's having an affair. Mark's in residence and flunking out of Saint Mary's and Adam is dealing drugs."

Poor old Dad choked on his noodles and had to take a glass of water. Colleen slapped him on the back. When he finally got his wind back, he kept dabbing his face with his napkin and sputtering, "How can this be? Is this true? This is so upsetting. Little Adam dealing drugs?"

Hilary put another mouthful on her chopsticks. "I don't know if he's dealing drugs, but he has weed in his room."

Ah, to be young again, Colleen thought.

"I can't believe your father would be having an affair." Dad was still sweating. It was probably the spices.

Colleen looked at him. "I couldn't believe it either…I mean, I can't believe it either."

It went right over his head.

Hilary backed down on that as well. "I can't say for sure that he is. I just heard Mom on the phone say that Dad was too tired for sex and she was getting sick of it, so I figured he must be getting it elsewhere."

Dad's mouth dropped open. Colleen felt sorry for him. She decided to press ahead. "And I suppose Mark is only getting average grades, so he's not really flunking."

"If I was bringing home C's, I'd get shit for it."

Colleen was going to have to get her dad out of the restaurant before his heart stopped. "Dad, why don't you go to the men's room and splash some water on your face? You're looking a little flushed."

He fumbled around with his napkin. "Yes, yes…perhaps I should."

Hilary was unaware that she was flustering her grandfather. The narcissism of youth was mind blowing. Colleen remembered it well. As soon as he lurched off to the john, Colleen got right to it.

"How are you and your mother getting along?"

"We're not. She thinks I'm a lesbian."

Thank God Dad was gone.

"And are you?"

"How do I know? I've only ever kissed animals."

"Good point."

"I know she's ashamed of me, so screw her."

"Oh Hilary, she's not ashamed of you, honey. Let me tell you about your mother. I hate to say it, but the only thing she ever thought she had going for her was her beauty. She gets her self-esteem from it. Your grandmother Hanover brought her up that way, so it's not really your mom's fault."

"How come you escaped?"

"Just lucky, I guess. She really is a good person. You and your mom will be best friends one day. Have a little patience. She tried so hard to have you. You're very much wanted."

Hilary grunted.

Early the next morning, while Dad organized their suitcases, Colleen snuck into her mother's room. She looked very small in her king-sized bed. She was wearing her black silk eye mask.

Colleen reached over and touched her mother's shoulder. "Mom?"

She sat straight up. "What?"

"It's me. Dad and I are leaving soon. We'll let you know when we get home."

"Okay. Goodbye, dear." She puckered her lips.

Only her mother would say goodbye to someone with a mask on. Colleen leaned down and her mother kissed her. Then she lay back down again. Colleen was at the door when she thought of something.

"Mom?"

She sat straight up. "What?"

"Are you and Derek okay?"

"We're getting a divorce."

Colleen came back in the room. "A divorce?"

"Don't sound so surprised. It happens all the time."

"But…"

"He was too clingy. Your father was never like that. It bugged me after awhile. Safe trip." Zorro fell back into bed.

Colleen got in the car and turned on the engine. Dad put on his seatbelt.

"Mom and Derek are getting divorced."

"I knew he wouldn't last."

"How did you know?"

"She's only ever loved me."

That's all he said on the subject.

She dropped Dad and his suitcase off at the house, told him she'd see him on the weekend, and then took the car to the Credit Union and asked to see the manager. A half-a-million-dollar cheque isn't something you can deposit at an ATM machine. Maybe a teller, but she didn't want everyone knowing her business.

The manager was delighted to hold onto her money for her and told her she should speak to one of their investment advisors. She said she'd leave that for another day. A lot of it she would put away for her old age, but she knew she was going to buy Ewan and Lila a new truck and a new tractor. And she wanted to build a few more craft stores in and around Cape Breton, creating more work for rural women. The artistry of the women in small communities was breathtaking.

Her big indulgence was going to be buying her own horse. She'd always wanted a horse. And a pot-bellied pig.

By this point, Colleen was desperate to get to the bungalow. She needed to breathe Round Island air. It was the middle of September and the weather was still lovely. When she unlocked the door the place was hot and stuffy. She stood in the middle of the room and thought about the things she could do now to spruce the place up, and then decided she wanted to leave it exactly as it was. Some things were never meant to be messed with.

Once she unpacked, she headed across the field towards the farm. It felt so good to get out of the city, with its traffic lights and road signs and miles of strip malls. Uncle Louis and Stephens had asked her to stay at their penthouse if she was ever in New York. Fat chance. She extended the invitation to them as well. If they did come she'd buy a movie camera to record their first impressions.

As always, Lucky was waiting by the brook. Lila said he waited there when she was away. It was sort of halfway between the properties. He knew to have his supper and stay at the farm to sleep, but every day he'd go down to see if she was coming.

She clapped her hands. "Hello, baby boy!"

He lifted his head. It's pretty hard to run and wiggle with excitement at the same time, but Lucky managed it. She rubbed his head and patted him all over before giving him a scratch by his tail. His back foot scratched the air and then he rolled over and wanted his belly done.

The two of them walked up to the farm. No one seemed to be around, which was unusual. She didn't see Ewan's truck, but

Duncan's was there. She called his name around the yard, but he didn't answer. Mystified, she went into the house. There he was, singing to the radio while frying up thick slabs of bologna. Polly gave her a wolf whistle.

It felt like home.

"There she is! I was wondering when you'd be back. The place hasn't been the same without you. Want a bologna sandwich?"

"Sure. Where are Ewan and Lila?"

"They're visiting one of Ewan's brothers in the hospital. He was in a car accident with his cab last night. Broke his leg or his arm or something important. He'll be out in a couple of days."

"Thank heavens for that."

She watched him flip the bologna over and over again.

"If you'd leave that alone it would cook faster."

He pointed the spatula at her. "Now there you go again, always telling me what to do. Were you bossy as a child?"

Colleen thought about it. "No, I was a big wuss."

"You've gotten bossy over the years, then, but you ain't the boss of me. Not yet, anyway." He flipped the bologna onto a plate. "There's bread in the breadbox and mustard in the fridge."

"Talk about bossy." She did as she was told and he made two sandwiches. They sat down at the small kitchen table and took big bites.

"This is so good," she said, "I don't know why more restaurants don't have fried bologna sandwiches on their menus."

He pointed at the side of her mouth. "You've got some mustard…"

She wiped at it. "Is it gone?"

"I'll get it." He reached over and kissed it off.

When he stopped, she didn't move.

"Well?" he said.

"Do that again."

He did it in the kitchen, he did it in the living room, and he did it in the upstairs bedroom. He was still doing it when Ewan's truck came up the driveway. He looked down at her. "They're back."

The two of them scrambled around like kids. They set a record for putting clothes back on, running to the kitchen and sitting down at the table just as Ewan and Lila walked in the door.

Polly jumped around and squawked, "Hi Mama! I want ice cream! Ice cream!"

"Hi Polly, hi everyone," Lila said. "Glad you're back. How did everything go?"

"Great!" Colleen took a big bite of sandwich.

"Your grandfather's funeral was great?"

Duncan stood up. "I think I better be getting out to the barn."

"I'll come with you," Ewan said.

Lila sat down at the table and pointed at her. "Your shirt's inside out."

"Pretty bird!" Polly added.

❋ ❋ ❋

A heavy rainstorm lashed the east coast later that week. Great gusts of wind bent over trees and power lines. The yard was full of branches and leaves and even shingles. The roar from the beach was deafening. Lila couldn't imagine how big the waves were or how high the tide was. At the door, she tasted the salt from the crashing surf melded with the torrential rain as it blew inland, and saw seagulls and crows flung through the air by mighty gusts. The light was an eerie underwater colour and it made the house dark and gloomy even at eleven in the morning.

Lila watched as Ewan, Duncan, and Colleen braced themselves against the force of the wind to check that the doors to the barns and sheds were locked tight with the animals safely inside.

Gales were a common occurrence. She remembered Annie's dad telling them about the August gales he'd seen as a kid. Boats were lost, wharfs gone, breakwaters decimated. He said living by the sea was a privilege and a hardship, depending on Mother Nature's whims.

Everyone on the island knew when to batten down the hatches and lay low until the great Atlantic storms rolled back out to sea, heading for Newfoundland.

Lila set about making fires in both fireplaces and lighting the oil lamps to keep the dimness at bay. She placed a big pot of corn chowder on the gas burner to simmer for lunch and put the kettle on to make the tea. She was taking scones off the cooling racks to put in a napkin-draped breadbasket when the phone rang. No doubt it was David to check up on Colleen. She went to the phone.

"Hello?"

It was David.

"Colleen is fine. They're doing their rounds and they'll be back inside shortly. We've lost our power, have you?"

"Yes, I was listening to the radio and most of this side of the island is affected."

"A good day to stay in."

"Lila…I don't know how to tell you this. Henry was found dead this morning."

"Oh no! Oh my god, what happened?"

"They don't know yet. John went to check on him and he was in his study, slumped in his chair. It was probably a heart attack."

"Where was Lee?"

"Up visiting Daniel, thank God."

"Oh, David, Annie and Henry are both gone." She started to weep over the phone. She couldn't help it. It sounded like David was too.

"He died alone. I can't bear it."

They stayed on the phone like that a long time, neither one saying anything, alone with their memories.

Lila finally wiped her eyes with her apron. "This getting old business is terrible. All our precious friends and family go one by one and it's like our lives are disappearing before our very eyes."

"I try and take comfort in the hope that they're together again," he said.

"Theirs was a real love story."

David didn't speak.

"Are you there?"

She heard him cough and clear his throat. "Lila, I've loved you from the first day I laid eyes on you sixty years ago. I'm to blame for what happened to us, the misery I put my family through, and I regret it every day of my life. The one thing I don't regret are the moments you were in my arms. Not all love stories end happily, but that doesn't mean the love wasn't real."

Lila put her hand to her throat. She couldn't find her voice.

"Lila?"

"I loved you too, David. I still do."

She heard him crying and wished she was there to comfort him. He whispered, "Thank you, my love," before he hung up.

❖ ❖ ❖

After the funeral, the family gathered at Henry's house. Colleen counted twenty people who were directly related to Aunt Annie and Uncle Henry: five children, thirteen grandchildren, and two great-grandchildren. Wouldn't Aunt Annie have been thrilled, and wouldn't her grandchildren have loved her.

All these funerals were starting to take a toll on Colleen. She felt like life was passing her by. People were dropping like flies and she was already forty-one. Forty-one! She was ancient.

The only thing that made it bearable was Duncan chasing her around the cottage after work. And the cottage was pretty small, so he caught her a lot. It was cold at night now that the month of September was disappearing. Their solution was to stay beneath the covers.

To think that this man had been under her nose the whole time. Lila said the exact same thing happened to her—they were late bloomers.

Colleen caught sight of Lee, waiting by the window. She was thirty now, but still looked like a teenager. Her sisters-in-law said that wasn't fair. She was quiet and her sunny expression was gone. She and her dad had been a team. Everyone was worried about her. John and his family were going to take care of her, with periodic trips to see her brothers. Spreading the honey around, they told her. Robbie said they were going to sell the house and put the money in a trust fund for Lee, for her future needs, whatever they might be.

Colleen decided to forgive Robbie for the fat remark he had made in this very backyard when they were kids.

She picked up an egg sandwich, popped it in her mouth, and savored it. It reminded her that Grammie had always made great egg sandwiches. She was also at a perfect vantage point to watch her dad and mom on one side of the room and Ewan and Lila on the other. They were four harmless senior citizens, with wrinkles and grey hair. Dad was losing his in the back. Lila was a bit stooped but her skin was soft and lovely. Mom's skin looked sallow, despite years of buying the most expensive cosmetics out there. The drinking hadn't helped her. Ewan looked younger than the three of them. His lifetime of hard work had paid off handsomely.

But the stories her dad told her about being a pilot in the war, flying in the dark, not knowing if he was going to make it back from a mission, were breathtaking when she thought about it. Dad had been eighteen or nineteen when he joined up and went halfway around the world; her nephew Mark's age, and Mark still had to get his parents' permission to take the car for a weekend.

Colleen asked Ewan about the war once, but he didn't want to talk about it. He said that door was nailed shut.

They were an amazing generation and the stories of their growing up always made her envious. She was born too late.

Back at Dad's house, it was just the four of them again, and no one felt like talking. Frankie and Mom would be leaving in the morning. Her sister got changed into exercise gear and went out for a run. Mom said she needed a glass of wine since it was such a terrible day. Dad told her he didn't have any, so she sulked. He got upset and then she got even testier.

Colleen got in the car and drove out to the farm. Lila and Ewan weren't back from the funeral. Duncan's truck was there and she knew exactly where he'd be at this hour. She almost ran to the barn. He was there, just like always.

He turned when he heard the door squeak. "Hi, you okay?"

Colleen went over and took the pitchfork out of his hand and pressed herself against his warm body.

"I'd like to be your wife, even though my parents' marriage was a bummer and Mom divorced her next husband too and my sister and her husband don't have sex, so who knows when that marriage is going to implode and I was married to the devil himself…"

"Jesus, woman. Will you shut the hell up?"

"Can I? Please?"

He looked down at her. "Only if you promise to make fried bologna sandwiches. Every time I think of them I get a hard-on."

She smacked his arm. "Is this any way to talk to your future wife?"

"I certainly hope so."

CHAPTER TWENTY-FIVE

1999

HILARY REMEMBERED THE LUNCH WITH Aunt Colleen when Colleen had said Hilary and her mom would be best friends one day.

Hilary was still waiting.

It would be different if she were a daddy's girl. At least she'd have one parent she was close to. But her dad was a little remote. He was kind and generous and she knew that he loved her and her brothers, but he wasn't the kind of guy you'd run home to and say "I've fallen in love!" or "I hate the jerk."

She saved that for her Grampy. Aunt Colleen was great too. Even Duncan was a source of comfort. He always had her laughing whenever she went to see them, which wasn't as often as she'd like.

Right now she was stuck behind a desk at Dalhousie taking first-year courses, which were basically geared to discourage you from everything. Dal was Grampy's university, and when he talked about it, it sounded fun, but Hilary had to go home every night instead of getting drunk with her friends in a dorm. The idea of living in residence appealed to her. She'd be out of the house, but her parents nixed the idea.

"Why would we pay for a room when you have a perfectly good one five minutes from campus?"

"It's not fair. You paid for Mark to live in a dorm."

"And look what happened! He flunked out his first year and we had to pay for it all over again."

"Which is the dumbest thing I ever heard. You should've made *him* pay for it."

Even her grandmother Hanover tried to get them to change their minds. She said she'd pay for it, but for some ridiculous reason her parents wanted to teach a lesson: you don't always get what you want.

Her parents were never consistent. She and her brothers were on the same page on that score. One minute they talked about mom's inheritance from grandmother and the next they downplayed the fact that there would be money. Hilary got the feeling that as soon as her grandmother was planted in the ground, her parents were going to abscond with the whole enchilada and never be heard from again.

That would suit Hilary just fine.

And then Mom would go and do something thoughtful, like buy her fair trade organic coffee and pick up vegetarian frozen dinners. There was one night Mom was in tears over a commercial on television asking for foster parents to help poor children and they showed a little girl about seven picking through a mountain of trash trying to find something to eat. The flies crawling on her face sent Mom over the edge. She got up from the couch, called the number, and now there were ten foster children's mug shots on the fridge. Every time Hilary looked at them, she'd think maybe Mom wasn't so bad.

And then Mom would ruin it.

This morning, for instance, Mom hollered at her to get up for school. She hollered at her to get out of the shower. She hollered at her about what she wanted for breakfast. This was a war waged every morning. Hilary didn't like breakfast. She wanted coffee, not food.

"Do you want a Pop Tart?"

"No."

"How about Captain Crunch?"

"NO."

"I have frozen waffles."

"NO."

"I read a magazine at the hairdresser's that protein is an essential part of your breakfast experience. I'll make you an English muffin and put peanut butter on it."

"NO."

There was a brief moment of respite. That meant her mother was waiting for the English muffin to toast. Sure enough, there was a ding from the toaster oven. "Come and get it!"

"NO."

Hilary was doing a lousy job on her hair because she couldn't concentrate "Shit!" Now she'd have to start all over again.

"Hilary! It's getting cold!"

Hilary marched out of the bathroom and into the kitchen. "Do you not have ears? I don't want it! God! You never leave me alone!"

Her mother took one half of the English muffin and threw it in her face.

It stuck.

Then it slid down and hit her white shirt on the way to the floor.

Her mother covered her mouth with her hand. "I'm sorry. I didn't mean to do that."

"You aimed before you fired."

"It's just that you can't talk to me that way, Hilary. I'm your mother."

At this rate, she was going to miss her sociology quiz.

"I'm sorry I yelled at you."

"Thank you," her mother said.

Hilary turned to go.

"Are you sure you don't want to take a banana?"

❋ ❋ ❋

Lila got a kick out of watching Colleen and Duncan together. They were middle-aged but acted like teenagers. They had this crazy lifestyle that involved them living all over the place, jumping from the bungalow, Duncan's father's farm, David's house in town, and the farm here. But it didn't bother them. Lila had never seen Colleen so happy and it did her heart good just to look at her.

Life was unexpected. One day you're damn near dead from grief, fear, or loneliness, and the next you're in sync with everything in the universe.

Lila remembered the years when Colleen was very unhappy and thought her life was just one dreadful day after another, and yet here she was laughing and hugging Duncan every time she walked by him. But that wasn't the only reason for her satisfaction. Besides the small craft store in the house, she was the owner of three small shops along the coast that opened in the summer. Her army of rural women kept her in plentiful supply and they were very successful.

And she adored her baby, her colt Dixie, who was all legs at the moment. When Colleen had bought her sweet mare Bonnie, she hadn't known Bonnie was pregnant. When Dixie was born in the middle of the night, Colleen cried for hours, she was so happy.

Lila heard it said that if you put everyone's tragedies or difficulties in a pile, you'd still pick your own because there was always someone worse off than you. Even when she lost Caroline, there was mercy in the fact that she was able to bury her child and visit her every day if she wished. There were mothers out there whose children disappeared and they never knew what happened to them. Lila knew that would be unbearable.

That summer when Hilary was down visiting her grandfather, she came over and weeded Lila's garden for her. She chatted away about this and that while Lila sat in her chair. She was a lovely girl, but a bit lost under all that anger, insecurity, uncertainty, and hormones.

"Colleen tells me that you and your mom fight a lot. Is this true?"

"You would too."

"I wish I'd had the chance."

Hilary stopped weeding. "You lost your mom?"

Lila nodded. "I was seven. I didn't have a father, either. I came to live with a dreadful relative and your great-grandparents lived next door. They watched over me and found me this place to live with the world's sweetest couple. I called them Aunt Eunie and Uncle Joe. I never fought with Aunt Eunie because I knew what it was like to be alone in the world. I'm sure I gave her a run for her money on occasion, but she only wanted the best for me. I was grateful I had someone who cared."

Hilary fell quiet.

She was here again at eighteen, down for the summer. She came faithfully every year, calling it her sanity break. It was hard to believe she was Frankie's daughter, that a woman so glamorous and refined could have a daughter who was such a rebel. Hilary looked like an unmade bed, with a sarong around her middle, rubber flip-flops on her feet, and at least three layers of tops. Her hair was a rat's nest, caught up in some sort of kerchief, and there were beads in some long strands. She didn't have the nose ring anymore, now it was in her eyebrow. A small tattoo was on the inside of her wrist. She had beautiful skin and wore no makeup. Lila thought she was stunning.

She and David never talked about it, but Lila thought she could see Caroline in that face. It might have been wishful thinking, but Lila wondered if maybe wishes did float around in the air and settle somewhere in your life when you least expected it.

It was a nice warm morning. Ewan had carried Lila out to her chair and wrapped a blanket around her, kissing her forehead. He had only left her because Hilary was there. Maybe that's why she was always around. Lila thought that Hilary liked weeding a little too much.

Lila's fatigue was constant now, worse than she let on, and had been for a while. Her ankles and belly were swollen from her congestive heart failure. It was hard to catch her breath and the few hours of sleep she did get at night were while she was sitting up, Ewan's hand resting reassuringly on her somewhere. Her heart was working too hard, trying to get oxygen, and she was winding down like an old clock. She and Ewan both knew it but they never talked about it.

"Hi, Lila," Hilary said. "Which row do you want to do?"

"I'll only supervise," Lila laughed.

"I love this time of day." Hilary went back to the row of peas and knelt down with her wicker basket.

Lila watched as the light crept over the lawn and into the trees as the sun rose. Everything around them was a beautiful salad green until you looked up into the pale blue sky. The multitude of colours from the flower gardens attracted big bumblebees and the hummingbirds Lila loved so much. She watched one ruby throat on a branch nearby, his tiny head going back and forth surveying and protecting his territory. As soon as another one tried to get to the feeder he'd tear off and chase it out like a Spitfire. It made her chuckle. She'd painted a lot of hummingbird pictures over the years and wished she had the stamina to do it now. Never mind. The real thing was more than delightful.

Her speaking voice was slow, but if she took her time she was all right. "Your great-aunt Annie and I would sit here on summer afternoons and Aunt Eunie would bring us lemonade. Now I wonder why we didn't go get it ourselves."

"She must've enjoyed doing it."

"Annie and I would make ourselves sick laughing about nothing. She was a character."

Hilary wiped her forehead with her glove. "I've always heard about Aunt Annie. Grampy tells the best stories about when you were all kids. It sounds so much more interesting than when I was a kid."

"Children today look at the television as if that's real life. They don't have one because they spend so many hours staring at it and not moving."

"My brothers were like that with video games. If I wasn't moving, it was because I was reading. I've decided my major is going to be English. I love to write."

"I never knew that. Clever girl. Dare I ask if you have a young man?"

"I don't have him and he doesn't have me. It's better like that."

"I admire young women today. I was horribly naïve and frightened of my own feelings. Do your parents like him?"

"They've never met him."

"Why?"

"It's private. It's ours."

Lila understood that sentiment.

She must have dozed a little, because when she opened her eyes, David was in the chair beside her. "David."

"I'm here to entice my granddaughter away. We have a date to go to Louisbourg and pick up crab legs and lobster."

"That sounds fun," she whispered.

"Are you all right? You sound a little weak. Should I get Ewan?"

"No, I'm sleepy, that's all. I'm enjoying the sun. He'll be here in a minute to check on me. You two go and enjoy your day."

David got out of the chair. "Come on then, kiddo."

Hilary came up and kissed her on the cheek. "Bye, Lila. Maybe I'll see you tomorrow, unless it's super hot, then I'll be at the beach."

"Exactly where you should be."

David took her hand and kissed it. "We'll see you later, dear."

She gave him a little wave. "Bye-bye."

❋ ❋ ❋

Ewan and Duncan cleaned out one of the pigpens and put new straw down for the two miniature black-and-white pigs that were coming in a few days. They would be company for Colleen's pot-bellied pig, Ira, the world's biggest sook. It was Duncan who saw them for sale on the Internet, and they were so darn cute he talked Ewan into getting them. Colleen was excited, but then she loved all critters. And they all missed Polly, who one day said, "I'm sick, Mama." They found her dead at the bottom of her cage the next morning.

Ewan, thankfully, was still as robust as ever, a few aches and pains on rainy days but nothing serious. But he was leaving a lot of the work to Duncan and Duncan's young nephew who lived down the road, because Ewan's mind wasn't on work. He saw Lila failing every day and the doctors basically said there was nothing more they could do. At one point years ago she could've had a heart valve repair, but her trauma in the hospital before and after Caroline was born put her off hospitals forever. If she was going to die she wanted it to be right here, and he knew better than to argue with her.

He saw Hilary and David as they left. They waved at each other. There weren't many young girls who would spend their mornings with a sick old lady to help him out. Frankie must have done something right to have a daughter like that.

He walked over to the garden and Lila was in her chair, head to the side away from him. It gave him a fright. He fought to stay calm. Bending down, he touched her face.

She turned and opened her eyes. "Hi, sweetheart."

Relief flooded every inch of him.

"Having a nap?"

"Yes. I dreamt that Annie was weeding the garden and David came along and told her they had to go. I saw them as plain as day."

"That's nice."

"I miss Annie."

"I know you do. Let's go in and I'll give you a little soup."

"That would be nice."

He carried her into the house and propped her up on the couch. She liked to stay there and look out the window at her hummingbird feeders. Colleen had a tray of soup and tomato and cucumber sandwiches ready, the same meal that Lila served to her so long ago. Ewan wanted to feed her today. He sat in a chair beside her and gave her a spoonful when she nodded her head. It was like feeding a baby bird.

He'd once found a mother robin dead under a tree and heard chirping from the nest above. He climbed the tree and found four baby robins, so young they had no feathers, opening their beaks, wanting their mother. He waited to see if the father would come back, but he didn't want to wait too long or they'd die. It took a ladder to get them down from the tree, and he devised a system where he had the four of them in a box that he divided in half with a piece of cardboard. Whenever they soiled the paper towels he'd lined the box with, he'd gently push them to the clean side and cleaned up the mess. He also fed them dog food every two hours. He'd put a little on a small flat stick and push it down their throats like their mother would. He'd whistle to them while he fed them and they grew up healthy and strong. When they were first learning to fly they'd land on his head. They even landed on the dog, who was so used to them he'd sleep right through it. When they finally flew off for the winter, he missed them, and then one summer morning the next year, he heard a commotion on his bedroom window ledge. There they were. They didn't jump on his hand like they used to, but it was enough to know that he'd taught them well. One of the barn cats managed to kill one of them because they weren't as afraid as wild birds, but the others were there all summer teaching their own young. Privately Ewan always thought it was his most impressive accomplishment.

He tended to wander back to old memories when he fed Lila, just so he didn't have to acknowledge what was happening in front of him. The looks on Colleen and Duncan's faces were enough to tell him he should be worried, but he refused to believe it would be today. He'd been saying that for weeks.

Not today.

That night in bed as he heard her ragged breath get weaker and weaker, he held her close. And then she spoke softly. "I want to see the stars."

It was happening, but he couldn't think about that. She needed his help, and he had spent his whole life helping her. He put on his clothes and a jacket, wrapped her in Aunt Eunie's quilt, and took her outside to sit on his lap in her old weathered Adirondack chair. He watched her look up at the Milky Way stretched across the night sky.

"It's beautiful..." she whispered.

He nodded.

"...my life with you."

"Lila..." He couldn't continue. He held her tight in his arms and rocked ever so gently. She sighed and he waited for the next breath, but it never came.

He sat out there in the dark with her the whole night. He had to. There was a cricket chirping, keeping him company.

Ewan did what he had to do. He endured them coming to take her away. He consulted with the funeral home and when they asked what her religion was, he said she was a tree fairy. He talked and shook hands and kissed people at the service. He had to endure all this so that she could be cremated.

All of the Macdonalds were there and there were a lot of them. He and Lila had had each other. That was it. That's all they needed.

When the ordeal was finally over, Ewan told Duncan and Colleen he wanted to be alone, if they could just make sure all the chores were done before they left. They did as he asked and hugged him goodbye, saying they'd see him in the morning.

He took Lila's ashes and walked along the very familiar path to the ballerina tree. He stood awhile and looked out at the water. This was a good place to be. The only place he wanted her to be if she couldn't be with him.

He opened the small container and looked at her ashes. They were exactly like the white sand on the beach below. She belonged to nature now; to the trees, and the wind and the ocean she so loved. He took her in his hands and gently scattered fairy dust around the base of the ballerina tree. She vanished into the ground, hiding under leaves, moss, twigs, and grass. That's what life is in the end.

You disappear into the earth.

Ewan stayed there until he was sure that Lila was safe. Then he walked back to the house and got all his papers from the locked drawer of his mother's desk and put them in order on the kitchen table. There was the deed to the house and land, papers listing the value of his property, the petting zoo and his animals, the shop, his and Lila's wills, his new truck keys and ownership papers. Everything had been dotted and signed with lawyers in Sydney, leaving Colleen as their heir. It would all be hers.

He and Lila had discussed it one night sitting in front of the fire. It made them feel good that they were leaving everything to someone who would love it as much as they did.

Once that was settled, he went into their bedroom and took Lila's housecoat off the hook on the back of the door. As he lay in their bed he held it in his arms. He didn't think he'd be able to sleep, but he heard Lila tell him she loved him. It gave him the peace he needed to close his eyes.

In the morning after Ewan had washed, dressed, and had a quick bite to eat, he took an old suitcase out of their closet and started to pack. After he'd packed all his own clothes, he took Lila's slip out of a drawer. He opened her jewellery box and took her wedding ring and the gold heart-shaped locket with their picture in it. Colleen had taken it years before, capturing their image from afar as they walked arm in arm out of the barn, both of them in rubber boots.

He walked over to her bedside table and retrieved the journal she kept there. Ewan had given it to her thirty years before, when the map on her wall was so covered with pins it was in danger of falling apart. Written on the inside cover was *Wonders of the World*.

She had quite a list of places she thought were marvellous—the rainforests in South America, the Great Wall of China, Egyptian pyramids, the Cabot Trail, the St. Lawrence River, the swamps of Louisiana, and volcanoes in Hawaii.

"You and I are going on an adventure, old girl." He wrapped up the journal, ring, and locket with Lila's slip and tucked them into one of the mesh enclosures inside the suitcase. The last thing he packed was the picture she'd drawn for him of his animals looking out of the barn door, the one he'd kept with him during the war. It was his most prized possession. Then he went outside and walked around the farm and said goodbye to all his friends, touching them gently, kissing them on the nose, breathing in the wonderful smells that were so familiar to him, the horses and the big warm cows. He was sorry he wouldn't see the miniature pigs that were coming. They were awfully cute. He even picked up every chicken and thanked them for their years of service.

These creatures were his family. All his life his comfort had come from them. When he was lonely growing up, they had listened to him and kept his secrets and were always glad to see him. They took care of him.

Ewan was at the kitchen table holding his airline ticket when Colleen and Duncan arrived. He smiled at them.

Colleen took everything in at once. "What's this? Are you going somewhere?"

"Yes. I'm taking Lila on a trip. Our first stop is an African safari. We can't wait to see a real lion and tiger."

Colleen's face crumpled. She fell into one of the kitchen chairs. "But we'll miss you."

"I'll miss you too."

She pointed at all the paperwork. "And this?"

"I'm leaving you the farm. Everything."

Colleen and Duncan looked at each other.

"That's not necessary," Duncan said. "We'll look after this place as long as you need us to."

"I'm not coming back."

"Not coming back!" Colleen cried out. "But you have to! The new pigs are coming!"

Ewan reached over and patted her hand. "And they are very lucky pigs. Take care of them for me."

Duncan cleared his throat. "Uh, I hate to ask you, Ewan, but do you have the money for this? The world is awfully expensive these days."

"I have a little nest egg that should hold me over for quite awhile. If not, I can always get a job cleaning out barns."

Colleen jumped out of her chair. "You'll do no such thing! Wait here." She hurried out of the kitchen.

Ewan looked at Duncan. "I hope you both have a very happy life here. I know I did. There's something magic about this place."

Colleen came back in with an envelope. She stuffed it in Ewan's pocket.

"What's this?"

"Never mind what it is," Colleen sniffed. "But you better use every bit of it." She grabbed him around the neck and hugged him tight. "You have to promise to stay in touch. You can't disappear off the face of the earth. It's not fair to those of us who love you, and we do love you. We're your family."

Ewan kissed her cheek. "Yes, you are. Don't worry. I'll call you."

"Promise me that if you get sick, you'll come home to us, or get us to come to you. Do you promise?"

He patted her back. "Okay, I promise."

A car horn honked outside. "That will be my brother taking me to the airport."

Ewan gave Colleen one more kiss and then shook hands with Duncan. Petting the dogs one last time, he took his suitcase and walked out to the car. He waved at the wonderful couple who gave him the peace of mind to take his sweetheart on her journey to see the world.

He was in the air when he remembered the envelope. It held a cheque for a hundred thousand dollars.

That crazy girl. He knew she had money but he couldn't take this. Just as he was about to rip it up, he paused. A few weeks before he'd seen a documentary on television about an orphanage for baby elephants whose mothers had been killed by poachers.

"That's what we'll do, Lila. We'll spread this money around as we travel."

The passenger beside him gave him a quick glance. "Pardon?"

"Don't mind me," Ewan smiled. "I'm talking to my wife."

CHAPTER TWENTY-SIX

2000

HILARY KNEW HER MOTHER WAS ready to pull her hair out. Her grandmother had gone off the deep end. She stayed in bed all day ordering things from the shopping network. Like she didn't have everything she could possibly need in that apartment. The worst was her obsession with skin care products. She had every item, of every cosmetic line, of every actress in North America. They arrived by the boxful and then kept coming because she didn't cancel the order. Every three months more cleanser, toner, and moisturizer arrived to be piled on top of the pile that was already there.

Her mom would call Aunt Colleen up and bitch about it, but she never had time to talk.

"How did my sister end up on Noah's Ark? I called her the other day and she was on her cell phone in the barn. I asked her what she was doing, and do you know what she said? Waiting for a placenta to drop."

That morning her mom put Aunt Colleen on speakerphone so they could say howdy to each other. Mom started up again and Colleen told her off.

"Look, you've got Mom down there and I have Dad up here. You think it's easy for me to be taking him to endless doctor's appointments? He won't drive the car anymore, and he won't live out here with us so that's an hour's drive to get him and take him to Sydney and then another hour to deliver him back home and back out here again. At least Mom is ten minutes away. Consider yourself lucky."

"You think it's lucky that I have to go into that apartment? She won't have a maid service. She says they rob her blind, which is ridiculous because even if they did, it would be a huge help."

"Welcome to middle age. It's nothing new. We've been silently losing good women for centuries, trying to take care of children, grandchildren, men, and parents all at the same time."

"Don't talk about children."

"What did the poor girl do now?"

Hilary slurped the last of the milk out of her cereal bowl. "I didn't do anything! Can you believe it?"

"It's Mark. He says he's gay. He wants to go live with his Uncle Louis and Stephens."

"Well, they are experts on the subject."

"And then last night Adam told me he accidently knocked up Lisa and would I be available to babysit five days a week until they both finish their degrees. Apparently they don't believe in daycare and her mother is too busy. I have to tell Edward tonight that his twenty-one-year-old son is going to be a father, and he'll naturally blame me."

"Oh my god, you're going to be a grandmother!"

"Don't call me that. I can't deal with it right now. It has to sink in."

"I'm going to be an aunt!" Hilary shouted.

"I feel sorry for the kid. Gotta run. The pigs are on the loose." Click.

Hilary got up from the table and put the cereal bowl in the dishwasher. "I have to get ready and pick up Grandma."

"Thank you for doing this. If I hadn't waited so long for this mammogram, I'd reschedule."

"That's okay."

"How does someone get a girl accidentally pregnant? Did he slip it in when she wasn't looking?"

"Eww…Mom!"

"And how do I tell your father about Mark?"

"Everybody knows about Mark, including Dad."

"They do? He does?"

"Mom, I have to go." Hilary gave her mom a hug. "Can you believe that I'm the good child now?"

Frankie patted her back. "You were always good, just bad."

"I'll be back soon."

"Good luck with that."

* * *

Hilary ran upstairs to get dressed and Frankie sat at the table. Her miniature Yorkshire terrier jumped up on her lap. Everybody knew about Mark? *Edward* knew? What gigantic umbrella of ignorance had she been living under?

* * *

Hilary got off the elevator on her grandmother's floor and was just getting to the door when it opened.

"Where were you? I've been waiting a good half an hour. We'll be late for my eye appointment."

Her grandmother was still a handsome woman, but seemed to be shrinking every time Hilary saw her, and her addiction to makeup became more and more obvious with each passing day. Her lips were pink, glossy, and sparkling. Something a twelve-year-old might love.

They took the elevator down to the street and had to walk to the parked car.

"Could you have parked any farther away?"

"Sorry, Grandma, there were no other spots available."

Hilary got her into the car and started off. They weren't one minute down the street before her grandmother complained about the sun being too bright, and then the radio was too loud, and the wind from the open crack of the window on Hilary's side was too cold on her neck. She fiddled with the heater and put on the defroster instead, then blasted the air conditioner. Hilary tried to fix it at a red light. When she didn't start the instant the light changed green, her grandmother shouted, "Go!"

There was no parking in front of the medical clinic and the parking lot was full. "I'm going to have to let you out in front while I find somewhere to park. Stay at the door and wait for me."

Grandma got out of the car and started up the stairs. Hilary zoomed around the block and around again and again, until finally she caught a break and saw a car attempting to pull out. She waited for the woman to manoeuvre her steering wheel back and forth, trying to not hit the car ahead or behind her. It took forever.

Honestly. Old people.

Hilary zipped into the parking place and fumbled around for change in her purse for the parking meter, then charged up the stairs to find her grandmother wasn't there. She looked around, back outside and then went to the lobby. She definitely wasn't there. Hilary didn't know the name of her doctor, which she realized too late, was a dumb move. There was a big sign listing all the offices in the building so she looked at it thinking she might recognize a name. Nothing rang a bell.

It took Hilary twenty minutes to find her. She ran into countless medical offices and quickly looked at their waiting rooms before heading back out. When she finally did track her down, looking small and anxious in a chair, Grandmother wasn't pleased.

"Where on earth have you been?"

"You were supposed to wait for me at the door," Hilary panted.

"I have a doctor's appointment. Why do you think I'm here? I can't be late."

Hilary sat in the chair beside her. "Sorry, Grandma."

A young woman who was obviously escorting her elderly relative looked to the heavens in sympathy.

Grandma complained that she was too hot, so Hilary helped her off with her coat. Then she was too cold. Hilary put it back on. Then she complained that it was taking too long. The other elderly lady leaned over and said, "It's like this wherever you go." They started a conversation about how inconsiderate doctors were and found out they both went to the same GP. That led to a review of their various ailments and symptoms and they talked so loud, Hilary was mortified. The others in the waiting room were either scowling or smirking behind old copies of *Reader's Digest*.

Her new friend was called in and they bid each other goodbye. Grandma started complaining again. They sat there for fifty minutes before they called for her. Hilary popped down to put more money in the parking meter, and then waited another hour before Grandmother emerged. She waved Hilary up to the desk.

"Listen to this so I'll remember it," she said.

The nurse showed both of them the prescription and went over what she had to do, how many drops in each eye every second day and then three times a week for two weeks and in six weeks she'd have to come back so the doctor could see if there was any improvement. Hilary kept nodding like she was in charge of the situation, but it was baffling to say the least. Let the pharmacist look at it.

The pharmacist. She'd forgotten about that.

She got her grandmother back down to the car and put her in. Her pharmacy couldn't possibly be any farther away. Once again, she drove up and down in the mall parking lot looking for a place to park that was close to the door. Several times Grandma pointed to a spot but when they got up to it, there was small car hidden behind the others.

Finally, success. They went in. Hilary gave the pharmacist's assistant the piece of paper and Grandma starting talking about what a good granddaughter Hilary was and wasn't she lucky and did she have any grandchildren? The assistant, who looked like a washed-out forty, said no and left in a hurry. Hilary felt bad about feeling so impatient with her grandmother after the nice things she said. There was one seat left in the small waiting area to the side. Hilary stood. For twenty-two minutes. Her grandmother didn't notice because she'd made another friend.

Back out to the car and Grandma asked if she'd mind going to the shopping centre to find a specific brand of support hose.

An hour and a half and four stores later they found them but they didn't have the colour Grandmother wanted. The girl said she'd check and see if their other store across town had them.

They did.

An hour there and back and Grandma said they deserved a cup of coffee. Hilary rushed to the nearest Tim Horton's but her grandmother she didn't want to go there, so they ended up in a restaurant big enough that they had to wait to be seated.

Forty minutes later, after coffee and a piece of cheesecake, Hilary got her back to the apartment and her grandmother wanted to know if she'd like to come in since she never saw her and she only had one granddaughter.

An hour later, Hilary kissed her grandmother goodbye, got in the car, and drove over to her boyfriend's apartment. When she opened the door, Reef gave her a big smile.

"Hi, babe, how was your day?"

She closed the door, leaned on it, and slid to the floor.

"I don't know how my mother does it."

❋ ❋ ❋

David was lonely.

They were all gone now: his parents, Annie, Henry, and Lila. Kay wasn't here either. He still had some old buddies he'd see at the supermarket, but Colleen was always in a rush to get him out and he never had a chance to say more than a quick, "How are ya? How's the family?"

Colleen kept pressuring him to sell the house and move in with them because she was worried about him living alone. But that was Lila's and Ewan's house, the place where they'd been happy. He guessed that hadn't occurred to Colleen and he didn't want to bring up any old memories.

He spent a lot of days looking through old photo albums. He and Annie on a skating rink, her pretending to be a famous ice skater with one foot straight back behind her and her arms opened wide. All the pictures of Annie had her either mugging for the camera or with a big smile on her face. God, he missed her; what a bright button she was, always chasing after him, always wanting to be with him.

And Mom and Dad. He and Annie couldn't have asked for better parents. Their home was a safe and loving place to be, their focus on their children and each other. David despaired when he turned on the television and saw the news about battered or homeless or drug-addicted children. Where were their parents? And the worst horror, parents who killed their own children. What was wrong with the world? Hate everywhere, wars still being fought, people starving or exiled, living in refugee camps.

He was very grateful to be living in Canada and especially in the Maritimes and even more especially to be from Cape Breton and his hometown of Glace Bay, where he knew his neighbours and their families. When he was a kid, it seemed like the whole town knew who he was—the milkman, the mailman, the grocer, the guy who fixed their car, the doctor who came to their house, and the man who delivered the coal. He said hello to people all day long and they always wanted to know how he was or what his parents were up to; friendly chit-chat that made him feel like he belonged, that people would miss him if he left.

Other days, looking through the albums left him feeling melancholy. All the moments in their lives that rushed past them, the days they thought were ordinary but now, looking back, seemed like heaven.

When he ruminated about all the mistakes he'd made, he got cross with himself and considered all the wonderful things he had, his two girls and his three grandchildren. He loved them and was proud of them. He and Kay did that.

The girls didn't know, but he and their mother often talked on the phone for hours at a time, reminiscing about silly things that wouldn't mean anything to anyone else, but were special to them. They were good friends. They shared the same memories and that was important, because she was the only one left now.

Colleen was picking him up in an hour. Today was the day they'd find out the results, but he knew. He went through the charade for Colleen's sake. How could he tell his child that death looked better than the life he was living now? But the pain and suffering he'd gone through weren't worth it anymore. He was tired.

At the doctor's office, Colleen cried when he told them that yes, David's stomach cancer had spread and since he'd ruled out chemotherapy and surgery, the doctor said there was nothing they could do, other than to keep him comfortable until the time came. He shook the doctor's hand and helped Colleen out of her chair. He hadn't anticipated how emotional she would be.

Back at the house, he made the tea. "Colleen, dear, these things happen."

"I wanted them to happen when you were ninety-something, not seventy-five. Seventy-five isn't old these days. Seventies are the new sixties."

"I bet the person who said that wasn't seventy-five and didn't have cancer."

"Do you want me to call Frankie and Mom?"

"No, dear, it's my news, I'll do it."

Colleen seemed a lot older, suddenly. When he looked at her, he'd usually see his little girl; now there was a middle-aged woman looking back at him, a sad middle-aged woman.

He leaned across the table and reached for her hand. "Don't worry. I'm not going to be one of those patients who insists on dying at home and the whole place has to be in an uproar. I know how busy you and Duncan are. One bed is as good as another. I'll make it easy for you."

He guessed that wasn't the right thing to say.

"Oh, Daddy!" She jumped up from the chair and put her arms around him, hugging him close. "Don't say that! I don't want it to be easy for me! You're not something that needs to be taken care of without any fuss. You're my dad and I don't want you to die!"

He patted her back and held her as long as she wanted.

It was nice to be loved that much.

❖ ❖ ❖

It was nice to be loved this much.

Hilary and Reef lay in each other's arms on his single bed. He absentmindedly stroked her arm.

"Feel better now?"

"You have no idea."

"Don't you think it's time I met your grandmother, and your parents, for that matter?"

"Yes, you're right. But when you do, you can't go spouting off about being a journalist travelling to hot spots around the world."

"For the record, I'm not a journalist yet. I still have another year at King's."

"You want us to travel together. That's news I have to deliver slowly and carefully. She'll have a stroke."

Reef got up on his elbow and looked down at her. "That's not what I said. I asked you to marry me. And what did you say?"

"I don't know, maybe."

"Do you know how reassuring it is when the woman you love says, 'I don't know, maybe'?"

"Why get married? Who gets married anymore? Statistics are we'll be divorced in three years. Think of all that paperwork."

He laughed and reached down to kiss her softly. "I want to marry you because my mother and father have been married for thirty years, my grandmother and grandfather have been married for fifty years, and my brother and his wife have been married for five years. It runs in my family. My mother wants me to have a wife. She says it will be the making of me."

Hilary touched his face, dragging her finger down his cheek and along his jaw. "What if she disapproves of me? I'm not Muslim."

"My mother has always told me that she will love who I love because I love her."

"She sounds nice. I have to meet them too."

"We can go to New York this summer. My brother and his wife are having their second baby."

"Okay. Come for dinner on Saturday."

"It's a date."

"You have to kiss me until then."

He scooped her up in his arms and laid her on top of him.

"Not a problem."

When Hilary got home that night, there were barely any lights on. Maybe her parents had gone out, but they didn't say they were. She opened the back door and her mother's latest hairy rat ticked across the kitchen floor on his toenails to greet her. She rubbed his head. "Hey there, Monty, or Milk Bone, or whatever your name is."

There was no one in the kitchen. She headed for the stairs, and then saw her mom sitting on the family room couch with her legs tucked under her, with only a small lamp on beside her. She had a box of tissue in her lap.

"Oh my god, what's wrong?"

"I don't want to tell you."

Hilary's heart started to race. "Are you and Dad getting a divorce?"

Her mother screwed up her face. "Why would your father and I get a divorce?"

"The no sex thing."

"I have no idea what you're talking about, but it doesn't matter. Come sit beside me."

This was going to be bad.

Her mother took her hand. "It's Grampy. His stomach cancer has spread. He doesn't have long."

Hilary went weak. She almost drifted down, her head in her mother's lap. Mom stroked her hair. "It's all right, honey. I know. I know."

She didn't know. Grampy was her best friend.

Grandmother was inconsolable. Colleen called her every morning. Frankie talked to her every afternoon and their dad called her in the evening. The only thing she did was lie on her bed and weep. It got to the point where they called the doctor's office.

Hilary went with her mother to her grandmother's apartment. The doctor said he would see her if they could get her in before the office closed, otherwise they'd have to go to the emergency department.

Her grandmother looked like a tiny limp rag doll.

"Mom, you have to get dressed and come with us. We need to get you better."

"He's the only man I ever loved. No one else. The only one I ever loved."

"That's nice, Mom, and he knows that. We all know that, but you're not helping him by carrying on this way. It's making it very stressful for him. If you love him as much as you say you do, you'll be strong for him. He needs you."

Her eyes opened wide. "You're right. He does need me. I have to go to Cape Breton this very minute. I'll stay with him and nurse him back to health."

"I'll take her," Hilary said. "Reef and I will take her."

"Who's Reef?"

"I told you. The boy who's coming for dinner on Saturday."

"He'd go with you?"

"He's good like that."

Her grandmother sat on the bed and watched the two of them like a tennis game. Her mother mulled over the plan. "If you take her up this week, I can come and get her the next, because I was planning on going anyway, after my doctor's appointment. But I better call Dad to see what he thinks."

Hilary was alarmed. "What doctor's appointment?"

"Nothing…just nonsense and hormones and menopause and every other blight known to womankind."

Grandma pointed at the phone. "I'll call him."

She told him she was coming up to take care of him. He said it wasn't necessary and when she started to cry, he backed down and said he'd love to have her. That was how her grandmother operated. The minute she got off the phone the tears dried up.

"I've got to get packed."

She jumped off the bed and hurried into the bathroom, her tiny body visible under her nightie. At the back she looked like a ten-year-old who'd been deflated a little.

"I love your bum, Grandma."

She shouted, "I always did have a nice ass."

Hilary paced by the living room window waiting for Reef to get there. Her mother had bought one of those frozen roasts that were ready in ten minutes, with frozen roast potatoes, frozen mixed vegetables, and canned gravy. The one food in the oven was the frozen crescent rolls. She had an ice cream cake she bought on the way home. Hilary was cold just thinking about it all.

She saw his headlights in the driveway. "He's here!" She said it louder than she meant to. Her parents looked at each other.

Reef came to the door with a cardboard bakery box wrapped with string, a bouquet of flowers, and a bottle of wine. He stood and smiled at them.

They stared back.

Hilary went over to him and put her arm through his. "Mom, Dad, this is Sharif Jamal. Reef, these are my parents, Edward and Frankie."

"Welcome to our home, Sharif," Dad said. "It's nice to meet you."

"You as well, sir."

Mom shook his hand too. "Hello…there's so much that Hilary hasn't told us about you. I look forward to our evening."

Reef held out the gifts. "The flowers are for you, Mrs. Roth."

Mom took them. "Thank you, they're lovely."

"And the wine is for you, Mr. Roth."

"I appreciate it, thank you."

Mom pointed to the box. "That looks interesting."

"It's for dessert, Basbousa. My father makes the best in the world, but this will have to do."

"How interesting. I've never heard of it."

Hilary was going to scream if her parents didn't start acting a little more relaxed. It's like they were in an amateur community play.

Fortunately, Reef turned on the charm and told them about himself. That he was born in New York City, the Bronx, and that his father was Egyptian and his mother was from Harlem. He mentioned that he was Muslim before they asked him and said his dad was an engineer and his mom was a nurse. They lived in Brooklyn now and his older brother and his wife and baby lived down the street. He mentioned that his mother's sister lived here in East Preston and that's how he knew about King's University. He told them his mother only let him move away because her sister was close by. He expressed how lovely Hilary was, and added their daughter was the nicest and smartest and most compassionate girl he'd ever met and his parents were going to love her.

"How long have you been going out together?" Mom asked.

"I can't remember," Hilary laughed.

"It's been one year, six months, and eight days as of midnight tonight. We met at the SUB building at Dal. We bumped into each other signing a petition. I forget what for."

Mom's face lit up. "That's where my parents met! What an amazing coincidence."

Hilary brought out the Basbousa and gave everyone a piece. "This looks delicious."

"What's in it?" Dad asked.

"Yogurt, almonds, sugar, lots of good things."

Her parents raved about it.

"That's what happens when you cook something from scratch, Mom."

Reef thanked them very much, shook their hands, and walked to the car. Hilary walked with him.

"Thanks," she said. "You handled them perfectly."

"They're nice people."

"They are, aren't they?"

Mindful that her parents might be looking out the window, they shared a chaste kiss, but he whispered "I love you," in her ear before he left.

Hilary went in the house. Her parents were clearing the dishes.

"Why didn't you introduce him to us a long time ago?" Dad asked.

"Because I didn't know how long he was going to be my boyfriend. I don't drag guys I date home. There's no point."

Mom rinsed the dishes before she stacked them. "You could've told us he was black. We felt like idiots gawking at him when he first came in."

"He wasn't what we were expecting," her dad said.

Hilary got huffy. "And what were you expecting?"

"A nice boy—not a really great boy."

Grandma sat in the front passenger seat while Reef drove. Hilary was stuck in the back. She couldn't believe Grandma flirted with him the entire trip. He kept glancing at Hilary in the rearview mirror, his eyes dancing, trying not to laugh.

As they crossed the causeway, Hilary's mood changed. All the times she had come this way, excited to see Grampy and Aunt Colleen and the beach at Round Island. This was a journey that always made her happy, and today it didn't.

What was her life going to be like without Grampy in it? She couldn't imagine that world. It made her feel empty and lonely inside. He and Aunt Colleen had always been the two people she could count on to understand her, and even when they didn't, they pretended they did. They were the three musketeers. Now there would only be two.

They stopped at the Cedar House to pick up the raisin and oatmeal bread he loved, and his favourite molasses cookies. There was also a strawberry-rhubarb pie just out of the oven that looked divine, so they took that too.

When Reef pulled up to the house, there Grampy was in the window, waiting like he always did. Hilary ran out of the back seat and left Reef to deal with her grandmother. Grampy opened the door and she ran into his arms.

She couldn't believe how bony and thin he was; his face was gaunt. It was hard to ignore the skull that now made its presence known under his skin.

There were no tears, because she didn't want to upset him.

"Hi, Grampy," she whispered. "I love you."

"Hi, Hilary. I love you too."

Grandma made an incredible scene, hugging and kissing him, crying the whole time. He finally told her to stop all the nonsense and by God, she did. That gave Hilary a chance to introduce Reef, who carried the baked goods and grandma's purse.

Grampy held out his hand. "It's nice to meet you, young man. Hilary talks about you all the time. I feel like I know you."

"And I you, sir. There's no one in the world she loves better."

Aunt Colleen waited by the kitchen door, not wanting to intrude. The minute Hilary left her grandfather's arms she ran into her aunt's, the two of them trying not to cry.

"I'm so glad you're here. He's been waiting for you all day."

That's when Hilary noticed the hospital bed in the living room. It was huge and intrusive, just like the cancer spreading through his body.

The welcome wore Grampy out, so he lay back in bed and the others sat around the room, eating sandwiches Aunt Colleen made for lunch. Hilary went into the kitchen and cut him a slice of oatmeal bread and put a thin layer of butter on it. She cut it into four pieces and brought it to him, and when he saw what it was he smiled.

"My favourite." He took a small bite.

"Remember when you'd take me to the Cedar House for lunch? You always had the seafood chowder and I had the fish cakes and beans."

"An odd request from a little girl, but our Hilary always was a different sort of child. Who else would want to hang around with an old man all summer?"

"You were lots of fun. Remember the time I sat in the frying pan and you told Aunt Colleen that sausages were called bum warmers!"

Grandma said, "Bum warmers?"

"Inside joke, Kay."

Eventually her grandmother went upstairs to unpack and freshen up. Reef and Aunt Colleen were in the kitchen tidying up and getting to know each other. Hilary sat by her grandfather's bed and held his hand while he slept. Aunt Colleen said he was on a lot of pain medication that kept him comfortable. They had a nurse who came in daily to check him out.

Hilary rubbed her cheek against his swollen knuckles. Nothing was quite as frightening when her grandfather held her hand.

The next day he had a request. He wanted Hilary and Reef to take him out to Round Island. He wouldn't get out of the car; he just wanted to see it again. Grandma wanted to go too, but Aunt Colleen made an excuse to keep her there. Her aunt also told her that she was sending for her parents and her brothers because Grampy seemed to be going downhill fast, now that his family was around him.

They bundled him up in a jacket with a blanket around his stick thin legs and once again, Hilary was in the back seat. They drove him down the dirt road and stopped by the bungalow to see the pink and red weigela bushes at the side. They were loaded with blooms, which Grampy said was because the spring had been so rainy.

After awhile, Reef drove down through the field and took the dirt road that led to the beach. He drove as far up onto the ridge as he could, so Grampy could see the sand and the waves. They opened the windows to let in that glorious Round Island smell that Hilary would know anywhere. She had once tried to figure out what exactly it smelled like, but it was a combined scent of a lot of things—salt and seaweed, fir trees and rose blossoms, clover, grass, fish, and clean, clean air.

"Annie and I would race each other down here when we'd come out for the summer, trying to be the first one to put our feet in the sand. Then we'd jump the brook and see who could run faster down to those big rocks near Long Beach. She usually won, which always bugged me."

Hilary and Reef laughed.

"There were so many cousins and aunts and uncles piled in the bungalow sometimes that we boys had to sleep under the kitchen table at night. If the bugs weren't bad, we'd sleep outdoors. To look up at those stars as I lay in that field made me wonder why I was here. I was so small in the face of all that glory. What purpose did I serve? Do you ever feel like that?"

Reef nodded. "Sometimes, but I know I'm here for a reason. I hope I can make the world a better place."

Grampy smiled at him. "That's what's so wonderful about being young. You feel you can change the world. Maybe in this new millennium you will."

He stopped talking and continued to look out over the water. Eventually he asked if they could walk him over to the big log up on the rocks, so he could sit on it. Hilary and Reef got him out of the car and, holding either arm, managed to slowly move him across the tippy rocks. He sat on one of the flatter sections of the weathered log and Hilary sat beside him. Reef said he was going for a walk. They watched him go.

"I like him, kiddo. He's just the kind of man I'd want for you."

"I love him, Grampy. He's generous and thoughtful and passionate about what he does. And the thing I like the best is that he talks about his family so much. He calls his mother all the time."

"Always marry someone who loves their mother. That's what my mom told us. I forgot about that piece of advice until after I was married. Our divorce seems to suggest Mom was right."

"What else did Great-Grammie tell you?"

"Marry someone with clean fingernails."

They both began to laugh. "Why on earth would she say that?"

Grampy shrugged. "There was no one dirtier than my dad when he'd come home at night. He'd always wash up first and change his clothes before he came down for dinner. Dinnertime was an occasion and we never rushed through it because Mom put such effort into it. He was respectful of that."

"I don't remember her."

"She was a lovely woman. She believed in God and her family. They always came first."

Hilary felt him getting tired. He hunched over and leaned on her. "Do you want to go back, Grampy?"

"Yes."

Hilary waved at Reef to return. He started to walk towards them.

"Thank you for this, Hilary."

"It was my pleasure."

"Now I have one more favour to ask you."

"Anything."

"I want you to go on a secret mission."

❋ ❋ ❋

The entire family was there when he died four days later. They cried, but in some ways it was a relief. He'd been in pain for so long. Colleen was the one holding his hand a few hours before he died, when he opened his eyes and said, "Am I dead yet?"

"Not yet, Dad. Soon. We're all here with you. You're not alone."

Colleen and Frankie were amazed at their mother when Dad finally slipped away. All the hysterics and crying jags they'd expected didn't happen. She kissed him on the lips, told him she loved him, and then went upstairs to be by herself.

Colleen and Frankie held each other in the kitchen. Reef was outside in the backyard holding Hilary in his arms while she wept.

"I like him, Frankie."

"I do too. I have no idea why she didn't introduce him to us sooner. It's like she was ashamed of us."

"Hilary's like Ewan, she's private."

Once the arrangements were made, the obituary written, and the funeral details done, the family had a two-day period where it was all hands on deck. Colleen and Frankie were selling the house and had to arrange for the furniture to be put in storage until they could figure who might want what in the future. But before that could happen they had to take figurines off the credenza and pile books into boxes and clear out desk drawers and bureau drawers and the endless things one accumulates over the course of a lifetime.

Reef and Hilary's brothers were carrying the big stuff into the vans, except for the living room furniture and the beds. They still had to get through the next forty-eight hours. Adam's girlfriend, Lisa, was only allowed to take dishes off the bottom shelves in the kitchen, so Adam informed everyone, in case she overdid it.

Frankie whispered to Colleen, "Like he's an expert on pregnancy all of a sudden."

"Don't mock. Young men today take fatherhood seriously."

"Save me."

Edward, Duncan, and the twins sorted out the garage and the basement. That left Colleen, Frankie, their mom, and Hilary upstairs cleaning out bureau drawers and the bathroom of his personal effects. At one point they were on the bed sorting through everything and Hilary picked up a set of cufflinks. "I remember these. He wore them to church."

Kay held out her hand. "Let me see. I bought them for him in Montreal. I didn't realize he still had them. You should've seen him in a suit. No one wore one better. People always noticed when he walked into a room."

Frankie got teary. "May I have his shaving bowl? I used to watch him shave in the morning and he always chased me down the hall, threatening to kiss me with his soapy face."

"Can I keep his big dictionary? Whenever I asked Grampy how to spell a word, we'd look it up together. I always felt important."

Colleen bent down and pulled out something sticking out from under the bed. She covered her mouth. "Oh my god, he had two girlie magazines under his bed."

Hilary laughed. "That's so adorable."

"Adorable? I don't want to think of Dad that way," Frankie said.

Their mother grabbed the magazines. "Give me a break. How do you think you girls came into the world? A stork? Your father was a fantastic lover."

Colleen, Frankie, and Hilary covered their ears and told her to shut up.

And then Colleen picked up his oval brush, the one he used every morning. His grey hairs were in it. "I'm keeping this."

Once they got into the photo albums, the four of them propped themselves up on the headboard and lay side by side covered with a blanket. Their mother went through it and told them who were in the pictures and what the occasions were. They laughed a lot.

Until the men came upstairs and asked them what they thought they were doing sitting on their asses. There was work to be done.

❂ ❂ ❂

Hilary was alone when she happened upon a small photo of a little girl. She didn't know who she was, except she was such a pretty little thing that Hilary couldn't stop looking at her. She turned it over and saw *My Little Cricket, May, 1949,* written in her grandfather's handwriting.

Whoever she was, her grandfather had thought she was special, so she put the picture inside the dictionary to take home.

They were exhausted and dirty by the end of the day. Her mother and aunt went to pick up Grampy's ashes and they brought them home and placed them on the living room coffee table. Colleen went out to the garden and picked some flowers to put by the urn. It was like a beacon for the rest of the day, everyone at different times going into the room to sit quietly with him.

The funeral was in the morning.

Hilary's grandmother, mother, and Aunt Colleen were staying the night with her and Reef, who was sleeping on the couch in the living room. Her father was staying with Duncan and her brothers and Lisa were scattered upon the cousins. They'd gather at the church in the morning.

When Hilary thought everyone was asleep upstairs, she tiptoed downstairs and went into the living room. Reef was on the couch waiting for her.

"Bring Grampy into the kitchen."

He picked up the urn and followed her into the pantry. "What do I do if one of them comes downstairs?"

"Hold them off. Kiss them if you have to."

"Your mother?"

"My grandmother would enjoy it."

She had a bag all ready with the things she'd need in it. She put out bowls, plastic bags, the scale, a measuring cup, and small scissors. "I feel like I'm in a meth lab."

Reef handed her the urn and she put it on the counter. She opened the top and there was her Grampy, now looking like fine cat litter. Very carefully, she put him on the counter, and cut a small hole in the bag. Her hands were shaking. "I don't want to spill him."

"You're doing fine."

She emptied what she thought was half of her grandfather's ashes into a bowl and measured it on the scale so she'd know how much brown sugar to put in to replace him. Reef opened the new bag and she poured him in it. They sealed it and Reef put him in his pocket.

Now all she had to do was put a bag of brown sugar in the bottom of the urn and put the original bag over it, so it weighed the same and if anyone looked in, they'd see ashes.

"Almost done."

They heard steps coming down the stairs. "You spoke too soon."

"Get rid of them!"

She hurriedly poured the brown sugar into the bag, but she made a mess and most of it ended up on the floor.

"Hi, Grandma. You couldn't sleep either," she heard Reef say.

"Lordy, you scared me. What are you doing wandering around the house?"

"You know what it's like to sleep in someone else's house. You're awake most of the night."

"True. My stomach's bothering me and we cleared out the bathroom. I need some antacids. There may be some in the kitchen."

Hilary scooped up the brown sugar that had gone all over the counter and even some off the floor, because she didn't have any more. It was awful to think of Grampy with dirty brown sugar next to him, but what could she do.

"I don't think there are any antacids in the kitchen," Reef said very loudly.

Oh God.

"I have some out in my car. We could go out there and get some."
"In the middle of the night?"
"It's a lovely night out. The moon is full..."
"Okay," she said.

Hilary put the sugar in the bottom of the urn, re-tied the original bag, and placed it on top and moved it around so it looked like more. She closed the top and ran to the living room and put Grampy back on the coffee table.

She was in a sweat.

Back to the kitchen to get rid of the crime scene and try to locate a broom to sweep up the sugar—but she couldn't find one. She scuffed the sugar under the counter with her slippers. The implements were next. Into the carry-all they went and back upstairs under her bed.

She waited for Reef to come back in with Grandma, but there was no sound. What were they doing out there?

Back downstairs she went and looked out the living room window. The car was gone. Poor Reef.

They eventually came back from an all-night store where Reef bought her a package of antacids. Hilary was in the living room with Grampy when they got back.

"You can't sleep either?" Grandma said. "Want something for your stomach?" She held out her bottle.

"No thanks, Grandma."

"I have to tell you Hilary, you better keep this boy. Forget all this bullshit about waiting until you're thirty to marry. All the good ones are taken by then. Sweet dreams."

When she disappeared up the stairs, Reef collapsed on the couch beside her.

"Did you finish your secret mission?"
"Grampy would be proud. Thank you."
"Your grandmother is a good kisser."
She shoved her elbow into his side. "You're making that up."
"You'll never know."

The funeral was a quiet affair. All of Annie's family was there and they had a fine reunion over tea and sandwiches in the church hall after they came back from burying Grampy next to his sister and parents. Whenever anyone asked Hilary how old she was and she said almost twenty, they couldn't believe it. She was the baby in the family, so they must be getting really old.

It was finally over. Her dad and brothers and Lisa drove back to Halifax. Grandma and her mom were staying on with Aunt Colleen to oversee the rest of the move and sale of the house. Hilary told them that she and Reef were going to spend the night at the bungalow and then drive back to Halifax the next day.

Kisses all around, and just as they were backing up out of the driveway, Mom came running out.

"Before you leave, go to the Superstore. We're out of teabags and your grandmother wants some chocolate digestives."

Colleen came out of the house and added ten more things, seeing how they were going anyway.

When they got to the parking lot, Hilary wasn't sure what to do. "Do we leave Grampy in my purse or here in the car?"

"Leave him in the car."

"He'll be lonely."

"Then keep him in your purse, or I can stay out here with him if you like."

"No, I want you with me. This is where Grampy and I would come to get our groceries for the summer."

They went into the store and Hilary pushed her grandfather around in the seat of the shopping cart. "This is weird, Grampy. What shall I buy?"

They picked up the groceries her mother wanted and were heading for the cash, when they passed the aisle with the sugar cereals her mother used to get.

"Grampy would never let me have this crap in the summer, so he bought the plain cereal in little boxes instead." Reef picked some up and put it in the cart.

They delivered their groceries and set off for the bungalow. By now it was mid-afternoon.

"I hope I can find this place. I only went here once."

They walked hand in hand past the long beach and then into the woods. At first she wasn't sure if she was right, but she remembered

Grampy saying if you could see the water on your left you were going in the right direction.

It seemed a longer walk than when she was with her grandfather, but there was a part of her that didn't want to let him go, so she wasn't hurrying. For the most part, she and Reef didn't talk.

And then there it was, the huge ballerina tree in the middle of the clearing, the wind blowing its raggedy branches to and fro.

"Does it look like a ballerina to you?"

"It looks like someone trying to hail a cab in New York. It's quite something, isn't it?"

"Grampy said this was his favourite place in the whole world. Round Island beach is the second. He used to play here with his sister Annie, and he told me that a tree fairy and a magic cricket live here."

"Your grandfather liked to tell stories."

Hilary looked at the ground. All of a sudden she wasn't sure if she could do it. Reef put his arm around her.

"I loved him so much. He was...a very special man."

She inhaled a deep breath, took her grandfather's ashes, and scattered them around the tree. It was over in a moment. She couldn't see him anymore.

"I need to sit down."

They went to the spot where she and her grandfather sat when she was a child. They leaned against a tree and watched the water below. She cried against Reef's shirt for a few moments and then she wiped her tears, took his face in her hands, and kissed him. He was perfect.

"I love you, Reef. I want to tell you here, near Grampy, that I would love to marry you."

"How did I know you'd say that?" He took a small box out of his pocket.

Her eyes widened. "Are you serious? Darn it! I ruined your moment!"

"This is the best moment of my life." He opened it. "This was my great-grandmother's engagement ring. I'll buy you your own, when I make some money."

"You will not. I love it!"

He put the heritage ring on her finger and they whispered promises and dreams to each other. They thought no one had ever loved someone as much as they did. That no one had ever felt this way before.

It was time to go. He reached for her hand and pulled her up. They paused by the ballerina tree.

"Goodbye, Grampy."

They walked hand in hand through the woods and onto the beach, heading for home.

"I can't wait to see the world and write about it," he said.

"I'm going to write stories," she said.

"I know. And there will be so much inspiration for you when we're travelling."

Hilary stopped and looked at the beach where she swam, the field where she ran, and the woods that held her grandfather's secret.

"I don't think I need to go that far to find good stories."

"What will you write about?"

"My kin."

ACKNOWLEDGEMENTS

I'D LIKE TO THANK MY family, friends, and neighbours for sharing with me their memories of growing up in Glace Bay, Mira, and Louisbourg during the thirties, forties, and fifties: Bill and Edie Phillips, Erna Jean Scott, Jean Crowell, Gladys Smith, Neila Johnston, Beverly Macdonald, Barbara MacDonald, Donald and Bev Smith, and Myrna Steele. I'll always be grateful.

HEIRLOOM RECIPES

Some of my favourite recipes from my grandmother's collection…enjoy! —L. C.

LEMON MERINGUE PIE
Filling:
1 cup sugar
1¼ cups water
1 tablespoon butter
¼ cup corn starch (dissolve in 3 tablespoons cold water)
6 tablespoons lemon juice
1 teaspoon grated lemon peel
3 egg yolks
2 tablespoons milk

Mix. [I'm assuming this means cook on stovetop until thick. She doesn't say! —L. C.]
Bake pie shell

Meringue:
3 egg whites
6 tablespoons sugar
1 teaspoon lemon juice
Whip!

CORN BREAD
½ cup sugar
¼ cup shortening
2 eggs, beaten
1¼ cups flour
4 teaspoons baking powder
¼ teaspoons salt
1 cup cornmeal
1 cup milk

Preheat oven to 400 degrees. Cream sugar and shortening, then beat in eggs. In another bowl combine flour, baking powder, salt and cornmeal. Add gradually to the cream mixture alternately with the milk, stirring just enough to blend after each addition. Pour into a well-greased 9 x 9 baking pan and bake 30–40 minutes.

MACARONI AND CHEESE
2 cups macaroni
cheese
butter or margarine
salt and pepper
1½ cups milk

Gradually add 2 cups macaroni to rapidly boiling salted water (little salt), so that the water continues to boil. Cook uncovered for 8–10 minutes, stirring occasionally until tender to a fork. Drain well. (When I drain the macaroni I let some cold water run through and then drain well.)

Put half of the macaroni in casserole, place layers of cheese on top. I use old cheese (sharp). Over this put some dots of butter and then the rest of the macaroni, more cheese, little butter or margarine. Salt and pepper.

Pour over this 1½ cups milk. Bake 375 degrees for around 40 minutes.

MOTHER'S WHITE FRUITCAKE
[This is Cynthia's recipe…my grandmother Abbie's mother. —L.C.]

¾ pound butter
2 cups white sugar
3 cups fine coconut
4 ½ cups flour (use ½ cup flour to dredge fruit)
¼ teaspoon salt
2 teaspoons baking powder

Mix together. Add:
    8 eggs
    ½ pound almonds [chopped? —L. C.]
    1 teaspoon lemon juice
    1 teaspoon vanilla
    1 teaspoon almond flavouring
    ½ cup milk
    1 package red cherries (8-ounce package)
    1 package green cherries (8-ounce package)
    1 package white citron
    3 packages pineapple
    1 package golden raisins

Bake at 275 degrees. [Usually 4 to 5 hours? It doesn't say on the recipe. —L. C.]

WHITE BREAD

2 cups milk
¼ cup sugar
4 teaspoons salt
¼ cup shortening
2 packages dry yeast
1 cup lukewarm water with 2 teaspoons sugar dissolved in it
5 cups flour

Scald milk. Pour into large bowl. Add sugar, salt, shortening. Stir until shortening melts. Cool to lukewarm.

Meanwhile sprinkle dry yeast over lukewarm sugared water. Let stand for 10 minutes (Keep at temp of about 80 degrees [I'm assuming she means Fahrenheit, which is about 26 degrees Celsius —L. C.]). Then stir briskly with a fork.

Add softened yeast to the lukewarm milk mixture, stir. Beat in flour. Work in the last of the flour with a rotating motion of the hand. Turn dough onto a lightly floured board and knead 8–10 minutes. Shape into a smooth ball. Place dough into a greased bowl. Grease top, cover and let rise until double in bulk, around 1½ hours. Keep dough in warm place (80 degrees [again! —L. C.]).

Punch down dough and cut into four pieces. Form each into a smaller ball. Cover and let rest for 15 minutes. Shape into loaf and place into greased pans. Grease top. Cover and let rise until double in bulk, about 1¼ hours.

Bake at 425 degrees for 30 to 35 minutes.

[A real time saver for the modern woman. —L. C.]

A READER'S GUIDE TO
Kin
BY LESLEY CREWE

Kin has an enormous cast of characters. Are there any you feel particularly drawn to? Are there any you dislike? Why?

Why do you think Crewe changed perspectives so much between the characters? Is there anyone whose perspective you wanted more of?

Crewe introduces Annie, Colleen, and Hilary in the same way. What traits and circumstances do these three characters share? In what ways are they different?

Lila is, from the moment we meet her, frail. And yet she lives through one of the worst losses imaginable, the death of her child, and even thrives afterwards. Where does she find the strength to live through her grief? What would you do or have you done in similarly devastating circumstances?

After all his professions of love, David ends up acting very badly towards Lila and to Kay. Does his subsequent journey redeem him?

There is a lot of detail about food in *Kin*, and even recipes from Crewe's ancestors included at the back. What are some of the most significant and memorable food-related moments in the book? What role does food play in the book? Does it have a similar place in your own life?

How is reading a book that's multi-generational different from reading a book that focuses on a more specific amount of time? Does the broad perspective we have of the characters change how you feel about them? Would your impressions of Ewan, for example, be changed if the book stopped before he and Lila reconciled? And does seeing a character die change your impressions of their personality?

Round Island is a very important place to a number of characters in *Kin*. Is this sense of connection with a place common? Do you have your own retreat from the world?

Each generation we meet in *Kin* is full of optimism and ready to change the world. Will any generation actually succeed in changing the world? Has any generation done so? Does it matter if they don't? Is it a goal we should keep striving for?

Lesley Crewe is the author of *Her Mother's Daughter, Hit & Mrs., Ava Comes Home, Shoot Me,* and *Relative Happiness,* which was shortlisted for the Margaret and John Savage First Book Award. Lesley was previously a freelance writer and columnist for *Cape Bretoner Magazine* and *Cahoots* online magazine. Born in Montreal, Lesley lives in Homeville, Nova Scotia.

www.lesleycrewe.com